"EVERYBODY STRAP IN. WE'RE GETTING OUT OF HERE."

Colonel Anderson's voice came over the speakers. Stung by machine-gun barrage, Air Force One was wounded. With all controls and electrical systems duplicated, and each section of fuselage structurally isolated from the next, it would take a massive blow to destroy the aircraft's integrity. But more dangerous were the leaks from the pressurized cabin. Each bullet hole bleeding air was a potential explosive decompression.

The President disregarded Anderson's orders, stepped to the desk and pushed a button on the red telephone. In a moment, he was speaking with the Bagman. "Your instructions," the President said, "are to open the Code Bag. I'll require today's entry code for SAC."

"May I have today's password?" asked the Chief Warrant Officer.

But before the President could say, "Vesper," the P-38 attacked again. . . .

AIR FORCE ONE

Edwin Corley

A DELL BOOK

Published by
Dell Publishing Co., Inc.
1 Dag Hammarskjold Plaza
New York, New York 10017

Dell ®TM 681510, Dell Publishing Co., Inc.

ISBN: 0-440-10063-1

Reprinted by arrangement with Doubleday & Company, Inc.
Printed in the United States of America

First Dell printing—July 1979

This story is totally fictional.

But the achievements made by the real people, who inspired it, are very real. Dedicated, loyal, highly qualified, they are a credit to the Air Force and to this nation.

Therefore, I dedicate *Air Force One* to:

The men and women of the 89th Military Airlift Wing at Andrews AFB, Maryland

DEPARTMENT OF THE AIR FORCE
HEADQUARTERS 89th MILITARY AIRLIFT WING,
SPECIAL MISSIONS (MAC)
ANDREWS AFB, WASHINGTON, D.C. 20331

March 1

SUBJECT: Presidential Aircrews

TO: All 89 MAWg Units and Wg Staff plus OL 1,
LASI

For your information, the following personnel
comprise the Presidential aircrew:

Aircraft Commander	Col. Thomas Anderson
Pilot	Maj. Paul McGowan
Navigator	Lt. Col. Carl Birney
Flight Engineer	CMSgt. Juan Hernandez
Radio Operator	TSgt. Lester Dent
Flight Traffic Specialist	TSgt. Ed Miller
" " "	A1C Angela Nemath
" " "	To Be Assigned

THOMAS ANDERSON, Colonel, USAF
Commander

Her official coming out was on October 12, 1962, when she arrived at Andrews Air Force Base in Maryland, just outside Washington, D.C. But she had been born and schooled months earlier, in the Boeing Aircraft Company's Renton, Washington, plant.

There was never any question that this was a "she." Temperamental in her testing—precocious, yet stubborn in learning to take to the air—she was designated a VC-137C Stratoliner, the military number for what is basically a Boeing 707-320B commercial intercontinental jet airliner.

No one blamed her. The pressure was intense. She was no ordinary passenger plane. Her destiny was to be the first jet assigned to an American President. She had to be more than qualified; she had to rise to the head of a class of outstanding quality. She was a Boeing 707. The first one which rolled off the line had taken the air world by its wings and shaken it until, with a sigh, it was decreed that flying would never be the same again.

Until now, the President's aircraft had borne a variety of names. President Roosevelt's C-54 had been called the Sacred Cow. President Truman had flown in a DC-6 named the Independence. President Eisenhower's series of planes had been known as Columbine II and Columbine III. When he first took office, President Kennedy had used an unnamed VC-118.

The new jet became the first plane called Air Force One.

At the time, no one knew how closely that name would be associated with triumph—and tragedy.

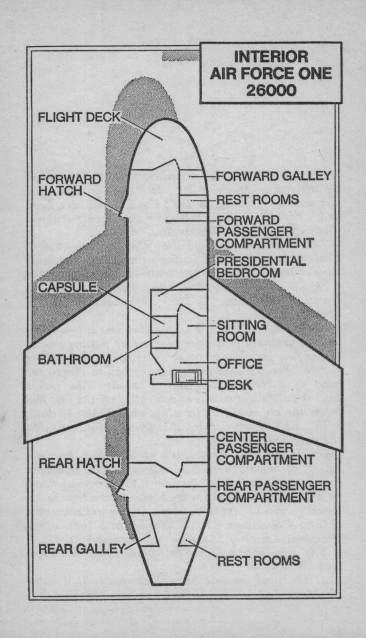

INTERIOR AIR FORCE ONE 26000

FLIGHT DECK

FORWARD HATCH

CAPSULE

BATHROOM

REAR HATCH

REAR GALLEY

FORWARD GALLEY

REST ROOMS

FORWARD PASSENGER COMPARTMENT

PRESIDENTIAL BEDROOM

SITTING ROOM

OFFICE

DESK

CENTER PASSENGER COMPARTMENT

REAR PASSENGER COMPARTMENT

REST ROOMS

PART ONE

Pre-Flight Check

1

Anderson's eyes were locked on the instrument panel. Outside the windows of the jet plane the giant complex of the Greater Southwest Regional Airport sprawled all the way from the Industrial District to the shores of Grapevine Lake. The lights of Fort Worth were on the port side; those from Dallas to the starboard.

"Two hundred knots," intoned the Pilot in the right seat, where a copilot would have normally flown. But this was a special airplane, with an Aircraft Commander in the left seat, and a fully qualified Pilot in the right.

"Two hundred," repeated the Aircraft Commander, Colonel Thomas Anderson. His blue regulation shirt was dark with perspiration. Anderson had nearly 16,000 hours flying four-engine jets. His landings numbered in the thousands. Still, every time he brought this special bird down to the runway, out popped the perspiration.

The Pilot, Major Paul McGowan, noticed it. He smiled, and gave the punch line to an old pilot's joke: "Colonel, we've reached the Point of Maximum Pucker."

"Altitude?" snapped Anderson. He disapproved of cockpit small talk, particularly at such critical moments as a landing.

"Passing through twelve hundred," said McGowan.

"Half flaps," said the Aircraft Commander.

The Telex headphone clamped over his ear crackled. "Air Force One, we have you for a straight-in approach. Winds from the southwest, gusting to forty knots. No other traffic in your immediate vicinity."

An unnecessary report. Whenever Air Force One neared an airport, all other traffic was vectored away from the runways and approach pattern. In John F. Kennedy's time, delays to civilian (and often military) landings had sometimes run as long as fifteen minutes.

Anderson felt his lips tense in a wry smile. Not that it had done President Kennedy much good. Within hours after Air Force One had brought him to this very airport, he lay dead in the Dallas Parkland Hospital.

His eyes scanned the instruments again. At this critical moment in the approach, he would bring the giant Stratoliner in blind. It was the job of his Pilot to visually monitor the sky. Anderson could not risk any momentary disorientation in the transition from instruments to the harsh lights of the night world outside. But he still felt an almost overpowering urge to look.

Calmly, he said, "Paul, do you have visual contact?"

"Negative," said the Pilot. "One thousand feet. One-fifty knots."

Air Force One shuddered under sudden turbulence. It felt exactly as if some unseen creature had taken the giant airplane in its jaws and shaken it like a beagle killing a rabbit.

The longer indicator on the altimeter lurched counterclockwise past three clock-like digits.

"Lost three hundred," said Major Paul McGowan.

Over his voice, the Tower said, "Air Force One, you're low. Correct your altitude to nine-five-oh."

"Nine-five-oh," repeated Anderson. He reached beside his right leg, to the pedestal between him and McGowan, and pushed the master throttle lever forward a click. He felt back pressure against his seat as the four Pratt and Whitney engines wound up six hundred revolutions more each second.

"Right three degrees," said McGowan. In normal cockpit routine pilots tended to use "right" and "left" rather than the more precise "port" and "starboard."

"Right three degrees," repeated the Aircraft Commander. He made a slow rotation of the yoke, coordinating the turn with his rudder. On the instrument panel before him, the straight line in the center of the artificial horizon tilted downward, making the tiny airplane indicator appear to turn right in a slow turn. He kept it so for a few seconds, then brought his controls back to their central position. The horizon steadied.

"Steady at nine-five-oh," said McGowan.

"Nine-five-oh." Anderson's voice was hard. The plane was bouncing violently now. There had been no bad-weather reports for the Fort Worth area when he had checked in just a quarter of an hour ago. He knew that weather reporting, vastly improved, was still an inexact science. He also knew that the President of the United States does not like to be bounced around.

"Colonel," said Technical Sergeant Lester Dent, the Radio Operator, "I've got a heavy radar return dead ahead. Looks like a bad squall."

"Can we go around it?"

"Negative."

Veteran pilots often spoke of their careers as "hours of boredom punctuated by moments of sheer terror." This was part of their modest denial that there was anything heroic or in any way special about those who fly. In moments of emergency, terror was the last intruder to enter the flight deck. A cold calmness was the usual response.

"Shit," said Anderson. "Tell the President to buckle up."

"Roger," said Dent. He touched a red button on his console. "Mr. President, we may be encountering turbulence. Please be sure your seat belt is fastened."

"Eight hundred," said McGowan. His voice was dead quiet. Later, over coffee—or, if they weren't flying for the next twenty-four hours, a beer—they would chuckle over these moments, describing them as "Maximum Pucker plus Three."

The jet was now wallowing as if plowing through a heavy liquid instead of the warm desert air.

The radio altimeter warning blared.

"Pull up!" snapped Anderson. He applied pressure to the yoke and, at the same time, advanced the thrust levers.

Air Force One shuddered violently, on the very edge of a fatal stall. The movements were so strong that Anderson had trouble keeping his feet on the bouncing rudder pedals.

He made a decision—one he had never expected to make as Commander of this dependable, sturdy airplane.

Pressing the Command microphone switch, he said, "Emergency! Capsule! Capsule!"

"Closing fast," said TSgt. Dent. "The screen's almost blanked out."

Anderson fought the controls. Outside, he heard a loud explosion. The flash, even though he was not looking through the windows, seared his eyes.

"Lightning strike," said Major Paul McGowan. "Number One's on fire."

"Hit the bottles," commanded Anderson. McGowan pressed the fire extinguisher switch. Somewhere on the flight deck, an alarm bell was clanging. The jet shuddered again and, in spite of himself, Anderson looked up from the instruments.

"Oh, my God," he said.

Directly ahead was a whirling black funnel cloud, blotting out stars and runway lights alike.

"Twister," said McGowan, unnecessarily.

"Hard left!" said Anderson, putting all of his muscle power against the unwilling yoke. With his own dual controls, McGowan helped. The rudder pedals slammed against their feet like pinion bars on a scrambling motorcycle.

Anderson freed one hand momentarily from the trembling yoke and tried to uncage a locked red switch just below the ball-bank indicator. The plane lurched back to the right.

"I can't hold her," called McGowan.

Another flash came from outside. Air Force One slewed sideways, almost throwing the flight crew from their seats.

"Number Two's gone," said CMSgt. Juan Hernandez, the Flight Engineer. "Turbine's blown."

The tornado was directly ahead.

"Straight and level," said Anderson.

"Tom, you can't!" McGowan protested. "That'll put us right through the funnel."

"It's the only way I can blow the capsule," said Anderson. "Get her level!"

Both men were straining against the yokes and virtually standing on the rudders.

"Too much drag from those dead engines," gasped Anderson. "Kill Three and Four."

This was a death verdict for the struggling airplane. With no power, she would wallow in the turbulent air and then slip down to an inevitable crash.

Without hesitation, Paul McGowan chopped the throttles. The scream of the jets outside wound down.

The two pilots fought the controls. Slowly, the right wing lowered.

"Hold her . . . there . . ." said Anderson. He released the yoke with his left hand, reached for the cage protecting the red switch marked "Capsule." He flipped up the cage and, as he reached for the switch itself, a red explosion flashed through the flight deck and all sound and movement stopped.

The silence of death. Lingering acridness of smoke. The memory of motion, although all had ceased.

Then a bright light.

A hatch had been opened.

A burly black man, wearing a brightly colored sport shirt and puffing on a foul green cigar, leaned into the flight cabin and said hoarsely, "Congratulations, Colonel Anderson. You've just killed three Senators, the Secretary of State, Barbara Walters, the President of the United States—and, incidentally, your worthless self."

"Fuck you," said Anderson, unbuckling his seat harness. He could feel cold sweat squishing against his back. Carefully, he slipped past the pedestal and stood, trembling, behind the radioman's seat. "Why didn't you throw in an H-bomb blast too? Just to keep things humming."

"Maybe next time," said John Mead, the senior simulator-standards programmer at the American Airlines Flight Academy near Fort Worth, Texas. "Want to take a break and listen to the cockpit tapes?"

Slowly, Anderson said, "I didn't get the President's capsule away, did I?"

"No," said Mead, mopping sweat from his gleaming brown skull. "The airframe disintegrated point-four seconds before you threw the switch."

"Goddamnit," grumbled the Command Pilot. "This is the first simulation that's ever gotten far enough to even uncage the switch, and then I blew it."

"Cheer up," said the black man, puffing at his cigar. "If it makes you feel any better, the computer prediction was that you'd never survive that second engine pop. With both port fans out, and in the edge of the cloud funnel, you were supposed to do a Dutch roll and impact with no survivors."

"Big deal," said Anderson. "So I lasted five seconds longer. I still killed the President."

Casually, Mead said, "Want to try again?"

"Can you recycle?"

"Not the whole flight. We'll fast-forward to destruct minus two minutes. That'll put you around twelve hundred feet and two hundred knots."

"Shove it to us," said Anderson, slipping back into the left-hand seat.

As Mead closed and locked the hatch to the simulator, he shook his head.

"Fly-boys," he said. "They're all crazy."

Nine P.M. Tomorrow was a travel day. Back to Andrews Air Force Base, just east of Washington, D.C., in the green hills of Maryland. Okay to have a beer or two, because the Air Force One crew would be flying as passengers.

The draft Pearl was cold, in frosted mugs. The jukebox played June Carter's latest version of "I've Got the Pill." Anderson, McGowan, and Lieutenant Colonel Carl Birney, the Navigator, were chewing on thick, red slabs of pizza.

"Okay," McGowan was arguing. "You finally saved the President. But it took you three tries."

Groaning, Anderson answered, "Plus a new set of piles." He patted his rump. "These Phase Three simulators are bastards. That first time we destructed, I really thought I was dead. I absolutely forgot that I was only piloting a mock-up controlled by computers."

Birney reached for another slice of the spiced Mexi-Pizza. "I don't know why I even ride in them," he said in a deep bassoon voice. "I can't take star shots or use dead reckoning. It's all radio and radar. Plus the black box."

At forty-three, and having flown with it most of his life, Birney, like most navigators, scorned the inertial guidance system—the omnipotent black box which, given a starting time and precise location, would lock into all systems and provide a position accurate down to a matter of square yards after a 7,000-mile random flight. Originally developed to guide the Navy's nuclear subs, inertial guidance was the nearest thing to navigation perfection yet attained by man. Its only weakness was getting cut off from a stable power supply. Then, starved for energy, it would become confused and inaccurate. Which was why Lieutenant Colonel Carl Birney had to fly aboard Air Force One. By now, every major airline had dispensed with navigators—and so had most Air Force missions. All, in fact, except this one. Glumly, Birney described his job as "backup man for the black box."

"You ride with us," Anderson corrected dryly, "because if you didn't, I wouldn't have anybody to play Liar's Poker with."

Birney chuckled. Anderson, forty-eight and overage for a chicken Colonel, had a reputation for never taking risks—except when playing Liar's Poker, when he became reckless and a sure pigeon. Once on each mission, out of pity, Birney would overlook Anderson's outrageous bluffs and let him win enough to pay for a round of beers.

Anderson was almost rail-thin. At six two, he tended to hunch over when he walked—a habit born of many cracked skulls against unforgiving aircraft doors. His voice was a soft, midwestern drawl. He would have been right at home in any John Ford Western movie.

Had he been willing to accept a Training Command, or a Pentagon job, Anderson would have had his star by now—and probably the second one too. But he clutched the role of Aircraft Commander to him like a security blanket. Once, when President Jimmy Carter had privately offered him a position on the staff of the Joint Chiefs, Anderson had gone right to the wire of resignation rather than leave flying status. Carter, a line man himself, understood—

and had even defended Anderson when the Air Force
brass interpreted the Colonel's refusal as defiance.
Anderson had been shipped off to head a SAC wing
on Guam. So out of touch were the brass that they
still regarded that Pacific island as a Siberia, instead
of the swinging tourist paradise it had become.

Now, sipping Pearl beer and crunching a Mexican
Pete's Supreme Pizza in a noisy highway restaurant
east of Fort Worth, he stroked back his tousled pepper-
and-salt hair and resolutely put Guam out of his
mind. Guam, and its sunny laziness, and twisting white
coral roads, and the death that waited there beneath
the sheltering palm trees.

McGowan persisted. "What I mean, Tom, is that
the third time around, you knew the tornado was up
there waiting for us. You anticipated it. That gave
you enough edge to buy a couple of seconds."

"Agreed," said Anderson. "But in most emergencies
that may come up, we'll be able to anticipate precisely
because we've trained ourselves to recognize them
before they happen. That's the value of the simulators.
It's like practicing your batting. You may know the
pitcher's going to give you a curve, but the problem is
in learning to hit it."

"Nobody throws curves any more," grumbled Mc-
Gowan. His angular face glowered under a sheaf of
jet-black hair that looked as if he had combed it
with his fingers. Which he had. His teeth were so
white that they looked false, and only rarely did they
relax into a smile. At forty, McGowan's career paral-
leled that of Anderson's in that he had held on to the
controls of SAC's B-52s longer than was good for his
professional standing in today's management-oriented
Air Force.

He scorned the gung-ho attitude of the Air Force
One mission, saying—usually while filling out efficiency
reports—"Even Steve Canyon would have only been
able to swing a 3.6 in this chicken outfit." What he

really resented was having to overpraise his crews, because an "excellent" rating would have been interpreted as merely adequate. It was much the same in
his native Los Angeles, where a movie producer, when
told that his latest film was "great," would ask, "What's
the matter, didn't you like it?"

Anderson looked at his watch. "Nine-thirty," he
said, avoiding the "2130" affectation of those pilots
who lived by the twenty-four-hour clock. "We're due
on the flight line at six. We'd better break this up
pretty soon."

Flying east was always a pain in the ass. You lost
an hour off the clock before you even got aboard. To
have any useful work time at Andrews, you had to
leave shortly after dawn had crawled over the mountains.

"Tired?" asked Birney. He made the word casual,
but it was one he had used often recently when speaking to Anderson.

"Hell, yes," said the Aircraft Commander. "Aren't
you? How many tornadoes a day do you want?"

"Speaking of tornadoes," said McGowan, nodding
his head toward the bar, "check that action."

Anderson and Birney turned their heads. Sitting
near the revolving Coors Beer sign, a tawny blonde
dressed in the absolute minimum between herself and
pneumonia in this chill, air-conditioned room, met
their eyes and smiled. It might have been for any one
of them.

"She's an Eskimo," said Birney.

"Sure," said McGowan. "Don't you recognize her?
She's one of the stews training out at American."

"She's the Good Fairy, Pinocchio," said Ánderson,
getting up and throwing a five on the table. "You
guys can wail all night. I'm bushed. See you in the
morning."

"Right," said McGowan, distracted by the blonde.

He gave her a wide grin, and she responded with a lift of one eyebrow.

With Anderson gone, Birney said, "He's awful tired lately. Have you noticed?"

"Shhhh," said McGowan, making a toasting motion with one hand, and indicating the just vacated chair with the other. "I think I'm in love."

"Sure," said the Navigator. "You always are."

Half a continent to the northeast, Senator Philip Hopper spoke, with the deadly whisper he used when confronted with an enemy to Morton Bailey, President Howard Foster's press secretary.

"*MOR*ton," said Hopper, putting the emphasis on the first syllable, "this is important to me. We both know that the President is going to be using Air Force One later this month."

Bailey, trying not to lie and yet protect what he knew the new President wanted to remain secret, said, "Senator, nothing's definite yet. As you know, the 747 is still undergoing tests out in Washington State and—"

"And there's no way in the world the President of the United States, whatever campaign promises he may have made, is going to fly again commercially. Morton, Howard Foster and I have known each other for twenty years, on the Hill and before." Tauntingly, knowing that it was merely the switchboard number, he added, "I can call him at home right now—456-1414, isn't it?"

Reluctantly, Bailey said, "I'll see what I can do, Senator. If I have it right, you want to accompany him on the next flight he makes using aircraft from the 89th Military Airlift Wing."

"Wrong," said Senator Hopper. "I'm not interested in any trips he makes aboard a standard Air Force jet. I want to be aboard the next flight of Air Force One."

"Sir," said Bailey, "any plane carrying the President

automatically becomes Air Force One. It can be a four engine jet, or a two-place Piper Cub. And if it's Army, it will be called Army One—"

"I know all that," interrupted Hopper. "When I say Air Force One, I refer to that fancy one-man flying carpet with rugs from Istanbul and interior decoration by Raymond Loewy. Shall I continue with the description?"

Morton Bailey sighed. "No, Senator. This will take a day or two. I'll call you back."

"Be sure to do that, *MOR*ton," said the Senator.

Naval Lieutenant (jg) Liv Matthews stared at the telephone near her bed: 11:14 P.M.; 10:14 in Fort Worth. He would be at the Ramada East. The crews always stayed there. Air Force billets were available, but long ago the decision had been made to keep Air Force One personnel apart from line pilots and crews.

She had the number in her permanent address book. When she had gone to Fort Worth for training, she stayed at the Ramada East too. It was only a ten-minute drive from the American Airlines Flight Academy, had an adequate restaurant and good TV reception. It had been there that she first met him, one evening after a long day of training, practicing ocean ditchings and water first aid.

The "fifteen-second man," they described him. It sounded like the punch line to a dirty story. She'd giggled when she heard Colonel Thomas Anderson called that.

Her boss, Lieutenant Commander George Agee, stifled the giggle. A Navy doctor assigned to the President, he said, "This is Colonel Anderson's second tour as the AC of Air Force One. He flew it six years ago, for eighteen months, when Colonel Gardner was killed in that car crash. In more than fifty flights, some of them halfway around the world, Anderson was never more than fifteen seconds off his ETA."

At that time, she had never flown aboard the President's airplane. So she didn't know. "What's so important about that?" she asked. "We all wait for the President, no matter how late he is."

"*We* may," said the doctor, "but a foreign King or Premier won't. The welcoming ceremony's planned down to the split second. It would be embarrassing for the President to arrive late and have a head of state waiting. It'd be just as bad for him to arrive early and have to wait himself."

They were dining in the Dodge City Room, which featured thick rib roasts and spicy barbecued steaks. Anderson, with a slim red-haired woman, seemed to be enjoying himself. The woman wore a blue pants suit and her hair hung down almost to her waist.

"His wife," said Agee.

"She's very young."

"Second time around." The Commander did not explain further, and Liv had not asked.

Later, they had joined the Andersons for a drink, and Liv met Martha Desmond at the same time she did the pilot. Marty, as she demanded that she be called, was in her early thirties and volunteered that she was a free-lance designer and that she had worked on the renovation of Air Force One with Raymond Loewy as a precocious teen-ager, just out of college, when Nixon had commissioned the assignment. Today, she looked hardly into her twenties. Her eyes were a deep green, and—without makeup—seemed as large and luminous as Sonoma grapes. Her voice had a persistent break to it, like a modern-day June Allyson.

"I'm spoiling Tom's weekend," she confided to Liv. "I know what he'd rather be doing tonight."

"What?" Liv asked innocently.

Marty Desmond Anderson stared at the nurse in disbelief, tilted back her head, and laughed.

Liv's finger trembled on the first digit of the number—a 1—then pressed it. The chirp of the direct punch dialing whispered in her ear, and then the others in rapid succession. The Ramada's operator answered, listened, said, "One moment," and then his voice—slow, slightly rasping, weary, said, "Colonel Anderson."

"Florence Nightingale," she said. It was their private joke. He had used it in jest the first time she reported aboard President Foster's temporary Air Force One, a jet left over from the previous Administration. Angered at first, she soon realized that his meaning was gentle, and aimed at her long blue cloak rather than at Liv herself. It had survived the intervening three months.

Originally, Foster had promised to abolish the expensive fleet of planes maintained at Andrews AFB for the President's use. Actually, the planes were more used—and abused—by the Senate and Congress than by the Executive Office.

The outgoing President had ordered a Boeing 747 Jumbo Jet before the outcome of the election, and the work was too far along to stop without incurring a huge loss. Reluctantly, Foster had decided to allow its completion. But overruns in schedule left him without an aircraft of his own, and after two attempts at fulfilling his campaign promise to eliminate presidential aircraft, Foster had gone on national television and explained why he had failed to do so.

The reason was simple: flying commercially, the White House had found itself buying out the full flight loads of two or three commercial jets, having to virtually rewire them to keep the President in communication with the White House and Defense outposts, and inconveniencing hundreds of passengers.

"I was wrong," he admitted on camera. "I'd rather fly back there in tourist and pay two bucks for my drink like the rest of you, but it's impossible. Next time, I'll keep my mouth shut until I know what the bottom line is. As for now, I promise you we'll run the operation as cheaply as we can. From now on, no freebies. Everybody pays first-class rates, including me."

And they did. Although it had been a long-standing custom for reporters to have their papers or networks billed for travel expenses, Senators and White House personnel were not accustomed to dipping into personal or office funds.

Still, opponents of White House spending such as Senator Philip Hopper criticized the Air Force One mission as wasteful. Others felt that this was partisan politics, aimed at restricting the President's freedom of movement—particularly in an election year.

"How's the Lone Eagle?" asked Liv. She had never been able to bring herself to use the other nickname. Maybe Tom Anderson did not even know it existed.

"Weary," he said. "They really threw it at us today. How are things back home?"

"Cold," she said. Although it was early March, the winter had not yet released its grip on the capital. "I nearly didn't get the car started this morning."

"Poor baby," he said. "When I get back, I'll stop over and pour some white gas down your carburetor."

She choked with laughter. "You'll *what*?"

He chuckled too. "It's perfectly harmless, believe me." She thought she heard a yawn. "What's new in the Pharmacy?"

Another private joke-code. The Pharmacy was the Pentagon. While he, as Commanding Officer of the 89th Military Airlift Wing, Special Missions (MAC), standing for Military Airlift Command, received advance information concerning all missions, often the President's doctor sometimes knew earlier. Because of special medical requests or immunization procedures, the news often leaked to the presidential medical group.

She was tempted to pass along the rumor she had heard earlier that day. But it was still in the early whisper stage. Something about cold-weather gear. But it was too slight to trouble him with tonight.

"Shop's closed up tight," she said. "I just wanted to be sure you were coming back tomorrow."

"We'll be in after lunch," he said. "So far as I know, Friday's a No-Fly. Want a martini at the Club?"

"No," she said. "Not at the Club. I'll call you around four. Maybe the Tiki?"

"Good," he said, openly yawning. She could hear the sigh in the earpiece of the telephone. "Good night, Flo."

"Good night," said the young nurse. She hung up the telephone and, in surprise, looked at her hand.

It was trembling.

In far-off Montana, a telephone rang in the darkness.

A gruff man's voice said sleepily, "Hello?"

"Are you serious about this thing?"

The man sat up. He had been dozing at his desk. "Absolutely. Why?"

"I've decided to help."

"Good. When will you know anything?"

"I'm not sure. The President hasn't been flying around much. But he's about due. Are you sure you can carry it off?"

"You know my combat record."

"But this won't be combat."

"I can handle it," said the man in Montana. "Just bird-dog that goddamned plane for me, I'll do the rest. I want to know where Air Force One is headed, and when she's due, and that's all I need from you."

"All right," said the distant voice. "Stay close to your phone."

"I'll be here," said the man in Montana glumly. "I can't even afford to go downtown to buy a beer."

2

In January of 1943, when he flew from Miami to Casablanca, Franklin Delano Roosevelt became the first American President to travel by air.

In that second year of America's participation in World War II, flying was still regarded as a daredevil occupation. But there was little choice for the President. A meeting with Churchill, De Gaulle, and other Allied leaders was imperative. And the U-boat menace to ship travel was even more hazardous than a transatlantic flight.

Besides, Roosevelt had a keen eye for drama, and an even more acute sense of history. Privately, he detested flying. But since he must, he would milk it dry politically.

On January 11, 1943, he took off from Dinner Key Seaplane Base in Miami, aboard a Boeing 314—identification number NC18605—for the four-leg flight via Trinidad, Brazil, Dakar in West Africa, then north to Casablanca.

The thirty-second President of the United States, leaving Miami aboard the Dixie Clipper, was shattering four precedents. Since Abraham Lincoln, no President had ever personally visited a war zone. Nor had one ever been to Africa—or even left the continental United States during wartime.

And, as Roosevelt knew well, none had ever flown.

The historic flight was a great success. So much so that by the fall of 1943, a secret plan known as an line soon. Another overrun of $370,000. Although the President's advisers that more trips such as the Casablanca flight were in the future, and they prepared for them.

Douglas Aircraft, at Santa Monica, California, was directed to build a transport plane for presidential use. A highly modified four-engine C-54A, fuselage No. 78, the new plane was moved to a top-security corner of the Douglas plant where only carefully screened workers were allowed access to its mysteries.

The tradition of a military pilot commanding the presidential airplane began with the Casablanca flight, piloted by Lieutenant Howard M. Cone, USNR—and · that tradition carried down through the decades and nine Presidents. Every officer and enlisted man assigned to the 89th was aware of it, and of the responsibility it demanded.

Over the years, operations for the Presidential Mission had been performed by several units, but its bloodline remained true to that first flight commanded by Lieutenant Cone.

The 89th's motto, emblazoned on the sign in front of the Operations Building, is *Experto Crede*—"Trust One Who Has Experience." An understatement in a world of men whose stock-in-trade is playing it cool.

Colonel Thomas Anderson was leafing through correspondence as the Air Force jet circled for final approach. As Andrews came into view, he glanced down at a new budget readout for the 747 which would be on line soon. Another overrun of $370,000. Although Anderson had not been involved in the 747 project, he knew he would take some heat from President Foster over this latest setback. It would not disturb him. As Commanding Officer of the 89th, it was his job to absorb the punishment along with the praise. But, looking at the official address of the 89th Military Airlift Wing, Special Missions (MAC), Andrews AFB,

Washington, D.C., he had to smile. Because Andrews was actually across the Potomac, in Maryland!

His neck itched and, absently, he scratched. He wore Class A blues, slacks and an informal blue nylon flight jacket with the Presidential Service Badge over the right pocket, silver wings over the left. The Presidential Service Badge bore a superimposed replica of the Presidential Coat of Arms. The badge is awarded, by direction of the President, to Armed Forces personnel assigned to White House duty for at least one year. It is recognition, in a permanent way, of their contribution to the service of the President of the United States. The uniform was immaculate, with knife-edge creases down the trouser legs. No thanks to his wife. Martha Desmond Anderson, while she often spoke of how handsome her husband was in uniform, had yet to press iron to cloth, or even launder a shirt. Anderson, without comment, bundled up his clothing once a week and turned it in to the base laundry. Unknown to him, because the sergeant who actually ran the laundry did not think it seemly for the CO's shirts to revolve in the same drier with those of the ground crew, sent the garments to a French cleaner on N Street in the capital and paid for it with purloined Air Force One matches, napkins, and the occasional inscribed highball glass. All were presented to favored customers by the manager.

Anderson looked at his watch. It was Richards Aqualung, with black dial and large, bright numerals. For the past year, with his heavy sweating, he had found it impossible to wear any watch which used base metal in its casing. They rusted off his wrist in weeks. So, hating gold, he had bought this stainless-steel model while on a trip to New York. He had changed bands twice, but there was not the slightest trace of pitting on the case of the watch itself.

Twelve-eighteen, Washington time. Despite a late takeoff, they'd make good time, picking up the jet stream, which, at this time of the year, was curving down through the heartland of the country. He had dozed, done some paper work, but—surprisingly—had felt no urge to go forward and harass the pilot.

Beside him, Major Paul McGowan slept, snoring quietly. Anderson reached over to shake him, drew back. He himself did not like to be touched while unawares.

"Paul," he said, raising his voice slightly. "Up and at 'em."

McGowan snored louder.

"Okay," said Anderson. "You asked for it." He leaned forward and, into the sleeping man's ear, whispered, "Fire in Number One."

McGowan leaped half to his feet, looking about wildly.

"Settle down," said Anderson. "We're on Final. Buckle up."

"Holy shit," said McGowan. "I must have been dreaming. I thought we had a fire."

"How about that," said Anderson, forcing back a smile.

There were dozens of messages waiting for Anderson in his office, but none from Marty. Nor, he remembered, had he heard from her during his four days in Texas. Well, there was no point in calling her now. She would be out to lunch with one of her clients.

Clients. She had many, but somehow few actual jobs materialized. Last year the IRS had contested her deduction of two rooms of their Silver Hill home for business. New rulings demanded more than the occasional file cabinet to consider a room as a home office. And her income had been less than her deductions. The compromise, an additional payment of nearly a thousand dollars in taxes, had cost her (and Tom) the aggravation of a full audit.

He'd had a flight lunch aloft, so a trip to the Officer's Mess wasn't necessary. With an efficiency born of the distaste he had for this part of his job, he attacked the necessary paper work and, when it was 2 P.M., began returning calls.

At three, he dialed the number of the President's personal physician. A woman Petty Officer answered, and he asked for Lieutenant Matthews.

"I'm sorry, sir," said the Petty Officer. "She's out. Can she return your call?"

"Yes," said Andersōn, looking at his watch. "I'll be here until four."

Actually, the Lieutenant was not out at all. She was engaged in a raging argument with Samuel Milnes, President Foster's senior Secret Service man.

"This is a question that should be discussed with Commander Agee," she said, trying to keep anger from distorting her voice.

Bluntly, the Secret Service man said, "He's not here, and you are."

"Not for long, if you have your way," she said hotly.

"Lieutenant, it's nothing personal. But it's simple arithmetic. I'm supposed to carry five men on board Air Force One. If you come along, one gets bumped and I'm down to four."

"You can transport as many men as you want aboard the advance plane," she said. "You already have men there for the Bucket of Guts."

Milnes frowned. The Secret Service touring car which always followed just behind the President's Lincoln Continental was sometimes called that by the men who rode in, and on, it. But it was lèse majesté for an outsider to use the name which, only half jokingly, referred to the standing order that in the event of any threat of violence every man was to instantly interpose his body between the danger and the President.

"The advance plane is jammed," he said. "Besides, I have to consider security in case it has to turn back or is diverted from our own destination."

"Mr. Milnes," she said, trying to bring rationality back to the conversation, "this isn't anything you or I can decide. We don't have the authority."

He resented this woman, half his age, assuming equality with him in deciding what was best for *his* President.

So, knowing but not admitting that he was wrong, Agent Samuel Milnes flared. "Lady, I'm taking my full crew. I don't care if you ride back with the press corps, or in the goddamned john, but you're not taking a seat that belongs to one of my men."

And, knowing she was wrong too, Liv retorted, "I suppose that's something Commander Agee will have to decide."

It was an unfortunate challenge to throw at a man who, twice in his forty-eight years, had put his life on the scales in protection of a President.

"No, ma'am," said the Secret Service man, his voice now flat and expressionless as the leaden sea before a hurricane, "I guess it's something for the White House to decide."

3

Such is the power of the White House that even those who hold great power in their own right scuffle like hungry beggars in a bazaar to grab one of its tiny, uncomfortable, crowded offices. For no matter who you may be telephoning, or why, your position is automatically established from the moment the operator says, "Hello, Mr. So-and-so? I have a call from the White House."

Anderson was linked to the White House in another way. He, and all key Air Force One personnel, carried personal beepers. These were no ordinary "Doctor, call your office" types. They could be activated anywhere in the world by a powerful shortwave signal which emanated from a linkage of antennas, microwave networks, land lines, and satellite transmissions.

Once, when the beeper had gone off at a most inopportune moment, Marty had squirmed from beneath the suddenly tense body of her husband and, in a mixture of laughter and anger, told Anderson, "I thought so! That bastard's bugged your prick!"

Anderson had laughed along with her as he dressed hurriedly, and did not make reference to her having called the President of the United States "that bastard."

They had been taking a long weekend in their cabin on Taylors Island in Chesapeake Bay, and there was no phone. He had to drive two miles to the nearest combination gas station and general store, where he direct-dialed 456-1414, gave his identification code, and was informed by the President's Chief of Staff, Arthur Cummings, that the lid was on for the weekend and he was authorized to stand down from duty.

Anderson cursed the entire two miles back to the cabin without once repeating himself.

"Standing down" was a false designation anyway. It was the pride of the 89th that, whether or not the CO was on the base, Air Force One could be airborne less than sixty minutes from the time a request was received. That time could be cut in half if the flight departed without full food service, relying on box lunches and frozen dinners.

Now, at a quarter of four in the afternoon, the beeper sounded. He switched it off and reached for the telephone.

As soon as Sam Milnes left her office, Liv called Arthur Cummings and asked if she could see him. He agreed, and she crossed over to the White House from the Executive Office Building, showed her identification to the guard, who, while recognizing her, still examined both sides of the ID card carefully, and entered through the basement.

The Chief of Staff's office was at the far end of the West Wing from the Oval Office. Liv took the elevator up, waited for a moment in the outer office while Julie White, his long-time secretary, buzzed Cummings.

Julie said, "He's on long-distance, dear, but it'll only be a minute. Would you like some coffee?"

Julie kept a Mr. Coffee machine on her desk, with four mugs that bore the presidential seal—reserved for the privileged few. When, on previous visits, Liv had accepted coffee, it was served in the polystyrene cups Julie kept in her top right drawer.

"No, thanks," said the nurse. "I'm saving up to buy a pound of my own."

Julie laughed, and then cocked her head.

"He's off," she said. "Go on it. I'll buzz him."

Wondering how the bird-like woman had been able to sense that the long-distance call was over, Liv went into Arthur Cummings' corner office. He was at the window, looking down at Lafayette Square. Without turning, he said "Ah, trouble approaches."

"Only if you start it," she said. "You and Sam Milnes."

He turned. Arthur Cummings was a slender, dapper man with a neatly combed "wet look" hairstyle which was serviced regularly by one of the best—and most discreet—hairdressers in Washington. At fifty-two, Cummings had been a very successful lawyer, had earned millions by judicious investments (and by never reaching for a dinner check), was still a bachelor much in demand at the most "in" parties, and, most importantly, had the complete trust and attention of the new President.

"You tortured him," said Cummings. "Poor Sam. He promised me he'd bite the poison capsule if you tried to get the truth out of him."

"Be serious," said Liv, sitting down without being asked. She and the Chief of Staff each knew, and appreciated, the other's worth. He knew very well why he was in this corner office. And he knew why she was on Commander George Agee's staff.

Still, he could not resist playing the Game. Washington, D.C., is a company town with only one industry—the Government. Like those company towns of song and legend, where your balladeer had to lift fifteen tons and still owe his soul to the company store, this Baghdad on the Potomac paid off with scrip which had to be spent on the premises or not at all.

The scrip was in the form of perks—perquisites—privileges, honors, invitations, favors from distant cor-

porations and universities and even governments. The
scrip was perishable. It could not be stored up for a
rainy day. It had to be used now.

So Arthur Cummings lifted a thick folder from his
desk and, as if he had not already been completely
familiar with its contents, pretended to read.

"Olivia Jane Matthews, Caucasian female, aged
twenty-eight. Born in Bethany, Missouri. Graduate of
Minnesota School of Nursing. Height, five three. Eyes,
blue. Blond hair." He looked up, added, "Presumably
natural. Weight, one twenty-four."

"One twenty-five," she corrected. "I ate a Big Mac
for lunch."

"Oh?" he said lightly. "Anyone I know?"

She did not answer, nor did she look away. Liv, in
her brief time in the capital, had already learned how
strong an aphrodisiac Power can be. Mousy little
politicians who, in their home districts, would have
blushed at a "dirty" word spoken by a woman, became instant garter snappers and chasers the moment
they set foot on Constitution Avenue. The double
meaning and oftentimes blunt statement of sexual
suggestions did not embarrass her, but neither did
they attract her.

Cummings pretended not to notice the gap in the
conversation. He continued to read: "Direct commission in United States Navy, January of this year. Current rank, Lieutenant, junior grade." He looked up.
"Surely you could have done better than that."

"Mr. Cummings," she said. "I wasn't trying to do
'better' than anything. I was quite happy at the Mayo
Clinic. It wasn't my idea to join the Navy and See
the World. As a matter of fact, so far all I've seen is
my office over in the EOB."

"Ah, yes," he said. "But you hope to see more soon,
from the windows of Air Force One."

She did not rise to the bait. "You sent Sam over to

brace me," she said. "Why? You, of all people, must know why I was assigned to the mission."

"Do I?" he asked. "Do *you*?"

Quietly, she said, "Yes."

No more. It was still something she preferred not to speak aloud. The dependence Howard Foster had felt for her, since those two weeks he had spent at the Clinic just a few months before the Democratic National Convention had chosen him as their candidate for the presidency, was a sharing between the two of them. Although sure that Commander Agee knew everything, she had never mentioned it.

The facts were on the record: Senator Howard Foster had gone to the Mayo Clinic for treatment of a benign tumor. He had been cured. A week before his Inauguration, the Navy approached Nurse Olivia Matthews and asked if she would join Commander George Agee as part of the President's medical team. Although not sure she was making the right decision, she accepted the commission.

Cummings said, "He doesn't really need you."

"I know."

"Then why don't you fly on the advance plane? Sam's right—the Secret Service team is spread pretty thin as it is."

"Mr. Cummings, I'm trying to keep this disagreement from blowing up any bigger than it is already. The President, for whatever reasons he deems important, requested me to join Commander Agee in being available for him whenever he wants us. I can't be available if I'm an hour ahead in the advance plane."

Cummings gave an ugly chuckle. "Well, if he gets too hard up, we've got a female stew on board now. Something for everybody. A woman steward for the first time in history. A Chicano Flight Engineer. A nigger Bagman. Some crew."

Despite herself, Liv felt her ears burning. "You're

right," she heard herself say, as if from some vast distance. "And a horse's ass for Chief of Staff."

Chief Warrant Officer Fred Stewart, the primary "Bagman," did not feel his ears burn. It was his rear end that was giving him difficulty.

Stewart was the President's shadow. Wherever Foster went, Fred Stewart would not be far away. And always with him was a sturdy black valise, secured by a combination lock. Only the Bagman, whoever he happened to be, knew that combination. At one time the valise had been known as "the Football."

When briefed on the purpose of the Bagman, Howard Foster had barked, "What the hell do we do if there's a nuclear alert and this joker has a heart attack on us?"

Seriously, Arthur Cummings had answered, "We chop his arm off at the wrist. The combination's engraved inside the handcuff."

Caught up in the laughter, Stewart had gone out on a long limb. He shook the chain that linked him to the valise and said, "Anything but that! I'll have the combo tattooed on my balls."

"Oh?" demanded Foster. "And does your girl friend have a Top Secret clearance?"

To be so near to the hub of power, and yet not actually possess any of it, was the constant frustration of the Bagman. In rebellion, legend has it, one Bagman arrived for duty carrying *two* valises. The usual large black one, and a smaller, brown one.

"Two bags?" asked the victim, an unfortunate military attaché. "What for?"

The Bagman, all innocence, had answered, "Sir, the black one is for World War Three, total nuclear strike."

"What about the little one?"

"That's in case we have to invade Cuba again."

At thirty-six, Fred Stewart was unmarried. The

Army was his wife and mistress. He had supported a younger brother through medical school, and now that Ernest was doing well, saved most of his salary and spent the rest on electronic kits from the Heath Company in Benton Harbor, Michigan. Two hours with a circuit board and a soldering iron were as thrilling to Stewart as a night on the town with a sexy starlet would have been for some of the other men in the outfit. Which was just as well. Stewart had been examined under a microscope before being offered this assignment, and one night with an un-cleared hooker would be enough to uncuff that valise from his wrist.

He was keenly aware that he was the tip of the black iceberg which made up so much of the peace-time Army. Highly visible, always on call, Fred Stew-art had deliberately decided to submerge his own life to the discipline of his unusual job. The usual tour of duty for a Bagman was two years. At its end, he would be given his choice of assignments.

Fred Stewart claimed he had just about decided to request duty at Little America in Antarctica. His joke, for his few friends, was "Babe, I've been so close to the heat for so long, I want to go someplace where it's cold!"

Liv Matthews reached Colonel Thomas Anderson at ten after four, just as he was turning out the fluores-cent light of his office.

"I'm sorry," she said. "I got busy."

"Unbusy now?"

"Uh-huh. What about you?"

Anderson had just called his home for the third time since his arrival. Still no answer.

"I'm loose," he said. "But I don't want to come all the way into town. Why don't we crash at the Apple Tree, on Route Five."

"Just this side of Fort McNair?"

"That's the one. Half an hour?"

"Colonel, you're on. Bring money. I'm ready for a double."

He started to make a clever reply, perhaps suggest that she pick up the check with her Navy pay, but didn't. Something in her voice gave the lie to the humor she was trying to project.

"That can be arranged," he said. And, after a good-bye, he hung up.

His four-year-old Plymouth Fury wagon was parked in its spot just a few yards from the Headquarters Building. Although it had rained earlier that day the Fury was spotless. And when he turned the key, the engine caught immediately. Gremlins, hard at work, he thought. At first he had tried to discourage his enlisted staff from performing little personal favors like making sure his car's battery didn't run down while he was away. But he gave up with good grace when it became obvious that his protests were not going to do any good.

The enlisted men of the 89th had perhaps the highest morale of any Air Force unit in the world. Of course, even by revised modern service standards, they lived well. Each man had his own private room—almost a suite. There were no dull-green wall lockers, or GI cots. The furniture was civilian style, with normal beds and chests of drawers, and even a refrigerator. Television, stereo—both were allowed, and their volume levels were controlled only by the consideration of other men in the same building.

Other *personnel*, Anderson corrected himself. Several enlisted women also had rooms in the 89th's quarters. At first, a separate latrine and shower had been assigned to them. But soon, at the request of the women themselves, the facilities—which were smaller and more private than normal barracks latrines anyway—were desegregated. An informal arrangement involving a "Do Not Disturb" sign hanging from the doorknob let those in the hall know which sex had possession of the john. It was a system that had worked well for some time now without incident.

Returning the salute of the Air Policeman at the gate, Anderson turned left on Allentown Road. It was a mile or so out of his way, but at this time of day, the Capital Beltway would be jammed with trucks and long-distance drivers, hurrying around the arterial in an attempt to get out of the Washington area before the five o'clock rush.

Another reason, he mused, for the high morale of the 89th was simply that the personnel were of such high caliber. While the standards for assignment to the Wing itself were not as strict as those for actual aircrew and maintenance personnel, the requirements were still harsh enough to automatically disqualify two out of three applicants. For some years now, the 89th had been an all-volunteer outfit. Anyone assigned to duty there had merely to inform his CO that he did not want the transfer, and without discussion his name would be erased from the roster.

Of course, just like the coach of a hot football team, the 89th personnel officer spent quite a bit of time recruiting. One of the pilots, relaxing at some distant Officer's Club, might hear of a wizard electronics repairman or a burly magician who could coax wonders out of ailing jet engines. Soon, after a quiet investigation of the man's military record, his background, and his financial and marital situation—even his drinking habits—the man would be summoned to the CO's office. He would be interviewed by at least two representatives from the 89th. If everything checked out, he would be invited to transfer in for a four-year tour. Most 89th personnel were career men, and the four-year tour fitted in with their overall service profile.

If he accepted, and would be in direct contact with the Air Force One mission, an in-depth FBI investigation would then be made. He would be warned of this at the beginning, and could refuse to go further without prejudice. Some, with youthful records of troublemaking, theft, or drugs, would decline the investigation. Nothing ever went on their service records —they were simply eliminated from consideration for the 89th.

Excessive drinking, marital difficulties, heavy debts —all were grounds for turning down a man. The risks of accepting someone who might be unstable, desperate for money, or a target for outside pressure were simply too great to accept.

Anderson reached Branch Avenue, which was also Route 5, and turned north toward Washington. Traffic was moderate going into the city, heavier coming out. Liv Matthews would probably be late.

He smiled as he thought of her. The tip of her silky blond head came barely to his shoulder, so unless they were seated, his impression of her was that of an impish face constantly peering up at him. She smiled easily, and when he was with her he tended to also.

Not that they had ever "dated." A casual drink, like today, over which they discussed the mission, the President, and, he admitted frankly, when he picked her brain to get an advance hint of some possible mission that was too nebulous for him to have been informed about. And training, for her duties aboard the plane.

So far, except for short flights in one of the backup planes, the President had made no trips involving the VC-137C, which, in the minds of everyone at the 89th was the *real* Air Force One.

But Anderson sensed that something was coming soon. The training had intensified. Each flier and crewman's proficiency had been honed to a sharp edge of preparedness. Like a runner straining at the blocks, the crew was ready, trembling in anticipation of the starter's gun.

Ahead, he saw a large red wooden apple hanging from the extended limb of an oak tree. He slowed, pulled into the driveway of the restaurant. His watch told him he was four minutes early.

Before leaving his office, he had changed into a regulation blouse. No crewman ever wore the Air Force One insignia into a bar, not even an overseas Officer's Club.

Although he did not come here often, the manager recognized him, came over to seat him personally.

"Colonel, good to see you. In the corner, where it's quiet?"

"Fine," said Anderson. They both knew that not only was the corner booth quiet, it was invisible from most of the room. No mention was made of this, or who Anderson was. There might be gossip later among the help, but it was never voiced publicly.

"Will you order?"

"I'm expecting someone. I'll wait."

"Some cider, then." The Apple Tree never hustled a customer to refill—and if a drink was not ordered, such as just now, a tall glass of fresh apple cider, non-alcoholic and free, was presented. With the prices charged for dinner and wine, the management could afford to be generous.

Waiting, and sipping the sweet cider, Anderson took out a small calculator. Most pilots used these battery-operated wonders now instead of the circular Jeppesen Computers they had learned to fly with. Still, they had to keep themselves familiar with the Jeppesens too, because that solid standby was still required during flight checks. Fuel burn versus range was the constant battle waged by long-distance pilots. Always having alternative fields well within reach was important to commercial flights; to Air Force One, it was vital. Every unscheduled landing was a fresh danger to the President, since a diversion to a new field might leave little or no time to arrange for security. When possible, Anderson always arranged for two Air Force bases to be his alternates. So far, in the few months of President Foster's Administration, no diversions had been necessary. But during the eighteen months he had flown for the previous President, after the Command Pilot had been killed in a car accident, Anderson had been forced to divert twice. Once was when a sudden shift of weather covered March AFB with fog without warning. He had been forced to land at Hamilton AFB, near San Francisco. The other was when Number Three began to vibrate and overheat. He'd set down at Maxwell AFB in Montgomery, Alabama, where he found that the jet engine had somehow, at nearly 33,000 feet, ingested an unfortunate Canadian snow goose flying alone, presumably blown off the flyway from Louisiana to Quebec by strong jet-stream winds.

The plane's wing had already been modified to land slower, yet fly faster, than any standard 707 in the world. Still, if he could increase the Lift/Drag ratio by . . .

"Is this a private brainstorm, or can anyone play?" asked a voice, startling him.

He switched off the calculator's display. Liv Matthews had slipped into the chair opposite him. She wore her trim Navy blues and, he noticed, filled them nicely.

"Oh, no," he said. "I've been burned once by you." The last time he had let her use his calculator, she punched up a series of numbers, hit the "total" button, and when she held the calculator upside down, it had (if you stretched your imagination) spelled out the word H-E-L-L, that being the way the digital readout of 7-7-3-4 appeared when inverted.

She slipped her leather purse from her shoulder and put it beside her, under the table. "How flies the Lone Eagle?" she asked, smiling.

"All alone by the telephone," he said. "Apparently

I don't have a wife any more. No messages, and she's not at home."

Oh, no, thought Liv. I'm not walking into *that* one. She gave a slight shrug. "Probably career stuff," she said. "I read somewhere that 'Mrs. Martha (Marty) Anderson, wife of Air Force One's pilot, is discussing the design of the new pair of DC-10s Braniff has bought for the New York–South America run.' The poor girl's working her fanny off. And where's my martini?"

Anderson had caught the waiter's eye. "On the way. You're probably right. Still, I'd like to talk with Marty once in a while."

Liv, whose recitation of the imagined gossip item, which she had actually heard at a party earlier in the week, and which had also contained the juicy addition that Marty Anderson had flown to Dallas, just a few miles away from her husband's training base, and the Colonel didn't even know she was there, let her voice soften. "I know," she said. "It's rough when you both work."

The drinks came. A Beefeater martini, straight up, no olive, for Liv. A tall Dewars White Label scotch for him and a glass of plain water, no ice. He would keep adding the water as he emptied the drink. At the end, he'd be drinking nothing but scotch-flavored water. He liked it that way. He hated the thought of not being in full control of his senses or his actions.

The nod of his head at the waiter had been enough to let the bartender know they wanted the "usual," which—for important guests—was filed on neat cards. He'd been here only three times in as many months, twice with Liv, but because of his rank and position, he was in the file.

Anderson lifted his scotch, tipped it toward the lovely young woman in her severe Navy uniform. "Good luck," he said.

"Keep 'em flying," she replied, sipping, "Mmmmm. Dry."

He smiled. "The bartender just leans down and whispers, 'Vermouth . . . Vermouth,' over the glass."

"Please," she said. "Not *two* whispers. I like mine very dry."

"So," he said. "What's new at the Pharmacy?"

She hesitated. "Well, it may be nothing. But everything points to someplace cold."

"That could be anywhere in the country."

She shook her head. "No, *really* cold. We're laying in stuff for frostbite, flu shots, that sort of thing."

He put his glass down so hard that it spilled a single drop straight up into the air, which, luckily, returned to the glass.

"Montana!" he said. "Hell, yes."

"How can you be sure, Tom? It might be Canada—"

"No," he said. "We never take the Man anywhere unless I've already checked the field out in advance. And I flew into Helena last month, on what was supposed to be an endurance checkout of the bird. Sneaky, sneaky. I bet he's going up there to light a fire under Governor Hoskins' behind."

"He's the one who bolted the party during the convention and threw the delegates to Kennedy?"

"None other. Hoskins is trying to set Montana up as a private little duchy, with those shale-oil revenues giving him a financial base. He thinks he can control output and blackmail the country into subsidizing Montana with Most Favored Nation price scales on everything from eggs to toilet paper." Anderson sipped at his drink. "But why is the pilot always the last to know?"

"Don't start marking up those maps of yours yet," Liv said. "It's only a rumor at this stage."

"Still, it doesn't hurt to be ready, just in case." He reached out and took her hand, made a big gesture of shaking it. Did he hold it perhaps a moment longer than necessary? As the thought crossed his mind, he released her. "Many thanks, Flo. For everything."

"Not to mention."

"I need ninety hotel rooms," said Warren Rogers. "Plus the entire seventh floor."

The manager of the Helena, Montana, Great Northern Hotel choked.

"You don't know what you're asking," he said.

"I do," said Rogers. "I know how tight rooms are. But if you start now, you can arrange it. You can get some guests to double up, and shift others out to the motels."

"But this is such short notice."

Rogers scowled. "What kind of notice do you suggest?" he asked. "Enough to let every nut in Montana know that the President's coming, so he can get out his thirty-ought-six rifle and find a good place to shoot from?"

"My God, no," said the manager. "Mr. Rogers, I appreciate the difficulties of your job. It's just that I—"

"Can you do it?" asked Rogers. Then, more gently, he added, "*Will* you do it?"

The manager hesitated. "If I can," he said finally.

"Not good enough," said Rogers.

"All right. I will. But two nights maximum. I've got a convention coming in from Texas and—"

"Two will be fine," said Warren Rogers, Advance Man for the President of the United States. "Naturally, you'll bill us for the accommodations."

"I wish I didn't have to," began the manager, "but—"

"*Commercial* discount rates," added the Advance Man.

4

The first presidential Advance Man was Fidas Madison, actually Mrs. Washington's footman. When the first First Lady went calling, it was Fidas who arrived beforehand and, knocking loudly on the door of the house which Martha would be visiting, announced his mistress.

When the Washingtons and their family moved from New York to Philadelphia, then the capital of the newly won United States, they took Fidas and his wife, and another footman, James Porter. The President ordered liveries for them in two colors from his coat of arms—white with "trimmings & facings of scarlet & a scarlet waistcoat."

Speedy, efficient, loyal, Fidas and James were paid $8.00 a month.

Warren Rogers earned considerably more than that now, but he often wondered if the buying power of his $42,000 a year matched that of the $96 paid to Fidas Madison.

Rogers had begun his career as a bill poster for the ragtag Shotgun Pace Carnival & Monster Midway, hitting small southern towns a week before the Pace trucks rolled in. He traded ride tickets for window space, free admissions for room and board at run-down hotels. He "squared" the law, passing out tens and twenties in smelly back-room toilets. He primed the local newspaper, cajoling free space for the terrifying Snake Girl, buying an ad only whenever the editor and publisher, usually the same man, insisted on cash for space.

Two weeks in a Macon, Georgia, jail, with a charge of bribery hanging over his head showed Warren the error of his ways. Released on bail, he skipped town and since that day, more than twenty years ago, had not set foot on a carnival midway again.

Married in his late teens, he had divorced Mona on his twenty-first birthday. A stripper with the Pace girlie show, she did not bother to contest the suit. Now, with Shotgun long since gone to that great Ticket Booth in the Sky, she still drifted from one cheap midway to the next. Warren sent her a small check every month, enough to keep her in beer and Garrett's Snuff.

After leaving Macon so suddenly, he had drifted into the legitimate theater, where his ability to organize travel soon earned him a well-paying job with the public relations firm of Howard Bandy, the self-acknowledged king of Broadway flacks. Bandy, no fool, soon realized that the extraordinary logistical skill of Warren Rogers was bringing him plush accounts he would not normally have gotten, and elevated the young man to a full partnership. So, for more than ten years, Warren dealt with rail and air timetables, snippy hotel clerks, restaurant owners who were persuadable in the matter of providing free, or half-priced, meals in exchange for a Broadway star's publicity-winning presence at a highly visible table.

His life changed suddenly, in Boston, when he met Senator John F. Kennedy. Warren was doing advance work for a new production of *Strange Interlude,* which was doomed to die in New Haven, and he knew it, having seen three performances at the Shubert Theatre. He met the Senator backstage, where Kennedy had come to congratulate Paul Ford, one of the unfortunate performers.

A twinkle in his eye, Kennedy told Rogers, "It occurs to me that you may be looking for a job in the next few days."

"I'll make out," Rogers answered, secure in the knowledge that three other road tours were bidding for his services.

But it was Tip O'Neill who spelled out for him what Kennedy had really meant.

"He can't offer you a job outright," said O'Neill. "But if you ask for one, he'll say yes."

"Oh? Are the Kennedys going back into the movie business?"

"*This* Kennedy," said O'Neill seriously, "is going all the way to the White House."

Intrigued, Rogers joined the gregarious Irishman for several tall ones around the corner, and by 3 A.M. had concluded a handshake deal to help the Kennedy team during the primaries. Two weeks later, he was freezing in Minnesota, where—thanks to superb planning, much of which was originated by Rogers— Kennedy trounced Hubert Humphrey in Hubert's own state.

At the Convention, however, Rogers became disenchanted with some of the backstage shenanigans— particularly those which originated in the devious and fertile imagination of Bobby Kennedy—and turned in his PT-109 tie clip. Besides, with four years until another presidential election, he needed another job anyway. It never occurred to him that, even more than a campaigning candidate, an in-office President required a top Advance Man.

Through the Kennedy and Johnson years, Rogers coordinated the far-flung activities of MGM's location filming. When Richard M. Nixon decided to take on Vice-President Hubert Humphrey for the nation's top job, one of his aides came to Warren Rogers and suggested that, since he had once helped beat Humphrey, it might be fun to try it again.

Rogers laughed in the man's face. "Me? Run out in

front for Tricky Dick? No way. Buddy, you're going to be looking for a new job yourself in a couple of months."

He was wrong. Hubert's association with Johnson and the Vietnam war brought him down. "Dump the Hump" killed him in the first election which allowed eighteen-year-old voters at the polls. Only much later would the nation really learn how much raw courage and dignity there was inside the bouncy little man from Minnesota.

A virile forty-six, after Watergate, Gerald Ford, and the jovial peanut farmer from Plains, Georgia; quite satisfied with his comfortable life in the film industry, Rogers thought politics and advance work were both behind him. MGM had gone into the hotel business, but he was on constant call—not to hit the road any more, but to give advice to those who did—and he was an always welcome extra man at the few Hollywood parties that rated the description of "A" in a world which now regarded "C" as perfectly acceptable.

Then he received a visit from Senator Howard Foster. He knew Foster from the Kennedy campaign, when—as a Congressman—Foster had helped stump West Virginia. Some said it was Foster who came up with the daring idea of facing the Catholic issue squarely, instead of attempting to avoid it.

"Warren," said Foster, "I need you. I'm going all the way, and I'm going to do it el cheapo. I don't want any fat-cat money, and you know what that means. We'll do telethons, and sponge off the Rotary Clubs. If I get the nomination, I'll pledge myself to using only federal funds. Not a dime more."

"It can't be done," Rogers said flatly.

But it could. And was.

Privately, Foster admitted, "Warren Rogers got me elected. That slippery little bastard can cut a dime into six slices and still have change for the phone."

Such a contribution, under any other grateful President, would have resulted in a well-paying, non-working appointment. But Foster rewarded Rogers by keeping him on as his number one Advance Man.

As for Warren himself? He sighed, said, "Never trust a politician," and continued fighting the battle of the bulging wallet for his boss.

The battle here in Montana, however, was getting rather heated. Governor Claude Hoskins did not want President Howard Foster any closer to Helena than Chicago. Learning, through his friends in the capital, that he might expect a visit from the angry President, Hoskins had done his best to louse up the facilities in Helena. His first ploy, that of choking the hotels with conventions and visiting oilmen, had already failed. He had tried an end run, attempting to cancel the mayoral election, which was the lure that had attracted Foster. The previous Mayor, discovered with his arm in the oil till well over the elbow, had resigned in disgrace and now faced several counts of grand theft, fraud, and malfeasance of office. The Deputy Mayor had declined the honor of running the state capital. So a special election was obligatory. And, with all that new Republican money from the shale mines, the Democratic candidate for the office was in deep trouble.

Warren Rogers did not like Montana. He did not like having to plug his automobile into what looked like a parking meter, for electricity to keep an inblock heater bubbling away to prevent his engine from freezing up. He did not like paying more than three dollars for two eggs, a strip of bacon, and a foul mixture that pretended to be coffee. Above all, he did not like the henchmen of Governor Claude Hoskins, who turned up at every step, impeding his job and grating his nerves.

Still, this was Hoskins' state. Protocol dictated that he be courteous, even if unwillingly, to the President.

But cold politeness could conceal a dozen hidden daggers.

When he found that most of the state highway troopers were suddenly scheduled to be at far-off Billings for an accident refresher course at precisely the same time as the President was scheduled to be in Helena, Rogers reached his limit.

He telephoned the President, cutting through the protective shield around the Chief Executive by using his rarely spoken code name of "Battler," and advised Foster that he should reconsider his decision to come to Montana.

After a moment, the President said, "No, Warren. That's what that bastard wants me to do. You go to alternative measures."

"Okay, boss. But it'll piss everybody off at us."

"Temporarily. Maybe they'll figure out what happened later. Meanwhile, blame everything on me."

"Hell," said Rogers, "I always do. Okay. I'll be in touch."

Next, he telephoned the President's Chief of Staff. "Arthur? Warren. Listen, Hoskins is throwing up a cloud of shit to give the boss a hard time. I'm going to cut through it. I want a Go–No Go signal between me and the pilot of Air Force One."

There was a long pause. "Is it that bad?"

"I don't know," said Rogers. "But if it is, I want some way to bail out before we're totally committed."

Cummings, when he spoke again, almost whispered. "Surely you don't believe it's that bad. Not from one of our own Governors."

"I don't know exactly *how* bad it is," said Rogers. "I may or may not be up Horseshit Creek, but either way, I want a paddle to get us out."

"All right," said the Chief of Staff. "I'll back you. But keep me posted."

"What I know," said Warren Rogers, "you'll know."

5

Halfway home, Anderson's White House beeper sounded from his briefcase. There was a Gulf gasoline station a few hundred yards ahead, and he pulled into it.

The pay telephone was out of order, its coin slots jammed with chewing gum. Anderson went over to the attendant.

"Sorry to ask you," he said, showing his special presidential identification, "but can I use your private phone? It's important. I'll pay for the call."

The attendant, who had all but come to attention when he saw the Presidential Seal and Anderson's photo and thumbprint, said, "Colonel, be my guest. Want me to leave?"

Anderson, already dialing, shook his head. Using an open line, there was no reason not to give the attendant a minor reward for his help. Anderson knew what the principal topic of discussion would be around the dinner table at the attendant's home tonight.

The White House operator said, "Colonel Anderson? Hold on while I patch through a call from Mr. Warren Rogers."

Anderson nodded. The Advance Man—things were starting to happen.

"Colonel?"

"Mr. Rogers. What can I do for you?"

"I'm lining up a trip, and I wonder if you've been advised yet."

"Negative. But I've got a good idea. How's the weather up there?"

Rogers laughed. "I told them they couldn't keep it secret. Since you ask, it's colder than a well digger's ass. But that's not why I'm calling. Colonel, I've already spoken with Mr. Cummings, and he agrees that you and I should have some sort of Go—No Go system in case of trouble."

"Mr. Rogers, this is an open line."

"Oh-oh. Well, I'm secure on my end. I'm calling from Malstrom." This was the Air Force base just outside Great Falls.

Anderson glanced at the attendant. "I'm patched through the switchboard, and nobody can hear on this end."

"Okay, what the hell? Jack Anderson's readers will know by morning anyway. Here's what I want, Colonel. When you firm up your flight plan, I want you to keep Malstrom as an alternative landing spot."

Anderson frowned. This was unusual. The Air Force base was less than a hundred miles from Helena Airport. If Helena were weathered in, Malstrom probably would be too.

"Can do," he said finally. "But I plan to have others out of the immediate area."

"That's up to you," said the Advance Man. "Okay, I just wanted to clear this with you briefly. I'll get it into a TWX later today, and we can work out the details."

"I'll be waiting," said Anderson. He hung up, reached for the change in his left pocket.

"No, no," said the attendant. "Glad to be of help. Anytime."

"Thanks," said Anderson. "I don't need any gas, but—"

"No bother," said the attendant, itching to get at the phone and call his wife. "Hit me next time."

"I will," Anderson promised. As he started his

motor, he saw, and smiled at, the attendant dialing frantically.

The house was empty, but it did not have that desolate feeling of a dwelling which has been unoccupied. The rooms were heated, the light was on in the downstairs bathroom, and the refrigerator was well stocked.

But Marty was not there. Nor was there a note.

Anderson felt an urge to go to her bedroom and look in the closet. Would her clothes be gone?

He did not give in to it. Instead, he poured a weak scotch and water and sat down at the desk in his small den. Using a legal-sized yellow pad and a black felt pen, he began organizing his thoughts about the upcoming mission. He wrote:

1. **MONTANA.**
   (a) Why? Hoskins? Shale oil?
   (b) Problems? Weather? Outside interference? Security?
2. **AIRCRAFT.**
   (a) Fuel load? Supplies? Crew? Duration of trip?
   (b) Flight readiness? Maps? Alternate fields?
   (c) Any chance of 747 being ready?

He looked at the last entry, then crossed it out. No way was there that he would fly the President in an untried aircraft.

Anderson was sometimes a methodical man. It had been well drummed into him as a cadet at the Air Force Academy that while there are old pilots, and there are bold pilots, there are very few old, bold pilots. He was capable of acting in a split second if the situation demanded it. But, given the chance to reflect and choose his alternatives, he took it. Just as in the simulator at Fort Worth, he kept himself in trim by imagining possible emergencies, and practicing recovery from them.

So, now, before he had even received the first official word that he might be piloting Air Force One to Montana, he had already begun planning the flight.

It wouldn't be shale-oil stuff, he thought. Most likely that mess with the Governor. Okay, count on political interference. Red tape. It was nothing new, and he had handled it before.

Now, back to the aircraft.

Her tail identification number, prominent under the United States flag, was 26000. She had been flying with the 89th since October 12, 1962, when she had been delivered from Boeing to join the President's air fleet.

She was a tired, gallant lady. President Ford had retired her in favor of tail number 27000. But that plane had recently burned on an Alaskan runway after being struck by lightning. And there was sentiment for 26000, so Anderson thought he knew why, when he took office, President Foster had ordered her recommissioned.

In May of 1963, she set her first record—flying from Washington to Moscow in eight hours, 38 minutes, and 42 seconds.

President Lyndon B. Johnson was sworn in aboard her, one bloody day in Dallas. And she brought the body of her fallen Chief home to Washington.

Later, she flew the first presidential around-the-world mission, carrying President Johnson to Australia, where he attended memorial services for the late Prime Minister Harold Holt, killed by sharks while swimming. The plane continued westward, allowing Johnson to visit servicemen in Southeast Asia, and Pope Paul VI in Rome.

The voyage of 28,000 miles was accomplished in five days. Of them, 59 hours and 30 minutes were actual flight time.

Number 26000, regarded by most 89th personnel as the only *real* Air Force One, was retired to backup duty in the seventies. But Howard Foster remembered her well, and when he learned that the Boeing 747 ordered by his predecessor would not be available until midsummer of his first year in office, he ordered the plane refitted.

"Good for me he did," said Tom Anderson more than once. "I'm not that hot with 747s. But I've flown the old girl as much as anybody around, so when they recalled her, I came along."

More cool, low-key pilot's modesty. Despite his constant run-ins with the high brass, no one, if asked who should head the President's aircrew, would have ever left Anderson off the short list.

Still, he thought, scowling down at his notes, is the old girl able to make the trip?

His hand picked up the felt pen and scrawled a bold YES.

With her modified wing, 26000 could land safely on a 5,000-foot strip. Once, Colonel Ralph Albertazzi, Command Pilot to President Nixon, had been instructed to plan a trip to Berlin. It was assumed, because of the wintry conditions and the short runway at Tempelhof—much of which was actually unusable because of the steep approach over buildings and a cemetery—that the President would transfer to another aircraft at Bonn for the Berlin leg. Albertazzi, known affectionately to his crew as "Steve Canyon," did not like this arrangement. He wanted to have his President on board a plane which was positively known to be safe. So Albertazzi flew a practice mission into the Berlin airport, where no four-engine jet had ever landed. He used only 3,500 feet of the icy runway. And when President Nixon later went to Berlin, he flew all the way aboard 26000.

So would President Foster, wherever he wanted to go, Anderson decided. She was a good bird, dependable and true to her bloodlines. With her official range of 7,140 miles (plus a secret fuel capacity of another 1,800, which Anderson in his first tour as CO of the 89th had caused to be built into her) she could make the less than 2,500 miles to Helena easily, with range to burn in case of weather diversions.

All right. Time for a crew planning session. He reached for the telephone, planning to call his adjutant, who would relay a message to all department heads to gather at 9 A.M. in the 89th's main conference room. Swept twice a week for recording devices and bugs, isolated from any microwave spying or even possible laser sound readings from windowpanes, which might, like the cone of a speaker, resonate with words spoken within the room, this enclave was only one of the highly sophisticated security systems which protected the secrecy of Air Force One's plans.

But before he lifted the receiver, it rang—a discreet buzz, as opposed to the telephone in the living room, which jangled wildly to alert everyone within a hundred yards that Ma Bell had someone on the line.

"Anderson," he said.

"Anderson here too," repeated a woman's voice.

"Marty?"

"Me."

"Where are you? I've been worrying."

"Don't. I'm a big girl."

"A big girl where?"

"New Orleans."

"Braniff?" he asked, trying not to let displeasure slip into his question.

"How did you know?"

"Something in one of the columns. How's it going?"

"Fair. I'm trying to talk them out of that fixation on Caldwell. Hard sale, roomie. I think Mary Wells sold everybody, including herself, a bill of goods. Who the hell wants to fly in an airplane that looks like a game of tic-tac-toe? Anyway, I'm getting through to some of the younger executives. At least, they're listening. We'll see."

"When?"

She gave the sigh that corresponded to a shrug. "Who knows? The wheels of God and Commerce grind exceedingly fine, but exceedingly slow."

He could not hide the irritation now. "What I mean, Marty, is when are you coming home?"

Her voice was expressionless. "When I do. Why, did you miss me?"

"Of course I did. It's like a tomb here."

"Good description. You ought to try it on from my side, when you're off with your taxi driving."

He refused to let her taunt him to an angry response. "Yeah, I guess it's just as hard for you."

"You bet your boots, buster." In the background, he heard someone laugh. It was a man. He wanted to ask, "Who's with you?"

But he didn't. Instead, he said, "Okay, hon. There's nothing scheduled for me until Monday at least. Think you might be back for the weekend?"

There was a long pause, and the background sounds had vanished. She was holding her hand over the mouthpiece.

He waited. Finally, she said, "I don't think so, baby. But you'll make do. Won't you?"

"I'll make do," he said flatly. He waited. She said nothing. "I miss you," he added.

"Poor baby," she said. He heard, in the background, the deep laugh again. "Bye-bye. I'll call when I can."

"Fine," he said. He waited for her to hang up, but she did not.

So he did.

At Andrews Air Force Base, where the giant jet with the tail number 26000 sat, sheltered, in a hangar so huge that on moist days drops of water condensed against its ceiling and dropped, rain-like, Chief Master Sergeant Alvin Booth, head of the 89th's security squad, signed in at the chain-mesh gate outside the hangar.

"Everything's quiet, Chief," said the guard. The two men had served together more than a year, but he still examined Booth's ID.

"You've got a button undone," said Booth, tapping the guard's chest.

"Sorry." The man fastened it.

"You weren't smoking?"

"Absolutely negative," said the guard.

Booth believed him. "Okay," he said. "I'm going to look around inside. Who's on the ramp?"

"Jergenson."

Booth nodded. Jergenson was one of his best men. "And the catwalk?"

"Morris."

"Okay, keep an eye out. The Old Man's back from Fort Worth."

Not that it mattered. Security would still be tight. To get aboard Air Force One involved signing your name, and having your ID examined, a minimum of three times. And—so far as Booth knew—no one outside of the immediate security team had any idea that there was another guard, high up on a catwalk which ran around the inside of the hangar's ceiling, equipped with a laser-aimed machine gun that could spew out nine hundred rounds a minute with deadly accuracy. TSgt. Walter Morris, who had the duty, was in communication with Base Headquarters, the Front Gate, the Officer of the Day, and the head Secret Service man via a tiny radio clamped to his belt, with a silent (to anyone more than a foot away) earphone in his left ear, and a contact throat microphone which he could activate by merely whispering. Any unwelcome visitor who managed to deceive or overpower the other guards would still have to get past the catwalk sniper

—who was always, as part of his qualifications, a deadly shot.

The outer guard had a "deadman's switch" under his feet, concealed in the blacktop of the walkway. If he left his post, or was removed from it, a silent alarm went off inside the hangar and automatically locked the entrance. It also signaled the security room at Base Headquarters. More than once the base had been shut down tight because of a new guard's carelessness.

So far, only one known intrusion of Air Force One's security had ever been tried. During the Eisenhower Administration, the Secret Service noticed a shabby man and woman lurking near the entrance gate when the *Columbine III* was arriving from a trip at National Airport. When searched, it was discovered that they each carried a realistic-looking water pistol. Their plan was to wait until the President was disembarking, rush the plane brandishing the pistols, and be shot down by the guards. It was a bizarre suicide pact which failed.

The incident had been hushed up. As, indeed, most facts about presidential flights had always been.

Buzzing his code ID at the hangar entrance, CMSgt. Alvin Booth remembered being briefed about the occurrence. He had been told, "They were just two poor nuts. But that doesn't matter. If they'd taken one more step toward the airplane, we would have had to shoot them down."

Drumming his fingers on the butt of his .45 automatic, slung at his hip, Booth wondered if he would be able to kill on what, at best, could be only suspicion.

He hoped he would never find out.

6

The telephone in Major Paul McGowan's Corvette went *buzz!* He was on the Anacostia Freeway, Interstate 295, near his exit at Tuxedo Road, when he would turn into the aptly named (in his case, at least) "bedroom" town of Cheverly.

It couldn't be business, or his beeper would have sounded.

McGowan was wrong. When he answered, he heard Anderson's voice.

"Paul? Sorry to bother you on the highway."

Paul scowled, but made no comment to hint at his displeasure. His car, with its telephone, 40-channel CB radio, and stereo tape deck, was his private isolation booth. The phone number wasn't listed—but, of course, his CO would have it.

"No sweat," he said. "I'm just headed out for a little tennis."

"You young punks! I'm afraid if I even put my feet up I'll go to sleep."

McGowan said nothing. Anderson went on, "Well, I'm glad I caught you. I want to schedule a crew meeting for nine A.M. Can you make it?"

A rhetorical question. When the 89th's CO called a meeting, everybody made it. Period.

"I'll be there," said McGowan. "What's up? Do we have a mission?"

"I wouldn't be at all surprised," said Anderson. "Okay, have a good game. I'm clear."

"Thanks," said McGowan. He gave his phone number to the mobile operator and signed off too.

He looked at the green digital clock mounted in the Corvette's dash. Nearly seven. She would be there by now, waiting, in the two-bedroom guest house he had rented from a friend who lobbied for various manufacturing interests. The house, with a quarter acre of trees around it, had been offered for nothing, but McGowan knew all too well what kind of price tag was actually attached to anything "free." He insisted on paying a normal rental. In cash, of course.

The traffic was moderate, but too heavy for him to enjoy driving. He missed the assignments at those far-flung bases of the Strategic Air Command where life was simpler, more natural, and, above all, uncrowded.

Paul McGowan was not a philanderer in the normal sense of the word. Exposed to the world's most desirable women, who could not keep their hands off him when they learned he was one of the President's pilots, he just gave a gentle laugh and fetched them a drink. He knew quite well that only his nearness to the seat of Power drew their fascination. Without it, he would be just another bomber jockey, and as welcome at their exclusive parties as a truck driver.

So he amused himself by flirting, then—to their surprised anger—politely rejecting their not so subtle offers. His favorite reply was "Sorry, but we're required to keep it in our pants for twenty-four hours before a flight."

Some actually believed him. Those were strung along for some time, until he confessed that he liked them too much to confront them with his giant libido, which, fueled by days—perhaps weeks—of abstinence, would simply be too terrifying for a woman of grace and quality. To his amusement, this actually increased his desirability.

Still, he did not fall. Long before, as a young pilot in Japan, during the lull between Korea and the Vietnam

War, he learned that it was only the most highly motivated and superbly controlled women who attracted him. In those quiet days of the late fifties, he found that the women who were only then shedding their butterfly chrysalis in favor of an Air Force uniform, or who were even beginning to invade the actual male kingdom of flight, appealed to him tremendously. They were the best in every way—intelligent, educated, strong-willed, hard as the outer skin of a mango—yet deliciously soft and ripe within.

His associates knew him as a hard-nosed, fly-by-the-book pilot, who tolerated no mistakes and no letdown in performance. He did not drink heavily, never gambled. He would turn in a bad fitness report on his closest friend—yet, oddly, now that he had joined the 89th, he complained that the efficiency ratings there were artificially inflated. Or perhaps not so oddly, because what he was actually saying was that men received higher fitness reports than they had earned, merely because that was required in order to belong to the elite.

It was no secret that Major Paul McGowan did not want to be assigned to the 89th. True, there were—at the moment—no combat missions to be flown, but training still had to be kept at its peak efficiency. He knew he could serve well in a Training Command, and resented his role as glorified taxi driver for the President. He saw no reason why the Chief Executive could not requisition an Air Force jet when a trip was necessary, the way generals did. To him, the Air Force One mission was unnecessarily expensive, not only in money but in the careers of the pilots and men it absorbed.

Still, he was a professional. He would take orders, and carry them out to the best of his ability, which was probably quite a bit better than the normal officer could achieve.

He turned into the driveway at 1781 Belmont Street,

pressed the automatic garage door opener mounted on his dash.

The garage door lifted, and he slipped the Corvette in beside the red Volkswagen Rabbit which already took up half of the parking area.

Good, he thought. She's home.

He gave three short beeps on the horn, so he would not surprise her when he went into the house. Angela was very cool, but she did not like to be taken for granted. She allowed him to pay the normal sum for this house, but that didn't mean he could go barging in anytime without warning.

The house was warm, pleasant after the drive. He always drove with his windows down—the sense of sound was just as important to him as sight when on the highway. Even with the heater running full blast, the Corvette was chilly in this late-staying winter.

"Angie?" he called. "I'm here."

She answered from the main bedroom. The other was closed up, with no furniture in it at all. He only came here twice a week, three times rarely. And she had her quarters at the base to keep clean. Even if she seldom used them.

Regulations were relaxed. One could live off base officially, and draw a quarters allowance. Or stay off base informally, while holding quarters there. In which case, no payment was made.

Angela Nemath had already been at Andrews when Major Paul McGowan reported for duty on January 23. A veteran of two years at Patrick Air Force Base in Florida, where she had worked with the base Public Information Office, squiring important visitors around the Kennedy Space Center, she had been the first woman in the Air Force to volunteer for duty aboard Air Force One.

Before joining the Air Force, at twenty-four, she had been a stewardess for Delta Air Lines. When it became known, through the underground news service, which keeps enlisted personnel posted about decisions their generals are making, that the President's airplane would soon be abandoning the men-only rule for Stewards, Angie dug out her flight logbook and hurried to the base Personnel Office. Two weeks later, she was interviewed and, shortly after New Year's Day, she was on her way to Andrews Air Force Base.

The new President was not fooling around; he had promised changes, and they came fast.

Granted, his attempt to utilize commercial air travel failed. Most of those assigned to the 89th privately suspected that Foster had always expected that result. Still, he had promised to give it a fair try, and he had.

With two other young women, and nine men, Angela Nemath, now wearing the three inverted stripes of an Airman First Class, had gone through the Stewardess Training School, operated by American Airlines for their own aircrews, and with Air Force trainees admitted under a contract. The Air Force women, who were ex-stews, had little trouble with the intensive course. Their male companions did. Even though most airlines were now employing male flight attendants, the training emphasized points that were more often thought to be feminine rather than masculine.

"It's a goddamned charm school," complained one Staff Sergeant, who did not pass the course. "Smile, bow, take their guff, clean up their mess."

Angie, sipping coffee with the young man, who was so obviously unsuited for the job that she found herself wondering why he had ever volunteered for it—and who the idiot was who had approved his assignment—nodded sympathetically. The fledgling Steward had just undergone thirty minutes with "Mr. Nasty," the professional heckler whose job it was to try to get the trainees to blow their cool. Nothing was ever right for Mr. Nasty. The coffee was too hot or too cold. Something always got spilled. He had a sarcastic way of talking that made everybody want to clip him against an ear with a drink tray. Oh, yes, drinks. Mr. Nasty got drunk with the speed of a canary immersed in a vat of bubbling wine. Then, as such drunks often do, he threw up, missing the barf bag.

Her own stomach turned as she remembered her first session with Mr. Nasty. No one admitted to knowing what he brought, in its own plastic bag, to masquerade as a drunk's accident, but it was smelly beyond belief.

One American Airlines trainee, two sessions ago, had simply stared down at the mess and said, coldly, "Mister, you put it there. You can pick it up." She left without bothering to turn in her training uniform.

The young Staff Sergeant was still trying. But Angie knew he wouldn't make it. And he didn't.

Three days later, she met Major Paul McGowan, and the world around her changed. She had been intimate with other pilots, both in private flying, and in the Air Force. Something about them appealed to her—their bright, inquiring eyes—and the way they always seemed to assess every risk in advance. Within the world they inhabited, they were the leaders. And, in her own way, so was Angela. It was only natural that their pairing would be achieved.

But it was different with Paul. That first night still blazed in her memory, and sometimes, recalling it, she still trembled. He had been violent, yet tender; considerate, yet recklessly daring. Her private rule, shared by many other women who flew to distant overnight stops, was that there were two worlds. One, the ground world, contained mundane things—homes, cars, debts, families—and wives. The other, sliced from Time and Space by the new magic of the jet age, existed only on that level. An overnighter in London could be enjoyed, and looked forward to again. But it was not repeated while on the home ground base of Los Angeles.

But now that rule had shattered. Here she was,

waiting. And every empty moment before she heard the garage door open automatically, and his silly little three toots on the Corvette's horn, was an agonizing eternity.

So now, as if it were only a casual reply, when she heard his voice she answered from the bedroom.

"I'll be right out, Paul. I'm changing. Make us a drink, will you?"

"It's on the way," he called back.

Getting the ice, he checked the refrigerator and its tiny freezer. No meat. She must have stayed at the base while he was in Fort Worth. He could drive two miles to the nearest market and get a steak. Or they could both go and have something at one of the new candle-lit restaurants along the highway. The food wasn't too good. Still, they had to eat.

Or did they? "Angie?" he said. "There's nothing here to eat. Are you hungry?"

"Starved!" she said.

"Oh," he said, unable to keep the disappointment out of his voice. "Okay, when you get dressed, we'll head over to Angelo's—"

The bedroom door opened.

She smiled at him. She had been changing, all right. From her uniform to a tiny wisp of panties and no top at all.

"Stupid," she said, smiling. "I meant I'm starved for you. Pooh on food!"

The two rum and Cokes were slippery in his hands, and he almost dropped them, setting them on the coffee table. But he got them there safely, and she was pressing up against him with the amazing, warm scent of her body filling his senses.

Airman First Class Angela Nemath shivered. "Mmmm, Major," she said. "You've got cold hands."

Near eleven, he slipped into his boxer shorts and padded into the kitchen. The tea kettle had been simmering all this time, and he poured hot water for instant coffee. Two tablets of smuggled artificial sweetener from that last flight to Holland. Half a tot of Jamaican rum.

"Ahhh," she sighed. "You know how to spoil a girl."

"I try," he agreed.

She sipped, stared at him.

"How much longer?" she asked.

"What?" he said, surprised.

"Come on, lover boy. Everybody knows about you. Faithful, but fickle. I was just wondering how long *my* tour is going to be."

Stunned, he asked, *"Everybody?"*

She laughed. "Everybody in panties, stupid. Don't you think the word gets around?"

"I'd hoped it didn't."

"Not with your flying buddies, dope. To them you're Mr. Clean. Once in a while you come on as Mr. Mean. But never as Mr. Dirty Old Man. So don't worry, your secret is safe. You see, you keep us all hoping for a return bout, so nobody ever gets mad and blows the whistle. Except, babe, you've been something special for me. All I'm asking is that you be a good Joe and tell the truth, so I can organize my life."

He stared down into his coffee. "I'm sorry, Angie. Maybe you've got me figured out, but I swear, it's never been anything that cut and dried to me."

She patted his knee. "I know. You're the original skipper of the ship that passes in the night. It's all right, I don't blame you, and I don't say you do it methodically in cold blood. It's just the nature of the beast." She tickled his groin. "Sorry, I meant to say creature. You're what you are."

He squirmed. "Hey, cut it out."

"It must be about time, huh?" she asked. "For the goodbye bit?"

"Hell no, Angie. Listen, I've thought a lot about us and—"

She pressed one hand over his mouth. "Hush, you insane person. No lies, remember? We both promised." She released him, got up. Her taut thighs and prominent tuft were only inches away. He moved toward her and she leaped back.

"Not on your life. Into your clothes, Major. We'll continue this interview later."

He stood, stroked her cheek. "When, later?"

"Sunday afternoon?"

"I'll let you know."

"Do." She led him into the bedroom. "Now be a doll and get covered up before I forget I'm only a lowly enlisted person, and rape you."

He laughed. Then, with one leg in his trousers, he remembered.

"Oh, Angie, I meant to tell you. Get in early tomorrow. Anderson's called a crew meeting."

She tensed. "There's a mission?"

"Sounds like it."

"Wonderful. I'll go back tonight. Tomorrow's laundry day anyway."

Their leave-taking was prolonged, and tender, and almost out of control. But at last it ended, and she was alone.

He had not, she realized only too well, answered her main question.

The telephone made a harsh jangling in the quiet Montana twilight. Vernon Justus picked it up on the second ring.

"Justus."

A voice said, "I think there's a mission coming up."

Justus pressed the receiver to his ear harder. "When? Where?"

"I don't know."

"I'm running out of time," Justus said. "If we don't move pretty soon, I may not be able to hack it."

"It's not my fault that Foster hasn't been using the plane. You just have to be patient."

"Sure," said Justus harshly. "I'll be patient. But the bank is closing in on me. Are you sure you don't know the destination? If it's more than a thousand miles away, I don't know if I'll even be able to afford enough fuel to fly there."

"I told you everything I know. If I get anything else, I'll let you know right away."

"Yeah," said Justus. "You do that little thing."

He hung up.

7

Anderson was at the base early. Although he had slept soundly, without dreams, the dull edge of fatigue still weighed down his feet.

He went directly to the hangar. Like any other visitor, he signed the control book and had his ID examined.

"How's it going, Singer?" he asked the gate guard. Anderson knew the names of, and quite a bit of personal background about, every member of his command. SSgt. Glenn Singer was twenty-six, married, flew light planes as a hobby, and planned a career in the Air Force.

"Nothing unusual, sir. Just before dawn, there was quite a cluster of shooting stars. Something special to see."

Anderson nodded. "Yes, this is the time of year for them. Stand easy, Sergeant."

His lower back ached as he strode toward the hangar entrance. That old injury usually signaled rain. Or, considering the chilly March temperature, perhaps snow. That had been one of the few landings he hadn't walked away from. And in a damned chopper! It had been his own fault too. Bored with his administrative duties on Guam, he decided to go for a chopper rating. So, overconfident, he had spun the whirlybird in on his third solo. A Board of Inquiry found that the rotor gearbox had jammed, but Anderson still blamed himself for not being skilled enough to land the bird anyway. And, although theoretically healed, the torn muscles in his back never let him forget one moment of carelessness in a lifetime of aerial perfection.

Anderson buzzed his code signal at the hangar door, and went in when he heard the answering confirmation buzz.

He paused, looking at the giant aircraft which sat in the center of the hangar. The overhead lighting gleamed on her aluminum skin, dazzling the eye with its highlights, emphasizing the perfection of her curved lines and silent engine pods, their almost disintegrative power sleeping now beneath tapered wings which stretched more than 145 feet in width—almost half the length of a football field.

The silence in the hangar was cathedral-like, abetted by the overhead spotlights. Anderson's footsteps echoed back at him as he walked toward the plane.

Her vertical stabilizer reached 42 feet 5 inches toward the hangar's roof—white, with blue trim on the leading edge. The American flag emblazoned on each side was the size of a bedroom carpet—9 by 12 feet. Below it, the numbers which carried so much tradition with them—26000.

There have been others, thought Anderson. But you were the first. He knew, with a trace of sadness, that the officials of the Smithsonian Museum were eagerly awaiting the decommission of 26000, so that its interior cabins could be turned into an exhibition room.

He decided to issue instructions for the plane to be rolled out later. Anderson made it a point to fly the Boeing 707 at least twice a week, and although the simulator training had wrung him out, it still wasn't completely the same as being at the controls of the real bird.

There was a clearly marked traffic lane around the left side of the plane. Normal visitors were required to use it. But today Anderson was more than a visitor. He was performing the pilot's traditional daily "walk-around" of the aircraft.

He was not looking for anything in particular. He knew that he could depend on the technicians for that. Every maintenance man had a minimum of three years in his particular specialty. And each applied his skills to Air Force One with an intensity unknown in any other flight operation. Where the FAA requires that airliner jet engines of this type be completely overhauled every 14,000 flight hours, the 89th maintenance men stripped down the four turbofans every 2,500 hours. And, if even minor malfunctions occurred, more often than that.

Anderson could fly on three engines without concern. The loss of a second would cause him to dump fuel and reduce altitude while looking for the nearest landing field.

Or, he thought wryly, remembering the simulator sequence, for the nearest tornado.

He continued the walk-around. His subconscious probed for differences, subtle changes from the last time he had seen the plane. He expected none, but if they prodded his subconscious, that would be his best indicator that something was wrong. It was this special awareness, this almost sixth sense, prompting a pilot to step up and test a fitting he had passed on a dozen previous walk-arounds, and find it loose. How did he know? No pilot could pin it down—but that instinct was the difference between the real professionals and the throttle jockeys.

No pilot was admitted to the 89th with less than 4,000 hours of flight time. All were highly skilled aircraft commanders. Navigators, whose skills would be most needed on foreign trips, were required to have 3,000 flying hours on overseas routes. Most had, also, enough four-engine flight time to take over the plane in an emergency.

Nearly everybody on board wore two hats. For instance, the Flight Stewards—in addition to being well versed in preparing and serving food and drink—were also trained customs specialists. While the President and his staff enjoyed diplomatic immunity, reporters and other passengers did not. The Stewards acted as U. S. Customs Inspectors when passengers returned from a foreign city, although perhaps allowing more latitude toward a straying minor smuggler of trinkets or fine linens.

The ramp guard snapped to attention and saluted. "Going aboard, Colonel?"

"Not this morning, Chief. Everything quiet?"

"As a mouse."

Anderson had expected nothing else. If there had been the most minor irregularity, he would have been informed.

"Carry on," he said, returning the guard's salute.

His echoing footsteps, as he left the hangar, did not have the brisk vigor he usually brought to his job. He had missed his mile of running this morning too. He reminded himself to challenge one of his officers to a half hour of handball before lunch.

The hangar door clanged shut behind the Commanding Officer of the 89th Military Airlift Wing, and locked automatically.

Senator Philip Hopper sipped his second cup of coffee and smiled at the President's Chief of Staff.

"I'm pleased," he said, "that you and I seem to be—if I may say it—flying on the same beam."

"Let's say we're going in the same direction," said Arthur Cummings. "You for your reasons, and me for mine."

The two were having breakfast in the large kitchen of Cummings' Georgetown house. He had been telephoned by the Senator the previous evening, and had agreed to see him this morning, so long as it was not in public.

"Your place will be fine, *AR*thur," the Senator had agreed.

Now, after his compliments on the lovely house, and Cummings' even lovelier wife, and the two teen-aged boys who were "manly chaps," Senator Philip Hopper got down to the point.

"Since we both seem to agree that government spending has gotten completely out of hand—and since the President himself has openly stated that he wants it slashed, right down to his own transportation budget—I think we can help each other."

"How?"

"I spoke with your Mr. Bailey yesterday. Confidentially, *AR*thur, isn't he rather young to be a presidential press secretary?"

"It's a temporary thing," said Cummings. "But so far, I think he's doing a fine job."

"Oh," Hopper hurried to say, "he presents a fine appearance on television. But he was most uncooperative to me."

"Maybe he had no choice," said Cummings. He made a point of examining his watch. "Senator, I have perhaps five minutes more."

"Of course. Well, what I want is simple. I want to be on board the next flight of Air Force One."

"Why?"

"To see it at first hand."

"Surely you've flown her before."

"Under a previous Administration, which we all agree was a wasteful and profligate one. I have strong views on what appears, to me, to be a waste of taxpayers' money. Certainly the President requires mobility. But on such a luxurious scale?"

"Such as?"

"Four huge jets, and a bigger one on the way? A

million dollars in communications equipment aboard
one plane alone?"

"Senator, the President must be in immediate communication with our strategic bases every second of
every day. What do you suggest he uses, two tin cans
and some waxed string?"

Senator Hopper frowned. "You know very well I'm
not suggesting any such thing. But surely there must
be some middle ground, between this huge fleet of
planes, costing hundreds of thousands of dollars every
day just to maintain and staff, and his flying on
TWA."

"Yes," Cummings said reluctantly, not wanting to
give the other man an inch, but wanting to be fair.
"And we're working on it."

"Good. That's what I want to hear. So why won't
you let me *see* what you're doing? I could make an
issue of it, but frankly I would rather not."

Cummings said, "Nor would I want you to. All
right, Senator, you've convinced me. I'll slip you
aboard the next flight."

"Thank you," said Hopper.

Smiling, Cummings said, "Better pack your long
johns this weekend. You're going to be leaving for
Montana early in the week."

The Senator's laugh was forced. "Montana?"

"You wanted the next flight, didn't you? I don't
know when another will be coming up."

"All right," said Hopper. "Montana in the winter.
That will be a new experience."

"I've got another new one for you," said the President's Chief of Staff. He consulted a typewritten card.
"Have your office send us a check for $1,245.90."

"Twelve hundred—for what?"

Cummings showed his teeth with delight. "That's
part of our cost cutback, Senator. Everybody who flies
on Air Force One pays first-class ticket rates. New
rule."

"But—a Senator—"

"Senator Hopper, starting with this flight, even the *President* pays."

The crew meeting went swiftly, lasting less than an hour. Anderson did not have to go into specific duties —every member of the crew had his own area well in hand. He stayed with general information.

"I haven't heard officially," he said, "so nothing goes out of this room. But it looks like Montana in the next few days. Get your stuff ready, but don't make waves. Don't run out buying red parkas."

They laughed, but he had made his point. Unless the White House itself announced a destination, no one in the 89th had ever been guilty of leaking one even accidentally.

Once, in the Nixon years, suspicion had fallen on the Wing because of sudden press mentions of two highly secret missions—"Night Watch" and "Looking Glass."

One pertained to a constantly airborne Command Headquarters, fully staffed with high brass, able to order a retaliatory strike in case of the President and his successors being killed in an attack.

The other was the President's own flying Command Center, available to airlift him away from Washington and provide him with airborne communications facilities more flexible than those aboard Air Force One.

Neither mission had ever flown any but practice missions. But they were there, if events warranted.

The leak was eventually traced to an electronics technician from a western manufacturer, who had shot his mouth off in the motel bar across the highway from the Main Gate of Andrews. He was recalled to San Diego, where his career went into total eclipse.

Major Paul McGowan nodded when Anderson mentioned a 2 P.M. practice flight. So did the rest of the aircrew, with the exception of Stewards, who did not ordinarily fly unless there were passengers on board.

"Okay," Anderson said. "Code Yellow, but try to enjoy your weekend anyway."

Code Yellow meant that everybody had to be within thirty minutes of the plane, and available to a telephone at all times.

The crew filed from the conference room.

8

Outside his office, the WAF SSgt. who worked with the First Sergeant intercepted Anderson.

"The Chief's over at the Finance Office," she said. "They fouled up the payroll again."

Anderson laughed. "As usual. I'm still trying to return that per diem I didn't use last month when the New York flight was canceled."

"Anyway," she said, "you've got a visitor, Colonel."

His mind was blank. "Who?"

"A Mr. Pike, from some New York magazine."

He frowned, and she added, "The appointment was set up last week, sir. You okayed it yourself for today."

"Oh, yes," he said. "That buddy of Mort Bailey's. I'm sorry, I forgot. Stall him for another five minutes. I need to make one phone call, and I'll be right with him."

"Yes, sir," she said. "I'll pour him some more of your coffee. He's drinking it like water."

"Make it weak," he joked. "Use the grounds over again."

Without being disrespectful, she said, "I already did."

He slipped into his adjutant's office and dialed Carl Birney's number.

Birney himself answered. "Carl," said Anderson, "I've changed my mind about today's flight. Something's itching at me. I don't know what. But let's go for altitude instead of destination. If we head for Montana next week we'll be at max cruise altitude. Let's tickle around a little up there today, let the old girl clear her lungs."

"Still a two-hour flight?"

"Two hours."

"Okay," said the Navigator. "I'll get us a fast-climb-out vector, and we'll fly a triangle at altitude. Let-down at maximum descent."

"Good," said Anderson. "See you on board."

"I thought we had a handball game."

"Scrub it. I've got a reporter waiting in my office."

Birney laughed. "Better you than me. Okay, Tom. Thirteen-thirty roll-out."

"Thirteen-thirty," Anderson confirmed. When discussing precise matters such as a flight plan, he reverted to the twenty-four-hour military clock; 1330 was 1:30 P.M.

Anderson tucked his tie into his blouse and entered his office through the back, private door.

"Mr. Pike? Sorry to keep you waiting. We were having a crew meeting."

"Yes," said the reporter, getting to his feet and putting out his hand. "Your secretary told me."

"Don't let her hear you call her that. She's a desk sergeant," Anderson corrected. "Mort said you were interested in the Air Force One mission."

"Yes," said Pike. He was a sallow man in his early thirties. His suit was severely cut and dark blue. His hair was long, and covered his collar. "Mort and I went to Northwestern together, a long time back."

Anderson restrained comment. To this young man, a "long time" probably meant all of six or seven years. Instead, he said, "Well, what can I do to help you?" He looked at his watch. "I hope you don't mind, but we have a flight today. Will an hour be enough?"

Anderson had learned, the hard way, to put an up-front limit on the time he could give a reporter.

Even that sometimes left matters strained, but most realized, and accepted with good grace, the fact that he had an Airlift Wing to run in addition to giving interviews.

"Plenty, Colonel," said Pike. "I've read all of the background material Mort gave me, plus quite a bit that I dug out myself. Just a few minutes of personal conversation ought to give me plenty to work with."

Anderson nodded as he sat down. He appreciated reporters who had done their homework.

Pike consulted his notes. "I'm going all the way back to the beginning of presidential transportation. Some of it was hard to dig out. Nearly everybody concentrates on Air Force One. Of course, they usually don't have as much space as I do."

"I'm really sorry," said Tom Anderson, "but the name of your magazine slips my mind. I'm sure Sergeant Lipscomb has it written down and would whisper it into my ear if I gave her the signal, but why don't I just plead overwork and forgetfulness?"

"An honest military man!" exclaimed Pike. "That's refreshing."

Without smiling, Anderson said, "Mr. Pike, I'll take that as a joke, which I assume it was. The incidence of honest men in uniform exceeds that of those in business, the arts, and particularly the media. The difference is that we live under strict regulations which do not forbid our own views, but rather restricts when, where, and in what detail we can express them."

"What is honesty, if you can't voice it?"

"That's up to the individual. If a point of integrity or honor is stronger than the military oath a man has taken, then it's his personal duty to himself to resign his commission, at which point he can thunder his opinions from the rooftops. And more than a few good men have done just that."

"But," Pike persisted, "that implies the military's aim was to cover up those opinions."

"Wrong," said Anderson. "The chain of command works two ways. The man at the top takes all the heat. He shields his subordinates from outside pressure, criticism, threats. In turn, it is his voice alone which speaks for his command. It's not a bad system, Mr. Pike. You should try it sometime. But meanwhile, you still haven't told me who you're writing for."

"*Inferno*," said Pike. The reporter sat back, as if waiting for some reaction.

Calmly, Anderson said, "I've read it now and then. I found most of the pieces which dealt with issues I knew about to be well researched and presented as fairly as could be expected, considering that the stated purpose of *Inferno* is to burn down the corrupt Establishment and allow a clean Phoenix to arise from its ashes. I trust Mort Bailey. He wouldn't have sent you here if he thought you intended a hatchet job."

Looking embarrassed, Pike peered at his notes again. "Okay. I see here that most of our early Presidents rode on horseback, or in a coach and four on state occasions. John Quincy Adams used to ride down to the Potomac to take a swim."

Anderson chuckled. "God help anyone who tried that today."

"The crowds?"

"The pollution."

Pike permitted himself a smile. "By 1839, the capital had grown to around 40,000, and the streets and avenues were hard to travel on, especially in the winter. Horse-drawn sleighs were used then."

Anderson nodded. "Does your research tell you which President first rode in a mechanical device?"

"John Tyler, in February of 1844. The President attended the trial run of the U.S.S. *Princeton,* the first screw-propeller steamship acquired by the Navy. There was an accident."

"The ship's gun blew up," put in Anderson. "The

Secretary of State and the Head of the Navy were killed. Tyler wasn't scratched."

Approvingly, Pike said, "I see you've done a little research too."

"Enough to know the basics. I'm always being asked."

"Then of course you're familiar enough to know who had the first limousine."

"Warren G. Harding," said Anderson. "But it was Calvin Coolidge who really took to the open road by automobile."

"He was also the first President to have a radio in the White House," said Pike.

"And," added the pilot, "Truman was the first to have a television set. Mr. Pike, this little game of 'Can You Top This?' is fun, but we could play it all day. If you're testing me, I assume you've reached some conclusion. How do I score?"

Slowly, Pike said, "I'd give you a B-plus."

"Too bad," said Anderson. "And here I thought I was impressing the devil out of you."

"You were," said the reporter. "Nobody else in government has ever gotten higher than a C-minus."

After a pause, Anderson said, "You've still got most of your hour."

"I don't need it," said Pike. "I have only one more question."

"Let's have it."

The reporter leaned forward and, in a soft voice, asked, "Do you know that someone is trying to destroy Air Force One?"

The question still ringing in his ears, Anderson was momentarily bewildered when the buzzer on his intercom sounded.

"What did you say?" he asked numbly. The buzzer sounded again.

"Colonel, I work for *Inferno*. I think we do a good

job of alerting the public to the excesses and evils of
big government and big business. But—"

BZZZZZ!

"—I'm still an American and proud of it. I've tasted
chain of command, Colonel. I served three years in
the Marines, two of them overseas, and not a minute
in Canada or Sweden. I've earned my right to dissent."

"Colonel—"

It was SSgt. Lipscomb. She stood in the door.

"Not now, Sergeant," Anderson said. "I don't want
any interruptions—"

"I'm sorry, sir, but it's urgent. I've put it on the
adjutant's line."

Anderson looked at Pike. The young man spread
his hands. "I can wait," he said.

"I'll make it fast," said Anderson. He gave Sergeant Lipscomb a look that said, as clearly as words,
"This had *better* be urgent," and went into the empty
adjutant's office.

"Colonel Anderson," he said into the telephone.

"My, my, how formal," replied a woman's voice.

"Marty! Listen, I'll call you back. Where are you?"

"What the hell do you mean, you'll call me back?
I'm at home. That's where you wanted me, isn't it,
O Lord and Master?"

"Honey, I'm in the middle of a big problem out
here. I—"

"You're going to be in the middle of an even
bigger one, baby, if you don't trot on home."

"Marty, I simply can*not* talk now. I'm sorry. I'll
call as soon as I can."

She was saying, "You'll talk now, if—" when he
put the receiver down.

As he hurried back to his office, Sergeant Lipscomb
said, "I'm sorry, Colonel, but she insisted it was
urgent—"

"Not your fault. But hold all calls."

"Yes, sir."

Pike was looking out the window. Beyond an inner fence, he could see the flight line.

"You run a busy operation, Colonel," he said.

"Never mind that," said Anderson. "What the hell did you say about somebody trying to destroy Air Force One?"

"Surely you must know that this outfit's got its enemies."

"Everything to do with government does. Come on, Pike, get to the point. You don't just walk in and leave a statement like that floating around in the air. What do you know?"

"Colonel Anderson, I'm not sure if I came here to do an interview for real, or if subconsciously I used that to maneuver myself into the position of saying what I did."

"In about two seconds—" Anderson warned.

"Settle down, Colonel. There's nothing urgent. Let me tell it my way. As I was saying, I feel I've earned my right to dissent. I don't completely approve of having a President who lives and travels in the style of an Arabian oil potentate. I knew all along that Foster's bullshit about cutting back was just a smoke screen, and when he had your plane rolled out less than a month after he took office, I zeroed in on it. I guess I used poor Mort, but Jesus, man, what do you have a lightweight like that in the front lines for anyway?"

Grimly, Anderson said, "So much for friendship?"

"Mort's one of my *best* friends," Pike said. "But that doesn't blind me to his weaknesses—or, if you'd rather, the limit of his capabilities. Sure, I took advantage of those limits because—"

"—if you hadn't, somebody else would have," Anderson finished. Privately, he agreed with the reporter. Bailey *was* a weak reed, scheduled to be replaced soon.

"We all play the game our own way," said Pike. "You may not like my rules, but then I don't like yours. Although, right now, for reasons I can't comprehend, I seem to be abiding by them. Colonel, I guess when you scratch a rebel deep enough, you uncover layers of conformity. I couldn't care less if President Foster has to hitchhike to work, but it pissed me off when I saw, the deeper I dug, that *you* were going to take the lumps instead of the fat cats who deserve them."

"What does 'you' mean? Me, personally?"

Pike gestured at the busy airfield outside. "You personally, and your men. Shit, that's precisely what guys like me are shouting our heads off to prevent. At first, when I found out what was going on, it tickled me pink. Then, when I saw who the real victims were going to be, it started working on me. Still, I didn't really make up my mind until I talked with you this morning."

Anderson said impatiently, "Something about a man in uniform, I guess."

"In a way. Let's put it that a guy who knows that John Quincy Adams used to skinny-dip in the Potomac can't be all bad."

"Neither are long-haired reporters who never come to the point," said Anderson.

"The point is simple. Somebody's out to destroy Air Force One. I've been present at secret meetings. I have recordings and my own notes. At first I went along with the scheme, but now I'm blowing the whistle on it. They'll probably tear off my press badge and make me break my tape recorder over my knee when I go back to *Inferno*."

"Who's behind it?"

The reporter licked his lips. His voice was harsh. "Senator Philip Hopper."

"Hopper? I don't believe you, Pike. A U. S. Senator behind a plot to blow up the President's airplane? That's insane." He wanted to say more, but Pike was leaning back in his chair, convulsed with laughter. "What the hell's so funny?" Anderson demanded.

"You," choked the reporter. "I say 'destroy' and the first thing the military mind thinks of is dynamite and nuclear bombs." He forced back the laughter. "Sorry. Listen, he doesn't need bombs, or even a pea-shooter, to knock your plane out of the sky. His weapons are rules and red tape and words."

Anderson felt a wave of relief. "Jesus, you had me going for a couple of minutes. You're not talking anything but politics."

"Don't underestimate politics, Colonel. Particularly the kind that Hopper's bringing to bear."

"I don't. Mr. Pike, I appreciate your warning me. But I'm already aware of the Senator's opposition to our mission. He's been pretty vocal about it."

"Are you also aware of the pressure he exerts within the FAA? And the House Appropriations Committee?"

"Vaguely," said Anderson.

Pike sighed. "I hate honest men," he said. "You think that just because *you're* honorable and obey the law that everybody else will. So guys like me have to give up tilting at our own windmills just to keep you from falling in the moat and drowning."

"Mr. Pike," said Anderson, smiling, "I'm no writer, but that's as mixed a bag of metaphors as I've ever heard. Seriously, I do appreciate what you've told me. And I'll make sure that it's passed along—without your name being attached, of course."

"Good," said Pike. "Because our slippery little Senator has some pretty hot meetings lined up over the weekend, and I plan to attend. I'll let you know what I find out."

"Don't go out on a limb," warned Anderson.

The reporter shrugged. "That's my favorite hangout, Colonel." He got to his feet. "I'll be in touch."

"Thanks," said Anderson. He hesitated. "I suppose you have a first name."

"Sure," said Pike. "It's Seymour."

"Oh," said Anderson.

"Yeah," grinned Pike.

In Helena, Montana, Warren Rogers conferred with the regional head of the FBI and the ranking Secret Service man. They had a large-scale map of Helena and the surrounding area on the hotel bed.

"Thank God it's winter," said the FBI man. "No motorcade."

"He still has to get in from the airport," said Rogers.

"I recommend a chopper," said the Secret Service man. "Limo backup in case of weather."

"Forget weather," said Rogers. "If it's bad he doesn't come." His finger stabbed the map. "We can set down right here, in front of this school."

"I like it," said the Secret Service man. "No tall buildings nearby. No problem in covering the school itself. Direct route to the hotel. Pink-light run all the way."

"What's a pink-light run?" asked the FBI man, who had never before worked on the planning of a presidential arrival.

"Slow, but don't stop for intersections," said the Secret Service man. "It saves manpower. We can't block all crossings, except during a formal motorcade. It's safe enough."

Rogers said dryly, "Unless you happen to be riding with President Ford. Remember when he got broadsided by that kid in Hartford?"

The Secret Service man winced. "Don't remind me. I wasn't even *in* Hartford, but the fallout got all over me too. Ford was all right, but some of those shitheads who worked for him—"

Rogers cut in. "Speaking of shitheads, have you heard the latest from the Governor of this fine state?

I got a tip that the highway patrol may be 'unable to offer major assistance' during the President's visit."

"And you think Hoskins is behind that?"

"None other," the Advance Man said bitterly.

The FBI man said, "Why doesn't the White House put pressure on him?"

Smiling coldly, Rogers answered, "Because Foster wants to wait until he gets out here himself, so he can cut off that cretin's balls in private."

"I'm sorry I couldn't talk before, honey," Tom Anderson told his wife when she answered. "I'm glad you're home."

"Bravo," she snapped. "So why aren't you?"

"I'm on duty. There's a flight scheduled this afternoon. If I'd known you were coming—"

"Cancel it," she said. "You're the big honcho out there, aren't you? Don't all those nifty little Lieutenants spring to attention when you raise a mere eyebrow?"

So, he thought. Eleven in the morning, and she was already drinking. Two, maybe three stiff shots of Bourbon. Not enough to slur her speech, but ample to narrow her reactions down to their most basic level, that of suspicious hostility.

"I can be home by six," he said, "We'll go somewhere nice—" And, he realized, there goes that nice two-day pot of stew. Sorry, Liv.

"Like hell we'll go somewhere nice," she said. "If it's six when you get here, you won't find me."

"Be reasonable," he said. "I can't scrub a mission just because my wife is impatient—"

"Why did you make me fly all the way up here if you weren't going to be available?" she demanded. "I was having a perfectly fine time in New Orleans. I nearly had the Braniff assignment wrapped up. Now that's down the tubes, I guess."

A little emergency bell tinkled in the back of his

mind. She had either lost, or sensed that she was about to lose, the assignment. Probably the latter. Marty had a powerful instinct for rejection, and usually managed to avoid it.

"I'm glad you're here," he said. "But you shouldn't have let it interfere with your work."

"Now he tells me," she said, giving a bitter laugh. "That's not the way you put it last night."

"Last night," he said patiently, knowing it would get him nowhere, "I said I missed you. Which was true."

"And you practically ordered me to get on the next plane," she continued.

"Honey, I never said—"

"Oh, no, not in so many words. But I can tell what you want. I'm good at that, remember? You used to compliment me on it. Before you found your new girl friend!"

He hesitated. Had someone been feeding her false reports about his friendship with Liv Matthews?

"Sure," he said lightly. "I'm brushing movie stars off both shoulders all day long."

"Oh, screw your movie stars," she said. "Which I'm quite sure you do, and which doesn't faze me one damned bit. It's that goddamned blue-and-white womb you crawl into every day. One of these days I'm going to find Mr. Boeing and shove that 707 up his ass!"

Trying to joke, he said, "I sometimes have the same urge. Marty, let's not shout at each other over a mis-understanding. I'm happy that you're home, and I'll cut everything as short as possible here. But you know I can't scrub the flight."

"Fine," she said tonelessly. "Then you can scrub one wife."

Marty hung up.

She waited on the flight line. Sleek, slender, the sun

gleaming on her fuselage. Air Force One was waxed often. It kept her pristinely clean. More than that, the lessened friction added five knots an hour to her airspeed.

The cockpit check was completed expertly. Each man had the sequences memorized, but no one trusted memory. A printed checklist was consulted for every item.

As if this were an actual mission, the two starboard engines were already running. The other two would be started the moment the forward door closed behind the President of the United States.

He was not on board this Friday afternoon. It was a good thing for the crew that he was not, or they probably would not have discovered the enemy which waited for them in the stratosphere five miles above.

9

She was officially rated for a ceiling of 35,000 feet, but 26000 had no trouble climbing through that altitude and when she leveled out at 38,000 feet it was with a reluctance that implied there was plenty more where that came from.

The sky was blue-black above them. The highest clouds were far below. Ahead was the hazy horizon. Anderson could almost imagine its curvature.

At one time, he had hoped for more than the mere sight of the earth's disk, he had hoped to circle it—and perhaps even reach for the moon. But when the first astronaut classes passed him by, and he became involved with multi-engine flying, somehow the years had passed—each with fewer regrets than the one before. He came to enjoy the discipline imposed by the big birds, to smile indulgently at those hot fighter pilots whose remarks implied that his only job was to ride as a semi-passenger, monitoring a sequence of black boxes which really did all the flying. Anderson knew better, and was secure enough not to have to defend himself.

Anderson had enlisted in the Air Force in 1961. Already an accomplished private pilot, thanks to soaring training he had taken near his home town of Middletown, New York, he attended a special prep school conducted by the Air Force, and in his second year of service entered the Air Force Academy. He took flight training in Texas, where he showed aptitude for multi-engine flying.

His first overseas assignment was in Thailand, flying supplies into Vietnam. He served two hitches there, and when in Hawaii on R&R, met Carol Flaxen, a secretary on vacation from San Francisco. A week later, when they flew in opposite directions, they were engaged.

When his tour of duty was up, he wrangled an assignment to Hamilton Air Force Base in Marin County, and two months later he and Carol were married in a little church atop a Sausalito hill.

Together, they served at eight bases during the next eleven years. The last was at Guam's North Field, after his refusal to accept a desk job with the Joint Chiefs of Staff.

"Heads up, Tom," said Major Paul McGowan. "We're coming up on our first intersection."

"Roger," said Colonel Thomas Anderson, ashamed that he had been caught daydreaming.

Only children were missing. Otherwise, he and Carol were as happy on Guam as they would have been anywhere. The on-base housing for senior officers was a far cry from the Quonset huts dependents had been forced to make do with a decade earlier. The Guamanian economy was booming, due partially to the concentration of U.S. military forces—but, ironically, mostly due to the free-spending Japanese. The former conquerors of this isolated island now descended in jam-packed DC-10s, latter-day invaders armed with wallets heavily laden with yen instead of rifles and machetes.

The Guamanians, most of whose family fortunes had been derived from reparations paid by the American government, who had rescued them from Japanese domination, flourished. One cynical correspondent, examining the records, wrote, "According to the payments the U.S. taxpayers made for destroyed coconut trees, they were planted half an inch apart on every square foot of the island. Which is interesting, considering that the payments we made for livestock killed during the bombardment and battle also indicate that Guam was six feet deep in hogs and cows at low tide. If the tide had been in, most of them would have been swimming."

Good-natured and nonviolent, the Guamanians—a Polynesian race who had emigrated here centuries ago by seagoing canoe—smiled and held out their hands in friendship . . . palms up.

Carol loved the Polynesian girls, and painted them in acrylics. Some of her studies won prizes and, to her delight, one was actually sold from an exhibit to a visiting Canadian, who promised to send her a Polaroid of it hanging in his study. He did, but it arrived too late.

One morning, on their way to the capital town of Agana, which was nestled into a gently curving bay on the west side of the island, Anderson told Carol about the correspondent's description of the island.

She laughed. "He ought to see it today. Six feet deep in Lincoln Continentals."

It was almost the truth. Going into the taxi business was a family tradition on the island. It was said, only half in jest, that the first Marine who stormed Agana Beach in World War II was met by a Guamanian with an oxcart who asked, "Taxi, Joe?"

Today, while not all Lincolns, the taxi fleet was suitably upgraded. No true cab driver would have been caught dead in a Checker or a Dodge Dart. Caddies, Lincolns, Mercedes, and the occasional Bentley made up the horn-tooting, middle-of-the-road-driving, laughing, friendly—and totally mad—cabbies.

While there were duty-free shops on Guam for the benefit of travelers, they were off limits to island residents, including military personnel. But Carol still liked to peer in the windows, sighing over lovely pearls and gold watches that, even on a Lieutenant Colonel's salary, they could not afford.

He was up for bird Colonel, and knew that he had to make it. Being passed over would be the beginning of a downhill spiral. They had discussed this possibility often.

Once, discouraged, he said, "Maybe they're right. If I pack in the full-time flying and get assigned to a Training Command, I can still put in a few hours every now and then. And we'd be a lot better off financially."

"Ah," she said. "Diamonds! Caviar! Exotic perfumes! Our own Honda!"

Seriously, he said, "Maybe I'd better run for sheriff instead. Otherwise I won't be able to afford you."

She laughed. "That poor man. Did they ever catch him?"

"As far as I know, he didn't do anything wrong," he said.

They were referring to a period, shortly after they had been married. He had been assigned to Keesler Air Force Base in Biloxi, Mississippi. Shortly after their arrival, the headlines in the Gulfport/Biloxi *Herald* had been about a local sheriff who had declared a three-year income of around three million dollars. And the IRS was after him for *under*stating what he'd earned. Reading the item in the Officer's Club, Tom and Carol had sat in awe for several moments before she finally spoke.

"Well, Tom, that proves it."

"Proves what?"

"Crime doesn't pay."

They laughed so hard that the bar steward turned up the jukebox.

On Guam, they laughed again, often. Particularly the day his promotion was leaked to him by the base CO.

He got home early. "Come on," he said. "We're going to Agana."

"Why?" she asked, pins in her mouth. As usual, she was making a dress. Short-waisted, she had trouble buying anything off the rack which did not make her look twelve years old.

"I hate your cooking," he said. "We're going to Benjo-wah's."

This was an Air Force joke about the local branch of Benihana's restaurant chain. In Japanese, their version meant "toilet." The food was good enough, but the alliterativeness of the joke name was too good to pass up.

Carol spoke no Japanese. But neither did she live with her head in a shoe box. She had long since learned the reason why, when someone called Benihana's by the other name, the men all grinned and looked away. It simply pleased her to pretend ignorance and let them enjoy their joke.

In Agana, he parked their little Toyota and they walked to the restaurant. At their table, he said, "Whoops! Forgot my wallet. It's in my jacket."

In the tropic heat, jacket and tie usually gave way to a flowing sports shirt. Under which, Anderson's wallet was hidden in his hip pocket.

He went two blocks to a small gift shop, which he had telephoned from the base.

He paid the smiling owner, slipped a tiny package into a side pocket, and returned to the restaurant with his wallet in his hand.

They ate to surfeit, enjoying the shrimp, fish, and thinly sliced beef which was prepared on a grill mounted in the corner of their table. They drank hot sake from tiny, flower-vase-like bottles.

Finally, contented, they paid up and strolled to the car.

"Colonel," said Carol Anderson, "you really know how to treat a girl."

"Stick with me, kid," he said. "The night ain't over."

Military wives often assume, in their private lives, a mirrorlike parody of their husbands' rank. Carol and Tom Anderson laughed about this. The wives of Captains were exceedingly polite to the wives of Majors . . . and expected the same politeness from the wives of lowly Lieutenants.

"Pecking orders," Carol once said profoundly. "No wonder they call them hen parties."

The present he'd bought for her tonight was calculated to please on two levels.

In the center of the setting was a black pearl she had admired more than once. It would touch her sense of beauty. As for the setting, it was a sterling-silver replica of a full Colonel's eagle. That would be his way of telling her that his long-awaited promotion had finally come through. And it would give her a good laugh when she wore it to the next party. Most of the officers' wives there would take it perfectly seriously, accept it as her absolute right—to Carol's secret amusement.

As they drove north, she asked, "Where to, Silent One?"

"Suicide Cliff, to look at the moon," he said.

"Aha," she declared. "I know what you have in mind to look at!"

"My intentions are pure," he protested.

"Shoot!" she came back. "In that case, it ain't hardly worth going all the way up there."

They laughed, and he speeded up slightly.

Suicide Cliff overlooked one of the loveliest bays on the island. It took its name from the hordes of Japanese soldiers and civilians who supposedly leaped from its heights to their deaths after the successful Allied invasion in 1945. Now, with a good, if twisting, road leading to a parking area along its seaward edge,

it was a favorite parking spot for couples. Again, ironically, many were Japanese.

As he slowed for the turn, she pressed his arm.

"Hon," she said, "You've got something important
to tell me, haven't you?"

"Always prying," he said. But he tensed his muscle
in that private signal they often used during lovemak-
ing when words were unnecessary.

"I can't wait," she said.

But she did. Because at that moment, the rented
Mazda came over the hill, on the wrong side of the
road. Its headlights were out, and the driver was
drunk.

Anderson woke up in a hospital. The woman seated
beside him leaned forward.

"Tom?"

"Carol? What happened? What . . . ?"

He stopped. This wasn't Carol.

"Nancy!"

His sister pressed his hand. "Shhh, Tom. I'll ring
for the doctor."

She pressed the bedside button.

His head throbbing, Anderson asked, "How did you
get here?"

Softly, she said, "You're back home, Tom."

"But, I— We were— Where's Carol?"

"Tom you've been unconscious for nearly a week.
They flew you home."

"Carol?"

The doctor arrived. "Well," he said. "It's good to see
you awake, Colonel. You didn't have a fracture, but—"

"Damn it to hell." he grated. "Will somebody tell
me where my wife is?"

Gently, Nancy Anderson said, "Nobody knew how
long you'd be in a coma. Her family waited as long
as they could."

"What? Waited? Why?"

Crying, she said, "For Carol's funeral. It was yester-day."

Anderson's eyes were stinging. He felt a heavy pressure in his chest.

Goddamnit, he'd been daydreaming again. He glanced at his Pilot. If McGowan had noticed, he made no comment.

"Take her, will you, Paul?" Anderson asked, snapping open his harness. "I've got to take a leak."

"Got her," said McGowan. Actually, the giant plane was on autopilot, but that did not relieve the crew from monitoring their instruments and controls as carefully as if they were doing the manual flying themselves. If the President had been on board, it would have been rare for either pilot to leave his seat, or even unbuckle. But Nature did call, on occasion.

Anderson went into the forward head and splashed water on his face. His eyes, staring back at him from the mirror, seemed to be sunk in his cheekbones. They were running. He moistened them and dried with a paper towel.

His hands were trembling. He took a deep breath, trying to steady himself. It hurt his chest. The pressure seemed greater than ever.

Damn it, he thought. Is it happening again? It wasn't supposed to, not if I watched my fatigue level and didn't get oxygen-starved. They said I'd be perfectly normal. It wouldn't affect my flying at all.

A spasm of coughing took him, and when it was over he felt dizzy.

He sat down on the toilet. The dizziness passed.

In a moment, he got up and made his way back to the flight deck.

When he entered, Carl Birney was choking with a hacking cough. He had his handkerchief to his lips, and when he took it away it was spattered with crimson.

"Jesus Christ," said Birney.

Anderson's head cleared instantly. He almost thew himself into his seat and, buckling up, said sharply, "We're in trouble. Paul, how do you feel?"

The Pilot said, "Okay, but—"

"Can the shit. Level with me."

McGowan said, "Kind of choked. My eyes are smarting too."

"Sergeant Dent?"

"Rotten, sir."

"That's it," said Anderson. "We're going down. Paul, alert the area. Get us a heading at 25,000 feet."

Without question, McGowan said in his microphone, "This is Air Force 26000 beginning emergency descent to 25,000. I repeat, emergency descent to 25,000 feet. Request immediate confirmation and new heading at 25,000."

The calm voice of an Air Traffic Controller came back, "Roger, Air Force 26000. I have you on my screen. You are clear for descent to 25,000 feet on your present heading. At 25,000, change course to one-nine-zero. Do you copy?"

"Affirmative," said McGowan.

The Controller asked, "Do you wish to declare an emergency?"

Paul looked at Anderson, who shook his head. "Negative, Traffic Control. We seem to have a minor equipment problem."

"Roger, Air Force 26000. Good luck."

"Air Force 26000 standing by," said McGowan. He switched off the microphone. By now, Anderson had throttled back, after switching off the autopilot, and the giant jet was descending at a steep angle. The altimeter needles whirled backward, past 32,000 . . . 31,000 . . .

Birney was still coughing. He gasped, "What's wrong, Tom?"

Grimly, Anderson said, "Ozone."

Unbelievingly, McGowan said, "At 38,000 feet? Since when?"

The ozone layer normally hovers high above the earth, above the stratospheric altitudes modern jet planes use. There, as manufacturers of fluorocarbon aerosols learned to their regret not too long ago, it serves the beneficial purpose of screening out the harsh ultraviolet sunlight which can cause skin cancer.

"Sergeant Dent," said Anderson, "get wet towels for the flight deck."

"I'll do it," said Chief Master Sergeant Juan Hernandez, the Flight Engineer. "You may need Lester on communications."

"Roger," said Anderson. The Mexican noncom hurried back to the galley. To McGowan, Anderson said, "Sometimes a cold winter pulls the ozone down, at least a light concentration of it. Our compressors must have been sucking it in and increasing the amount with our pressurization system. We've been getting an overdose ever since we reached altitude."

Birney, whose cough had begun to subside, said, "Good thing we didn't have the Man on board."

"Passing through 28,000," McGowan said automatically. "Is that why we made an altitude check today, Tom? To check this out?"

"No," Anderson said. "I just had a hunch."

"Some hunch," Birney said admiringly. "Well, it's back to the old drawing board for next week's trip. Nothing over 30,000?"

"Twenty-eight would be better," said Anderson. Hernandez had returned with the wet towels. Anderson held one over his face with one hand and breathed through it.

The heaviness in his chest had nearly vanished, and his eyes were clearer. Through the towel, he said, "Starting to level out."

"Leveling out," repeated McGowan. "Twenty-six thousand."

As the nose of the jet lifted slowly to bisect the horizon, Anderson discarded the towel. He pointed to the control yoke.

McGowan nodded. "I've got her."

Into his own microphone, Anderson said, "Air Traffic Control, this is Air Force 26000. We are at 25,000 feet and starting our turn to one-nine-zero. Over."

"Roger, Air Force 26000. We have you proceeding on one-nine-zero at 25,000 feet. What is your destination?"

"We will be proceeding to Andrews Air Force Base. Can you give me a turn point?"

"Can do. Make your turn to course nine-five, at Bedford intersection. On nine-five, you will descend to 24,000. Do you copy?"

"Affirmative," said Anderson. He looked over his shoulder at Birney, who nodded. "Turn nine-five at Bedford intersection, and descend to 24,000 feet."

"Roger," said the Controller. "We'll be passing you along to Dulles Control in six minutes."

"Acknowledged," said Anderson. "Meanwhile, I want to report high ozone levels at altitudes above 30,000 feet in this area."

"Roger," said the Controller. "I'll put it on the wire. We don't have any traffic that high right now, but it's good to know about." The radio was dead for a moment. "Area alerted," said the Controller. "Thank you much, Colonel Anderson."

"Thank *you*," said Anderson. "Air Force 26000 out."

"Ah," said McGowan, "fame."

The crew was back to normal. Ozone, an unstable form of oxygen, can cause sickness at incredibly small concentrations. The Occupational Health and Safety Administration permits no more than 0.1 part per million during a normal workday. The concentration in Air Force One when Anderson began his descent was a dangerous 0.6 per million and, while ozone itself would not have incapacitated the crew, the complications from its irritation might have. It is hard to fly a four-engine jet while coughing blood into a handkerchief.

"Well," said Birney, "you've got my vote. How did you recognize it, Tom?"

"I ran into it once down in South America," said Anderson.

The lie came from his lips before he could stop it.

Great, he thought, taking the controls from Mc-Gowan. Now I'm bullshitting my crew.

He *had* run into a similar problem in South America. But it had not been ozone sickness.

Birney looked up from his work desk. "Bedford intersection in two minutes. Prepare to descend to 24,000."

Anderson, his eyes flicking across the instrument panel, acknowledged. "Two minutes."

Like all good pilots, his mind was miles ahead of the aircraft. After the turn, it would be less than thirty minutes to the Andrews area, on the ground in less than forty.

He might be able to leave the base by 5 P.M. after all.

10

"We're here to talk about a cancer," said Senator Philip Hopper.

He had learned, by studying the most powerful speakers in politics, how to start the ball rolling with a shocker. It worked today, in the comfortable conference room he had "borrowed" from the Charles Hotel. Hopper held a sizable blind ownership in the quiet, out-of-the-way hotel, which catered to visiting dignitaries.

Hopper was actually a small man, barely five eight. But the lifts in his custom-made shoes and the careful way he always positioned himself—whether addressing another person or an audience such as he faced today —gave the impression of stature.

When his thick black hair started turning gray, Hopper made the choice to go all the way, instead of letting the white crawl slowly up his sideburns. Now, with a shock of snow-white hair that made his unlined face even more youthful, he was an impressive figure in any crowd, and on any television screen.

"Yes," he repeated. "A cancer that is sapping the vitality of our nation."

The audience of nine men and two women waited. They were the elite of Hopper's followers. Three were publishers of powerful metropolitan newspapers. Two were in policy-setting positions at major television networks. One of the women anchored an evening news program which was broadcast by more than two hundred stations. The other edited the most successful woman-oriented magazine in the nation. The rest of the men were in high government positions. One headed the Federal Aviation Administration. Another chaired the House Appropriations Committee.

Although Hopper was, and had been for his twenty-one year political career, a Republican, only two thirds of those in the room owed loyalty to that party. The others were Democrats or independents.

They shared two common causes, however.

One was to support Senator Philip Hopper (R.-Iowa).

The other was to see him in the White House four years from now.

It was just after 3 P.M. Friday afternoon. At that moment, five miles above southern Virginia, Colonel Thomas Anderson was putting Air Force One into a steep dive to escape from the ozone layer.

Senator Hopper's purpose here today was to put Air Force One into an even steeper dive. One into oblivion.

There were no press present at this meeting. One persistent reporter, Seymour Pike from *Inferno*, had almost been admitted, but at the last moment Hopper decided to exclude all media. Time enough later to let the working reporters in on what was happening. Those from TV, newspapers, and magazines who were here today wore their second hats of opinion shapers, not reporters.

The silence was thick enough to cut with a knife. But no one spoke. Senator Hopper liked to present things at his own pace.

"Our new President," he continued, "*HOW*ard Foster, has made a strong pitch for economy in government."

There was polite laughter. Everyone knew what was coming. It was an obligatory part of any Hopper discourse.

"Promise: He told us he would slash the White House staff on the day he was handed the key. Result: Three months after he moved in, the staff has increased eighteen per cent. Promise: He said he would continue the moratorium on new military hardware. Result: There's a shortage of aircraft engineers, because every weapons shop from Long Island to San Diego is gearing up for new production."

His audience squirmed a little at this one, because while everybody was in favor of cutbacks, they all wanted them in somebody else's home town.

"And Bigmouthed Promise of all: Our new President assured us that he would abandon the senseless luxury of having a private fleet of aircraft at his disposal, and use more conventional means of transportation, just as you and I, and even the Prime Minister of Great Britain, do."

He pulled back a small curtain that had covered a blackboard.

"Here is the cancer I spoke of. It is only the visible tip of a growth that consumes as much of our national budget as the entire Marine Corps did in 1941."

He permitted himself a tiny smile at this breathtaking analogy. Actually, in 1941, the budget for the tiny Marine Corps was minuscule.

"I am referring to the President's private Air Force, the 89th Military Airlift Wing at Andrews Air Force Base, less than twenty miles from this room."

His finger pointed at the board. "Let me list what President Foster has at his disposal out there."

He leaned forward. "You all know what a Boeing 707 is. You've all flown in them. Beautiful plane, if you happen to be an airline. Well, friends, our new President *is* an airline. Do you know how many of those huge jetliners he has?"

Hopper shot up a hand, fingers and thumbs extended. "Five! Five four-engine jets—more than some of our regional airlines own. And two of those jets have telephone switchboards that cost you and me over a million dollars a set."

He was exaggerating somewhat here. The million dollars covered eight separate communications systems. Still, it was a large sum of money.

"But it doesn't stop there," Hopper continued. "The President has an even bigger jet on order. A 747 Jumbo, specially modified so he can travel with his own automobile and even a collapsible helicopter. How's that for luxury?"

One of the television executives started to ask a question, but the Senator cut him off. "Let me finish, Bert, and then we'll chew the rag. I haven't even gotten started on my inventory of the Foster Private Air Force. He's got twelve Lockheed Jet Stars, which can carry fifteen passengers each. Uncounted prop planes, including half a dozen Super Constellations, a flock of twin-engine Aero Commanders, and, so help me God, *fourteen* multi-engine planes listed as 'supplementary aircraft.' Add in five or six big rotary-wing jobs—that's choppers to you, Miss Sue"—he smiled at the anchorwoman—"and Foster has enough air firepower not only to start a war with anyone in this hemisphere but by God, to *win* it!"

"What does all this cost?" asked one of the publishers.

"Nobody knows," said Senator Hopper. "Oh, we can figure easily enough how much it costs per hour to keep a 707 in the air. Last election, the Democratic National Committee paid just under four thousand dollars an hour for flight time, six hundred an hour for ground time." He gave a cynical laugh. "Assuming a four-hour coast-to-coast flight, and eighteen hours on the ground, that comes to $25,800 for nearly a day's use of the plane."

The network anchorwoman said, "That seems pretty fair."

"How fair it is," said Hopper, "is only obvious when

you add in the fact that the plane flew back deadhead
—empty, Miss Sue—gulping down sixteen *hundred*
gallons of fuel an hour. A week later, it went *back* to
the coast to pick up the President. His fat-cat friends
flew back commercial. It cost the fourteen of them
three hundred bucks apiece—which the DNC paid for
—for a total of only $4,200. Out-of-pocket costs to the
taxpayer for *four* coast-to-coast flights by Air Force
One, conservatively estimated, $70,000. And that's
just for mileage! How about maintenance? Equipment
write-off? Air Force personnel, who are paid by the
Department of Defense? The space and support facilities out at Andrews?"

He paused for emphasis. "You see, that's what I'm
getting at. The hourly operating costs of this private
Air Force are staggering enough. But the huge flow
of money is consumed by the unitemized services and
facilities which are charged to the military. I don't
think an estimate of five hundred million a year is any
too high."

Hopper scrawled a number on the blackboard. Five,
followed by so many zeros that it was impossible to
count them swiftly. "The average President makes
perhaps fifteen flights a year. Divide that into the total
cost, and you'll find that this little boondoggle adds
up to thirty or forty million dollars per flight. If you
feel like heavy breathing, now's the time to do it."

The anchorwoman spoke. "Senator, surely the Wing
performs other duties."

"Of course they do. But every one is in some way
related to the President's personal transportation requirements. Junkets for foreign visitors? He authorizes
them."

Dryly, one of the network men said, "Well, we can
hardly give them a Greyhound Tour Pass and aim
them toward Kansas City."

Hopper eyed him suspiciously. "No," he admitted.
"But do we need a fleet of aircraft sitting here, or

burning up fuel on practice flights, as a hedge against the very few foreign dignitaries who are so important that we really have to roll out the red carpet? What would be wrong with chartering? Pay the going rate and let the airlines worry about maintenance and personnel?"

"Security?" suggested a publisher.

"We'd have to change procedures, but our security people can protect airline planes as well as they do Air Force Ones. Gentlemen—and ladies—look at the numbers. Assuming we chartered one plane every day of the year, and assuming that we paid $50,000 for each charter—which is quite high, may I add—at the end of the year we would have had better utilization of aircraft, more comfort and flexibility for our visitors . . . and the total bill would have been just a little over eighteen million dollars. For the *best*, I remind you. Not Scoobie-Doo Airlines, but TWA, American, Eastern."

One of the government executives laughed. "Leave out Eastern. They still think Eddie Rickenbacker's running the show. They'd serve box lunches, if they could get away with it."

"Never mind Eastern," said a network man. "How about Delta? They'd overbook a funeral procession. And Frank Borman is a friend of mine."

Hopper realized he would lose his audience if he let the jokes continue. "Very funny, gentlemen," he said. "But think for a moment how much that wasted five hundred million hits you right where it hurts, at tax time."

"Senator," said "Sue," who was actually Susan Earhart, anchorwoman on the UBC Evening News. "I think your five hundred million is a bit high. But even cutting it in half, I have to agree that charter payments could easily be handled out of the interest that much money would earn sitting in any commercial bank. I don't think it's immodest of me to suggest that my face is as well known as President Foster's—"

"Better, better!" cried the network man, laughing. "And a hell of a lot prettier."

"Thank you, Herb," she said. "Not everyone can look like Walter Cronkite. What I'm getting at is that I fly commercially all the time. I get my hate mail every day, my kidnap threats. Maybe I'm living on borrowed time, but I don't have even one teeny-weeny Secret Service man riding with me. I'm not suggesting that the President travel coach, as he jokes about, but why *not* charter a plane?"

"Or requisition one from the Air Force," said Clarence Willoughby, head of the FAA. "That's the way it used to be done."

He did not add that when it "used to be done" was in the early days of World War II.

Good, thought Hopper. It's back on the track.

Truthfully, he had often admitted to himself, if he ever became President, he would never in a million years fly on a commercial airline, or requisition an untried Air Force crew. But that was in the future. To reach that future, he had to embroil Foster in a controversy that the President could not emerge from with clean hands.

Hopper had done his homework. He knew that the numbers he threw around so casually were only wild guesses. He knew that the 89th performed hundreds of missions a year completely unrelated to presidential needs. But, he justified, that was their own fault. They had tied themselves so closely to the President's coattails that if he got mired down in a mudslinging contest, some of it was bound to stick to them.

His own figures, unofficial, told him that last year the Wing had handled more than 21,000 passengers, including some 1,500 foreign visitors important enough to warrant White House visits. He knew, too, that the 89th's ready rate was more than 85 per cent. At any given time, fewer than 15 per cent of the planes were not ready to take to the air on literally a moment's notice. And he knew that the Wing's delay rate was less than 1 per cent, meaning that out of each hundred flights, only one had been delayed for *any* reason, including weather.

But such numbers did not advance his case, so he did not mention them. And his audience, skilled as they were in communications and in government, never questioned his conclusions.

"Sue is absolutely right," said Hopper. "I think there may be several solutions, but chartering is certainly near the top of the list. Look at the immediate savings. Right now, the 89th Wing has more than a thousand airmen, two hundred officers, and three hundred civilians, working out at Andrews. Every one could be eliminated—"

One of the publishers raised a warning voice. "Senator—"

"By that," Hopper hurried to add, "I mean transferred to useful duty. None of them would have the slightest bit of trouble. Even I admit that they're the best in the business. But they've been siphoned off from service where they could benefit the nation as a whole, instead of the ambitions of one man."

He was coming on too strong, and realized it. Pulling back, he added, "I don't blame President Foster himself for the situation. He inherited it. He said he wanted to dispose of it. But the truth is, he's trapped. He's got his own work to do. It's up to us to help him —and the country."

"How?" asked Sue Earhart.

"By presenting the truth. Forget the glory of the big blue-and-white bird, soaring high over the capital. Let's tell the public how much it really costs. Forget national pride. Instead of bragging how much bigger and better Air Force One is, point out how much more efficient and sensible the alternatives would be."

One of the publishers said, "If we take the gloves off, Senator, it won't take the White House too long to figure out what's happening."

"So what?" Hopper shot back. "What can they do?" He glared around the room. "The days of Enemies Lists are over. The White House won't even stop delivery of your paper, the way Kennedy did to the *Herald Trib*. Foster's Private Air Force has plenty to worry about. Ask any one of the regulatory agencies." He nodded to the head of the FAA. "The truth is, the whole mission violates the law every day of the year. But up until now, nobody's had the balls—excuse me, Sue—to put the bell on the cat."

She smiled at him. "I'm sure *you* do, Senator." There was an edge of sarcasm in her voice. Sue Earhart did not like Senator Philip Hopper. But she saw in him a man who could help her advance her own ambitions before he was discarded or passed by in favor of another leader. "I, for one, will help in any way I can. I don't like taxes any more than you do."

This brought a chuckle from most of the men in the room. At almost a million dollars a year, Sue Earhart outearned them all.

Smiling toward her, Patty Jo Green, who had to struggle through life on a mere $211,000 a year (plus stock options in the magazine), said, "I'm with Sue." (Only in principle! With all that money, why doesn't she put some of it on her back? Peasant blouses. My God!) "We've got three pieces penciled in for this summer, on the Washington scene. There's plenty of room in them to get the message between the lines. Not to mention our syndicated column, which runs every Sunday around the country."

Sue nearly yawned. Rolling everything up into one gooey ball, Patty Jo might be able to communicate with five million people in a month. She, Sue, talked to more than sixty million every evening, five days a week.

The other pledges came in fast. Senator Hopper rocked on the balls of his feet. He had known he could depend on this elite group. More than the support they could give him through their own outlets, though, the important thing was the power they wielded as opinion shapers. By Monday, their roll call of a mere eleven would have swelled to eleven *hundred*, all influential followers who, in turn, could deliver eleven thousand . . . and so on, like a monumental chain letter, gathering momentum.

"One more thing," he said, waving his hand for silence. "I'll have all of the pertinent facts delivered to you by messenger this evening. But we aren't dealing in mere numbers and charts. I intend to go further."

He paused, let the hook sink in before he hit it hard.

"I am in opposition with our President on this matter. But, and I hope you all join me in this, it is *loyal* opposition, as our English neighbors would put it. Under no circumstances would I ever do anything to jeopardize President Foster's safety."

They waited expectantly.

"So, while I cannot—no, *will* not, for I know the answer—give you our destination, I can tell you that when Air Force One leaves for a secret mission next week, I will be on board."

He chuckled. "It took some doing, because the White House knows all too well how opposed I am to this wasteful operation. But I persuaded them to put my name on the manifest, and when the President's plane lifts off, I will be there. And when I return, I hope it will be with the pledge I leave with you now:

"Next week, I will fly on the last flight of Air Force One."

11

German fighter pilots, many of whom found themselves floating earthward in parachutes after their
Messerschmitts had been blown apart, grumbled unhappily about *"der Gabelschwanz Teufel."* The Fork-
Tailed Devil. Better known as the Lockheed P-38
Lightning—the only twin-engine American fighter
built during World War II—*der Teufel* had scored
an impressive number of kills on nearly every battle-
field of the war.

Vernon Justus stood in the main hangar of the Fort
Benton, Montana, Municipal Airport. The name was
almost as big as the field—a single 3,500-foot asphalt
strip running roughly east and west in the sheltered
valley. A battered SuperCub, with "Justus Flying
Service" painted on its fuselage was available for
charter—and most of its runs were into Great Falls,
some fifty miles to the southwest. Now, after one of
the worst winters in history, the Justus Flying Service
had not had a customer for more than two weeks.

His bank note was long overdue, and an official had
been out to the field earlier in the week, snooping
around. Probably adding up which assets to throw
a lien on, Justus thought angrily.

He patted the gleaming side of the P-38, which took
up nearly half of the hangar. She was his only real
asset. The SuperCub was mortgaged to the hilt, and so
were the buildings. Goddamned politicians! Between
their manipulated "Energy Crisis" and rampant infla-

tion, they had forced him—and thousands of other good Americans—to the wall.

Vernon Justus was nearly sixty, but he looked years younger. His slim body was well muscled, and he still had most of his hair and all of his own teeth. Women still noticed when he entered the room. Ask Joyce. Only twenty-eight, and as hot for his body as if he were half his real age. Dumb, though. She kept after him to marry her, as if she thought she could break down a lifetime of bachelor habits by simply asking.

Well, this time next week, it wouldn't matter either way.

It was cold in the hangar, and his left arm was stiff and aching where he'd taken that cannon fragment over Okinawa. Lousy 14 per cent disability! Thanks for nothing.

He was already an ace—he downed his fifth Zero on his twentieth birthday. And he was sharp—as good a pilot as any in the squadron. Was it his fault that he hadn't been old enough to get into the war sooner? If he'd been out there from the beginning, he might have done better than Dick Bong, that lucky bastard. Bong got every one of his forty confirmed kills flying a P-38. And Vernon Justus knew for cold fact that he could outturn Bong, outclimb him—and, damn it, outshoot him. If they'd only given him the chance.

But a lucky Zero chopped up his arm just when the big battle was beginning, and he was out of the air for a fateful seven months. By then it was all over but the shouting.

Thanks a lot, kid. Here's your Purple Heart and your ruptured duck. We'll send you a few bucks every now and then to pay for your arm. Write if you get work.

Jesus, where had the years gone? Blown down a hundred runways in a dozen countries, paper scraps caught up in the prop wash of how many rattletrap planes?

But no more wars. He'd tried when Korea hotted

up. His arm was fine. They just didn't like what was in his head. Lousy shrinks, telling him that he wasn't fit to go out and kill more gooks. Shit, the Japs had shot him in the arm, not the noggin.

He'd come close to flying as a mercenary in Biafra. But some snitch turned him in, and he couldn't get a passport. Some thanks, from the country he'd flown, and fought, and been wounded for!

Justus climbed up and slipped into the cockpit of the P-38. Man, it was just like the old days, feeling the stick between his knees, smelling the familiar odor of gasoline and oil vapors, the sweetness of polished leather cushions and headrest.

What a mistake they'd made, discontinuing this bird! He had practically snatched this one from the scrap heap, back in the late fifties. It had taken him ten years of scrounging—for money, for parts, for instruments—to put her back in top flying trim. Right now, he would pit her against any prop plane in the world, including the P-51. Racing was coming back. Maybe—

No. It was too late. Hell, he could barely afford the price of enough aviation gas to take her up for an hour on weekends. He'd been stockpiling fuel, so that he could fill her up when the time came. And that last outlay for the fifty-caliber machine guns had stripped his bank account.

Originally, the P-38 Lightning had been armed with four guns in the nose, for a field of fire that would literally blow an enemy out of the sky. With a ceiling of more than 28,000 feet, the plane could scream down out of the sun at Jap formations, hitting 700 miles an hour. Too fast to evade, too powerful to shrug off, the P-38 had enough range to fly more than 3,000 miles.

But Justus had not been able to find—or afford—four machine guns. He had to settle for two.

He smiled tightly. Two would be enough. He had

located the ammo belts himself. At an altitude of around 30,000 feet, a single round would—punching into a pressurized cabin—be capable of destroying anything in the air.

What luck, that he had gravitated to Montana six years ago. He'd hoped to be able to build up a good business flying hunters into the mountains. During the oil boom in Alaska, he had built up a good stake bush-flying there.

But Montana was different, he learned. Too late, as usual. There wasn't the huge number of fields he had found in Alaska. And the highways were better. So the hunters, many with four-wheel-drive off-road vehicles, didn't need him.

And, apparently, neither did the businessmen in Fort Benton. The hustler who had unloaded the airfield on him for 50 per cent down, the rest to be paid from earnings, had obviously known there wouldn't be any earnings, for he vanished into that limbo reserved for pilots who do not want their location known.

Justus had cursed Montana soundly and often. Too often, as the scar over his right eye attested. One local cattle rancher had called him outside after Justus spent nearly an hour bad-mouthing the state. Justus tried the first blow, missed, and was knocked unconscious. The rancher waited until Justus came to, bought him a drink, and said, "Next time, friend, I break both your ankles."

Justus believed him, and from then on kept his mouth shut.

A month later, the rancher's barn burned. He lost the winter's feed for his breed stock and had to board them around the country at considerable expense.

Blame might have been aimed at Justus—except that he had been away all week on a charter to Vancouver.

No one noticed that Buddy Lane, a drifter who did

odd jobs around town, drifted *out* of town on the Greyhound bus, wearing a new suit and drinking from a pint of Wild Turkey wrapped in a brown paper bag. His ticket was stamped "El Paso, Texas."

Justus, shivering in the frosty hangar, stroked the red button mounted on top of the hand-fitting hard-rubber control "joy stick," and made a BRRRRRRP! sound.

It would be that easy.

Air Force One landed at Andrews, greased in by Colonel Tom Anderson. He stayed with the crew until the ship had been powered down, then took the heavy valise all pilots called their "brain bag" and left the flight line.

Liv Matthews was waiting at the gate. Her face was white.

"What happened, Tom?" she asked. "We got a flash that you had an emergency, but that was all."

"Ozone," he said. Funny, he thought. When you get psyched up for a flight, your conversational skills go to hell. Everything is brisk, clipped. "Affirmative. Negative. Ozone."

He softened. "You shouldn't have worried. Nobody shoots down the Lone Eagle."

She smiled. "They wouldn't dare. Are you all right? Ozone can hang around, doing nasty things."

"Fine," he said. "We caught it early. But it's just as well it happened today. I hate to think of all the yelling if the President had been on board."

"How about all the yelling if you leave me alone tonight with my two-day-old beef stew?"

He glanced down at the ground without meaning to.

She caught it. "Oh. That way?"

"I'm sorry, Flo, Marty flew up this morning. She's upset. I think she lost the Braniff account."

"Sure," said the nurse. "Say hello for me."

"I will," Anderson said, knowing that he would not.

She looked after him. He seemed so worn, so haggard. As a medical nurse, her instincts warned her that something was wrong.

But as a woman, she refused to see or accept it. He's tired, she told herself, and he's just been through an emergency situation. He'll be all right.

Medical judgment lost to womanly protectiveness.

Airman First Class Angela Nemath was sitting in her red Volks in the HQ parking area. Major Paul McGowan, on the way to his own car to deposit his brain bag, saw the red Rabbit and went over to it.

"No sweat," he said, in response to her unasked question. "We ran into a little trouble, but Tom spotted it coming."

"Then he's all right?"

He snapped a glance at her. "What do you mean, 'all right'?"

"It was only that, last week, you said something about him being too tired."

"Hell, we're all tired," said McGowan. "Don't believe anything I say in bed."

"Not *anything*?"

He almost tousled her hair, then remembered that he was in the parking lot of the 89th Military Airlift Wing, talking to a subordinate enlisted woman. "Well," he hedged, "anything about the mission. Look, we've been hauled in from all over the world, to activate a plane that's been in mothballs for years, and run a taxi service for a President few of us have even met so far. Anderson's got a right to be strung out. I know I am."

"Too strung out for Sunday?"

He made a kiss-kiss with his lips. "Nobody's too strung out for that," he said.

Lieutenant Colonel Carl Birney washed up. His

craggy face was bleak in the mirror, harshly lit by the fluorescent lamps.

Tom reacted well enough to the emergency, he thought. Faster than any of us.

But the doubt still nagged at him. Just before, the Aircraft Commander had been drawn and weary. His mind was obviously elsewhere. We had to remind him of basic cockpit procedures he should have picked up on by himself.

Had the ozone affected him before the rest of us?

Birney dried his face. He tried to brush the fears from his mind.

They retreated below consciousness. But they did not go.

"My God, what you doing out here?" asked Joyce Cox. "You must have the balls of a brass monkey."

Vernon Justus managed a grin. "You ought to know," he said.

"Stop talking dirty," said the young woman, "and let's go in the office where it's warm."

"You go on," said Justus. "I'm checking these controls."

"Check them any more," she grumbled, "and you're going to wear them out. Baby, what we'd *better* start checking out is how you're going to pay the bank. Otherwise, they're going to zoom down and gobble up your airport."

"I've got it figured out," Justus said.

She blinked at him. "Since when? Last night you were moaning about how you were afraid they were going to take your P-38 away from you. As if I'd let them."

"How can you stop them?"

"I talked with my lawyer. Baby, you sell me this plane for a hundred bucks. Then, if they grab off the rest of the stuff, they can't touch *it*. What do you say?"

He was curiously touched. The tall, boyish woman obviously meant what she said. She would enter into a collusion to defraud the bank if he asked her to.

"Thanks, Joyce," he said. "But I've got everything worked out."

"Jeez," she answered. "I sure hope so."

"Wait in the office," he said. "I'll be in there soon."

"Promise?"

"Five minutes."

"I'll make some coffee."

"Weak."

"How else, with the price?"

She left. Yes, he thought, how else, with the price? And who had manipulated those prices? Coffee, sugar, gasoline, beef? All out of sight, because the crooked politicians got together with the big companies and screwed the little guy.

Screwed him the same way the government had screwed Lieutenant Vernon Justus back in 1945.

Well, Judgment Day was coming. And not far off.

Funny. Suddenly he was in the right place, at the right time. And he had the right weapon.

This morning, he had been on the verge of giving up. The bank was closing in, the other creditors were phoning him twice a day. He had been ready to take the P-38 and fly south. Let them try to put an attachment on it out of state!

Now none of that was necessary. One phone call had made all the difference.

The President was coming to Helena, to blast the shit out of the Governor. Monday, Tuesday—one day next week.

Justus knew almost as much about Air Force One as her own commander. And he knew, for sure, that if there was a nearby military base, the plane would land there rather than at a civilian airport.

Malstrom Air Force Base was just outside Great Falls. A Strategic Air Command post, with the Headquarters of the 24th Air Division stationed there, it would be the logical touchdown for the President's airplane.

Justus had flown around the Malstrom area often. He knew, because he had tested their defenses often, out of a perverse wish to know just how sharp they really were, how careless they were about slow-moving prop aircraft. A radioed warn-off was the most severe response he had ever received, and that when he was practically over the SAGE Regional Control Center. Later, he'd asked what SAGE stood for, was told it was an acronym for Semi-Automatic Ground Environment, and went away knowing no more than he had in the beginning.

Of course, with Air Force One arriving, the security would be much tighter. But that did not bother Justus.

With its 52-foot wing span and twin 1,475-horse-power Allison engines, he could hurl the P-38 more than 30,000 feet into the stratosphere. Pouncing on his target, diving at 700 miles an hour, he would be there and gone before radar caught more than a glimpse of his image return.

Lieutenant Vernon Justus, the victim of countless rejections and short counts from his government, had decided on the perfect retribution.

When Air Force One, carrying the President of the United States, began its letdown over the high plains of Montana, he intended to come hurtling down out of the sun and blast it from the sky.

THE WHITE HOUSE
WASHINGTON, D.C.

March 14

TO: Commander, 89th MAC, Andrews AFB

SUBJECT: Flight Readiness

The Presidential aircrew and equipment is hereby placed on Yellow Alert for probable mission sometime within the next 84 hours. Overseas kit will not be necessary.

Until further notice, this alert will be automatically extended by 24 hours each 2400 hours EDT.

ARTHUR CUMMINGS
Chief of Staff

She slept quietly in the hangar—but it was only a light doze. Air Force One was aware of the activity around her. She felt the surge of gentle energy as her circulation system—her hydraulics—filled with freshly pumped fluids. Her nerve endings—the electronic sensors which reported on the many subtle reactions within her engines, and her life-support systems, and her mechanical muscles—tingled as the crew chief tested them.

Her health was monitored in other ways. A gallon of jet fuel was sucked from her tanks for analysis. In the past, a daily jet had whisked samples to Wright Patterson AFB. Now the tests could be made at Andrews, saving considerable time and expense—and depriving certain Pentagon Air Force staff officers of a milk run to obtain monthly flight time.

This fuel had been checked yesterday, when it rested for twenty-four hours in a special fuel truck under heavy guard. It would be checked again tomorrow. Once, in Vienna, an entire fuel load was condemned because rust from an old storage tank got into it. Within ten hours, that tank had been condemned and filled with concrete.

Dozing, she received a pedicure. Each giant tire was examined carefully for air pressure, tread wear, and overall condition. Once, while landing at Quonset Point Naval Air Station in Rhode Island, she had blown two tires with President John F. Kennedy on board. Since then, her tires had been rotated to other, less sensitive aircraft automatically when they reached 25 per cent of estimated life span.

Other crewmen gave her a beauty treatment. She was cleaned and waxed, and paint touch-ups were made on her blue-and-white trim.

Finally the daily ritual was completed, and the hangar door clanged shut, leaving Air Force One alone again except for two floor security men and an expert marksman up on the catwalk.

PART TWO

Cleared for Takeoff

12

Warren Rogers refused a second drink. "No, thanks,
Mr. Mayor," he said. "I've still got some homework
to catch up on."

Mayoral candidate William Guthrie smiled. "Thanks
for the vote of confidence. Let's hope the good people
of Helena concur."

Rogers shrugged aside the thanks. "You'll be a shoo-
in. I haven't wet-nursed advance campaigns this long
without learning a little. Why do you think the President's coming out here?"

Guthrie said, "I assumed to help me win."

Rogers laughed. "Hell, if there was the slightest
chance of you losing, you wouldn't catch him on this
side of the Mississippi. He's a good man, but like every
politician I know, he doesn't like to get caught with
the dead body. Oh, sure, his visit will give you a boost.
But you'd have won anyway."

Uneasily, Guthrie said, "Anyway? Does that mean
there's a chance he may not come after all?"

"There's always that chance," said the Advance
Man. "War could break out somewhere. He could get
the flu."

"My God," said the candidate.

"Cheer up," said Rogers. "I told you that you'd win
anyway, didn't I?"

"It's not that," said Guthrie, trying to smile. "It's
just that I know for a fact that if he doesn't show up,

after all the work she's done, my wife will wait until I'm asleep and then slit my throat."

"I know the feeling," said Rogers. "Well, Bill—if that's okay—?"

"Sure, Warren," said Guthrie. "I guess you want to brief me."

"Wrong," said Rogers. "I want you to forget all the loyalties you've built up around this town, and lay the pure, unadulterated truth on me. I don't want any surprises while the President's here. Don't hold anything back, because I'll find out anyway, but if I have to do it the hard way, your wife may not get first slice."

"What do you want to know?"

"How serious is Governor Hoskins? He can't really mean to spit in Foster's eye and hope to get away with it."

"He puzzles me," admitted Guthrie. "I've known Claude for most of my life. He's always been pretty sharp. Looking out for Number One is his way of life. This hostility toward the President isn't like him. I know he made a mistake at the Convention, but until now, he's always cut his losses, taken his lumps, and come out ahead in the long run. This deliberate obstruction to the President's visit seems suicidal."

The Advance Man considered for a moment. "If he's as sensible as you indicated, and that's what my own reports on him say too—then there's only one other possible reason for his actions."

"What's that?"

"He thinks he can get something out of this."

Guthrie poured himself another weak drink. They were talking in the small apartment he kept in Helena. His "ranch"—actually a gentleman farmer's version of cattle raising—was nine miles out on the Great Falls highway, near the Houser Lake Dam.

"Warren," he said slowly, "Claude's ambitions must be larger than the state level. Take this election. If—

when," he corrected, nodding at Rogers' upraised finger, "I win this election, it'll be a minor embarrassment to him, but that's all. This is the state capital; it's his town, and he'll have all the real clout, no matter how much kicking and screaming I do. So my candidacy isn't why he's throwing up roadblocks for the President."

"Then he really wants to embarrass Foster?"

"Maybe. But, knowing Claude, I think it goes further than that. He's embarrassing himself too, and I'm sure he realizes it. No, I think he's drawing up genuine lines here, and daring the President to cross them."

"Why?"

"To . . ." Guthrie hesitated. "To actually hurt him in some way."

"Physically?"

"No, no, not that. But my every instinct tells me that he wants to take something away from the President—some of his power, or his prestige, or his credibility."

"Again, why? Hoskins isn't a national figure. What would he gain?"

"The approval of someone who is a national figure?"

Warren Rogers tapped his fingers on the table.

When he spoke, it was with an expression of new awareness. "You may just be right," he said. "Your jolly little Governor might be playing stalking horse for some joker back in Washington. Beautiful." He consulted his watch. It was late Friday evening in the capital now. A bad time to try to catch anybody on the phone. Dinners, parties, TGIF dashes out of town . . . the business of government was pretty much like any other business.

Was this important enough to take directly to the President? Assuming he could pull an end run around one Arthur Cummings?

He decided to hold off for a while, and dig some more. Nothing would be moving over the weekend anyway. He knew that President Foster had scheduled a working visit to Camp David.

"The Governor's announced that the state police wouldn't be much help, because of some training thing over in Billings," he said. "Is that on the level?"

"Apparently. It's an annual thing. But it's unusual for any substantial number of troopers to attend all at once. I think Claude's got his neck out on that one. If you called the Commandant—"

"No," said Rogers. "Not as long as I have your assurance that the city police are dependable."

"I talked to Pete Judson, the Deputy Mayor, this afternoon. The Chief of Police is already working with your Secret Service men. The police here are professionals and nonaligned. You can count on them."

"All right," said the Advance Man. "Now, let's keep these details quiet as long as possible. We've scheduled the visit for Wednesday, with his arrival in time for lunch."

"I know," said Guthrie.

Rogers sighed. "Leaking already, huh?"

"The hotel people are calling all over town trying to move guests."

"Okay," said Rogers. "I'll make an official statement on Monday morning. You can break it then too. The President will helicopter in from the airport, make a four-block dash for the hotel."

"No official motorcade route? Folks'll be disappointed."

"Don't worry," said Rogers. "Foster likes to press the flesh just as much as Nixon did. The folks can get a good look at him outside the hotel. Then lunch, and an endorsement speech by the President."

"Will he be staying over? My wife—"

"Only if something unexpected makes him decide to. I wouldn't count on it."

"But you took the rooms for two days—"

"A cushion. Be grateful, Bill. Not many mayoral

candidates get even this much." He did not have to add: especially in out-of-the way cities like Helena.

Hopefully, Guthrie said, "Well, I guess I'll meet him at the airport anyway."

"Wrong," said Rogers. "You're not Mayor *yet*. It's the Governor's place to greet the President."

"But what if he doesn't?"

"I think he will. Whatever's up his sleeve, I don't think he could pass up all that national TV coverage."

"I guess not," said Guthrie. "Okay, don't get the idea I'm complaining. I know what a break I'm getting. What else do you need from me?"

Rogers consulted a scribbled four-by-five card. "Get your guest list for lunch Wednesday to me no later than ten A.M. Monday."

"With background information and so on?"

Rogers shook his head. "Don't need it. Just the full name of each person, and his Social Security number."

"But— You mean, you can check people out from just that?"

Rogers smiled tightly. "Bill, you'd drop your teeth if you knew how much data I can get just by knowing that little old number."

"I thought Social Security information was privileged."

"It is. But the number's used in other ways. Some states make it your driver's license number. If you enlist in the armed services today, you don't get a serial number, you use your own Social Security number. It's on your bank accounts, it's on your credit information forms, it's on your hospital records."

"In other words," said William Guthrie, with a flash of pioneer anger, "we all now have a personal National Identity Number, just like Nazi Germany. Seriously, Warren, how does that strike you?"

"As a citizen, it makes me madder than hell," said the Advance Man. "I get spooked knowing that my entire life, and my family's, and everybody I know, are all trapped there in the computer banks, instantly available to any bastard who has access to the right button."

"My point—" said Guthrie, before he was interrupted.

Rogers went on. "But as the President's Advance Man, I'm overjoyed to have a fast way of checking out everybody within gunshot range of my boss." He gave Guthrie an embarrassed gesture of spread hands and added, "Oh, and, Bill, when you turn in that list of numbers, don't forget your own."

Shaking his head sadly, Guthrie said, "And my wife's?"

Laughing, Rogers said, "Particularly hers."

"I didn't think you were coming over tonight," said A1C Angela Nemath. She had heard the tiny beeps from the garage and waited at the door until she heard the buzzer.

"You weren't supposed to either," said Major Paul McGowan. He had put the key back in his pocket when he saw the red Rabbit already in the garage.

"You could have called. I have my lover hidden in the closet."

"I'm civilized. I'll just boot his ass out the window."

"That won't hurt. We're on the first floor."

"I *said* I was civilized. May I come in?"

She pouted at him. "Give me one good reason why."

He moved his hand toward his fly. She slapped it. "Oh, you're beyond help! Come on in, before you hurt yourself. This garage is freezing."

"Where do you think I got this icicle?" he asked.

"Enough," she said. "Come on in. Are you drinking?"

"Smallishly," he said. "There's nothing scheduled for tomorrow, as you know. But with those itchy characters over at the White House . . ."

"Weak Bourbon and branch water," she decided. "Paul, why *are* you here?"

He hesitated. "I called the main gate, pretended to be the OD checking on crew personnel. He said your car had left the base. I figured you'd be here, so—"

"Seriously, *were* you checking up on me?"

"No. Should I be?"

"Maybe."

"Okay," he said. "Next time I will. But tonight, love, I swear it was only a small case of the blues. I just didn't want to go back to that empty apartment."

"Why not?"

"You."

She had finished making their drinks, and served his to him in an Air Force One glass.

He examined it. "So that's where all our crystal has been going?"

Angela shook her head.

"Our crystal has been going into the huge-mouthed handbags of the wives of Senators and Secretaries of State, despite the frantic efforts we lowly cabin attendants make to protect it from them. Darling, I kid you not, do you know what Mrs. Sol Cushman made off with two weeks ago when we rolled the plane out for that special luncheon? Two glasses, an ashtray, and five books of matches. Not to mention that she went through napkins like she was eating spare ribs. Funny, though. None of those napkins ended up in the trash."

"The wife of the Secretary of State is a klepto," he said, sipping his drink. "What's your excuse?"

"They're all kleptos," she said. "Meanwhile, you're the backup pilot, and I'm one of the Stewards. We're entitled."

"Stewardae," he corrected. "Feminine."

"Shove it. If *we* can't let a little of the glamor rub off on us, who can? But those fancy ladies, with their names in the Blue Book and their pictures in the *Post*

every Sunday . . . my God, but they have sticky fingers.
We watch them like hawks, and we still lose half a
dozen glasses every time there's a gaggle of them on
board."

"Well, you can't really blame them," he said. "It's
their way of letting the world know they were important enough to lunch aboard the President's airplane.
I know we make a big deal out of trying to prevent
souvenir hunters from snatching stuff, but if we felt
that strongly, all we'd have to do is use plain unmarked glasses and ashtrays. We maintain an attractive nuisance. Besides, it does Tom's soul good,
scrounging to keep us in silverware."

"I think it's indecent," she flared. "He's the CO.
Why should he have to beg for free glasses and serving plates?"

Calmly, he answered, "Because if he sent *me* to beg,
I'd strike out. Do you think the president of Corning
Glass would give me the time of day? But when
Colonel Thomas Anderson comes to visit, the gates
of the storehouses swing wide."

"Seriously, Paul," she said, "those old bags are strip-
ping us clean. We do our best. When we go for a new
drink, we always try to take the used glass. But they've
got a thousand slippery tricks. 'Oh, I gave my glass
to that nice young man,' and you can't come right out
and call them a liar, or search their purses."

"Why don't you just do your best and let it go at
that?" he suggested. "Leave it to our brave commander
to scour up some more glassware."

"Damn it," she said, "that's one extra burden he
shouldn't have to carry."

He studied her. "Well," he said. "Why this sudden
concern for Colonel Anderson?"

"I'm worried about him."

Carefully, he asked, "Why?"

"Because he seems to be shouldering all the responsibility."

"You bet your sweet ass he is," said McGowan, surprised at the sudden bitterness in his voice. "That's what the job is, that's the job he wanted, and that's the job he got."

She leaned back in her chair. "Why, Paul," she said. "Are you jealous of him?"

"Jealous? Hell, no. If you want the truth, Angie, I'm sorry for him. Sure, he's got the problems of Command, just like the British had the White Man's Burden. And they both sought it to the exclusion of everything else. Baby, I'd rather fly than fuck—present company excepted. But even I have a line where I draw back and say, 'Hey, wait a minute. There's a limit.' But guys like Anderson have their heads screwed on differently. They have what the ground crew call 'calibrated eyeballs.' They can take one look at a torque bolt and tell you that it's ten pounds under. Or one glance at some poor pilot who forgot to iron his necktie, and tell you that he doesn't have what it takes."

"Why are you so angry?" she asked. "*You* have what it takes."

"I've got goddamned *more* than it takes," he said. "And I'm wasting it playing bus driver for a lot of spoiled politicians."

"There can't be a war on all the time," she said. "Somebody has to do the routine work. My job isn't exactly Thrill City, but I do it the best I can."

"Come on," he said. "You're the first woman on Air Force One. Don't tell me that doesn't thrill your little cockleshells."

"You're making fun of me," she said. "All right, you're not happy in your work. Transfer out."

"I would," he said. "I would in a minute. But they tar you with a black mark that stays with you forever."

"Black?" she asked evenly. "Or yellow?"

His face flushed, and he choked back an angry reply.

He sipped at his drink, and in a moment said, "We're talking about Anderson."

"He looks very tired," she said, glad to avoid the argument. "I think he's under a lot of strain."

"You'd be under strain too, if you—" he stopped.

"What?" He did not answer. "What, Paul? You were going to say something."

"It's none of our business."

"But it is. He's our commanding officer. More than that, he's the Aircraft Commander of Air Force One. Now, what were you going to say?"

How about this? he thought. A goddamned enlisted woman is bracing me to repeat things I haven't even said to myself.

"Let it drop," he said. "I shouldn't have even mentioned it."

"But you did, and I won't let it drop."

"Suppose I order you to?"

He was surprised to hear her laugh—a short, snorting outburst, almost manic. "You, order *me*? On base, yes. On board the plane, yes. But here, in our little den of iniquity? Major, don't make me throw up. In this room, we're just people. Maybe not exactly the people I thought we were. I believed we were something special to each other. Otherwise, do you think I would have ever— Paul, you take an awful lot for granted. In my whole life, I have never—"

"I know you haven't—"

"This was different—"

"For me too—"

"But you're an *officer* and I'm only enlisted dirt—"

His voice overrode hers.

"SHUT UP!"

Stunned, she fell silent.

"Damn it," he said. "I love you. What the hell are we fighting about? Didn't you hear me? I said, I love you."

Softly, she answered, "I heard you."

"Then quiet down and let me think."

"It's the first time you've ever said it . . ."

"Please, Angie . . ."

"I'll be quiet."

"Shhh."

She stood and held out both her hands. "Come with me."

"Damn it, hon, I've got to—"

"Come."

He followed her into the bedroom.

"We're going to keep talking about it, you know," she whispered. The bedroom was dimly lighted by light spilling from the bathroom. "I know it bugs you, but I'm not just some broad you shack up with—"

"Damn it, Angie, I've already said—"

She pressed a finger to his lips. "I know. You love me. And I'm glad. But listen to me, will you. I've got a stake in this too. I'm *proud* to be in the 89th." She giggled. "I'm not particularly proud to be sacked in with one of my officers. They have rules against fraternization. Or is it cohabiting?"

"You're a nut."

"Could be. But, Paul, don't shut me out. So we're bending a few rules now—they're little rules, old-fashioned ones, which may or may not pertain today. But what counts is, and don't laugh at me, are we really doing our jobs full out? A little screwing around —with or without love—is one thing. But I warn you, Major, I am gung ho in my job, and I mean to stay that way."

"Gung ho," he yawned, "is Marine talk."

She punched him in the ribs. He hissed with shock. "And *that*," she said, "is pillow talk, the new wave. Now, give. What's the matter with Colonel Anderson? No shit, Paul. I'm serious."

Carefully, he said, "It's his own personal bag."

"I'm no gossip."

"All right." He sat up and reached, automatically, for the cigarettes he had given up more than five years ago. In their place, he sipped at his drink, which had melted down to mostly water.

"It's as simple as this. I think Tom flies that much, and pushes himself that hard, just so he doesn't have to go home too often."

"Come on."

"I mean it. I think Tom suspects that Marty is playing around on the side, and he doesn't want to face it. So he removes himself from the area."

"Of *course* she's playing around," said Angela. "Don't tell me that you didn't *know*!"

"No," he said. "I don't, not for sure. I suspect that's what Tom's afraid of, but that's all."

"Well, he's very perceptive. After all, isn't the husband always the last to know?"

"Do you speak from experience?"

"Sorry," she said. "Well, if that's his problem, my guess is that it won't go on much longer. She's getting careless. One day soon she'll put him in the position where he *has* to notice."

"Angie, how do you know so much about Marty Anderson?"

"She's a big item in the columns, if you know how to read between the lines, and I do. And I didn't give up my outside friends when I enlisted. The stews on the major airlines have a pretty powerful communications system."

"To which you're still plugged in?"

"Five by five," she said. He laughed. The radioman's jargon was strange, coming from her lips. He was, he realized, learning more and more about this girl each time they were together.

"I'll tell you something else," Angie went on. "I think Marty *wants* him to catch her off base."

"Why? Anderson's straight arrow. He'd leave her."

"Which may be precisely what she's after."

"I doubt it," he said. "That woman doesn't like to lose."

"Who says she'd be losing? If she runs out on the Colonel, she's on her own. This way, because he's an old-fashioned gentleman, the likes of which you don't hardly find any more, he'd give her a quiet divorce. Probably alimony, or at least a settlement."

He laughed bitterly. "On the pay of a Colonel? Babe, the man makes less than $30,000 a year—before taxes."

"So she'd nick him for a hundred a week. That'd keep her in Kleenex."

"Women," he said. "No souls at all. You see a man as a hunk of ore, ready to be mined. All right, agreed that's what she's up to. There's nothing we can do about it."

"I didn't say there was," she said. "But if that's what's been wearing him down, don't you think it's dangerous for him to be flying in that left seat?"

As if from a distance he saw her, leaning toward him earnestly, her naked body rosy in the light reflected from the red curtains. Carefully, he said, "I'm not sure I get your drift, Angie."

"Paul—maybe he ought to be replaced."

On the Metroliner, speeding toward New York, Sue Earhart leafed through the confidential file given to her by Senator Philip Hopper. Most of its contents were cost breakouts, which, according to her Corgi combination calculator, alarm clock, and stopwatch, supported Hopper's estimate of five hundred million dollars a year for the President's air fleet.

There was plenty of hard material here with which she could, when next reporting on a presidential flight, drop into her commentary and, without editorializing, get a picture of waste across to her viewers. With most other TV news people, the technique might have appeared obvious—but Sue had a reputation for being hard-nosed. When someone with whom she disgreed faced her in a one-on-one interview, she did not hesitate to speak her own mind or to attack statements she did not like. It was already well known that she disapproved of Howard Foster, and she would be able to sting him easily with a series of tiny barbs which, in their cumulative effect, could be extremely painful.

There was no uneasiness in her mind about her actions. Since the investigative reporter had become a national folk hero during and after Watergate, it had become generally accepted that there were no private boundaries any more. Where, in earlier days, a compliant press corps might have looked the other way at an aging Senator's drinking problem, today they would hoist a few with him and steal his fingerprinted glass as evidence of transgression. Perhaps Sue Earhart was more aggressive than some of her companions in the media, but she was envied, not blamed, for this.

Her last call before leaving Washington had been to Morton Bailey, who regarded himself as her friend. She smiled at that thought. Bailey was a callow, none too bright young man who had fallen into incredibly good luck when, after a heart attack put his boss in the hospital, he was able to keep Foster's press activities on an even keel during the last two weeks of the campaign. Sue knew that Bailey's success had been due largely to superb work by Foster's Advance Man, Warren Rogers. The old pro didn't need the bouquets, and had generously allowed them to fall Bailey's way.

"What's this about the President going to Montana?" she asked.

Bailey made noncommittal sounds, until she said, "Don't worry, I got it from a good source. Your name won't be attached. But I think I can do you a favor."

"Such as?"

"Put me on the flight."

"Sue," he complained, "I'm up to my ears in requests from old-time White House staffers. They'd set my pants on fire."

"Not," she said, "if I did pool coverage for them."

"You? Pool? But you're in broadcast."

"No matter. I cut my eye teeth in a city room. Get me on board, and your good buddies will have some interesting copy for once."

Bailey considered. What Sue was proposing was very unusual. He wondered if her network would sit still for it. A nationwide celebrity herself, Sue would in effect be giving her competitors first shot at a two-layered story. One, the usual no-problems routine of an Air Force One flight. Boring. Two, the reactions of one of the world's most famous women to an event which, while ordinarily dull, could take on sparkling life if properly presented. And, he thought God knows Foster needs a little color on his plate.

He made a decision. "I'll see what I can do," he told her.

She stuck in the knife and twisted it. "Would you like me to call the President directly? We're old friends from his Senate days."

"No," he said, realizing that he was caught between the rock and the hard place. "If any press at all are allowed, I'll make sure you're fitted in. But no camera crew."

"Of course, darling," she said. "Just little old me. You have my home number, don't you?"

He did not, so she gave him the unlisted phone in her Central Park South apartment.

Sue had finished the basic material given to her by Hopper, and was now glancing through the dossiers of the key Air Force personnel.

She'd already read Anderson's and had put it aside.

Smiling, she thought: Okay, Colonel Anderson. Here I come!

Major Paul McGowan sat in his car for a moment in the parking lot. The heated words he and Angie had exchanged still echoed in his mind.

"Replaced!" he had shouted. "What the hell for?"

"For his own good," she said. "I'm no pilot, but I've known enough of them to be able to see when someone isn't flying at his best."

Furious, he said, "I'll just *bet* you've known enough of them. On all those cozy *lay*overs. Well, Miss Smarty, observations made in bed don't qualify you to criticize your commanding officer. Where do you get off, suggesting that *any* pilot be replaced—let alone Tom Anderson?"

"I didn't say he should be replaced," she flared. "I asked *if* he should be!"

"Same difference," he said, throwing on his shirt. "Listen, baby, stick to your beverage trays and counting cocktail napkins, leave the flying to the pros."

"I'm pro enough to be assigned to helping the President in an emergency," she said, pulling the sheet up around her body in belated modesty.

"Sure," he said, knowing it would hurt her. "Because it makes for good press copy. But, baby, if there's ever any trouble, you can bet that Sergeant Miller will be there before you."

"That bone-headed chauvinist? He doesn't even know how to make an old-fashioned."

"Maybe not, but he knows how to lower the boom if anybody makes a move toward the Man. Let's see *your* Golden Gloves medals."

"*Major*," she said, her lip trembling, "I would appreciate it if you would put on your goddamned Air Force pants and haul your military ass out of here."

"Gladly," he said. "And I might suggest, *Airman,* that you report back to base where you belong."

She threw the nearest thing to her hand at him. It was a pillow, and be brushed it aside with a harsh laugh.

"Lousy shot," he said. "Maybe Anderson's not the only one who needs to be replaced."

"Meaning me?" she demanded.

"Who else? Sweetheart, I put you on that plane, and I can put you off—"

He stopped, astonished that he had said the words. It was not in him, usually, to be cruel.

She sank down to her knees.

"*You*? You had me assigned?"

He tried to retreat. "In a way. I mean, you earned the spot, but—"

It was too late. She would not listen now.

"Go away," she said. "Please go away."

"I'm sorry," he said. "You made me furious."

"Please," she said. "Now."

He left.

Now he sat outside his apartment building in the chill March night, and wished he did not have to go inside alone.

13

Anderson drove directly home. He considered calling ahead, but decided not to. Telephones were too easy to hang up.

Marty's car was in the driveway, the new Mustang he'd given her for their first wedding anniversary four months ago. The motor was running. He opened the door and switched off the key. He waited for a moment, expecting her to come out with a forgotten purse or gloves. But the house door remained shut.

Anderson went inside. The lights were on in almost every room. Marty had never learned economy. He switched off those in the dining area and all but one in the living room.

She was in the bedroom, stretched out on the spread, breathing heavily. Her hand held her address book. There was an empty glass on the bedside table, near the telephone.

Apparently she had started the car, remembered a phone call to make, and had dozed off while looking up the number. It was probably just as well. Not normally a good driver, she became a road hazard when she was drinking. Which, he observed sourly, seemed to be most of the time lately.

He took the book from her hand, closed it—almost, but not quite, glancing at the page to see if he recognized any of the names. He got an extra blanket and covered her. Her hair was tousled like a red flower against the pillow. He started to kiss her, but she snored as he bent over, and it broke the moment. He turned off the light and went down the hall to his study, pausing to slip out of his jacket and tie.

Marty would be out for at least four hours. He had seen her like this more than once. Until her body had metabolized the alcohol, there would be no waking her, not by hot coffee, cold showers, or any other means.

It was just as well. There was work he could get done, while things were quiet. He knew the silence would not last. Once she was awake, he could count on Marty to stir things up.

Boeing had sent him three modification reports on the Boeing 707. When changes were made to other aircraft, it was his job to examine them and see if they were desirable for the 89th's planes. The same was true whenever new equipment and instruments were designed. In many cases, the equipment or modifications were excelled by changes which had already been made to Air Force One, but sometimes the civilian sector led the way.

One example was the slow-scan image reproducer which had recently been added to the plane's communications system. Essentially a television transmitter using short waves which could be broadcast worldwide, instead of the normal line-of-sight TV transmission, the basic equipment had been conceived by ham radio amateurs. An 89th communications specialist had run across the specifications in *QST*, the official magazine of the American Radio Relay League. Incredible as it seems, military technicians were still using phone wire systems to transmit pictures, maps, and other visual material. Five months and nearly four hundred thousand dollars later, Air Force One could transmit a photograph or replica of a document while aloft. It could also receive them.

The street went both ways. The adjustable wing, which extended forward and below the leading edge, worked in conjunction with the flaps to increase lift over drag, giving Air Force One the ability to use fields so short that often conventional prop planes found them unsuitable. It had been developed for Air Force One, and was later adapted to commercial use.

Anderson found nothing in today's reports that sparked his interest. He slipped them into the folder marked "File" and put them in his brain bag.

He stretched and yawned. He had spent nearly an hour at the base, preparing a report on the ozone incident, and making sure that its presence in the upper atmosphere had been passed along to all military and civilian control facilities. He was virtually sure that the Ground Controller had done so too, but in something this important it paid to follow up.

If Marty had not been in her present condition, he would have taken a nap. But he did not want to be asleep when she awakened. It would be just like her to take the car and drive away.

Leafing through his Pilot's Guide, he began to choose alternate landing sites if Helena and Great Falls should be weathered in. He made note of the Advance Man's desire to make Malstrom AFB an alternate, then chose bases near Cheyenne and Albuquerque as well. And, of course, Air Force One would be carrying enough fuel to return them to Andrews if necessary. Or would it? Flying under 30,000 feet would eat up extra fuel. He would suggest the alternates to Carl Birney on Monday—or sooner, if the mission date was advanced. Such a suggestion was, in effect, an order—but Anderson did not run that kind of outfit. If the Navigator had other ideas, he could express them—and if they were valid, Anderson would probably agree.

One of the Stewards would have to shop for food. No, he reconsidered: Two. The new attendant, A1C Angela Nemath. Sergeant Miller could show her the ropes. By going in civilian clothes and appearing to be a young couple, they would be able to use one of the markets which had already been "burned" by previous shopping. It was his rule that supplies for the airplane were bought for cash, without any indication being given that they were other than private purchases. For additional safety, no market was used twice by the same Steward. So the circle around Andrews was getting bigger and bigger, as buyers widened their range. Certain special food items and most of the liquor were sent over from the White House. But the last President had been a virtual teetotaler, and the press crew had threatened open rebellion. So a special booze slush fund was created to take up the slack. If new President Foster knew about it, he gave no sign. Nor, with the temporary aircraft he had used while 26000 was being spruced up, did he send any appreciable amount of liquor to the plane. Still, the reporters and other guests drank well and frequently, thanks to the booze fund.

They did it from lovely glasses ornamented with the Presidential Seal, and flicked their cigarettes into similarly adorned ashtrays. Whenever possible, they absconded with the glasses and ashtrays.

The plane was in good shape for the upcoming trip, but he knew there would be inevitable losses, through theft and breakage. It was almost time for him to go on another raiding party.

He had a sucker list, passed along by the previous Aircraft Commander. It contained sources for dinner plates, for flatware, for glasses, ashtrays, matches, and napkins.

All were "donated" by their manufacturers. Gorham, or Corning, or some other maker of fine porcelain would outfit the plane with a full set of serving pieces and accessories. When enough had been lost, broken, or stolen, the remainder would be removed from use, and the Aircraft Commander would move to the next name on his list. No manufacturer was approached more than once in a three-year period, unless the President himself made a specific request.

Only one in recent memory had. Specifying a particular maker and pattern, Richard M. Nixon soon had Air Force One dinnerware on his tables in Key Biscayne and San Clemente.

Naturally, all donors wanted to publicize the honor which had befallen them. Privately, they could do so. A salesman could mention the fact to a client. But no publicity or advertising was permitted.

It was another example of the government's general hypocrisy, thought Anderson. To properly equip the plane's galleys would have cost less than two thousand dollars. Instead, he spent valuable time fine-stroking the president of some glass company—perhaps even taking their top brass for a luncheon flight aboard the plane—and by the time the gifts were delivered, fifteen or twenty thousand dollars in military time, fuel, and aircraft write-off would have been spent. But the dishes were "free," and that delighted the hearts of White House cost cutters.

He felt a twinge of pain in his stomach. Probably a belated gas bubble from the sudden descent that afternoon.

Remembering Liv Matthews, he considered telephoning her. But it was getting late. She knew by now that he wasn't coming for dinner. He did not feel like food anyway.

He decided to make himself a weak drink. When he got up, his knees sank under him as a wave of dizziness whirled through his brain. He held the back of the chair until the vertigo passed.

Liv was right, he thought. That ozone hangs around and does nasty things.

The twinge of pain prodded his stomach again.

Instead of making the drink, he went to the bathroom.

A minute later, he was staring into the mirror,

sweating heavily. "Jesus, not again," he whispered.
"Not *now*."

He had flushed the commode, but not before he
saw, clearly, that there was blood in his urine.

He splashed water on his face. His mind raced.

*It must have been that damned ozone! I've been
careful not to get oxygen-starved.*

His face, glistening wet, accused him.

*But you've been driving yourself. Getting too tired.
You know better than that.*

I'll play it easy all weekend. And take the pills.

*The pills were so you could pass your physicals.
You're not supposed to take them on any regular basis.*

Just to get through this next flight. Buy time to turn
around.

*That's what you've been saying for more than a
year. When are you going to face the truth?*

Soon. Soon . . .

Carol had been dead nearly a year when he met
Martha Desmond at a party given by *Flying* magazine.
He was the guest of honor, having been chosen by a
vote among a dozen base commanders as the Air
Force's most representative pilot.

The choice embarrassed him. "What it means," he
confided to a friend at McCord AFB in Tacoma, Washington, where he was stationed, "is that I'm so dull
they can all point at me and say, 'See? Air Force pilots
aren't *all* bloodthirsty throttle jocks.' Some honor."

"Don't knock it," said his friend. "You get a week
in New York. That can't be all bad."

It wasn't. At the party, which took place on his
second night in town, he met Martha Desmond. After
the past months of hard work and study—anything to
keep from thinking about Guam and Carol—it was an
unexpected release to find a beautiful young woman
giving him her total concentration, her large hazel
eyes apparently locked to his face, even when she spoke

herself. She was a "designer," whatever that was. He pressed her to make conversation about herself, but she threw the initiative back. And it was pleasant to find someone so interested in him, and his work.

He did not take her home—she had come with a young advertising man—but he promised to call her the next day.

He forgot, so she called him. That night they went to the latest Broadway musical, for which she happened to have impossible-to-buy tickets, and had supper afterward in the Tavern-on-the-Green.

This time, he did take her home. She invited him in for a drink, he accepted, and it was almost dawn when he left.

Except for casual bumps of hands when passing drinks, chunks of sharp cheddar, and napkins, they did not touch during the night.

Instead, they talked. She listened quietly when he spoke about Carol, cried when he told her how he went alone to her grave and, when no one watched, buried the little silver eagle with the black pearl at the base of the simple plaque which read: CAROL DEAN ANDERSON and her dates of birth and death. She almost touched him when he described his first month back on the flight line, when he flew with an abandon that frightened his crew and horrified his superior officers. One day he took an F-86 straight up into the clouds and tried to twist its wings off. Instead, he made himself airsick and when, totally embarrassed, he landed, the destructive mood had left him.

Martha—by now Marty—described her own past and ambitions concisely and without embroidery. She had worked with one of the country's top design firms, left to go on her own, was struggling to make a name. She was still on the sunny cusp of thirty, had never married, didn't intend to.

"All of my married friends are having affairs on the

side," she said. "They seem to be having so much fun I think I'll make the affairs the main event and forget about the marriage."

He laughed, thinking she was joking. She put some music on her tape player—the old musical *Bells Are Ringing*. Her eyes misted when Judy Holliday sang "The Party's Over."

"Pardon my snivel," she said. "That song always gets to me. It reminds me of all the parties I've been to, and wished would never end. But of course they always do."

At the door, with dawn painting the sky pale red, she said, "If you want to kiss me, you can."

Surprised, he said, "No. Not on the first date."

She laughed. "You're something, do you know that? What time?"

He looked at his watch. "It's almost five-thirty."

"Not now. What time will you pick me up?"

"Well . . ." He hesitated.

She decided for him. "Seven. For dinner."

"I've got to check in with PIO. That's the Public Information Office. They've got some TV spots for me to do."

"They still let you out of the cage every now and then to eat, don't they?"

"Seven," he said, surrendering. He had been wary, unwilling to accept sudden friendship—but her persistence wore him down. "Do you have any place in mind?"

"Do I ever," she said. "Leave it to me, Colonel. You're in skilled hands."

She was as good as her word. The cab delivered them to a tiny restaurant on East Fifty-fourth Street. He had only glanced at the menu, which was in French, and while the fare seemed to consist of rather ordinary cuisine, the prices on the a la carte side horrified him. Mussels were $9.50—an an appetizer. Bread and butter was $4.00.

"Forget that thing," Marty said. "They know me here. Jean will serve us himself."

The owner-maître d' came over. "*Bon soir*, Miss Desmond. It is good to see you again. I have had many compliments on the decor."

She waved a hand around at the quiet, tasteful room. "I designed this joint," she told Anderson. To Jean, she said, "We've got a growing Air Force fly-boy. Feed us."

"Leave it to me," said the manager.

The food was exquisite. Simple, unpretentious—and served in generous amounts. Reassured by the American Express decal on the cash register, Anderson gave himself up to enjoying the meal, and the two wines that came with it.

Steeling himself for the inevitable toll, he thanked Jean for an outstanding meal and asked for *"l'addition."*

"Christ, your accent stinks," said Marty. To Jean she said, "Thanks for the chow. You put on a good act for our visitor."

"Anytime, Miss Desmond," said Jean. "Good night."

In the cab, Anderson said, "You didn't tell me you were paying for that."

"Pay? Me?" She laughed. "Jean *owes* me. I designed that slum for nothing but expenses. Plus the thirty per cent rake-off I got from the suppliers. He saved a fortune. If I took friends there every week for a year, he'd still be way ahead."

"Well," he said, embarrassed, "thanks anyway."

"Don't mention it," she said. She looked at the driver through the bulletproof shield dividing the compartments. "Driver," she said in a normal conversational tone, "what time is it?"

After a moment, Anderson said, "He didn't hear you. But it's—"

"I know what time it is, baby," she said. "I just wanted to find out if he could hear us. Listen, Thomas, it's been a fun two nights, but you're only in town for the rest of the week. Now, what do you want to do? We could go to Coney Island."

"At this time of night?" It was after ten.

"You're right. They don't get rolling until after midnight."

"Which Coney Island are *you* talking about?" he asked.

"The new disco, over on Third," She laughed. "And you were thinking of—"

"The other one, where you ride the roller coasters."

"Well," she said casually, "we can always go to my place and fuck."

He choked. "I'll say this," he said. "You put things right out there in front."

"No jokes, Tom." Her hand stroked the inside of his thigh. "We don't have time to do the ritual courtship dance. You're flying back to Tacoma on Saturday. We both know what we want. And there's so little time. Why waste it?"

"No reason," he said, drawing her to him.

So they went back to her apartment and fucked.

A week after he'd returned to McCord, she called him from Seattle. Somehow she had wangled an assignment there, redesigning the interiors of three Ozark airline jets which had been returned to Boeing for refitting.

He drove up, they had dinner, he stayed over, and nine days later they were married in a brief nondenominational service at McCord's Base Chapel #1.

With typical scrounging efficiency, he managed to cut their honeymoon costs by accepting a two-week special mission to Caracas, Venezuela. Marty flew back to New York alone, down to Maiquetía on Viasa-KLM two days later. Anderson was at the airport to meet her, having ferried a new military version of the 727-

200 stretch jet to Bolívar Military Airfield forty miles south of Caracas. He was weary, having spent the day flying check rides with his Venezuelan counterpart, a suave but friendly colonel named Alberto Betancourt. ("No relation to the former President, my friend. Nor to the famous Caracas advertising man.")

The new Bolívar Airfield was crisply modern, well equipped and swarming with the latest military planes —fighters, transports, bombers. The energy crisis had made Venezuela the richest country in South America.

Betancourt was an excellent pilot. He greased the big jet in for a series of flawless landings, as Anderson rode right seat. Their crew was Venezuelan, returned only that week from extensive training at Braniff's Flight Academy.

"Colonel," said Anderson, "you don't need me. You've got this bird by the tail."

"Oh, no, my friend," said Betancourt. "You will be our guest for two weeks, perhaps longer."

"But you don't *need* me," said Anderson.

Betancourt chuckled.

The 727 went haywire. One wing dropped, the nose came up, and every warning bell on the flight deck began to clang. Almost thrown out of his seat, Anderson instinctively reached for the controls, then drew back.

"What a devil woman of a plane!" Betancourt shouted. "She is out of control. Such fire! So headstrong! I shall never master her alone, my Colonel! Please—tell me what to do, or we shall crash."

"Stop fooling around, Alberto," said Anderson, "and start flying this thing."

"My mind has gone blank," complained Betancourt.

"All right, I'll stay the two weeks," said Anderson. "But get this bird straightened out, or my bride's going to arrive and find herself a widow."

Betancourt smiled, as the jet slowly resumed straight and level flight. "We are honored that you should choose Venezuela for your honeymoon. Mrs. Anderson will take many delightful memories home. You must leave all the arrangements to me."

"We're fine," said Anderson.

"Do you have a hotel?" Anderson had been assigned quarters on the air base, but they were hardly suitable for a new wife.

"My crew has put up at the Hotel Avila, while they wait for their hop back to the States. It sounds nice."

Betancourt made an explosive *poof* noise. "It is *very* nice—for sleepy old ladies and visiting professors. But not for romance. My friend, this is my country and my city. Put yourself in my hands. You are the guest of the Venezuelan Air Force, and if you so much as put your hand in your pocket, we will have you handcuffed. Leave everything to me."

Protesting, Anderson finally let himself be convinced. It was obvious that, like it or not, he was going to get the full blast of South American hospitality.

It began when Marty debarked from the Viasa-KLM DC-10. He and Betancourt were waiting outside the visitor's gate, and Anderson saw a uniformed man step up to her, salute, and lead her through a side gate without passing immigration or customs.

After they embraced, Anderson introduced Marty to Colonel Betancourt. She gave him her broadest smile, shook hands. "A real *carioca*, I presume."

"I, a sophisticate? Hardly, Señora Anderson. I am merely Juan Bimba."

"Mr. Average Man? I hardly think so, Colonel."

"We shall see," he said. "Come. The sergeant will follow with your luggage."

"What about customs?" asked Anderson.

"For a guest of the Air Force? You joke. Come, the car is waiting."

It was an air-conditioned Mercedes, hardly necessary

in the City of Eternal Spring, which Caracas is called by its residents.

"Where are we going?" asked Marty.

"I don't know," said Anderson. "Colonel Betancourt claims he has something special in store for us. Personally, I think we're being kidnapped to keep me from telling the world what a rotten pilot he is."

Marty was already familiar enough with pilot talk to know this was a high compliment to Betancourt's flying ability. She picked up the conversational ball.

"He couldn't be any worse than you, darling," she said, fluffing her red hair, which, lit by the sun through the incredibly clear air, glowed almost incandescently. "Do you know, Colonel, the first time this clod took me flying, he got us so lost that he had to follow the railroad tracks back to the airport?"

"It is a sad fact," Betancourt commiserated, "that pilots are often lost, while railroad engines always seem to know where they are going."

The countryside was verdant, brightly colored by many patches of flowers. Bougainvillea—pink, scarlet, salmon, even white—crawled up the hillsides. Tango —Golden Rain—sheltered orange blossoms within its vines.

"This is all government land," said Betancourt.

"You mean a military reservation?" asked Anderson.

"No. An area of—forest. To remain free."

Marty said, "Like one of our National Parks."

"Yes."

At that moment, they passed a rude shack of a house, perched on stilts. Chickens pecked under the porch, and half-naked young children played among them. Anderson remembered having seen several along the roadside.

"Do you let people live inside the forest?" he asked.

Betancourt shook his head. "They are squatters."

"Then they're illegal?"

"No, my friend. Since the last revolution, Juan

Bimba has held tremendous power. You see, at long last, Venezuela is a true democracy. And since we have so many Bimbas, the vote is in their hands."

"What's that got to do with squatters?"

"No man may be evicted from his home. Not for nonpayment of rent or taxes, not for trespassing, not for anything. Juan Bimba by himself may be only a poor farmer, but collectively he is a genius. The police can prevent a squatter from building a house—but once it *is* built, Juan Bimba owns it and about half an acre, in your measurements, around it."

"Why can't they be stopped from building?" asked Marty. "It's a shame, the way this beautiful valley is being ruined."

Betancourt said, "At sundown, the hillside will be empty, except for grass and vines. In the morning, there is a new house. A new family of Juan Bimbas. Who, with all their friends and neighbors, began building the house at nightfall, and finished it before dawn."

"This Juan Bimba sounds like some guy," said Anderson.

"He is," said Betancourt. "In the end, he is our true strength."

"Oh, no," said Marty Anderson. "I'm not going up in *that* thing."

"That thing" was a cable car, a *fenecula*, which held around twenty passengers and which vanished up into the clouds that rimmed the mountain range between Caracas and the sea.

"It is safer than walking," said Betancourt. "There has never been an accident, and it has been running for more than twenty years."

"Fine," she said. "You boys have your fun. I'll wait for you down here."

"But you cannot, Mrs. Anderson," he said.

"Watch me, buddy!"

"I meant, we are not coming back."

"I was afraid of that very thing," she said. "No thanks."

Patiently, he explained, "What I mean, señora, is that your hotel is up there."

"Cut this señora stuff," she said. "I'm starting to feel like Katy Jurado." Then, reacting, "*What*'s up there?"

"The Hotel Sheraton Humboldt," he said. "The most beautiful hotel in the world. It is built atop Mount Avila. From one side, you look down at Caracas. From the other, you can see the Caribbean."

"Oh, boy," she said. "Tom, tell me the nice man is kidding."

"I'm afraid not, hon," he said. "Come on. It can't be that bad."

"Want to bet?" she grumbled. But since there was really no other choice, she followed them and boarded a car which had just arrived, moisture from the low-hanging clouds still dripping down its metal sides.

The doors were locked, and their car lurched around the cable turnaround and began its journey back up into the clouds. Soon they were swaying almost a hundred feet above the crests of the hills below, and twice that above the valleys.

Most of the others in the car were lightly dressed Venezuelans, some carrying wicker baskets.

"Don't tell me," said Marty. "Juan Bimba out for an afternoon picnic."

A stout woman, overhearing her, beamed a smile, and said, "*Sí. Musiu. Bueno.*"

"*Bueno* to you too," said Marty, nodding. The woman fumbled in her wicker basket and, shyly, held out a purple orchid. It was bigger than any Marty had ever seen.

"No, thanks." She smiled.

In a low voice, Betancourt said, "Take it, Mrs. Anderson. She's not trying to sell it to you. It is her gift."

"But really—"

He persisted. "Her feelings will be hurt."

Marty took the huge orchid. "Thank you," she said. "*Gracias.*"

"*De nada,*" said the stout woman.

"That is our national flower," said Betancourt. "*Flor de Mayo,* the Flower of May. But it grows all year, some place in the country."

Marty found a pin and attached the flower to her blouse. She smiled at the woman again. "*Muchas gracias,*" she repeated.

The car arrived at the summit, bursting from the clouds just a few hundred feet below the upper cable-car station. It was made of squat concrete and looked rather like the New York City Port Authority Bus Terminal. To its right, a narrow road stretched up the ridge of the mountain to a tall building that dominated the mountain peak.

"The Humboldt," said Betancourt. "At one time, we called it the White Elephant. The government participated in its construction, and like everything connected with governments, it was a colossal failure. But, with new management, it is now our treasure. There are three restaurants, a nightclub—even an indoor swimming pool. And, to keep it exclusive, there are only suites."

"Terrific," said Marty. "What did you do, Thomas, run off with the base payroll? How are we paying for all this?"

"Ask the Venezuelan Air Force," he said. "We're their guests."

Marty beamed at Betancourt. "How very nice," she said.

In appreciation of Marty's arrival, Anderson took the next day off. It was actually at Betancourt's insistence. The Colonel had joined them for dinner at one of the Humboldt's excellent restaurants, where he

had guided them to such local delicacies as *hallaca*
—cornmeal combined with beef, pork, ham, green
peppers, and dozens of other bits of vegetables. It was
served with *hervido*, a soup made with chunks of
chicken, fish, and vegetables.

Unasked, the waiter brought a bottle of *Pompero
anejo*, a dark local rum, with ice and mixes.

Near the end of the evening, Betancourt toasted
Marty, then said, "No flying tomorrow, my friend.
You and I, we have tasted too deeply of the *anejo*.
Besides, I have meetings in the city. Wednesday, we
will go to the base early and wring our new toy out."

"I figure two hard days," said Anderson. "All kidding aside, you're good. But I want to go over a few
procedures with you. After all, there have been quite
a few military modifications."

"Wonderful," said Marty. "Two days. And what am
I supposed to do, sit up here on this mountain and
listen to the echo?"

"There will be much to keep you occupied," said
Betancourt. "Caracas is a city of fine clubs. In the
morning you will visit the Army Tennis Club, near
the Tamanaco Hotel. For lunch, you will be taken
to the country club and golf course in the heart of the
city. It is for all military personnel and honored
guests. In the evening—"

"Don't tell me," she said. "The Taps Café, run by
the official firing squad."

He spread his hands. "For years, this country was
controlled by the military. The city built up around
those areas, such as the country club, which catered
to the military leaders. Now they are bits of green
surrounded by cement."

"Just ducky," said Marty. "I think I'll pass."

"If you wish," said Betancourt.

"Try it, hon," said Anderson. "It's only for two
days."

"Okay," she said. "I'll make a try. But what if I like it? Can you match it Stateside?"

"Not all of it," he said. "But we're not Stateside. Enjoy yourself. That's why we're here."

"That's why *I'm* here," she said softly. "I'm only just beginning to understand why *you're* here."

At 23,000 feet, Colonel Alberto Betancourt said, "It is too bad, my friend. Your wife is jealous of your other love."

"She's just tired."

"No. She mistrusts the ties you have with the sky, and these machines that take you there. She does not feel the same love you do for flying, so she sees it as competition for your attention." He sighed. "It is too bad. Here, matters are much simpler. A woman is a woman, and does not wear the pants, as you say."

"Wait until the feminists land," said Anderson.

"They have landed," laughed Betancourt, "and they were slaughtered on the beaches. Not by our men. Oh, no. Yes, we are *macho*. But it was our women who repelled them. Our women are wise enough, although they often pretend silliness, to see that the spoils of the world are equally divided as things are. They do what they do, the men do what they do, and in the long run, each gets a fair share of life."

"Somehow," said Anderson, watching the altimeter, "I don't think my wife would agree with you."

Betancourt made his familiar *poof* sound. "Of course not," he said. "Where is the excitement if they always agree?"

"Twenty-eight thousand," Anderson reminded. "This bird tops out at around thirty."

"Ah," said Betancourt, "but we have added the superchargers. The Andes are high, my friend. When crossing them, I want plenty of empty air between me and their peaks."

"What's over the Andes?"

"Peru. Chile. Our new President is a far-seeing man. He plans to make this plane his own version of your Air Force One. He wants to be as free as the breeze in his ties to earth. We do not need your big jets for the small airports we have down here. This beautiful little goose will cruise high above the rock-filled clouds, yet land on the smallest meadow."

Dryly, Anderson said, "You'd better make sure your meadow is covered with tarmac or concrete, or you'll sink in up to the wings."

"A figure of speech," said Betancourt. "I have the controls, Colonel Anderson."

"You've got her," confirmed Anderson.

He watched as Betancourt took the 727-200 through 30,000 feet. To 32,000, and still climbing.

Anderson had examined the airplane carefully before accepting it at Seattle. "Tell me, Alberto," he said, "why does your President's airplane need bomb racks?"

Calmly, the Venezuelan answered, "Perhaps we must land someplace where the Tower will not grant permission."

Anderson laughed. Somehow, the answer seemed very funny. He laughed until he choked.

Betancourt gave him a curious glance. "Are you all right, my friend?"

"Never better," said Anderson, his voice cracking.

"Thirty-five," said Betancourt. Outside, the engines were laboring in the thin air. Within the cabin, both men felt the altitude too. The plane's pressurization system had not been designed to take such an altitude. And Betancourt was still climbing.

Very seriously, Anderson asked, "Alberto, do you think you can put this bird into orbit?"

Betancourt replied, "Of course." Then, disturbed by the tone of the American's voice, he asked, "Or perhaps you would rather do so yourself?"

"No, no," said Anderson. "It's your plane now. But who the hell wants to go down? What's there. The same old crap, day after day. Let's hit ninety-minute orbit. Then we'll be heroes. You can squat in the forest, and I'll get me a motorbike."

Slacking back on the throttles, with the altimeter showing 36,400 feet, Betancourt asked, "Why that?"

"Always wanted one. Never had it. Could buy one now, but they'd laugh at a bird Colonel on a bike."

"Then why want one?"

"Because I want to be eighteen again. Ride that mother out on the back roads, rev her up and chase rabbits at night. Come on, Alberto. Be a pal. Put this bird through the orbit window." He reached for the throttles. "Give her the gun, pal."

Betancourt caught his wrist. It was like trying to hold a wet eel. Anderson seemed fantastically strong. He wrapped his fingers around the throttle knobs and pushed forward. The three Pratt & Whitney JTSD-9 turbofans wound up and the plane's speed surged to 590 miles an hour, with all gauges hovering near the red line.

"Please, Colonel!" said Betancourt, trying to pry Anderson loose from the controls. It was a futile effort. "Lopez!" he called. "Help!"

The flight engineer leaped forward. He added his strength to Betancourt's. The struggle transmitted itself to the yoke, and the plane began to yaw.

"Hit him," commanded the Venezuelan pilot.

Sergeant Lopez struck Anderson a rabbit punch behind the neck. The American fell forward, bashing his head against the instrument panel.

"Going down," said Betancourt. He hit a switch, and oxygen masks fell from the overhead. "Put a mask on him."

He did not feel the need of one himself, but he attached it anyway, and soon realized, as his head cleared, that he had been performing at the outer limits of his endurance. The oxygen starvation must have hit Anderson much sooner, making him irrational and disassociated.

They were below 20,000 feet and heading for the airfield when, groaning, Anderson came out of it.

Dazed, he writhed in his harness for a moment, then —suddenly aware that something was wrong—snapped to an alert position and reached for the controls.

"It's all right, my friend," said Betancourt. "I have her. We are on our way home."

"What happened?" Anderson asked.

"I think I took her too high. The pressurization system failed us. You passed out."

Anderson groaned, rubbing his neck. "It feels like somebody slugged me."

Betancourt made no comment, and gave a warning shake of his head to the flight engineer.

By the time he greased the jet onto the runway, Anderson was recovered enough to complain. "Good thing I don't have a bad back, or I could sue you for whiplash over that landing."

The entire crew underwent a complete physical. The Venezuelans passed, although the flight surgeon warned Betancourt, "Don't fly so high next time."

"I'm going to have the oxygen system beefed up," promised the pilot.

Privately, the same surgeon told Betancourt, "I am worried about the American. He passed blood in his urine. He has complained of abdominal pains. I want to conduct further tests."

"All right," said Betancourt. "But this is very confidential. Not even the higher command must know."

"I'll do my best," said the surgeon.

He drew blood, analyzed urine, gave Anderson stress tests with an EKG attached. They lasted well into the night.

Anderson had a late supper with Betancourt. "What's going on?" he asked.

Honestly, Betancourt told him, "My friend, you may be a sick man."

"Bull. I had my physical six weeks ago."

Betancourt shrugged. "A friend of mine was examined, told he had the body of a twenty-five-year-old, and dropped dead in the elevator."

"Thanks much," growled Anderson.

"Of course," said Betancourt, "I failed to mention that it was because a terrorist put thirty-four machine-gun bullets into him."

"Alberto, I don't know how to repay you for cheering me up."

"*De nada*," said Betancourt.

"I think I ought to call Marty."

Betancourt consulted his watch. "No," he said. "She will not be home yet. When the Air Force wives find a new fish, they rarely release the poor creature until three in the morning. By then, your Marty will have been dragged through every fancy club in Caracas. She will have met every eligible bachelor, because even though she is married, our energetic wives believe it is always wise to have a suitor waiting offstage in case of accident."

"Like I nearly had today?"

"More like my friend had in the elevator," said Betancourt. "Anyway, when she is finally taken home, her head will hit the pillow with much the same impact as yours hit the instrument panel."

"That's never happened to me before," said Anderson. "I've flown without oxygen barefoot above twenty thousand. No mask, no pressurization, nothing."

"And how old were you?"

"Not as old as I am now," Anderson admitted.

"My point exactly. My friend, do not worry. Our flight surgeon is not only highly qualified, he has lips similar to the purse strings of a miser. Whatever your secret, it will be safe with him."

"I didn't know I had any secrets," said Anderson.

As it turned out, he did.

"Porphyria?" he said. "Hell, no, I don't know what it is. I can't even pronounce it."

The flight surgeon consulted a thick book. "It is very rare," he said. "We believe it is congenital, carried from birth. But it is only activated by unusual stress, combined with lack of oxygen. It was noticed particularly in Mexico during the Olympics there. Several runners showed symptoms."

"Passing out?" asked Anderson.

"That, along with disorientation. You see, Colonel, the effects cause a breakdown of the hemoglobin. It is a vicious circle. At the moment when the brain calls for more oxygen, the blood refuses to carry it. The result is often neurological disturbance, and if the syndrome persists, the victim can go into shock if internal damage is great enough."

"Doctor," Anderson said, "you know I'm a pilot. I've lived with stress and low oxygen levels for most of my life. How come this never showed up before?"

The flight surgeon shrugged. "Who knows? But now that it has made its presence felt, you would be advised to limit your flying."

"Or?"

"Or the next attack might be worse. Particularly if you were not so fortunate as to have as fine a pilot as Colonel Betancourt at the controls with you."

"Let's level, Doctor. You know I'm in the U. S. Air Force. They'd ground me in a minute if they knew about this."

"Just as I would ground Colonel Betancourt."

Anderson looked down at his trembling hands. "I see," he said.

The flight surgeon hesitated. "However, Colonel, I must inform you that this condition is between you and me. Colonel Betancourt specifically instructed me to keep the matter secret. I think you would be ill advised to continue on flight status. But my findings will not be revealed outside this room."

"I see. What if I cut back? Avoid overwork? Never let myself get oxygen starved?"

"Perhaps you could fly for a while longer. We are none of us getting any younger, Colonel. From here on, for both of us, it is all downhill."

"But maybe a year or two? That would be safe, wouldn't it?"

"If you continued passing your physicals."

"How can I do that? Won't the damage show?"

"I'm afraid it will. But there are some new drugs in the steroid family. Taken a few days before an examination, they would elevate your red blood cell level temporarily. In conjunction with iron shots, you should pass all but the most thorough examination." The flight surgeon showed Anderson a large hypodermic needle. "In fact, I was preparing to give you such an injection now."

"Doctor," Anderson said quietly, "stick it in. Then I want you to help me."

He had staved off a return of the symptoms for more than a year now. None of his physicals had been more than routine. He flew carefully and, he was sure, safely. But now . . .

That goddamned ozone layer!

Still, the effects had not been as severe today. He hadn't passed out, or become irrational.

I can control it. Just for the next few months.

He had half risen, to go to his private first-aid kit where he kept the drugs given to him in Venezuela, when Marty came through the bedroom door.

Her amazing metabolism had burned off the alcohol completely. Her step was steady and her eyes glinted toward him as she said, "Okay, sit down, fly-boy. We've got some heavy talking to do."

14

Vernon Justus was alone in the small airport's combination radio room and snack bar when the telephone rang.

"Airport," he answered.

A voice said, "It looks like everything's set for Wednesday."

"Are you sure?"

"Practically. Colonel Anderson's given orders to have the galleys stocked on Monday. He always does that two days in advance."

"Good," said Justus. "I'm all ready here. Are things set at your end?"

The voice hesitated in answering.

Justus prodded. "Well?"

"Are you sure this will work?" asked the voice. "To tell the truth, Vernon, I'm starting to worry that we're in over our heads."

"You leave the worrying to me. All I want to know is if your part of the operation is ready to roll."

"I guess so," said the voice.

"Where are you calling from?"

"I'm in a pay phone."

"I didn't hear any money drop."

"I used a credit-card number."

"Whose?"

The voice managed to chuckle.

"Colonel Thomas Anderson's."

* * *

Perhaps it was just as well that Tom Anderson hadn't decided to share Liv Matthews' two-day pot of stew, because the nurse was not even at home.

Instead, she was on her way to Camp David, sharing a Marine helicopter with Lieutenant Commander George Agee and three newspaper reporters. The Catoctin Mountains of Maryland were beneath the chopper, and she could see the clump of buildings and radio antennas of the President's hideaway clearly through the approaching dusk.

Agee, who disliked helicopters thoroughly, was fighting uneasiness by giving Liv the guided tour. This was her first trip to the retreat.

"Roosevelt came here to relax and get his mind off the war," said the doctor. "He called it Shangri-La."

"After the movie," said one of the reporters.

Liv, who had never read the book, or seen *Lost Horizon* on television, and who had not even been born when the Frank Capra film appeared in theaters, nodded wisely. It was always a safe response.

Swallowing, fighting nausea, Agee went on. "Eisenhower changed its name, in honor of his grandson."

"That," Liv said brightly, "would be David Eisenhower."

The chopper seemed to be wallowing on its side now, and Agee was positive that his face must be bright green. Three red landing targets were painted on concrete pads a hundred feet below. There was still snow up here in the mountains, and the rotor blades tossed it about in a mini-blizzard.

"Yes," croaked the unhappy doctor. The infernal machine leveled out and touched down without a bump. The whine of the blades—no, he corrected himself, having once been called on the subject by an irate chopper pilot, the rotary wings—wound down and became a *flub-flub* sound.

Cheerfully, one of the reporters said, "Beat the odds again."

Glancing around, under the glare of four high-intensity lights mounted on poles, Liv said, "They don't want anyone to get in here, do they?"

She nodded toward three high wire fences surrounding the area. There was a wide no-man's-land between the inner fence and the next one, and coils of barbed wire stretched like metal hedges around the perimeter.

"Wrong," said the talkative reporter. He had long hair, but a pleasant smile. "The fences are to keep us *in*. After around twelve hours here in Siberia, you start getting cabin fever. I understand that, when he was up here writing his famous memo, John Dean almost managed to tunnel out. But the ferrets caught him. They have listening devices, just like in *The Great Escape*."

As they bundled into a waiting Buick, he held the door for her. Agee and another reporter had gotten into the front seat.

"After you," said the talkative reporter. "It's always nice to have snuggly ladies in the middle."

She laughed. "Snuggle against me, buster, and you'll get the shock of your life. I wear an electrified girdle."

Slipping into the seat beside her, he said, "Lieutenant Matthews, you have never worn a girdle in your ever-loving life."

"Oh, boy," said the other reporter in the rear seat. "Pike the Panther is at it again."

"Pike?" said Liv. "Not Seymour Pike, from *Inferno*?"

"Guilty," said the reporter.

"I've read some of your pieces," she said. "How in the world did you ever get invited to Camp David?"

"They've got a firing squad waiting for me," he said. Then: "Have you really?"

"Really what?"

"Read me."

"Of course. I liked the series you did about the welfare hotels. But I'm not too thrilled about your opinions of the Navy."

"Military," he corrected. "I'm an equal opportunity muckraker. I disapprove of all four services, not to mention the Coast Guard."

"Then why are you here?"

"I'm not sure," he said. "My office got a call from the press secretary, and I was invited. That's all I know."

This was the truth. He had no way of knowing that Anderson had made a call to Morton Bailey and suggested that Pike be included on one of Air Force One's upcoming missions.

The young press secretary had been delighted. "I'm glad you liked him, Colonel," he said. "Pike's got the rep of being a hatchet man, but I knew him in college, and he's as honest as they come. He won't slant the story; if you show him his opinions are wrong, he'll change them."

Anderson told Bailey nothing about the anti-Air Force One plot Pike had revealed to him. He had intended to do a little sleuthing himself after the practice flight—but then there had been the ozone emergency, and the Marty-caused rush to get home. So, at this moment, nothing more had been done.

Winter had lingered in the Washington area this year. And at Camp David, several thousand feet up in the mountains, its ice and snow were not even beginning their annual retreat.

It was most unusual for a President to come up here at this time of year. Camp David was at its best during summer, when the cool mountain air refreshed visitors after the heat and humidity of the capital.

"You're going to love the names on the lodges," said Pike. "Real rustic."

"Have you been here before, Mr. Pike?" Liv asked.

"Never. But I do my homework. Most Presidents stay at Aspen. It's the biggest, and most comfortable. But that's not the best name. You can pick Laurel. Or

Walnut. Sycamore isn't bad. Or maybe Dogwood, or Birch."

"Why," she said, delighted, "they're all trees."

"Wrong," he said with a sinister laugh. "Pray tell, where did the one named Rosebud come from?"

"*Citizen Kane*," she said, happy to be able to drag in a movie she had seen herself.

"Is he a tree?" asked Seymour Pike.

At a late supper at Hickory, the big lodge—complete with bowling alley—next to the Camp Office in the center of the compound, Liv found herself seated next to Pike. They had walked over from Aspen, after the brief group meeting with President Foster. Earlier, she and Commander Agee had spent nearly an hour with the President, giving him a complete physical examination. What equipment Agee had not brought was readily available from the sick bay.

"Isn't it beautiful up here?" she said, sipping a second cup of coffee.

"Sure," said the reporter, "if you don't look too close."

"You're cynical."

"No," said Pike. "I'm merely clear-sighted. Don't kid yourself, lovely Lieutenant. All you saw on our little stroll was the pale light of the moon on the snow-banks and the gentle sway of the pines? I thought medical people were observant."

"What did *you* see?" she challenged.

"I saw the entrances to two bomb shelters," he said. "I saw sentry posts with Marines all bundled up in Arctic gear, rifles at the ready and two-way radios clamped to their belts. I saw TV cameras scanning the entire area, and while I didn't see him with my own eyes, my research tells me that way up high, in a post which commands all approaches to Aspen, there's a hard-eyed guy with a thirty-caliber machine gun linked to a Starlite sight."

"A what?"

"A lens so fast that he can shoot in complete darkness, if all the power goes out."

"Well," she said slowly, "I guess you can't blame them. Not after the Kennedys and all."

"No," he said shortly. "It's their prison. Let them lock each other up."

"I thought the President was very nice to you," she said. "If you were surprised I'd read you, what did you think when *he* practically quoted your material?"

He allowed himself a smile. "I thought that he'd obviously gone to some trouble to impress all of us. I wasn't the only one he quoted. He knew everybody's work. What does that prove? That he's got good staff assistants who fixed up some nifty crib sheets."

"Seymour," she began earnestly.

He waved his hands. "No, please. Not that."

"Well, I'm certainly not going to call you Mr. Pike. What's left?"

"My nickname?"

"Which is?"

He chuckled. "Studs."

"Seriously—"

"All right. I'm not nuts about it, but at least it doesn't make me barf. Speedy."

"*That* is supposed to be better than Seymour?"

"Trust me," he said.

"How did you get it?"

"Back in Akron. I ran copy on the local paper. The Akron *Beacon Journal*. I ran faster than any kid in the city room. You ever read *What Makes Sammy Run*?"

"No. About Hollywood, wasn't it?"

"Yes, but also about the newspaper business, and a twisted little kid who had to get it *all*, right now, and didn't let anyone get in the way. If they did, he ran over them."

"That doesn't sound quite like you."

"It isn't. I was going to be editor of the paper by the time I was twenty. Then I saw the light."

"What was that?"

"The new boy in the city room, only two weeks on the job, jumped right over me and got the assistant sports spot I'd been aiming for. Why? Because he was dating the publisher's daughter."

"I'm sorry," she said. "But that's the way things happen all too often."

"Right," he said. "So I decided that running was the wrong way to achieve fame and fortune. Burning idols, that was more sensible."

"Not—"

He touched her hand. "Relax. I'm speaking metaphorically, which is the way all good reporters do. Ever read Don Marquis? *archy and mehitabel*? You see, there was this smart cockroach, and this promiscuous alley cat, and . . ."

He sipped the last of his coffee. "I know where there's some booze," he added conversationally.

She hesitated. Then: "Why not? Just one."

"Over at Laurel," he said. "Don't worry. You're well chaperoned. The other two guys are there. Probably playing poker. Do you indulge?"

"In poker?"

"Or anything else."

"Slow down," she said. "I'll have that drink. Period. Fair?"

"Agreed," he said. They bundled up, and he held the door for her.

The night air was so cold it hurt to breathe it. Their breaths were like bursts of steam from Old 49 chugging up the Rockies. He ran ahead, scooped up some snow, balled it, and let fly. She ducked, but it hit her shoulder. Stumbling, she recovered and began making her own huge snowball.

"No rocks," he yelled. "No icies!"

She threw her snowball, too high. He leaped up, like

a wide receiver, grabbed it from the air and took off, zigzagging between the trees.

There came a metallic click.

"Halt!" commanded a loud voice. "Right there!"

Pike skidded in the snow. "Hey!" he shouted. "We're friendlies."

A light glared at him. The voice said, "Just hold it right there, mister. Who are you?"

A joke flirted on Pike's lips, but he decided against it. "Pike, reporter."

"Why were you running?"

From the darkness, Liv called, "We were—well, throwing snowballs."

The light moved over, picked up her Navy uniform.

The voice said, "It isn't a good idea to run inside this compound, Lieutenant. Take it easy, will you? Some of these guys shoot at shadows."

"*Very* easy," agreed Pike. "We're sorry."

The metallic sound again. A shell being ejected, unused, from the chamber.

Chagrined, Liv and Pike continued to the lodge, where—as he had predicted—the other two reporters were engaged in a cut-throat game of stud poker.

He made her a drink, another for himself, and popped two beers for the poker players.

Without looking up from their game, one said, "Well, how does it feel, Pike? The Man as much as said you're going to be aboard the next flight of Air Force One. That ought to give your editor the jollies."

"How about your own?" he asked. "The invitation seemed to be a general one. Not a bad mix either. You're from a rag famous for its liberal views. Your pal's so conservative he wears both a belt and suspenders."

"And you," said the reporter calmly, "are so far to the left that your sun must come up in the west."

"Some batch," Pike agreed. He joined Liv at the sofa

near the window which would, when daylight came, face the dawn.

"Why are you here?" he asked. "We never got to that."

"No secret," she said. "Commander Agee saw the chance to give the President a brushup medical examination. It's always hard to find enough time. This fitted in."

"And so do you?"

"What do you mean?"

"Fit in. Around the big man's schedule."

"Of course," she said. "That's my job."

15

"I see you're awake," said Anderson.

"You mean 'sober,' don't you?" flared Marty. "Yes, to both questions. How long have you been home?"

"Since five-thirty."

"You could have wakened me." She remembered the car then, and gave a glance toward the driveway.

"I turned it off," he said. "As for waking you, we both know that wouldn't have worked." He nearly added, "You had to sleep it off," but did not.

"Well," she said, "I'm awake now."

"Do you want some coffee?"

"No, I don't want some coffee. Or tea, or milk, or anything."

"All right," he said evenly. "What do you want to talk about?"

"Us."

"Very well."

Her hand shook as she lit a cigarette. "You don't make it easy, do you?"

"If I could, I'd try."

"Oh, so calm. The super fly-boy, cool as ice, never flapped. You dragged me up here, and then didn't have the decency to even talk with me on the phone. You hung up on me."

"I had an emergency," he said. "When it was over, I called you back."

"You always have an emergency. If it isn't that big blue-and-white baby of yours, it's making speeches up on Capitol Hill, trying to drag more money out of Congress, or accepting a two-bit award somewhere."

"That's how you met me," he reminded.

"To my sorrow!"

"Marty, I'm sorry you're so unhappy. I don't mean for you to be."

"Then why have you turned into a goddamned flying machine? I haven't seen you for nearly six months. By the time I get up, you're out there with your precious airplanes. We never have lunch—and dinner not much more often. My career's gone down the drain. When I do get a break, like this Braniff assignment, you always foul it up."

He started to answer, and she waved him into silence. "All right, you didn't come right out and say, 'Come home,' but that's what I thought you meant. So here I am, and where were you? Out at Andrews, as usual. Thomas, it's just too much. I can't bear any more."

Quietly, he asked, "What does that mean?"

"Whatever you want it to mean." She whirled and headed for the kitchen. "Oh, the hell with it. I'm going to have a drink."

He did not try to dissuade her. It would have been foolish.

The ice clinked into the glass, and he heard a liquid gurgle. Then silence. When he looked up, she was standing over him, glass in hand.

"Well?" she demanded. "Don't you have anything to say?"

"I don't know," he said. "Marty, I don't want to fight with you. But it isn't doing either of us much good for you to keep heaping abuse on me. When you met me, I was a pilot; when you married me, I was still a pilot. It didn't seem to bother you then—in fact, I thought that it attracted you. I haven't changed."

"But *I* have, is that your version?"

"As I see it, yes." He gestured to a chair. "Sit down."

"I'm capable of standing," she said. "Despite your insinuations." She took a healthy swig of her drink. "All right, have it your own way. I *have* changed. I've learned to see the world without those beautiful tinted glasses you all wear. And it's *not* what I expected."

Gently, he said, "Exactly what did you expect, Marty?"

"Oh . . . travel. Parties. Important people. All the good things." Her eyes brimmed. "And we could have had them too, if you'd only come down out of the clouds and taken advantage of your opportunities. You're the President's pilot! Why haven't we been invited to the White House? Where were our tickets for the Inaugural Gala Ball? Why don't we have a nice house in Georgetown, instead of living out here in the sticks in a housing development?"

"We didn't have much choice," he reminded. "It was either live on base or somewhere thirty minutes of the gate. Georgetown's too far away."

"Bull! I make it door to door in twenty-seven minutes."

"You also picked up a speeding citation, and you're lucky they didn't bust you for DWI."

"Always an answer, right? Well, they don't pass out debating points in this event, Thomas. You're in the game of life now, not playing Snoopy versus the Red Baron."

"All right, Martha. What do you want? A divorce?"

She laughed. "Oh, no, you don't get rid of me *that* easy."

"What, then?"

"I want what's mine. I'm the wife of someone who, God knows why, is supposed to be the most important pilot in the Air Force. All right, I want to be treated accordingly. I see your picture in the *Post* all the time. Where's *my* picture? *People* magazine did two pages on you and that damned airplane. Where was I?"

"I think you were in Acapulco, Marty. They couldn't photograph you if you weren't here."

"Ahhh," she said, gulping down the remainder of her drink. "They wouldn't have anyway. All they care about are those big handsome shoulders of yours, and that fucking airplane." She looked at him with the sly expression of one who is about to reveal a Great Truth.

"Do you know what I'd do if I could?" asked Martha Desmond Anderson. "I'd blow that goddamned Air Force One right out of the sky."

When Major Paul McGowan dialed the telephone, he waited four rings, then a sleepy voice said, "H'lo?"

"This is Paul."

"Oh."

"I'm glad you didn't go back to the base."

"Would've," said the sleepy young woman. "Couldn't get my Rabbit started."

"I'm sorry."

"No problem."

"I mean about the things I said tonight."

She was coming awake. "I know. Me too."

"Don't go back to base tomorrow. I'll come over."

"All right," she mumbled. "Only—"

"What?"

"Why don't you talk with the Colonel? See if you can help."

He hesitated. "I don't know . . . even if you're right, he's still the CO."

"Couldn't hurt to try."

"I guess not. All right, Angie. I'll give it a shot. You go back to bed. I'll call you around noon."

"Do that," she said. She made a kissing sound.

Feeling silly, he repeated it. "Night," he said.

On most military bases, Sunday morning is a time for sacking in, with only the most essential duties being performed. The young enlisted men and officers would probably have had a late night and would be recuperating. More senior enlisted and officer personnel would be spending a welcome quiet day with their families.

The Japanese had observed this pattern, and used it to advantage on Sunday morning, December 7, 1941, at Pearl Harbor.

Andrews Air Force Base was no different. Just after 10 A.M., a passer-by could almost hear the base snoring. Traffic on the base roads, with their 25 MPH signs, was sparse. The usual two-man Air Police station at the Main Gate was manned by one AP, who easily handled traffic in both directions.

The mess halls had opened for breakfast, did a trickle of business. The snack bars would pick up the real breakfast traffic later in the morning. Most other services on base were closed. The laundry and tailor shop, the Post Exchange, the base theater (which would, however, open for a 2 P.M. matinee), the bowling alley, and the Service Club—all slumbered through the lazy morning. The chapels were open, of course, and so were the tennis courts, where a few hardy souls braved the brisk air in heavy warm-up suits.

At the 89th's Operations Building, the pace was little faster. The usual full-time staff was on duty, but the phones rang seldom, and since there was no 89th traffic in the air just now, the radios chattered with reports from other flights, of no interest to the 89th's radiomen.

The guards at the hangar and—within it—around Air Force One were vigilant, however. When TSgt. Ed Miller, the Senior Flight Steward, boarded the plane, he was subjected to the usual sign-ins and identity checks. His name was one of the few on the list of authorized personnel who could board the plane at will. Others, even though they might be regular crew members, had to be announced from Anderson's office unless an actual mission was in progress.

Miller had gone to bed early Saturday night. Single, he did not drink, and since he had already seen the movie at the nearest base theater, he watched television in his comfortable barracks room for a while after evening chow, then turned off the light and slept.

He had received the brief memo from the CO's office, instructing him to shop for the plane on Monday. That was fine with Miller; he liked to get off the base and run wild through the aisles of the finer markets. A frustrated gourmet cook, since on base he had no kitchen unless the Mess Sergeant looked the other way while he prepared some delicacy for six or eight crew members on a slow evening, Miller always tried to have at least one surprise for the passengers and crew of Air Force One. He had served through most of the last Administration, and had more than once received the accolades of the previous President himself.

But this Foster was different. Miller often grumbled that the new President would eat a frozen TV dinner and never know the difference. The substitute planes they had been using did not help either. The facilities on them were primitive. Miller rejoiced when he heard that 26000 was being rolled out again.

Number 26000's main galley had a six-burner electric stove, with a real oven, in addition to the usual microwave ones carried aloft. Miller scorned microwaves, referring to them as "zap machines." He would allow his staff to zap meals for the reporters or Secret Service. But those destined for the President or important passengers were cooked slowly.

To Miller, the men on the flight deck rated as "important," and ate accordingly. It complicated his schedule, however, because in spite of the care taken in choosing and preparing food, the flight deck was served at two-hour intervals, to avoid the possibility of simultaneous food poisoning. On a long flight, this was no problem. On a shorter one, it meant that if Anderson ate, McGowan went hungry. Or vice versa—Anderson often refused a meal if it meant that his Pilot would go without.

Miller, whose ear was eternally glued to the produce market, knew that the huge Florida avocados were appearing at reasonable prices. While the cost of food was no problem when buying for Air Force One, he still made it a matter of pride to shop well, and to get the best value for money. Fresh shrimp were coming in from the Gulf too. Perhaps he would plan shrimp-stuffed avocado as an appetizer.

"Morning," he said to TSgt. Walter Morris, who was standing the ramp watch. Morris always took the unwelcome Sunday tour, to spare his men the boredom.

"Miller," said the security man, holding out his hand for the Steward's ID. In a ritual that none of the crew ever let become comical, although most of them had known each other for months or even years, he compared Miller's photo with that on the card. "Sign in, please."

Miller did, and boarded. He had a small notebook with him, and he wasted no time in going directly to the small supply cabinets for each galley. He knew, without checking, that staples which were nonperishable were already stocked. Yet he examined them anyway. He always presumed that the plane would be full, though it rarely was. It was a necessary presumption; one does not step out at 30,000 feet to pick up three more steaks for unexpected guests.

On a lunch flight, such as the one to Montana, there would be a choice of four entrees for each passenger. Even though the President was attending a luncheon in Helena, he would eat on board the plane. Presidents had learned, the hard way, that food at ceremonial luncheons was to push around on the plate, not to consume. LBJ had been one of the rare Presidents who actually ate what was put before him. But since that was usually barbecued ribs, or blood-rare steaks, or chili, Johnson was not as hard to please as other Presidents with more refiined palates. And, of course, the press and the Secret Service must be fed, because once the destination had been reached, they would be working too hard to even find time for a McDonald's hamburger.

Each galley had a large refrigerator and an adequate freezer compartment. Miller had been agitating for some time, trying to convince the previous CO of the 89th, and now Colonel Anderson, that the President's plane simply cried for more freezer space. When told that weight was the problem, he would point disparagingly at the Xerox machine, which took up the space of two seats, and cry dramatically, "That monster weighs as much as *five* freezers!"

He was never able to be convinced that, to a reporter, a Xeroxed copy of the President's latest speech was more welcome than food, drink, or blondes.

Ticking off the condiments he would buy for Wednesday, TSgt. Ed Miller frowned.

They were going to make him take that little blonde on his shopping trip. She, with the least seniority of anyone in the Stewards' department! Talk about your reverse discrimination. That was another reason he did not approve of the new President. The way the women were starting to take over the mission was appalling. Now they had a nurse too.

Miller had no great affection for women anyway. He had been raised in the spinster home of an aunt, after his parents were both killed in a boating accident. Miller had survived only because his mother stuffed him into her own life jacket, then drowned before his horrified eyes. Her fearful struggles for life still haunted his dreams, and he had been forced to turn his eyes inward, to avoid looking out.

Still, he was no woman hater. It was simply that there was man's work, and there was woman's work.

It never occurred to him that what he was doing aboard Air Force One was—in the normal community —woman's work.

He kept his views to himself. If the CO ordered him to take the Nemath girl shopping, he would do so. And he would not do so grudgingly, withholding his knowledge. He would train her as thoroughly as any of his other attendants.

But he did not have to like it.

Major Paul McGowan was on base early too. Normally he never came in on a Sunday, but remembering his promise to Angie the night before, he had called Anderson and asked if they could get together at HQ. To his surprise, Anderson agreed at once. He sounded almost relieved to get out of the house, McGowan thought.

McGowan arrived first and had the coffee brewing by the time Anderson came in. Both men wore casual civvies. On off-duty time, which this was officially, there were no dress uniform requirements—or even traditions.

"Still batching it?" asked McGowan.

"No," said Anderson, without emotion. "Marty's back."

"Did she get the Braniff job?"

Oh, thought Anderson. How did you know about that?

"No," he said. "Just as well, as far as I'm concerned. Otherwise, they'd have shipped her off to Peru."

He rummaged through some folders on his desk. "I'm getting the stuff together for Wednesday's flight," he said. "I'm just as glad you called. I always like to be ahead of the whistle, in case they advance the trip without warning."

They spent nearly an hour going over plans for the Helena flight. Without the Navigator, nothing was completely firm, but the navigation skills of both pilots were nearly as good as Birney's, so they did not expect major changes. They worked well together, with a minimum of questions.

"It's a good route," said McGowan.

"If the politicians leave us alone," said Anderson.

"How so?"

Anderson explained what he had learned about the efforts of Senator Hopper to discredit the Air Force One mission.

Carefully, McGowan said, "I think the Senator's an asshole. But frankly, Tom, I agree with some of the points he makes. This setup is incredibly wasteful. The President would get better service—and save us taxpayers millions—by chartering."

"And you'd risk the President's life on board a charter flight?"

"Why not? Millions of other Americans risk theirs, if you want to use the word 'risk.' Supervised charter operations are as safe, and far more efficient than what we've got going here."

"What happens," asked Anderson, "when the President decides to fly to Japan, and can't get the money approved by Congress?"

"Who said anything about that kind of chicken-shit?"

"When you're dealing with special budgets, *somebody* has to approve them."

"Look, Tom, all I meant was that a certain amount of money should be set aside for presidential transportation, and it should be spent in the most efficient way possible."

"What we do," said Anderson, "*is* the most efficient way."

"It's certainly the most expensive," said McGowan. "I'm sorry, Tom. I was assigned to fly this mission, and I will, the best way I know. But I didn't shut off my head. We're dealing with the ultimate in waste out here. My God, a commercial airline counts a plane's

ground time in minutes, not days, and red ink spills
all over their books for every moment lost. Meanwhile,
our very own Air Force One spends most of the time
in her hangar, being waxed and polished by airmen
who don't have anything else to do. I'm sorry, Tom,
but that is *waste*."

Coldly, Anderson said, "Maybe you shouldn't be
flying this mission at all. If you disagree that much
with it, you ought to transfer out."

McGowan shook his head. "Wrong, Colonel. I'm
career, just like you. I take my orders, do my job, and
keep my mouth shut. Except during moments like this,
when I thought I was talking off the record with a
fellow pilot and officer. Was I wrong?"

"Completely," said Anderson. "Paul, I know you're
a great pilot. But there isn't any room in the 89th for
anyone who isn't prepared to give one hundred per
cent."

"Is that so?" said McGowan. "What about you?"

"What's that supposed to mean?"

McGowan leaned forward. "That you aren't giving
a hundred per cent yourself, Tom. You haven't for
some time. I'm not the only one who's noticed. Birney
keeps mentioning how tired you seem. And there are
others. I won't put them on your shit list by giving
names, but quite a few of us have noticed how you've
slowed down."

Calmly, Anderson lied, "I've been fighting a virus.
The antibiotics make me sleepy." His voice hardened.
"But sleepy or not, remember who caught that ozone
problem? Where were you sharpies then? I had to fight
my way all the way back from the john to get masks
on you turkeys."

"But what were you doing *in* the john?"

"What is anyone doing in the john? Major, you're
out of line. If you have a charge to bring against me,
there are channels available."

"No," said McGowan. "I don't want charges. What

I want is to be sure that you're completely in command of that left seat. Despite what you may think of my general attitude, I'm as much in favor of keeping the President safe as you are."

"I don't doubt it," said Anderson. "But remember one fact, Paul. There cannot be two commanding officers. Either you do it my way, or you ship out. A MAC wing isn't a democracy."

"I'll do it your way," said McGowan. "But I'm putting you on notice, Tom. There's a grave doubt in my mind about your ability to command. I won't let it go so far as to endanger the mission."

Anderson chuckled. "All this from a hot-shoe who hates the 89th and everything it stands for?"

"You pegged it," said McGowan. Then, quietly, "How about lunch at the Officer's Club?"

"No," said Colonel Thomas Anderson, looking down at the folders on his desk. "I want to spend some time on this goddamned paper work."

"Can I help?"

"Thanks, no. It's the usual garbage. File and forget. Paul—thanks, but you don't have anything to worry about."

"I hope so," said Paul McGowan.

Learning that the Marine helicopter was going to put down at Andrews before proceeding across the river to the Pentagon, Liv Matthews decided to debark there. Agee, who was continuing on, said, "Early call in the morning, Lieutenant."

"Yes, sir," she said. "I'll be there."

Foster, as always, had tested out as healthy as a horse. The small scar left by his Mayo Clinic operation was almost invisible. Liv knew, because Foster had insisted that she be present during the examination. She, he proclaimed, was his good-luck charm. Liv still had not been able to decide if the middle-aged President really believed that, or—in his widowerhood—

merely liked to have a good-looking young woman around. Whatever the reason, she was glad to help. The weeks at the Clinic, for all their fear, had not seemed to touch him. But after only a few months in the White House, gray was showing at his temples.

The chopper landed on its target near the 89th's Operations Building. Only Seymour Pike made a comment as Liv gathered up her small suitcase and purse.

"Say hello to the big honcho in the sky for me," he said.

She felt herself blush. "Do you know Colonel Anderson?" she asked.

"Intimately," said Pike. "Ask him."

She did not reply, merely ducked under the whirling blades and strode purposefully toward the Operations Building.

"Speedy," said one of the other reporters, "can't you stop yourself from trying to hit on every girl you see?"

"Sure," said Pike. "But where's the fun in that?"

Liv's arrival was a perfect excuse for Anderson to put away the boring files he had been reading.

"Flo," he said. "What brings you this way?"

"A Marine chopper," she said. "We had to go out to Camp David to give the President his monthly checkup. I hope you didn't keep calling me, because I wasn't home."

Feeling guilty, he said, "No, I figured that." He looked at his watch. "Hey, what about some lunch?" He hadn't wanted to join McGowan, but he really was hungry—having left the house without even coffee.

"Sounds great," she said. "Do you have much more work to do?"

"No," he said.

"I'd hope not. It's Sunday, after all."

"Officer's Club?"

She wrinkled her nose. "Sausages and ham and gunk. Why not scrambled eggs at the Diplomat?"

He shook his head. "Sorry. All crew are on Yellow. I have to stay within thirty minutes of the base."

"Pooh. They should have made it thirty-five minutes. Then you'd be able to go to a decent restaurant."

"Sadists," he agreed.

"My place?" she suggested.

"I wouldn't want to be any trouble."

"What trouble? It's a free ride, which is precisely what I was hoping for when I bailed out here." Actually, if Anderson had not been on the base, she was authorized to sign for a car and driver.

He stacked his file folders. They would wait, chuckling, for him to come back tomorrow. There was never any end to them. Like Medusa, each snake head which was cut off became two new ones.

On their way to his car, she saw McGowan's Corvette. "Isn't that Major McGowan's car?" she asked.

Anderson glanced at it. "Yeah," he said. "We were doing some work this morning."

His voice was so sour that she did not follow up on the question.

"Let me drive," she said.

Sharply, he asked, "Why?"

"No reason," she said. "Except I like to, and you must be tired."

"I'm fine," he said. But he let her take the wheel.

He had taken his medication this morning, and given himself the iron shot. He did not like handling the hypodermic. It made him feel like a junkie. But the slight vertigo was gone, and his hands were steady.

As she drove, skillfully, Liv briefed Anderson about the strange meeting at Camp David the night before.

"It looks as if the President is deliberately loading the press compartment with his enemies," she said. "Almost everybody he invited to Camp David has criticized Air Force One at one time or another. Particularly Seymour Pike."

"Oh," said Anderson, amused that his plan had worked, "was Pike there too?"

"Too! Foster had practically memorized some of his articles, word for word. Mr. Pike was one surprised young man."

"What do you think of Pike?"

Surprised, she asked, "Why?"

"I met him recently. I was impressed."

She considered. "Well, despite the rag he works for, I believe he's honest. But that may be merely a temporary condition. He's out for Number One."

"Does he have a conscience?"

She hesitated. "Yes, I think he does. Why all the questions, Lone Eagle?"

"I'll tell you one day," he said. "Meanwhile, keep on your own side of the road, if you can."

She had drifted across the yellow line. To him, as she pulled back in lane, she complained, "If I'd known what a backseat driver you are, I'd have made you do the driving."

"No," he sighed, half dozing, "you're doing fine."

She drove in silence for half a mile. "Tom?" she said after a while.

"Mmmmm?"

"I'm not easy," she said. "I just like you very much."

"That's nice," he said, without emotion.

Although he had gone to the Officer's Club, Paul McGowan did not have lunch. Instead, he ordered a tall manhattan, and called Angie.

She answered on the third ring.

"Hi," he said. "I'm still at the base. Shall I bring lunch?"

"Raid the Colonel," she said. Angie was a fanatic over Kentucky Fried Chicken. "I know it's really plastic and I'm eating an advertising campaign," she said once, "I just can't help myself. If I ever meet the chubby little old man with his Vandyke beard, I'll throw him right down in the street and kiss him."

"It's as good as done," said McGowan. "The chicken, not the Colonel."

"What about the rest?" she asked.

"I'll tell you when I get there," he said, conscious of the fact that his call was going through the base switchboard. "Half an hour."

"Code Yellow," she replied. "Hurry, but don't speed."

He laughed and hung up. Finishing his drink, he walked back to 89th Ops, and as he entered the parking lot, thought he saw Anderson driving away with a woman at the wheel of his car.

He looked again, but they were gone.

TSgt. Ed Miller had finished his inventory of the Air Force One galleys. He signed out at the ramp, and again at the gate.

"Working on Sunday?" asked the gate guard.

"Just checking for bombs," said the Steward.

The guard laughed. Only after Miller had strolled down the ramp and turned into the parking lot did he think: *What a funny thing for that guy to say!*

It was also Sunday in Helena, Montana, but not for Advance Man Warren Rogers.

His room was filled with FBI men and three of the top Secret Service staff.

"I'm not so worried about the city," said Rogers. "You have that all sewed up. But what if there's bad weather, or an accident, or anything, and the plane has to divert to Malstrom?"

"It's an Air Force Base," said the District Chief of the FBI. "With SAC security. Nobody penetrates their gates."

"But how does the President get back here?" asked

Rogers. He already knew, but this drill was an important part of psyching up the security forces.

"There's an Air National Guard chopper standing by at Malstrom," said the chief of the Secret Service squad. Actually, temporary chief, because now that the mission was definitely on, Sam Milnes was already on board an airplane, winging his way west.

"Do they have enough range to reach Helena?" demanded Rogers.

"Five times as much," said the Secret Service man. "They'll land at the presently approved site, and things will proceed normally from there."

"What about demonstrations?" asked the Advance Man.

"The route isn't being publicized, nor is the landing site," said the Secret Service man. "At the hotel, the police have been instructed to keep any offensive placards in the back, out of the President's line of sight."

"And," said Rogers, "out of camera range."

"We'll do our best," said the agent. "You know how the President is. He doesn't like us interfering with free expression."

Rogers turned to the senior FBI man. "What about hotel personnel?"

"All checked out and cleared," said the FBI man. "We ran personality profiles on everyone who will be in contact with the kitchen and the President's table. A couple of the younger waiters were reassigned, but only because they scored low on a couple of key questions. We don't question their loyalty or honesty. It's just best not to take chances."

"How about genuine nuts?"

"We've got half a dozen letter writers under observation. The kind who write nasty letters to the White House, verging on threats, but not going far enough for us to nail them. They won't get within a mile of the President or his hotel. Two known activists happened to be in town, probably to stir up trouble for Mr. Guthrie."

"Where are they now?"

"On the way to San Francisco."

Rogers fought a smile. "I presume they left voluntarily."

"They could hardly wait," said the FBI man. "Particularly when we explained that their other choice was to spend a few days in the local jail while some outstanding warrants were checked against them."

"Did you have such warrants."

"Would we lie? Of course we had them." The FBI man chuckled. "We merely didn't get around to mentioning that they were for unpaid parking tickets in L.A."

"This," said the Advance Man, "is turning into a police state."

Misunderstanding, the FBI man said, "Well, you can blame that on Governor Hoskins."

"You make better scambled eggs than the Diplomat anyway," said Anderson.

Liv, pouring more coffee, said, "Thank you, sir. The chef is flattered."

Anderson glanced at his watch. Liv noticed. "Do you have to go?"

"Pretty soon."

"I'm glad Marty's home. You haven't seemed very happy lately."

"I've been tired."

"I know," she said. "I guess it's harder work getting ready to fly the mission than it is to actually do it."

"Not to mention," he said, "that I'm not growing any younger."

"Airline pilots fly until they're sixty," she said.

"It isn't the same," he said, sipping the rich brown coffee she had made from a can of Blue Mountain sent to her by a friend in Jamaica. "Combat flying burns you up. It's not just the fear of being hit or shot down. It works on you—you dream about the bombs you've dropped, and where they may have fallen. I don't know a single combat pilot who hasn't come awake yelling at one time or another."

Softly, she said, "But that was a long time ago."

"Yes, for me. But it's always that final moment for those we killed." He looked at his hands. The fingers were twitching. "Don't get me wrong, Liv. I'm not apologizing for what I did, and I don't feel guilty. It was a war, and we did what guys in a war are supposed to do. I never deliberately dumped on a civilian target. Most guys didn't. Those who did—well, we felt sorry for them. But bombs don't have brains. They fall where gravity takes them. It wasn't Hiroshima, it wasn't Cologne. Mostly it was supply trails and jungle outposts, without names. But that burns a pilot up just as completely as the big ones."

"Well," she said, "stop painting yourself as the Old Man of the Sky. You've got the most important flying job in the country, and you seem to be doing it pretty good. That doesn't sound like a burnt-out case to me."

"No," he said. "I guess not. Maybe it's just Blue Sunday."

"That's supposed to be Monday," she said. "How about a drink?"

"Better not," he said.

"I'm having one," she said. "And you know very well that there's no way in the world you'll be flying tomorrow. Not that those scotch-flavored waters you drink would interfere even if you were."

"All right," he acquiesced. "Just one."

"It'll do you good," she said. "I've been worrying about you lately."

"That's wasted effort," he said. "I'm constructed of old shoe leather and wire. Even a Navy nurse ought to be able to see that."

"It's obvious," she said, managing to laugh. "But,

Tom, be serious. Your fatigue has gone on longer than I like. I know you're under strain and God knows you're overworked, but—"

"Overworked and underloved," he said. "Where the hell is that drink you promised?"

Fussing in the little kitchenette, she said, "Not my business, but it's obvious that you and Marty are having some problems."

"Our share," he admitted.

"Need a friendly ear to bend?"

"Thanks, but no."

"Didn't think so. The Lone Eagle goes his own way without complaint and without anyone else's help."

"Ouch," he said. "Am I really that stuffy?"

Handing him a very weak scotch, she said, "I meant it as a compliment. You're very much your own man, Tom. I admire you for it. But sometimes I feel sorry for you too. It can't be all that much fun. Take me. I admit freely that I'm a blubberer."

He smiled. "A what?"

"You know. I'm suffering in silence, and somebody says, 'Hey, Liv, what's the matter?' Bingo! In seconds I'm on his shoulder, both faucets turned on, and making *blub-blub* sounds. So whoever it is hugs me hard, and says, 'There, there,' and I feel better."

"Sounds good," he said.

She put her drink down and held out both arms.

"Why don't you try it, pal?" she asked.

16

Tom Anderson was already on his way to Andrews when Marty woke up. He had slept in the guest room, the only outward sign he gave of his anger. Otherwise, as she had baited him and torn away at his defenses, he kept his voice calm and had not responded in kind. Only his question about divorce revealed how disturbed he really was.

Now he had retreated again to the safety of his well-guarded Air Force base. And she was supposed to sit around the house and wait until he decided to return.

Not little Martha! She slipped out of her nightgown and padded into the bathroom. While the shower water was warming up, she examined herself in the full-length mirror. What she saw pleased her. High, firm breasts curved above a supple torso, unmarked by flab or stretch marks. And, she thought proudly, her legs still measured up to the appraisal they had won often out in Washington State—"best in the West."

She slipped into the shower and turned on the pulsating "magic fingers" of the shower head. She sighed as a warm glow spread through her body.

Tom had been transferred out of McCord just in time, she remembered. Her affair with that sportscaster from Seattle had gotten out of control. He was even calling her at home during the day. Like most men, he simply could not understand when he was no longer welcome. Poor Ken. She would watch him on the six o'clock news, and it was pitiful the way he would, knowing she was watching, slip one or two of their private code words into his boring descriptions of football or tennis. He even added a corny little sign-off, supposedly aimed at all of his viewers: "Love you!" For a while it took on a local fame similar to that achieved nationally long ago by Jimmy Durante with his "Good night, Mrs. Calabash . . . wherever you are."

Marty redirected the shower head so its pulsating streams beat against her taut stomach. The TV ads had been right, for once. Properly used, the water massage *could* turn you on . . . and more, if that's what you were willing to settle for.

It was tempting this morning. But no, she had other plans. With an abrupt motion, she turned off the water and reached for a towel.

Naked, and still glistening with moisture, she sat down at her makeup table in the outer room of the large bath, and dialed the white Princess telephone.

Wayne Livingston answered on the second ring.

"Hi," she said without introduction. "I'm back."

"You've *been* back," he said. "I called New Orleans."

"I wanted to think," she said.

He chuckled, She could see him doing so, his thick black mustache balancing the strong nose and jaw. At forty-two, Wayne Livingston looked like a thirty-year-old professional quarterback, not a twice-divorced lobbyist who represented an organization of food packers.

"Think?" he repeated. "That's what I like about you, Marty. You're always trying something new."

"I'm sorry I didn't call," she said. "Tom and I have been having the most awful row."

"I rather doubt that," Wayne said. "Your Colonel strikes me as the calmest man I've ever met."

"You've met—But I—"

"Didn't I mention it? We lunched one day last

month. He was promoting some free chow for his plane."

She had stopped combing her hair. "You never mentioned it. Neither did he."

"He never mentioned it, my dear, because it never occurred to him that you and I know each other. And I never mentioned it because . . . well, frankly, until I renewed my native cynicism, I felt a little guilty."

"Oh, yes," she said bitterly. "He has that effect on everybody. You ought to see him out at the island. He doesn't need the bridge, he just walks across the water."

"Martha," he said quietly. "I'm sure you didn't telephone me on this chill Sunday morning to bore me with more complaints about your husband."

"Well . . ." She stalled, trying to sense his mood. Was he angry because she hadn't called the moment she returned from New Orleans? Or just having his fun toying with her verbally, as he did so often before they both found release in the king-size bed with its red satin sheets? "It's just that I really wanted to see you. I hoped I'd have some good news for you, but the Braniff assignment went sour and—"

"Poor Martha," he said. "Do come over, if you wish. I have nothing scheduled for the day. But please, my dear, do not try my patience. We both know very well that the Braniff matter was never an assignment at all, but a carrot dangled before you by a handsome young executive with more balls than morals, and more money than good sense. I congratulate you, however, for being astute enough to get out before the walls came falling down."

"I came back because Tom—"

"Dear girl, you came back because you have a native instinct for survival. The young man's angry wife and private detectives were only hours behind the sweaty trail you both left through Texas and the Deep South. Your young man is in danger of losing both his job and his wife unless he takes instant vows of poverty and chastity. His star has gone dark. Yours, on the other hand, is as bright and secure as ever."

She did not answer. When Wayne was in this mood, and particularly when he knew the truth, it was best to give in. When he detected a lie, the stinging comments turned swiftly to brutal anger.

"I should have known not to try and fool you," she said, biting down the humility the words cost her. "I was just being proud again."

"Never stop," he said. "Deceive the entire world, pet. But not me. Never me."

"No," she said. "Never you."

Was I always a bitch? she asked herself, taking Brandywine Road to Suitland Parkway. Connecting with Rhode Island Avenue, on a day of light traffic such as Sunday, she would be in Georgetown within half an hour without speeding. Unknown to Tom Anderson, she already had two moving violations on her license. One more, and it would be suspended.

No, she decided. As a girl, she had been strong-willed, determined to get her fair share. One summer, she remembered, their father had taken Eugene, her brother, and Martha horseback riding. She had been terrified, clinging to the animal's mane, and pleading to be rescued.

"It's all right, Marty," soothed her father. "You don't have to ride if it frightens you." He'd lifted her, weeping, off the horse, and bought her a Coke.

That afternoon, when Eugene rode again, he and his father returned to the barn to find her waiting, already weeping in fear—but determined to get the horseback ride that she had coming.

"You don't love me!" she often accused her mother. "You love Gene because he's a boy."

No amount of persuasion would convince her any differently.

Miraculously, she survived through high school as a virgin. Some boys joked, to conceal their actual awe of her, that "she keeps razor blades in there." Developing the incredible beauty a natural redhead can have, with cream-like skin and the grace that comes from an inborn talent for athletics, Martha Desmond entered college well versed in the lore of sex, but a child when it came to understanding its physical effects.

That lasted exactly a month. Too much unaccustomed wine; a car seat spread under a concealing willow tree; a senior, majoring in engineering who was a BMOC . . .

The pain lasted only a moment, and on that night she found what she was, in all the world, best at.

Her ardor frightened the senior, who avoided her for the rest of the semester. At first, she was angry. Marty was not accustomed to rejection. Then, comparing notes with those other girls who, while never allowed to be close friends, at least were companions, she saw where her mistakes had been.

Never again would she make those same mistakes. After that first month, Martha Desmond attended the best parties, rode in the best cars with the most popular boys, weekended at the fine homes of affluent students, and used sex as an instrument of pleasure for herself—while it was often a searing weapon against the young men who foolishly convinced themselves that they were the aggressors. Luckily, young hearts which have been broken mend easily, or she would have left a trail of tombstones behind her as long as the Oregon Trail.

Crossing the Mall, between the Capitol and the Washington Monument, she nodded. From then on she *had* been a bitch. The term was the world's, not her own. If you took care of Number One, made sure that you got what was due, and did not weep crocodile tears over those who weren't as clever, then they said you were a bitch.

All right. She was content with the world's assessment, and with her life. She drifted into design, was lucky—and talented enough—to work with Raymond Loewy's firm for almost three years. Afterward, she managed to retain the expensive, freewheeling life style she had become accustomed to enjoying.

Then Tom Anderson came along, and for the first time in her adult life, she let down the barriers, and he destroyed her as completely as his bombs had destroyed the bridges of Southeast Asia. She found herself pursuing him to the West Coast. For more than six weeks—a very long time in her accelerated way of life—she supposed herself to be supremely happy. Her husband was in charge of huge airplanes and treated with deference by all around him. She was too. For the first time in her life, other women clustered around her—asking her advice, wheedling for the small favors her husband might extend to theirs, making her feel important and wanted.

Then Tom changed. After their trip to Venezuela, he stopped taking her out almost every night. He spent more time at his desk. When he came home, he was often tired and irritable. And, most important, he almost always fell asleep early—often before she had joined him in bed.

She blamed herself. She knew she was being rejected, but could not find the reason. She changed her hair, her perfume, her clothes. Sometimes her wishes came true. But more often they did not.

She reverted to the woman she had been before Colonel Thomas Anderson came along. She took vicious delight in pointing out the new gray in his hair.

During the afternoons, she was almost never home any more. Sometimes she was in a bar downtown. One encounter was particularly embarrassing, when she

had been accepting drinks from a tall and rather boyish man in civilian clothes. They had gotten to the
point of joking about taking a ride up to Mount
Rainier to "look at the peaks," when of course both
of them were actually referring to her braless doubleknit blouse. At that moment, an Air Force enlisted
man had come in, taken one look at her, and without
even attempting to be discreet about it, dragged the
other young man away, hissing, "Jesus Christ, Boyd,
don't you know who that is? She's the CO's wife!"

A few junior officers at McCord had fearful and un-
forgettable episodes with her in out-of-the-way motel
rooms, and quaked in their shoes when she rebuffed
them on their having another meeting, wondering if
their next station would be at Thule, in the land of
eternal ice.

Marty turned left on Rhode Island Avenue, the old
Route 1. She would be at Wayne's small town house
in another ten minutes. She felt herself tingle. There
was a danger about him that thrilled her. She had
never felt it from any other man. Never before had
she been so dominated. It was not always with words
either. He had not hurt her often, physically, but for
one two-week period she had been careful not to un-
dress in a lighted room, to hide the welts on her
buttocks Wayne had given her with an old-fashioned
leather belt. She had spent two hours in a midtown
hotel room with a visiting British record producer,
lied to Wayne, and then had been found out.

She blushed now, remembering—although she had
been screaming with pain—halfway through the
whipping she had felt the gushing warmth of a humiliating and totally unexpected orgasm. Afterward,
Wayne had taken her to bed, and had been patient
and gentle. Sobbing against his chest, she swore to
leave him—but when he said he would see her the
next night, she had pulled him to her and whispered,
"Yes. Yes!"

Washington, which lured her—when, otherwise, she was certain she would have broken her marriage with Tom—had turned out to be a great disappointment. When he told her he had accepted the new President's offer to be his Command Pilot, visions of White House receptions and grand parties with herself as the radiant hostess turned her again, for a while, into a loving and responsive wife.

But it took only a few weeks for reality ta kill the dream. If Tom's hours at McCord had been long, they were even longer here. And he spent days away from home, flying practice missions and getting Air Force One into condition. She found herself alone for days on end.

It was during one such time that she had met Wayne Livingston. For once, they had been invited to a decent party. It was for cocktails and a buffet at the home of Arthur Rand, the new Vice-President. Mrs. Rand, when Marty phoned and said with honest regret that Tom would be at the Boeing plant in Seattle, said, "Oh, what a bother. Why don't you come anyway? I have an extra man, and it will all work out nicely."

So it did. The moment she walked into the room, Marty knew who the "extra man" was. She sensed his presence across the spare ribs and cold potato salad. Their handshake, when it came, was almost anticlimactic.

"Mrs. Anderson," he said, nearly purring. Tall, austere, suit lent him more dignity than any cummer-mustache, Wayne was the only man present not in a dinner jacket. It was their loss. His simple, almost austere, suit lent him more dignity than any cummerbund and black tie could have.

Marty remembered almost nothing about that night. They ate, they drank, they danced, and he took her home with him.

"My car?" she whispered, when he announced his plans.

"There's a parking lot two blocks to the right. Leave now and wait for me there."

"But—" she stammered, as flustered as a young girl on her first date.

"Make your goodbyes," he ordered.

She backed away from him slowly, thinking: What the hell have I gotten myself into?

But she bade the new Vice-President and his wife a gracious good-night, with thanks from her absent husband. Offered a lift home, she said, "No, I have my car. It was a wonderful evening, Mrs. Rand. Good-night."

Through some mysterious warning system, the attendant had been signaled of her departure, and had the car waiting, the heater on, and wipers scraping off the new snowflakes. He refused a tip, in a gentle Jamaican voice. "The Vice-President takes care of that, ma'am," he said. "Drive carefully."

She saw the red neon blinking through the slow sift of the snow. PARK – ALL NIGHT – PARK.

This is crazy, she thought. I'm not getting involved right now.

She drove past the parking lot.

Two blocks later, she made a right turn around the block, and found her way back, where she waited, the wipers making a steady clumping noise that matched the sound of her heart beating in her ears.

This Sunday morning she was lucky. She found a parking spot half a block from Wayne's house. Parking in Georgetown was chancy at best; on weekends it was usually impossible. She was fully prepared to turn the car over to the valet at the Georgetown Inn and pay six dollars for the service.

It would have nearly drained her resources. She had meant to ask Tom for some money, but that is a hard request when accompanied by nagging criticism. She pulled a wry face. The hell with him. He wouldn't fight back, so what he got, he deserved.

Wayne lived almost directly across N Street NW from the famous novelist Herman Wouk. Once, a few weeks ago, there had been a party there. Marty, feeling depressed, said, "I never met an important writer. I wish you knew him."

"I do," said Wayne, reaching for the phone. "Do you want to join their party?"

"Oh, Wayne, I'm not dressed—"

That was true. Actually, she was buff naked. But what she'd meant was that she had worn a simple pants suit, which was hanging neatly in the bedroom closet. Passion was one thing; wrinkling a $250 pants suit was something else.

He laughed. "That can be corrected." He slapped her rump. "Let's. It might be fun."

She pouted. "More fun than being here with me?"

He pinched her. "I've 'been here with you,' as you so charmingly put it, three times since dinner. I need to recharge my batteries. Come on, hit the shower while I wangle us an invitation. You'll like Herman. He looks more like a banker than an author, but he has a sense of humor that can pry a chuckle from even these jaded lips."

Yawning, but feeling a tingle of anticipation, Marty stretched, her breasts rising and, as she had hoped, drawing an aroused glance from Wayne. "All right," she said. "I suppose we'd get along. I really liked *From Here to Eternity*."

He bent forward and, gently, bit her nipple. She gave a little scream, half pain, half pleasure.

"That," he said, "was James Jones. Come here."

She squirmed away. "But what about the party?"

He captured her and, as he had known, found her wet and open. "We'll have our own party," he said.

17

"We'll use your car," said TSgt. Ed Miller. "Nobody at the market will recognize it."

A1C Angela Nemath smiled. "Honestly, Ed, do you think they photograph every car in the parking lot ten times a day?"

"Let's get one thing straight right now," he said. "It wasn't my idea to bring you along. It's easy to see that you have somebody pushing for you topside. You're the lowest in rank and seniority, and if you were a man, you'd be on galley cleanup for at least six months. But since you're obviously somebody special, here you are. So be it. But listen good, *Airman*. You'll do the job, and do it right, or you'll find yourself out of the 89th before you can pronounce 'transfer.' Do you read me?"

Stung, perhaps because much of what he said was true, she replied, "Loud and clear, Sergeant."

"We'll see. Write down your mileage. You can turn it in. They pay sixteen cents a mile."

Who cares? she thought. But she wrote down the starting mileage anyway.

"We're going to that big Safeway in District Heights," said Miller. "They've got a new shipment of veal."

Surprised, she asked, "How do you know?"

He started the Rabbit. "I have a friend down in the wholesalers. He tips me off."

She said, "Why don't we just buy directly from him?"

"Nope," he said, pulling out onto the main base road. "Too dangerous. This way, nobody has the slightest idea we're buying for the plane. I trust my man, but there's no chance of his accidentally tipping anybody. I get a list of the markets he's supplied— half a dozen or so—and there's no way he or anybody else can know which I go to, or what I buy when I'm there."

As they passed through the main gate, she said, "But you don't really think anybody's out to poison the President, do you?"

"Why not?" he said. "They're out to shoot him, aren't they?"

Anderson and the rest of the primary crew had reported in early this Monday morning. He was tired and irritable. Marty had called, in the early evening, explaining that she was visiting with "friends" and would not be home.

Navigator Carl Birney glanced over the rough flight plan Anderson and McGowan had put together.

"Looks all right," he said. "Give me an hour at Ops, with the weather genius, and I'll let you know."

"The storm track's way down south," said Mc-Gowan. "We shouldn't have any problems with the jet stream."

"Particularly down at 28,000," said Anderson. "Remember that ozone layer."

"Fuel consumption's going to be lousy," grumbled the Navigator. "Sure you couldn't crank in another couple of thousand feet?"

Anderson shook his head. "Not with the Man on board."

"Yeah," said Birney. "Okay, I'll get some coffee over at Ops. Briefing?"

"Two-thirty," said Anderson. "Just in case they

move up the flight. Be sure we're covered for tomorrow as well as Wednesday."

Birney nodded and left. I didn't have to remind Carl of that, Anderson thought.

Alone with his CO, McGowan cleared his throat. "Listen, Tom," he said. "About what I said yesterday—"

"Forget it. We're both tired, but more to the point, we're getting keyed up for this mission. It's just like combat, Paul. The waiting is the hardest."

"You're right," said McGowan. "But I was still out of line."

Anderson fought down a wave of irritation. "What do you think of having Moore fly the advance plane?"

"He's ready. Why not? Fenton can hold down the right seat. How far ahead do you want them?"

"Forty-five minutes ought to be plenty. Schedule them for eight A.M. takeoff. We'll go at nine, and pick up the fifteen minutes en route. The President doesn't like to leave too early."

"We'll lose speed at 28,000," said McGowan, punching numbers on his calculator. "Still, we ought to be in the Helena area no later than nine-thirty their time."

"Let's pin that down to exactly nine thirty-four," said Anderson.

McGowan smiled. With his "fifteen-second man" nickname, Anderson had discovered that it was more impressive to arrive at an odd time rather than exactly on the hour or half hour. The Command Pilot was unaware that everybody who had anything to do with the mission, including the regular White House reporters, were in on his secret.

"We'll have both starboard engines fired up at eight fifty-six," said McGowan. "The President boards at nine A.M., roll-out at nine oh-one, in the air no later than nine-five."

"Do it," said Anderson.

In his White House corner office, the President's Chief of Staff, Arthur Cummings, was going over the near-final manifest for the upcoming flight.

The crew, of course.

Aircraft Commander: Colonel Thomas Anderson.
Pilot: Major Paul McGowan.
Navigator: Lieutenant Colonel Carl Birney.
Two flight engineers, a radio operator, and five flight stewards, who would be assigned by the Aircraft Commander.
Two 89th security men to guard the plane itself.
Five (no, four, he corrected himself with a frown) Secret Service men for the President's guard.
Chief Warrant Officer Fred Stewart, the Bagman.
Lieutenant Commander George Agee, the President's doctor.
Lieutenant (jg) Olivia Matthews, Agee's Nurse.

That took care of the crew and the forward section of seats. Now, for the press compartment, in the rear of the plane. John F. Kennedy, in search of privacy, had his bedroom and office there—where the ride was the bumpiest. President Richard M. Nixon had the plane's interior rebuilt, and now the presidential suite was midships, with a narrow aisle running down the left side of the plane for passage from forward to rear without passing through the suite.

Press Secretary Morton Bailey had requested four spaces for pool reporters. Cummings frowned at the list, but it was marked "With the President's approval," so the frown was the only reaction he was at liberty to give. He wrote down the names on the printed manifest form.

Sue Earhart, anchorperson for the UBC Evening News.

Seymour Pike, writer for *Inferno* magazine. (This deepened his frown.)

Scott Meadows, White House correspondent for *The New York Times*.

David Braun, aeronautics reporter for the Associated Press.

With the President's approval! What the hell was Foster up to? If he had deliberately decided to invite the four top names off his Enemies List, he couldn't have done better. Cummings made a mental note to discuss this with Foster, if the occasion arose. The timing would have to be precise—the President had, as he settled into office, taken more and more to solitary decisions, unexplained and undiscussed.

There was still plenty of room back there.

Cummings added the name of John Williams, the President's personal photographer. He considered placing the fifth Secret Service man, demanded by Sam Milnes, back there, but rejected the thought. The press were critical enough; a Secret Service man would only convince them that they were under surveillance. Instead, he crossed out one name in the forward compartment and added another.

Now he turned his pencil toward the large center compartment, between the President's suite and the press area.

There were two secretary's desks with electric typewriters. The White House had not furnished their names yet. It was rare for Heather Thompson, Foster's personal secretary for nearly fifteen years, to fly with the President. She remained at the office, coordinating the steady stream of messages. Sometimes, Cummings thought wryly, she functioned more as the President's Chief of Staff than he himself.

First, the VIPs.

Senator Philip Hopper headed that list. He had already phoned Cummings this morning, reminding. "*AR*thur, I presume all's well concerning the flight?"

The junior Senator from Montana, Christopher Healy—a Republican, but a political enemy of Governor Claude Hoskins and therefore a friend of President Foster.

Six White House staffers, including Mort Bailey. Other names to be supplied later.

Arthur Cummings himself.

His pencil hesitated. Then, firmly, he wrote: "The President of the United States."

TSgt. Lester Dent, Chief Radio Operator of Air Force One, worked his way through a careful checklist of his equipment. Shielded by the metal hangar, in previous Administrations the plane had to be pulled out onto the parking area to test radio and radar equipment. But, at Dent's suggestion, antennas had been mounted atop the hangar, and cables run down which could be connected to the plane's inputs.

There were eight basic communications channels, which put the plane and the President in touch with military bases around the world, with the U S. and foreign capitals. Two links were for ordinary telephone calls, which were made air-to-ground, much the same as nautical ship-to-shore phones. Two hooded machines received and sent coded messages, their contents masked off even from the Aircraft Commander. In this one matter, Sergeant Dent had the authority to disobey anyone on the flight deck who asked to see in- or outgoing copy on the code machines. The matter had never arisen so far. Four more were powerful radio transceivers.

Dent's pride and joy, the slow-scan television receiver, encoder, and printout, sat beneath the code machines. Any drawing, photo, or other image measuring eight by ten inches or less could be placed under a rubber mat and, in less than thirty seconds, would be transmitted around the world and received by another slow-scan machine tuned to the particular frequency used by Dent. That frequency was changed daily, and while the machine would not meet rigorous Top Secret requirements, there was little chance of anyone accidentally intercepting Air Force One's transmission.

Testing the slow-scan now, with the receiving point at CIA headquarters, Dent grinned as he imagined the surprise of the operator at the other end when the image was taken from the pickup machine.

Inside the rubber mat was a very realistic cartoonist's portrait of Barbara Walters sitting on a TV set.

Dent had torn it from an old copy of *Chic* magazine, and Ms. Walters, smiling, was totally nude.

Moving casually, yet efficiently, three of Air Force One's maintenance men strolled around the plane. A nod toward a section of fuselage which was a shade duller than the rest of the aluminum skin took the place of words: Wax it. The senior maintenance man stopped at the twin assembly of the nose wheels.

"How about that?" he said, jerking a thumb toward one tire.

Examination revealed that a tiny bit of rubber, smaller than a fingernail, had flaked off the sidewall of the huge tire.

"Looks like a gouge," said one of the younger maintenance men. "These babies only have three landings on them. They're good for—"

In ripe language, the senior maintenance man suggested what the tires were good for.

A chagrined maintenance assistant said, "Right, Chief. I'll have them replaced this morning."

On board the plane CMSgt. Juan Hernandez used a mimeographed checklist to examine more than five

hundred pounds of spare parts which were stored in
the cargo hold. In the past, a backup plane had usually
followed Air Force One. In recent years, at a tremendous saving in costs, parts for the jet were stocked at
most major Air Force bases, and the plane herself
carried 143 crucial parts, enough to repair all but the
most serious breakdowns.

Although the cargo compartment was kept locked,
Hernandez had personally inspected the parts last
week, and he would inspect them again next week.

"Diet Dr. Pepper," said TSgt. Ed Miller. "Get three
six-packs. The President likes it."

She put the soft drinks in the heavily laden shopping cart. "I thought this was a one-day trip," she said,
pulling up her doubleknit blue sweater, which had
been creeping down one shoulder.

"You never know," said Miller. "Back when Johnson was President, he used to like root beer. There
was plenty on board, they thought, but he had four
or five glasses, and gave some to the pool reporters.
Well, when he wanted some more, the Steward on
duty had to tell him that he was sorry, they had Diet
Cola, Cokes, and Fresca, but they were all out of root
beer."

Almost as an afterthought, Miller put two six-packs
of Dad's Root Beer into the cart.

"LBJ jumped out of his chair and yelled, 'I want
plenty of that blankety-blank root beer on this plane
at all times. That's not too hard for you morons, is it?
You can buy the goddamned stuff anywhere. Send out
an order to all bases, worldwide. Stock up on root
beer.' And he wasn't kidding. After that mission, the
Steward he'd chewed out transferred from the 89th."

"I," Angie said calmly, "find part of that story hard
to believe."

"Such as?"

"I don't believe LBJ ever said 'blankety-blank.' "

*   *   *

The water arrived by special truck shortly before noon. Since Miller was shopping, the senior Steward in his absence signed for the three five-gallon bottles of Rock Point Spring Water.

This was the brand of bottled water the President drank at home. On trips, it accompanied him. All ice cubes and tea or coffee were made with this particular water. So were his light scotch-and-waters. One bottle would, when Miller returned, be dispatched to the plane itself, to be placed in its special container which provided water for the President's sink in his private washroom.

The delivery of bottled water was not for fear that the plane's own supply might poison the President. It was in line with standard traveling procedures. Any change in water might cause that malady known as "the Tropical Two-Step," "Montezuma's Revenge," or simply *touristas*, to strike. Reporters, special guests— even the crew—might suffer from the runs, but never the President.

The third bottle would be dispatched to the President's hotel room, where it would be guarded by hard-eyed Secret Service men, forbidden to drink from its cool spigot.

At ten-forty, Washington time, when an official request from the President's military attaché went out to military bases across the continental United States, requesting assistance for an upcoming presidential flight, hundreds of individual units began to make their plans.

Air Force One would be tracked from the moment of takeoff to its landing in Helena. On the highest priority would be the half-hourly reports from the plane's Navigator, giving his location taken from readouts of the inertial guidance system and from his own computations. In addition, as a backup, military radar tracking stations would have the plane on the scope for most of its trip. Finally, Air Traffic Control centers would have its transponder in view, pinpointing 26000's position, altitude, heading, and speed.

On overseas trips, Coast Guard and Naval rescue vessels were posted at 500-mile intervals. During flight within continental borders, field agents of the FBI and Secret Service kept in touch with the nearest military installation, or Air Traffic Center, and were always within miles of any forced landing.

In the history of presidential flight, none had ever occurred.

On particularly sensitive missions, escort fighters were sometimes sent up to shepherd Air Force One to a safe landing. Dubbed "Quail" in official FAA Special Flight Operations manuals, such fighters were required, according to the manual to:

Maintain "approved separation at all times. Consider altitudes/flight levels assigned as continuously occupied even though both aircraft elect to fly with less than approved separation."

Which meant, simply, that though the "Quail" fighters might be sitting on Air Force One's wings, the Controllers should wink, look the other way, and assume officially that the escorts were actually occupying the next-higher altitude/flight level, a thousand feet above.

There was also a kicker in the regulations, which compromised Chapter 6 and Chapter 7 of Special Flight Operations.

The one with which Colonel Anderson, and all presidential pilots, had become most familiar went:

731. SPECIAL HANDLING

a. Clear the aircraft according to pilot request as soon as practicable. Do not ask the pilot to deviate from his planned action except to pre-clude an emergency situation.

b. Issue radar advisories to the flight inspec-tion aircraft where adequate coverage exists and to the extent permitted by workload.

c. Suggest flight path adjustments as required, for any aircraft which will enter or penetrate an area in which a flight inspection is being per-formed.

it was followed, on the next page, by:

SECTION 2. PRESIDENTIAL AND VICE-PRESIDENTIAL AIRCRAFT

740. MOVEMENT INFORMATION

Honor any request of the pilot concerning movement of the Presidential or Vice-Presidential aircraft if it can be fulfilled in accordance with existing control procedures, Also, honor any re-quest of the pilot, Secret Service, White House staff, or Office of the Vice-President for the relay, via FAA communications circuits, of information regarding the movement or proposed movement of these aircraft.

741. RADAR FLIGHT FOLLOWING

Provide Presidential and Vice-Presidential air-craft with the same radar flight following and traffic information provided all civil turbojet air-craft when operating along the appropriate route and at the appropriate altitudes. Forward time and altitude over compulsory reporting points to an FSS.

* * *

While not strictly entitled to it, presidential flights had taken advantage of the special regulations applying to those aircraft engaged in flight inspection of navigational aids. This cut red tape, saved time, and gave Air Force One a green light to the runway without offending commercial fliers.

But if the book were followed strictly, paragraph 740 would come into effect, with its key stipulation, *"if it can be fulfilled in accordance with existing control procedures."*

Major Paul McGowan went on board Air Force One and found Angie helping TSgt. Ed Miller stock the galleys. He knew from experience that Miller would come on board early tomorrow to prepare some of the basics for Wednesday's in-flight meal. If the flight were moved up, he would be here during the night.

Avoiding Angie's eyes, he patted his stomach and said, "Lunch, troops?"

"Touch my veal, sir," said Miller, "and you die."

"At ease," said McGowan. "I'm saving up for tonight." Carefully, aiming his words at her, he glanced at Angie and added, "I plan to have a big dinner and maybe even howl a little. It's about time we got a real mission. How about you guys?"

Miller just shrugged.

Angie, all casualness, said, "Major, you just read my mind."

18

Vernon Justus, making a miserly assessment of fuel on hand, decided that he could safely take the P-38 aloft for an hour and still have enough high-octane gasoline left to top off the tanks on Wednesday morning. His nerves were jangled anyway, and flying always calmed him down.

He hooked the ancient tractor's tow bar to the front wheel of the Lightning and towed it out onto the runway. The weather had turned nasty, and there was the sting of sleet against his cheek. But the sky above was clear, and he knew he would climb out of the clouds by 10,000 feet.

Unhooking the tractor, he examined the fairing that hid the two machine guns mounted in the P-38's nose. They were well concealed; nobody would ever have guessed that behind the black panel lurked a devastating barrage of fifty-caliber bullets.

At the office door, he paused to hang a sign on the doorknob. It bore an old-fashioned drawing of a biplane looping and the legend OUT FLYING!

Joyce would be out in another hour. Not that it mattered. Business was slow at best, and during the cold months, nonexistent.

He glanced across the hardtop at the Lightning. She was a beauty. Her twin booms, extending like graceful fingers to the double, rounded vertical rudders, joined by a wide horizontal stabilizer, were the very essence of speed. Double air scoops on each boom gathered the thin air of the stratosphere, to keep the two 1,475-horsepower Allison engines breathing.

The pilot's compartment, set deep into the center of the main wing, was relatively roomy compared to most World War II fighters. From it, with no fuselage hump behind, and no motor in front, Justus would command a wide field of vision.

The P-38 was at its best screaming down from an ambush position above its target. With Air Force One limited to a top altitude of 28,000 feet by the ozone incident, Justus would have the advantage of height. He had already plotted the only three landing glide slopes possible for Malstrom AFB, and had selected a holding pattern from which he could intersect all three in less than two minutes after he appeared on the Malstrom radar screens. That would not be nearly enough time for the base to scramble protective escorts. And he'd be too close to the President's plane for them to risk SAM missiles.

And once he had Air Force One in his sights, all he needed was thirty seconds.

Senator Philip Hopper sat alone in his office, consulting his notes. He had compiled a very complete profile of the upcoming Air Force One mission.

He now amused himself by computing, with a slide rule—he despised the new calculators because all their workings were hidden, uncheckable—the cost per minute of operating the President's plane.

By confining his costs to in-air time, Hopper came up with an impressive figure.

Assuming three flights a month, Air Force One flew 36 times a year. Some trips were only three or four hours round trip. Others, to the Coast, or overseas, were longer.

Hopper assigned an average of eight air hours to each flight. That came to 288 hours a year. Or 17,280 air minutes.

Which, divided into the total budget (estimated by him) of $500,000,000 a year, came out to:

$28,935.18 a minute!

Hopper smiled. It was a number he could work magic with.

Although he did not know it, he would have had to spend four times that much for a single one-minute commercial on any top-rated television program.

He examined an air routes map, tracing the flight path from Andrews to Helena, Montana.

His finger stopped. He cursed.

Air Force One which normally flew to the nearest Air Force Base—in this case, Malstrom AFB in Great Falls—was scheduled instead to fly directly to the Helena airport.

Suddenly all of his plans had to be changed.

Senator Philip Hopper reached for the telephone.

The clouds below were curved in fantastic shapes. Their tops gleamed sparkling white, their billows swirled and swooped in the rising air currents.

This was *flying*, Vernon Justus thought, diving at an outcropping of cloud which had blossomed two thousand feet beneath the P-38's nose. He put the cloud's center in his sights, pressed the locked red button on top of the stick, and said, "Brrrrp!"

Sure kill. He hauled the stick back, stood the Lightning on its tail, and then fell over again into a steep dive. He found the cloud directly in his sights once more, and repeated the shoot-down procedure.

His watch told him that it was time to return to the sleet and cold of the sulking earth. He did not want to leave his eyrie, but prudence warned that he must.

Feeling the vibrating power of the plane, he lowered her nose and watched the airspeed indicator move toward the right of the dial—650 . . . 700 . . . 720 miles an hour, in a 45-degree dive. The airstream outside buffeted the 21,000-pound plane. A mere gnat in comparison with modern fighters, the P-38 was perhaps the last airship which was completely controlled by the man riding inside her. Later fighters were, in Justus' scornful opinion, mere electronic gun platforms that carried a passenger. He, like so many other ex-fighter pilots, hated jets. They had no souls. They lacked the savage female personalities of the temperamental, often vicious prop planes. In the Pacific, every fighter had a name. Tin Lizzie. Miss Hot Rocks. Lady Cream. In later wars, few jets were ever named. They were only machines, borrowed for a few hours by whichever pilot was assigned to their cockpits.

Everything went to hell after the war, thought Justus, spiraling his P-38 down between layers of clouds. Bigger meant better. The hell with the little guy, the hell with sticking up for quality instead of quantity. That first Univac computer, big as a city block, was the beginning of the end for *people.* Now that they've got computers down to the size of a suitcase, humans are obsolete.

Well, by God, he'd show them different! Let them keep their ultrasonic jets, and their information retrieval systems which dehumanized a man, and their insane pride in destroying individual pride.

Wednesday morning, they would learn that one crippled individual, in a plane thirty years obsolete, could bring their precious system to its knees.

The P-38 fell out of the clouds less than five hundred feet above the runway, and he began his final approach.

Marty kept a chill silence during breakfast. Amazingly, though, she had gotten up to make it for Anderson this Tuesday morning. Her Sunday night in town with "friends," he thought, seemed to have calmed her down a little. She'd returned late Monday evening, made empty conversation which did not relate to their problems, went to bed alone, drinking only two weak Bourbons.

"We're flying out to Helena tomorrow," he told her. "We may return the same day, we may stay over. Anyway, I'll be back Thursday for sure. Why don't we go over to the island for a day or so? Just the two of us?"

"Why?"

"Why not?"

She hesitated, started to say something, changed her mind. "We'll see," she said. "Go do your big important job."

He met her eyes. "You'll be here when I get back?"

"Tonight? I don't know. But I'll be around for the triumphant return after your Helena trip. You can bet on it."

"Okay," he said, dismissing the subject. There was no time left for arguing. He was due at the base. He leaned forward to kiss her, and she presented her cold cheek.

She waited until the engine of his car roared and she heard the crunch of wheels in the driveway. Then she examined the copy of the Air Force One itinerary she had copied down at 2 A.M. while Anderson slept.

Picking up the telephone, she began to dial.

Joyce Cox was waiting for Justus when he taxied the P-38 into the hangar, revved up the engines to clear the carbs, and shut down.

"Cold day for flying," she commented.

"It's nice up top," he said, scrambling down from the cockpit. He helped her chock the wheels, and they entered the office from the hangar's side door.

"Somebody's been calling you," she said. "Twice."

"Any message?"

"No. They said they'd call back." She poured him a cup of coffee. "I'm glad you took her up. You always feel better afterward."

"Might as well enjoy it while I can," he said.

She studied him. "Did you think about what I said? About selling her to me cheap?"

"I thought about it," he admitted. "But I've got something else in mind."

"You can't let them take her away."

"I'm not going to."

"How will you stop them?"

"Leave that to me." He turned away and began to read the latest copy of *Flying*.

"Did you eat?"

"I grabbed a sweet roll," he lied. She recognized it, knowing there was no place, between the small apartment he kept for them downtown and the airport, where he could have bought one.

"Well," she said. "*I'm* hungry. How about some scrambled eggs?"

"If it isn't any trouble," he mumbled. Justus had long since lost any taste for food. To him, it was fuel. You topped off the tanks to get as much flying time as possible. The plane didn't enjoy the gasoline, it merely used it for energy. He himself never ate for pleasure any more, but to survive.

Joyce opened the small refrigerator and removed four eggs, a package of bacon, and a stick of Blue Bonnet Margarine. She turned on the small gas burner.

The telephone rang. Justus picked it up.

"Airport."

The voice said, "There's been a change in plans. Air Force One isn't going to land at Malstrom after all."

Justus stiffened. "Repeat that."

The voice did. "The new destination is Helena Airport."

Justus swore. "That screws everything up."

"Maybe it's just as well."

"Wait a minute," said the pilot. "I think—Listen, it may still be on. There's an old dirt field just a few miles east of Helena. Let me check it out. Can I reach you?"

"No," said the voice. "I'll call you tonight."

"Okay. Nine P.M. my time."

"All right."

The connection was broken.

Curiously, Joyce asked, "What was all that about?"

"A charter," he lied. "Some hunters. Hey, those eggs smell good."

Arthur Cummings put down the telephone. His brain seemed to reel.

What is right? he asked himself. How do you know when you've made the proper choice? He had been torn by doubt before making this latest call, and was still undecided.

It is the nation which really matters, he told himself. Politicians, Congressmen, Senators—even Presidents—come and go. The nation endures. Is my loyalty to the man, or to the office?

He pushed the telephone away.

The soul searching was academic now anyway. He had done what he thought he must do.

Flying the SuperCub, with its slow landing speed and durable undercarriage, Vernon Justus decided to try a landing at the abandoned airstrip east of Helena, Montana.

Ten miles above the Canyon Ferry Dam on the upper Missouri River, the strip had been carved out of the hills by the Corps of Army Engineers fifteen years ago. Since then, it had been kept up, more or less, by sportsmen who flew into it for hunting and fishing parties.

He buzzed the field, which was called, among

hunters, the Naked Edge. Only fifty feet wide, there was a sheer drop-off to the north, and a sloping hill to the south. With the P-38's 52-foot wing span, he would have to cheat toward the drop-off and somehow keep his wheels on solid earth—or, in this case, snow and ice.

A flier's good sense told Justus that by buzzing the field with the slow-moving SuperCub, he could decide whether or not the P-38 could be landed safely. And, more important, if it could be lifted off again. But he rejected this valid advice from his experienced subconscious. If he were going to crack up, better to do it in the SuperCub, which was more forgiving on impact. Taking the Lightning into a crash was like riding down in a steel coffin.

On his first pass over the strip, Justus spotted two ice ridges which, while not barriers, would have to be approached carefully. The wind was low, so he could come in from either direction. An approach from the west would put the ridges at the far end of the strip.

He made a steep turn and buzzed the strip again. This time, he spotted a patch of snow which looked soft. It was dead center on the strip, however, so he would have to live—or crash—with it.

Okay, he thought. Let's do it.

He glided in, just above the stall, his fingers white against the throttle, ready to pour on the coal and lift him out if a sudden hazard appeared.

The SuperCub's wheels touched, bounced, settled again, held.

He was down. He chopped the throttle and began to tap the toe brakes.

The plane slowed. He saw the ice ridges ahead and, tromping on the left brake and applying rudder, made a gentle ground loop.

He killed the engine and got out. The chill wind sighed against the plane's wings.

Carefully, he paced the entire length of the runway twice, stomping on suspicious patches. The soft spot he had imagined was actually a thin layer of snow over bare ground. The ridge were real enough, but not as bad as he had thought. If necessary, he could bounce over them.

His paces measured the strip at exactly three thousand feet. A westerly approach would be best, because that was almost uphill, and over flat ground. To land from the east would mean slipping in after he passed over a rim of trees. That would cost him at least four hundred feet of precious runway.

Justus nodded. It would be feasible to get the P-38 down, and off again. His only danger would be in being spotted from the air while he waited.

He found a wide spot in the strip, against the hill, which was in shadow and nearly under the spreading limbs of pine trees. With a dark tarp—heavy plastic would weigh least—he could cover the plane and be practically invisible, except to low-flying aircraft, which were rare in this area.

It would all have to be done by darkness tonight, though.

He hurried back to the SuperCub, cranked her up, taxied to the far end of the strip, and took off, clearing the ice ridges by a full six hundred feet.

Joyce, fully qualified in the SuperCub, still did not like the idea.

"Land on a dirt strip in this weather? Are you crazy?"

"I've already shot the field and made a touchdown. It's okay," he said.

"Why?"

"I'm hiding the P-38 out," he lied.

"I told you, my lawyer says you ought to sell her to me."

"Screw your lawyer," he said. "Are you going to help me, or do I boot your ass out of here and call Mike?"

Mike, a former backup pilot for Justus, was also a previous boy friend of Joyce's, and she now detested him with that particular hatred that comes only to ex-lovers.

"No," she said. "I'll fly the SuperCub. But how do you know that someone won't find the Lightning out there and strip her?"

"I don't," he said. "But it's a hell of a lot better than letting the bank stick her in storage."

Although not a professional pilot, Joyce had flown enough to understand, and to say no more.

Shortly after five, they took off. There was no possibility of her SuperCub keeping up with the P-38, so Justus headed directly for the strip, knowing that she would follow with the aid of the marked-up chart he had given to her.

He landed safely, although the ice ridges gave him a bone-jarring jolt. Taxiing the Lightning into the shadowed wide spot of the strip, he took out the plastic tarp and, fastening it with masking tape, began to cover the plane.

Seymour Pike, in his hotel room, was packing a suitcase. He had been sternly admonished by the Secret Service that he must pack his own bag, not let it out of his sight, and deliver it to the Air Force One baggage car, which would be at the hotel at 7:30 A.M. No, he could not send the suitcase down by a bellhop. He had to carry it personally and get a signed receipt. Half an hour later, a limo would pick him up for the run to Andrews.

Why couldn't he just carry his suitcase and save a trip downstairs?

Because that wasn't the way it was done.

Pike looked at his watch and reached for the telephone.

It was time to make his call.

Joyce was still shaking from her landing when Justus climbed into the SuperCub and, flying from the right seat, took off again.

"Jesus, Vernon," she quivered, "you said this was an airstrip, not a Band-Aid."

"Relax," he said. "You did great."

"I nearly tinkled in my pants, that's what I did," she said.

"Take over," he said. "Give me a one-eighty."

"I've got it," she said, taking the controls and making a slow turn. He stared down into the dusk. Yes, he could barely make out the P-38, but only by knowing where it was and looking for it.

"Okay," he said. "She's safe down there."

"I hope so," said Joyce.

He made the landing and, as they tied down the SuperCub and started for the office, he heard the telephone ringing.

Governor Claude Hoskins sensed that the meeting was running long. "Philip," he said. "I've got a plane to catch."

Senator Hopper nodded. "Five more minutes," he said. "I'll drive you to the airport myself."

"Fine," said the Governor of Montana. "Do you mind if I use your phone? I'll charge it to my office."

Hopper laughed. "Governor," he said, "this is my business phone. Feel free. It all comes out of the same pocket."

"Yeah?" said Vernon Justus.

"You said to call."

"Everything's fine," said Justus. "The change in destination doesn't affect tomorrow."

"Are you sure? Everything seems mixed up to me."

"Don't argue. Just do what you're supposed to."

"All right," said the voice. "But remember, nobody is going to be hurt. You promised that."

"I know what I promised," said Justus. "If you do your part, it'll all be fine."

"It had better be," said the voice. "Remember, I'm involved in this too."

"I won't forget," said Vernon Justus.

Sue Earhart covered the receiver of the telephone and called, "I'm on the phone. Make yourself a drink. I'll be right out."

Seymour Pike, picking her up for dinner, which he had been awarded in a surprise answer to his casual invitation, said, "No hurry. I'll switch on the boob tube."

She replied, still covering the phone, "Don't bite the hand that's feeding me."

As he said something she did not hear, she almost whispered into the mouthpiece, "I've got to go. There's someone here."

She hung up and went out to greet her escort. In the bedroom behind her, a neatly packed suitcase waited for the early-morning arrival of the Air Force One baggage car.

Joyce Cox awoke at five-thirty in the morning. She yawned, rolled over, felt emptiness beside her, and sat up.

Vernon Justus was gone.

She padded around the small apartment. His clothes were still there, and so was his prized .357 Magnum pistol. Wherever he had gone, he apparently intended to return.

Or did he?

Disturbed, she dressed and drove four miles to the gloomy airport.

The light over the office door was lit. She went inside. Someone had made instant coffee; the hot pot was still warm, and there were dregs in a cup.

She went out, with a flashlight, to the flight line.

The SuperCub was not there.

19

Held just a few moments before 5 P.M., with no broadcast media invited, the press conference in Senator Philip Hopper's office made a giant impact, but a slow-moving one. No print reporter was going to give the broadcast media the slightest chance to hit the airwaves with what amounted to an old-fashioned "scoop." So they telephoned their reports directly to city editors with fervent cautions to keep everything under the hat until the next edition hit the streets.

It was a brilliant game plan which, while earning the Senator the abiding anger of radio and TV reporters, still presented his message nationwide *after* the lid was on in the White House. It would have required an obviously deliberate act by the President or one of his aides to remove the Senator from the Air Force One manifest, and he knew full well that they would not dare such an action.

So, to the reporters who, in two or three hours, would be reporting his words to the nation and the world, Senator Philip Hopper announced, "Tomorrow, if there is any way I can achieve it, I will be riding on the absolute last flight of that expensive toy known as Air Force One."

A reporter tried to ask a question, and Hopper waved him aside, saying, "I'll answer you later." He went on: "Perhaps it does not seem excessive to you that our President utilizes a form of transportation which costs you, the taxpayer, approximately five hundred million dollars a year. Do you know how much that is? Take a five and put eight zeros behind it. Does that mean anything to you? If not, get yourself a lot of dollar bills and pile them up. When you reach a height equivalent to the Washington Monument, you will have spent only *half* what our President does on his comfortable junkets."

He glared at them. Glares were always popular. They implied honesty and righteous anger. "Perhaps that means nothing. Well, five hundred million dollars would completely rebuild the slums of Harlem. Five hundred million dollars would have paid the entire cost of the American Revolution. Or, if you so desire, it will provide six or seven flights a year for your President."

All of the above figures were false, picked out of the air. But not one reporter ever bothered to check on them. It had always been so.

Sourly, he admitted to himself that he was putting on a performance. He gave them what they wanted and expected, they repaid him with the newspaper space he wanted, and it was a quid pro quo.

He softened his tone. "Nobody, and particularly myself—remember, my friends, I was close to both of the Kennedy boys, and wept at their untimely deaths—wants to see our President in danger. But the truth is that our commercial airlines can provide charter aircraft with as much security and probably more comfortable accommodations than the Air Force, with its inflated budgets and overstaffed bases, can ever hope to. I have great respect for our military pilots—but they are fighting men, not glorified bus drivers. I dare not use his name, for it would destroy his career, but one of the top pilots assigned to fly the President has used those very words to describe his humiliating assignment."

Another glare. "Yes, *humiliating!* When a man has risked his life in aerial combat, what a comedown to be reduced to hauling a cargo of presidential cronies around the sky! How shameful to so reward our heroes! Yes—and if you do not believe me, merely consult the record—that is the policy of the United States Air Force. My friends, it's the Peter Principle magnified: promote a man out of what he is capable of doing, and what he enjoys doing, into a job which he is *in*-capable of doing and *detests* doing! Waste five hundred million dollars in the process, and you will have achieved what is referred to as Air Force One."

He whipped off his glasses and presented his most ferocious glare. "Questions?"

"Senator," said the man from the Washington *Post*, "why are you so opposed to this particular operation?"

"Because, as I told you, that much money could move an entire ghetto of people into the twentieth century. Next?"

"Why, then," said a woman from *Newsday*, "are you going on tomorrow's flight?"

"As a firsthand observer," said Hopper. "I do not report that which I do not know. I've flown on the planes of previous Presidents. I felt then as I do now. Tomorrow, I will decide if President Howard Foster has fallen into the same trap which captured his predecessors. Next?"

A man from the San Francisco *Chronicle* asked, "Why aren't there any broadcast people here tonight?"

"Because I want this message to be passed to the people without being converted into broadcast short-hand. You all have roughly the same deadlines, and plenty of time to make them. Whatever your reaction to my statement, you will have the time to evaluate it properly."

The man from the Chicago *Tribune* laughed. "You know what the networks are going to say about you, don't you, sir?"

"All too well. So what?"

The New Orleans *Times-Picayune* asked, "Do you

really believe you will see anything on tomorrow's flight that will be meaningful to us in context with your stand on Air Force One costs?"

"I believe I will," said Hopper. "In fact, if you'll permit me a little crystal-balling, I'm almost *sure* I will."

20

Advance Man Warren Rogers' phone call caught Anderson just as the Colonel was leaving his office for the day.

Rogers said, "I keep feeling there's something behind me and that it's gaining. But that may be just my native cowardice. At this moment, Colonel, I'd say it's Go."

"No problems?"

"Plenty of them, but nothing I can't take care of. I'm still worried about our friendly neighborhood Governor. I just found out why nobody's seen him for the past couple of days. He's been in Washington."

"State?"

"D.C. He's due home this evening. I've relayed this to Art Cummings, and my guess is that Governor Hoskins will find a few "Please call back" messages from the White House. Art's going to light a bonfire under his ungrateful ass."

Anderson did not answer. It was not his place to criticize public officials, even unfriendly Governors. "I'll call you before we take off," he said.

"Don't bother," said Rogers. "I've got a late night ahead. I'll be in touch with you en route. I have to check in with Cummings anyway."

"All right," said Anderson. "See you tomorrow."

"You can count on it," said the Advance Man. He hung up and went back to the hotel bar, where mayoral candidate William Guthrie nursed a perfect manhattan.

Worried as usual, he asked Rogers, "What's happening? Has the trip been canceled?"

"Nothing's happening but business as usual," soothed Rogers. "The trip's still on schedule. You can tell your wife."

Guthrie laughed. "I know it seems silly to you, but women get very excited about these things."

Noticing Guthrie's trembling hands, Rogers said, "It's a good thing us men don't. Somebody's got to keep things running."

"Here comes Pete," said Guthrie.

Rogers looked up and saw the stocky figure of Peter Judson, the Deputy Mayor of Helena, threading his way between the tables.

"Sorry I'm late," said Judson. He waved at the barman. "Dry martini, straight up." Back to Rogers: "Jeeze, those Secret Service guys are nit-pickers. Do you know that the Chief had to give them the Social Security number of every one of our policemen?"

"Well," said Rogers, "it doesn't make sense to keep the crowds back and then put an uncleared guy with a .38 Special right next to the President."

"Oh, I know you're right," said Judson. "But it took time, that's all." His drink came and he sipped at it, winced. "God, that's good!"

Rogers consulted his notes. "All right, since Sam Milnes is on top of security, I'll assume that's all taken care of."

Privately, he knew that he would assume no such thing, and would be briefed later tonight by a Secret Service man. But it was his policy, while covering all bases, to remain as casual and unflapped as possible in front of civilians.

He looked up and asked Peter Judson, "What about the airport?"

"We've detailed thirty patrolmen to man the fence."

"I mean the airport itself. They've been notified?"

"The airport is governed by a five-person commission," said the Deputy Mayor, "I spoke with them this afternoon, and they assured me that the airport manager and all personnel have been instructed to offer every courtesy and facility to the President's party."

Rogers nodded. "The plan is for a direct transfer into the chopper, but with the President, you never know. He likes to work the fence."

Judson looked puzzled. Guthrie, fast becoming an expert, explained, "That means working the crowd, Pete. Shaking hands, kissing babies."

"Stuff politicians do," agreed the Deputy Mayor. "Thank God I'm out of all that."

Seriously, Guthrie said, "You realize, Pete, that if I win, the first thing I'll do is ask for your resignation. I can't have a Deputy Mayor who refuses to serve if some nut shoots down my Piper Cub."

"You won't have to ask," said Judson. "I can't wait to leave. But nobody shoots down planes any more."

Governor Claude Hoskins landed at Helena Airport, where he held a mini press conference. To three TV news crews and a small group of newspaper reporters, he said, "No, I was not called to Washington. My old friend Senator Philip Hopper invited me there for the weekend, and since the press of duty was not overwhelming, I accepted."

NBC asked, "What about the President's visit?"

Hoskins smiled coldly. "What visit is that?"

"Why, his trip to Helena tomorrow."

The Governor said, "To my knowledge, I have received no official notification of any presidential visit to the Treasure State."

The NBC man persisted: "Official or not, surely, sir, you must have—"

But Hoskins would not meet his eyes or recognize the question. He pointed at a local newsman who had always been favorable to the Governor. "Mr. Hayes?"

"Do you have a prediction on Tuesday's election for Mayor?"

"No," said the Governor, "but I have a private hunch."

"What's that, sir?"

"The best man won't win." And Hoskins, to the boredom of the national reporters, who could not have cared less about local politics, launched into an attack on William Guthrie.

The President's visit was not mentioned again.

"He's a snake," agreed Warren Rogers. He and Guthrie were in the Advance Man's room, watching the late news. He had tried several times to reach Governor Hoskins at the state capitol building, without success. He had also called Arthur Cummings in Washington, routing the Chief of Staff out of a formal dinner in honor of visiting writer Jan de Hartog, who had returned to the United States from his native Belgium to accept a belated book award for his novel *The Captain*, which, in a reissue, had found its way to the top of the *Times* paperback best-seller list.

"You fucking well know he's been notified," snarled Cummings. "By phone, by telegram, and by courier hand-carried letter. He's on notice. The President intends to eat his ass out so completely tomorrow that when he's done, it'll fall off, leaving a neat round hole."

Before hanging up, Rogers expressed his heartfelt desire to view such a delightful occasion.

Now, to the nervous William Guthrie, who was fast becoming one of his favorite people, he added, "Don't worry about a thing. I have it on good authority that our slimy Governor isn't going to stay up there in that catbird seat much longer."

Seriously, Guthrie said, "The way he's playing it,

Warren, old Claude might just ignore the President's presence altogether."

"No, he won't," said the Advance Man. "Remember, we talked about this before. I don't care how independent Hoskins is, no Governor can refuse a summons from the President of the United States, and if Hoskins doesn't come to his senses by tomorrow, that's precisely what he's going to receive. The American public will accept lying, cheating, stealing, and even rampant stupidity from their politicians. But they won't buy discourtesy. If Hoskins doesn't already know that, he will soon."

He leaned down and switched off the TV set.

Guthrie glanced at his watch. "It's late," he said. "Maybe I'd better take off."

"Are you driving out to the ranch?"

"No," said Guthrie, pulling on his jacket. "Lisa's in town."

"Hell, why didn't you mention it? We could have taken her to dinner with us."

"Wrong, buddy. She's got two beauticians over at the apartment, completely rebuilding her face. I doubt if I'll recognize her when I get home."

"In that case," said Rogers, "Hang around. I'm not going to bed any time soon. The calls are still coming in."

"Just a short one," said Guthrie. "I'll make them." At the small bar which separated the room from its adjoining "kitchenette"—actually a small refrigerator, a two-burner electric surface unit, and a half-sized sink—he put ice in two glasses, splashed Jack Daniel's over them. "You know," he said, "before you hit town, I was looking forward to being Mayor. I mean, even in Hoskins' state, I thought I would be a pretty big man, and for a shit-kicking ex-farmhand, that's just about the top of the heap." He sighed, handed Rogers one of the glasses. "Boy, you ruined me."

"How's that?"

"I've been sitting here, watching you pick up that phone and dial the White House, call the President's pilot, order cops and Secret Service men and FBI agents around their positions on some kind of map you must keep in your head . . . Warren, you've got more power in that one phone-dialing finger than I'll ever have as Mayor of Helena." He lifted his glass. "Here's to you, pal. May your finger never falter."

Rogers, touched, said, "Take consolation from this, good buddy. What power I have is strictly at the whim of that man in the Oval Office. He can throw me out on my ass tomorrow morning. When you get elected, the people hand you a lease for four years."

"That's fine," said Guthrie wistfully. "But I'd still like to dial the White House one day."

The Advance Man indicated the phone. "Be my guest. The number is 456-1414. When you get the operator, ask for the Duty Officer. I've got to check in before I go off call for the night." He gave a bitter laugh. "As if that would stop them from waking me up at three A.M. if somebody wanted to."

"You're kidding, aren't you?" asked Guthrie.

"Like hell I am," said Rogers. "Listen, you said you wanted to call the White House. So call."

Reaching for the telephone, William Guthrie said, "Boy, I wish Lisa was here."

21

"That goddamned Rabbit won't start again," said Angie. "I must have flooded it, and now the battery's down."

Major Paul McGowan looked up from his coffee.

"What's the tragedy?" he asked. "I'll call Triple A for a hot start."

"We don't have time," she said. "I used them the other day, and it took a couple of hours for them to get here."

"All right, I'll drive you to the base."

She looked at her watch. "We'll have to leave soon. I need to get my uniform and gear together, and I'm due on board the plane at eight."

It was now ten after seven on Wednesday morning.

"Five minutes," he said. "You make good coffee."

"You make good love," she said softly.

"Hush. You're being insubordinate."

"We're right together," she said. "Why does it embarrass you to say it?"

He put down his cup. "I don't know," he replied, honestly. "I guess I'm not a talker. I'm a doer."

She patted his cheek. "You are that, my pet." She picked at her bright blue robe. "I'll zip into my Sears special. The gingham frock. My uniform's out at the base."

She wasn't joking. Off duty, she liked to wear frilly little things which contrasted with her uniform. That was one of the things which attracted McGowan to her—the side of femininity which she accepted without question or discomfort.

He was already dressed in slacks and sports shirt. His full uniform hung in his office at Base HQ, and he had showered on awakening. "You've got four minutes," he said.

"Yes, sir!" she answered, saluting. Then, her robe falling away, revealing her soft breasts, she kissed him hard.

"At ease, Airman," he commanded. "We'll have none of that."

"We'll have plenty of that," she said. Then, smiling: "But not here and now."

"Three and a half minutes," he said.

When he had arrived home shortly after seven on Tuesday, Anderson found, as he had suspected, that Marty was gone. As usual, there was no note. This time he checked her closet. She had not taken anything, so far as he could see. Afraid of the Pill, she used a diaphragm. He resisted the urge to open her dressing cabinet and see if it was still there, nested in its box of talcum.

He had felt good all day. The tiredness had vanished, and there had been no symptoms since his self-medication. The upcoming mission posed no problems, at its scheduled 28,000 feet. He had forced himself to move more slowly than usual, and his fatigue had been driven down beneath visible levels.

Get through this mission. That was all that counted. His own health, the problems with Marty—everything must wait.

Impulsively, he picked up the telephone and dialed.

Liv answered: "Hello?"

"It's me."

"Which me? Robert Redford? Paul Newman?"

"How about poor Tom Anderson?"

"Ah," she said. "The Lone Eagle returns."

"Are you busy?"

"No," she said. "My bag is packed, the alarm is set dawnishly, and for your information, the pot of stew has gone bad."

"That's unfortunate," he said. "I was feeling hungry."

She bit back a sharp remark and said, "I guess I could choke down a shore dinner."

"Barney's?"

"Where else?"

He hesitated. "The crew is on Yellow," he said. "Barney's is outside the circle."

"Ten minutes outside," she said, feeling rebellious. "You don't really expect an alert this time of night."

"No," he admitted. "But—"

"Barney's," she said. "It's almost seven now. I'll make reservations for eight."

Defeated, he said, "Fine. I'll see you there."

Aching to ask, "Where's Marty?" Liv said, instead, "Don't rush. I'll bring a book and wait in the bar."

"Wear civvies," he said.

"Sure thing," she said. "My topless jump suit."

It was late for such a meeting, but Senator Philip Hopper had much ground to cover. He apologized to FAA Administrator Clarence Willoughby. "I know it's late, Clarence, but I've been running all day."

"My pleasure," said Willoughby. "I understand you're off to Montana with the President tomorrow."

"As the unwelcome guest," said Hopper.

"Good luck to you," said Willoughby. "I admire what you're trying to do."

"Thank you," said Hopper. "Perhaps you can help. We've never spelled out details, but I believe you're in sympathy with diminishing the great costs—and the even greater power—the President expends on personal air transport."

"I am," said the FAA Administrator. "Naturally,

I can't go on record, being an appointed official, but—"

"Hold on to your seat, Clarence," said the Senator. "I'm going to ask you to take a stand this evening. It will be a dangerous one, an unprecedented one, but if we achieve our goal, I can assure you that less than four years from now you will be the Vice-President of the United States."

Recognizing that he was at the crossroads of his career, Clarence Willoughby asked, "What stand is that, Senator?"

Hopper told him.

"My God," said Willoughby. "You're right. It *is* unprecedented."

"But completely legal," reminded the Senator.

"Yes, yes, it's that. Still, the President can override me."

"I doubt that he'd dare," said Hopper. "The regulations were set up to pertain to *all* air traffic. He has no authority to violate them. If he does, he's open to criticism from all sides. So my assessment is that he will divert the flight."

"But he will still reach Helena," said the FAA Administrator.

"Only at great inconvenience," said Hopper. "And looking like a fool."

"It's too risky," said Willoughby. "I can't do it, not even for you."

"Think carefully about that," said Hopper. "Assume the worst, that Foster demands your resignation. You're in the legal right. With my support, you'll land on your feet. But if he fired you for something else, and you didn't have me behind you, where would you be?"

Willoughby gave a ragged sigh. "That Korean money. You told me it was untraceable."

"It is. Unless those canceled checks surface. With

your signature on them— Well, you remember what they did to that Senator from California."

"This is blackmail," said Willoughby.

"Only slightly," said Hopper. "It's for your own good, *CLAR*ence. Trust me."

Trembling, Clarence Willoughby said, "I suppose I have to. All right. You can count on me."

They had eaten well, and although Anderson had touched no liquor or wine, in preparation for tomorrow's flight, he had still enjoyed himself in the roughhewn restaurant by the Tidal Basin.

"All right," he said. "I know I'm ten minutes off the range, but you were right. The meal was terrific."

"I liked it too," said Liv Matthews. She was radiant in a soft blue blouse and flared peasant skirt. Not overdressed for the casual restaurant, she still exuded an impression of sophistication.

"Thanks for prying me out of the house," he said. "This was one hell of a lot better than watching TV and eating worms."

She touched his hand. "Tom—is it that bad?"

He nodded. "It's getting there. Frankly, Liv, I'm just about at the end of my string. I've run out of concessions to give."

"I'm sorry," she said, meaning it.

"Not your problem."

"Still—"

He shrugged. "What did I expect? Marty's a fast-moving, vital young woman. I'm an over-the-hill transport pilot with more glory than brains. She guessed wrong, while I kidded myself. Two zeros add up to double zero."

She flared. "I will not permit you to speak that way about yourself! You're a superb pilot—how the hell do you think you got your present assignment?—and you're an important person in the eyes of everyone . . ." She corrected herself: "Well, *almost* everyone who knows you. What's more, you are definitely *not* over the hill!"

"Many thanks," he said, smiling. "It's nice to have an admirer."

"Tom," she said, "I realize you've got aches and pains. All humans do. But don't let her castrate you."

He almost stared at her. This was the first time Liv had ever ventured an opinion on Marty.

"I know," she said. "I don't have any right to criticize your wife. Well, I'm not. I'm laying it on *you*, my friend. You can cope quite well everywhere else. How about trying it in your own house?"

"I'll be damned," he said. "One would almost think you cared."

Unwanted tears misting her eyes, Liv answered, "Oh, you big dummy, I do. I do."

She wanted to say, "Tom, Tom, please tell me what's wrong with you?"

But she was afraid to ask.

The night, in Montana, is very long and cold during the month of March.

Vernon Justus slept, fitfully, in the rear seat of the SuperCub. He had brought a blanket, but it did little to shelter him from the chill mountain air.

The wind had risen, and he made sure that the tarp was fastened down securely on the P-38. Still, he heard it whispering against the loose edges, trying to creep underneath with delicate fingers.

He kept the AM radio on, not caring whether or not he ran down the SuperCub's battery. He would not be using the plane again anyway.

He had always known this day was coming. No dreamer, he had seen his friends die, and even while he mourned them, had known that someday he would join them in the bloody trough of their graves. He was actually surprised that he had lasted so long.

No thanks to those bastards in Washington. They

had written him off long ago. Well, today they would be surprised. To the Air Force, he was a misplaced dinosaur, a remnant from an age which was rather best forgotten.

They would call him mad, crazed. He did not care. He had long since lost the savor for life. Like the dying sailor in *Moby Dick*, as the dismasted ship plunged into the sea, he would snatch a gull from the sky and bear it down to share his own watery grave.

Those who name jealousy as the ultimate passion have never experienced the lust for revenge.

When he took Liv to her car, Anderson kissed her for the first time.

He had opened the door for her and, as she fumbled in her purse for the keys, his arms surrounded her and then they were clinging together and it was as if he were eighteen again and feeling that drifting, almost indescribable sensation of warmth, flesh against flesh, tingling and time-defying ecstasy that he had nearly forgotten.

"This is no good," he said calmly. "I'm forty-eight years old."

"Pooh," said Liv punching her finger into his belly. "You're a terrific guy, and you're up to no good. Unhand me, before I scream."

He backed away. "I'm sorry, Liv," he said. "I didn't mean to—"

"Shut up," she said. "I wanted you to. I've wanted you to for longer than I like to remember. But not now, not with tomorrow's flight on your mind. When we get back. All right, Lone Eagle?"

"All right," he said. Then: "Liv?"

"Yes, dear?"

"Don't call me that any more. I've never liked it."

She laughed. "I won't. Get some sleep, darling. You've got a hard day ahead."

"Drive carefully."

"I will. You too. Night."

He shut her door and, through the closed window, mouthed, "Good night."

So now it was nearly 8 A.M. of Wednesday, and he was already at Andrews. Marty had called an hour earlier, waking him, and saying that she was once again with "friends" in Virginia. "Will you be home tonight?" she asked.

"I'm not sure," he said. "Tomorrow afternoon would be safer. I think the President's got more on his plate than he can handle in one day."

"All right," she said. Then, uncharacteristically, she added, "Be careful."

"I'm always careful," he replied.

He wasn't hungry, but he forced himself to drink some orange juice and eat a slice of toast with his coffee. The fatigue was back again, weighing him down. He took two vitamin plus iron tablets, resisted the urge to use the dwindling supply of steroids. He was not comfortable with his fears about what they might do to his flying performance.

In his mind, he still smelled Liv's subtle perfume. Never one to remember his dreams, he suspected nevertheless that she had been in them.

Still half asleep, he had started his car and, leaving the window open, started for Andrews.

"I've made a decision," said Angela Nemath. "Paul, I'm not going to be your kept woman."

McGowan, driving, almost ran off the road. "Where the hell did that come from?" he demanded.

"I've already told you," she said. "I know there's a duration, set and administered by you, for any of your affairs. Well, in case you're interested, I don't choose to play that game any more."

"Meaning what?" he asked grimly.

"It's simple," she said. "I don't want to break up

your playboy life. But *you* hit on *me*, if you remember.
It was your own decision. So is the next one."

Knowing the answer, he still had to ask the question. "Which is?"

"You have to make a choice. I'm sorry, Paul. I didn't
mean for it to go so far. I was intelligent, deliberate,
and fully aware of what I was getting into. Fun and
games for both of us, no claims, no demands. Except
for one thing I couldn't anticipate. I happened to fall
in love with you."

Flustered, he said, "This is all happening too fast,
hon. I can't come back at you without thinking."

"I'm not asking you to," she said, pressing his arm.
"Let's get the mission out of the way first. But I didn't
want to be dishonest with you. I'm sorry."

Turning into the main gate, he said, "Don't be
sorry. It's not your fault."

"Park in your space," she said. "I'll walk over to the
barracks."

Without answering, he pulled into the HQ lot, and
that was his mistake.

Colonel Tom Anderson had just parked his own
car and was getting out of it as McGowan arrived. He
nodded at McGowan and Angela Nemath and went
into the office building.

"Oh, my God," said Angie.

"Get changed," he said numbly.

"He saw us," she said.

"It can't be helped. Hang loose. It's my problem,
not yours."

"Be careful," she warned.

"Get ready for the flight," he repeated.

Anderson was waiting for him. Anger showed in his
eyes.

"I thought better of you, Paul," he said.

"It's not what you imagine," said McGowan.

"No? Unless I'm mistaken, you have a new girl
friend. Which, morals aside, wouldn't be any of my

business." His voice grated. "Except that she's an enlisted woman in this wing!"

"Her car broke down," said McGowan. "I just gave her a lift."

"Damn it, Paul," said Anderson. "Lying only makes it worse. Airman Nemath lives on base. You don't. Just tell me one thing, for today's mission. Have you been drinking?"

"No," said McGowan angrily.

"What about her?"

"I don't know—" Then, Anderson's accusing eyes on him: "No. She hasn't either."

"All right," said the Aircraft Commander. "We'll hold this over until we get back from Montana."

"You're not being fair—"

"That's all, Major," said Colonel Thomas Anderson.

As the first pink streaks of dawn lit up the sky, Vernon Justus crawled out of the SuperCub and, from the four jerry cans he had brought, began topping off the P-38's tanks with high-octane aviation gasoline.

22

Air Force One had been rolled out of her hangar and waited, in the slanting rays of the morning sun, in front of the Operations Building. She was pristinely clean, her aluminum skin sparkling under the thin coat of wax which had been applied during the night.

Takeoff was more than an hour away. But she had already been awakened and nourished with nearly five hundred gallons of top-grade jet fuel, topping off her tanks.

A power cart, plugged into her through a heavy umbilical cable, supplied electricity for lights, airflow to heat the cabins, and to save the aircraft's own batteries.

TSgt. Ed Miller was already on board, brewing coffee and packing Danish pastries into the refrigerator. He knew, from experience, that they would both be in heavy demand shortly after takeoff. A1C Angela Nemath assisted him. She still felt trembly over the confrontation with Colonel Anderson in the parking lot. The three other flight attendants were moving carefully through the various cabins, making sure no scrap of paper or cigarette butt marred the plane's fresh-from-the-wrapper appearance.

The Aircraft Commander and Navigator Carl Birney were at base Ops, filing the flight plan.

The Operations Officer said, "Colonel, we've had reports that the ozone layer isn't as low as it was. Do you want a higher altitude?"

"Negative," said Anderson. "Not with the President on board."

"You'll arrive without enough fuel to turn around and make Andrews," warned the officer.

"I've got three good alternates," said Anderson. "I'll take the tradeoff."

Shrugging, the Operations Officer said, "You're the pilot."

Major Paul McGowan was already on the flight deck, going over the pre-flight checklist. The encounter with Anderson had flustered him. For the first time in his professional flying career, he had a guilty feeling about his performance. He forced it from his mind. Nothing must interfere with his concentration.

CMSgt. Juan Hernandez was conducting his own pre-flight check. The static tests he made now would be repeated once the jet engines were fired up. He had conducted a complete pre-flight last night; today he would do it again.

TSgt. Lester Dent, happily freed from the antenna hookup of the hangar, worked his way through each of the communications systems. He even turned up the public address system and, in a voice that could be heard for half a mile down the runway, tested, "One, two, three, four . . ."

At his Washington hotel, Seymour Pike had already been awakened early by the front desk.

"Mr. Pike, there's an officer from the White House waiting."

"I'll be right down," said Pike, yawning. He jammed on his clothes, took his suitcase, and went down the elevator to the lobby.

An Air Force Captain greeted him. "Mr. Pike?"

"That's me."

The Captain took the suitcase. "You packed this yourself?"

"Toothbrush and all," said Pike, smiling.

The Captain did not smile back. "Has it been out of your sight since you packed it?"

"Only when I went to sleep."

"Has anyone been in the room?"

"Va va voom," said Pike.

The Captain wasn't having any jokes this morning. "Room service, anyone?"

"No," said Pike.

"Thank you, sir," said the Captain. "Passenger boarding is at exactly 0845."

"I'll be there," said Pike, feeling foolish.

Already in the baggage van, which was guarded by two clear-eyed Air Policemen, who had been driving all over Washington for the past two hours, was the luggage of most of the guests who had been invited on the flight. It would be transported directly to the plane and placed aboard—but not until it had been X-rayed by the security team.

Slowly, moving in trickles which became streams, rivers, and finally floods, people were converging on Andrews Air Force Base, and the plane known as Air Force One.

The White House staff was already hard at work. Arthur Cummings had held a predawn conversation with Advance Man Warren Rogers. If Governor Claude Hoskins had happened to be awake, his ears would have burned.

"He'll be at the airport," said Cummings. "The cocksucker's just making noises."

"Well, he didn't make any in my direction," said Rogers. "He's been hiding out."

"He agreed readily enough when I called him yesterday," said the Chief of Staff. "I think he's getting his jollies making people sweat. And I have no doubt that there's something up his sleeve other than his back-stabbing arm."

"My," said Rogers. "Your tone of voice would cut glass, Great One."

Cummings laughed. "I didn't mean to snarl at you. I get this way before every trip."

"I know the feeling," said Rogers. "Well, *ciao*. It's four A.M. here, and I'm going to pound the pillow for another couple of hours. Nighty night."

Across town, William Guthrie woke up. The lights were on.

"What—?" he mumbled. Then: "Lisa? What are you doing?"

"I'm fixing my face," said his wife.

Guthrie groaned and slipped back into a doze.

Clarence Willoughby, Administrator of the FAA, had not slept at all. A widower who lived alone in a modest apartment near the Watergate, he had spent the night drinking black coffee and reading hundreds of pages of regulations and precedents.

As dawn came, he finished. Pouring another cup of coffee, he wondered if he should wait, or wake Senator Philip Hopper. He decided on the latter.

Hopper was already up. "Yes, Clarence," he said. "What is it?"

"We're on sound ground," said Willoughby. "Our arrangement with the Air Force has been based on courtesy, not statutes."

"Then you can put out the order?"

"Yes, sir."

"Hold it until ten-thirty A.M., Washington time," said the Senator. "By then, we'll be too far along to turn back."

"There will be no public announcement," said the FAA Administrator. "My directive will go on closed wires, and won't be revealed until some actual action is taken."

"Excellent, *CLAR*ence," said the Senator.

The advance plane was almost completely loaded. The twenty-one-foot presidential Lincoln Continental, leased from the Ford Motor Company, had already been driven aboard and tied down securely. With its automatic roof, which raised or lowered by the touch of a button, and retractable foot stands for Secret Service agents, plus layers of armor plate, particularly directly under the President's seat, the Lincoln's actual cost was unknown. It was, however, a matter of public record that the two touring cars owned by the Secret Service had cost $65,000 each.

Scrubbed-face Secret Service men were already on board the plane, reviewing their assignments. By the time Air Force One arrived at Helena, they would have joined the agents on the scene in controlling crowd security, blocking any possible rifle angles, and in the unordered but always observed practice of suppressing banners and signs which were too discourteous to the President.

They had just been joined by a bewildered Bagman.

CWO Fred Stewart, attempting to board Air Force One early, had been stopped by the ramp guard.

Impatiently, he flashed his ID.

"I know who you are, sir," said the guard. "But you aren't on the manifest."

Stewart bit back a harsh reply. The security man was only obeying orders.

"May I see the list?" asked the Bagman.

The guard handed it to him.

In the first group of personnel, Stewart saw his name. But it had been scratched out and replaced by the name of a fifth Secret Service man. The change was initialed: "Approved, A.C."

"Thank you," said Stewart.

The guard, who had been consulting some typed sheets of paper, said, "They've reassigned you to the advance plane, sir. You'd better hurry. They're boarding now."

Stewart thanked him and hurried toward the advance plane.

Sue Earhart, who had been informed that she

would not be allowed to take a camera crew on board
the plane, even before takeoff, briefed her writer-
director. "Get plenty of stuff of me here before the
brass shows up. A Talking Head, with the plane in
the background. I'll give you enough to run on the
midday news. And make goddamned sure you get
some good footage of me boarding. As soon as I'm
out of sight, tilt down and zoom in on that Presidential Seal."

"Right," he said. "We'll get the whole takeoff too."

"End it with a whip pan," she said. "Then you can
get a setup on the parking lot. Cut them together, and
it'll look as if I've just taken off and little Muffin is
watching me."

"Muffin" was her white miniature poodle, waiting
ill-temperedly in Sue's car, with a slightly disgusted
research girl.

Lieutenant Commander George Agee had just finished a comical exchange with Lieutenant (jg) Olivia
Matthews in his tiny White House office.

"You're definitely aboard the plane," he said. "But
Sam Milnes got his way too. The fifth Secret Service
man made the manifest."

"Who got bumped?"

"The Bagman."

"The guy with the football?"

He chuckled. "One and the same. My dear, like it
or not, apparently—in the President's eyes at least—
you're more important than starting a nuclear war."

Out at Andrews, correspondents Scott Meadows, of
the *Times*, and David Braun, of the AP, were sharing
coffee and rolls.

Meadows, his short white hair like a skullcap glistening in the morning sunlight, said, "What do you
think the President is up to?"

"Nothing nice," said Braun. "Judging by those of
us he's invited, he's decided to confront his staunchest
detractors with something to make them change their

minds. It makes me uneasy. I feel as if I'd been invited on a nice Caribbean cruise, but it's really the Bay of Pigs invasion."

Arthur Cummings had, in point of fact, just broached that very matter to the President, who was organizing his papers in the Oval Office, and had been told, quite politely, to mind his own business.

John Williams, clicking off a roll of High Speed color film, chuckled. He did not particularly like Cummings. The feeling was mutual. The Chief of Staff was offended by the fact that someone who looked like a hippie, with a bushy blond Afro and blue jeans that often had frayed cuffs and actual *holes*, should have unlimited and uncontrolled access to the President when he himself had to at least allow Heather Thompson to buzz ahead. This morning, before he had sent the completed manifest out to Andrews, he'd had to wait nearly five minutes before seeing Foster and posing the choice between the Navy nurse and the Bagman. He made no mention of the fact that the fifth Secret Service man could easily have flown on the advance plane.

But Foster chose Lieutenant Matthews, and CWO Fred Stewart was banished to aerial Siberia.

Pushing, Cummings said, "Sir, don't you think that Warrant Officer Stewart should be aboard with you?"

The President had merely shaken his head.

It was not uncommon, despite popular fiction, for the Code Officer, which was the official name for the Bagman, to be separated from the President. So Cummings had no real basis on which to challenge the President's choice. And he had learned long ago never to join battles that he was unsure of winning.

Colonel Thomas Anderson, returning to his office for a few moments of attack on the Everest mountain of paper work, was told that he had a phone call.

Marty said, "Good morning, fly-boy."

"Hello," he said. "You're up early."

"I haven't been to bed," she said. He listened carefully, but, to his trained ear, she seemed sober. "Tom, I've decided not to wait until you get back from Montana."

"Wait for what?"

"Take this as official notification. I've decided to leave you."

He waited a moment, then said, "I see. I'm sorry to hear it."

"Sorry but glad, right? Listen, it's no good, it never has been. I know I've been lousy to you, but that wasn't what I started out intending to do."

"I know it wasn't," he said. "Look, we've got all the time in the world. Let this hang until I get back."

"No, I can't," she said. "For me, my options have run out."

"It's only a day or two," he said.

"No," said his wife, and hung up.

Listening to Marty's conversation with her husband, Wayne Livingston smiled wryly. He waited until she had completed her call and hung up, before saying sardonically, "Well, my pet. What brought that on?"

Surprised, she said, "I thought it's what you wanted me to do."

"Wrong," he told her. "We were discussing honesty and fair play in the abstract. I merely suggested that the kind and honorable course to follow would be to release your poor colonel without inflicting any more misery upon him. I never dreamed you would act on such obviously unrealistic advice."

Her hand reached for the telephone, hesitated. "Wayne, what the hell are you saying? You as much as told me to break it off with Tom. Now you're going back on your promise?"

He lit a long Pall Mall Gold with a platinum lighter from Mark Cross. "You should listen more carefully, my dear. I 'promised,' as you put it, to cherish and adore you, and to—so long as my waning

powers endure—provide you with that physical thrall
you find so necessary. I most carefully never mentioned marriage, long-term 'arrangements,' or even
becoming 'roomies,' as the younger set so charmingly
puts it today. Frankly, Martha, I was shocked to hear
you cut the ties so positively with Colonel Anderson."

"You bastard!" she said. "You no-good son of a
bitch."

He consulted his wristwatch. "Not this early, dear.
Save the foul language for after lunch. We *are* lunch-
ing, I presume."

"After this? In a pig's ass!"

"Please," he said. "I'll have to wash your mouth
with soap."

She tried to draw herself up in haughty disdain, but
since she was completely nude, the gesture was doomed
to fail. The absurdity penetrated her anger, and although she fought it, a smile twitched at the corners
of her lips.

"There," said Wayne, laughing. "It's not all that
bad, when you think it through. You wouldn't have
wanted me around on any permanent basis anyway,
Marty. I'm far too astringent. Never fear. I'll help you
back on your feet again." He punctuated this promise
with a stinging slap across her bare behind. "Since
it's done, you're probably better off without your gallant birdman. You'll do much better now on the party
circuit. New divorcees always do."

"So speaks the voice of experience?" she said, gig-
gling as he drew her down onto the bed.

Joyce Cox answered the airport telephone. A strange
voice asked for Vernon Justus.

"He's not here," she said. She nearly added that she
didn't know where he was.

"Tell him," said the voice, "that everything's moving according to schedule. But what I said goes. No-

body gets hurt, especially the President. Do you have that?"

"Yes," she said. She had jotted it down automatically, without really listening to meanings. Then they dawned on her. "Wait a minute, what do you mean—?"

But she was talking into a dead receiver.

The advance plane took off at exactly 8:15 A.M. on Wednesday, the ninth of March. Its departure was noted by the press crews on hand, and some of them photographed it. Others saved their film and videotape for the main event.

The base had taken on an urgent posture. This morning was the 89th's reason for being. Casual in attitude, cool in performance, nonetheless every man and woman assigned to the mission offered their best performance to the task. They joked, they pretended indifference, they scorned the rubbernecking visitors. But the shadow of the White House loomed over everything. It was a long and all-encompassing shadow, which no one could avoid.

The air crackled with radio messages. Incoming flights were warned to be on the ground prior to 8:31, or they would be diverted. Some, realizing they could not make the deadline, opted to orbit the Andrews area or to land elsewhere. Others streaked toward the runway.

At 8:30 A.M., the Andrews AFB strips were shut down. Air Force One would be using runway 19. Although the advance plane had taken off from the same runway minutes before, a security car now drove slowly down its 9,300-foot length, two men examining every inch for debris, potholes, dead birds—anything that might endanger the President's plane.

While most runways, those on military bases and at commercial airports, were swept regularly, it was surprising what was often found during a security check.

The oddest discovery had been spotted early one morning at MacDill AFB in Florida. Absolutely dead, blocking one quarter of a runway, lay a kangaroo. None had been reported missing, none ever was. But there it lay, all two hundred pounds of odorous mammal, thousands of miles from its Queensland home. Beer cans, bottles, pieces of metal which had fallen, unnoticed, from airplanes—these were common. But kangaroos?

Inside the Operations Building, passengers were being rounded up. The crew had already boarded and were going about their duties. Coffeepots were bubbling, fresh orange juice had already been poured into small glasses with their blue Presidential Seals. The President's compartment had been triple-checked. Scattered through the cabins was the daily shipment of fifteen magazines, five morning papers, and enough comfortable pillows to stock a sorority house party.

At a signal, twenty minutes before the hour, the press and other passengers began boarding.

Each signed his name at the ramp guard's desk. Each had his credentials examined carefully.

Each, unknown to himself, was photographed by an automatic camera.

Most were surprised to be met by a beautiful young woman in the Air Force blues of a WAF. This was almost like flying commercially.

The Flight Stewards wore maroon blazers with blue trousers, and light blue shirts, bow-tied. Each had the presidential emblem on his jacket. It was worn by everyone serving aboard the plane, and after a year of service was awarded for life.

A blazer had been ordered for Angie, but since it wasn't ready, she wore regulation Class A uniform. Her presidential emblem was stitched over her right breast, and made her appear to be lop-sided.

The Stewards had just finished mounting the two Presidential Seals which always heralded the arrival of the Chief Executive. One was attached to the interior of the plane's door. The other hung on the wall over the President's desk in the office section of his compartment.

No matter how cynical, how disapproving, a visitor to the plane might be, he tended to speak in hushed tones once aboard. The decor, with its blue-and-gold trim, radiated confidence and authority.

A previous pilot had expressed it well: "When I'm up there in that left seat," he said, "I'm not flying Nixon, or Ford, or Carter. I'm flying the *President*. I don't care what his name is, or which party he belongs to. Whoever he is, he's my Commander in Chief, and I put out one hundred per cent no matter which way I voted. We don't live in the last century; our President has to be mobile and in constant communication with the world. Air Force One can keep him that way. Whatever it costs, the mission is worth it."

It was a hard position to argue with, one held almost universally by the personnel of the 89th. Their loyalty was to the office, not the man.

Senator Philip Hopper, boarding, felt the same chill that came to almost everyone. He knew his purpose for this trip, he was firm in his ideals, he had no intention of changing his views . . . yet his own voice lowered as he thanked the Flight Steward who showed him to his seat in the middle compartment.

He found himself questioning the instinct that had led him to make this morning's telephone call.

While the obvious and public function of executive helicopters seems to be, primarily, to chauffeur the President to and from Air Force One, the command pilots of Army One and Marine One know quite differently.

In fact, providing fast hops from the choked Washington, D.C., perimeter to Andrews was only a secondary mission for the go-anywhere, anytime, choppers.

Although new Sikorsky helicopters were already available, with more range, capacity, and comfort, President Howard Foster had vetoed their purchase for White House use. So, this Wednesday morning, Marine One, chosen by lot for the flight to Andrews, was still a VH-3 aircraft, in use since the Nixon years.

While basically the helicopter familiar to combat veterans, the difference in flight was so great that the Sikorskys might have been completely different aircraft. Thick insulation and special muffling equipment made the flight many times more quiet. Even at speeds, pushed over the red line, of 170 miles an hour, the interior of the VH-3s was quieter than the passenger compartment of a Boeing 727—which is, itself, a very quiet machine.

Heavily padded walls, lounge chairs, and full air conditioning gave the Sikorsky choppers an aura of comfort and plush luxury.

But beneath the frills, a tough, combat-ready aircraft was ready to absorb abuse and stress. Unlike most choppers, the presidential craft were equipped with a flotation hull which could float for days in case of a ditching.

Their great speed, lessening undue exposure of the President to hostile outsiders, and without using too much of his valuable time, made the helicopters an ideal method of conveying him over relatively short distances. Yet, as the command pilot knew, this convenience was merely a by-product.

The first, and cardinal, mission of the helicopter fleet was to keep the government of the United States alive in case of an enemy attack on Washington, or if some natural catastrophe should occur.

Often not even known to wives—or husbands—of key government figures, everyone working in crucial departments had a code number. Those assigned the

number One or Two were to be the survivors. Without option of calling their families, or of refusing
evacuation, they were to be rounded up by special
security teams, placed aboard the choppers, and air-
lifted to safety, while their co-workers and families
were abandoned. Survival of the government was
paramount, to the exclusion of all other considera-
tions.

Meanwhile, since catastrophic occurrences happen
only rarely, the chopper fleet kept busy by airlifting
White House VIPs and visiting firemen around the
Washington area.

This morning's assignment, winging the President
and his staff to Andrews, was a routine chore. Still, it
was prepared for as carefully as if it were really as
important as it seemed.

The Marine honor guard was in full, flamboyant
dress. The pre-flight of the machine had been excru-
ciating, with those calibrated eyeballs measuring every
millimeter.

The flight plan was as usual—swooping up from
the South Lawn, heading directly for Andrews AFB
and the chopper's painted target just beyond the
89th's Operations Building. Total time, less than
twelve minutes.

Each of the specially converted choppers, which cost
more than two million dollars apiece, were called on
only once or twice a week to serve the White House's
needs. Often, their only flight time was logged between the White House and Camp David.

It was unusual for the President to use local machines. Under normal conditions, two of the Washington choppers would have left Monday morning
and flown all the way to Helena to be ready for the
President's arrival. There had been some grumbling
among the crew when it was learned that a helicopter
from Malstrom would be used.

On foreign trips, for example, two helicopters were

always dismantled and shipped ahead in a C-133 cargo plane to await the arrival of the President and his staff. The huge expense was accepted in the name of safety.

Each helicopter, with its unique white roof and a fuselage that combined the two rival service greens— Marine and Army—carried a special emergency book listing nearby hospitals in case there should be a medical emergency in flight.

A "chase" chopper always followed the President's craft, in case it went down because of malfunction or hostile action. Equipped with a winch, it could hoist the President up in a matter of seconds.

This morning, the job of the presidential helicopter was to wait on the South Lawn, with the clock's second hand ticking away, while the President did not appear for an on-time boarding.

On board Air Force One, Liv Matthews saw Colonel Tom Anderson for the first time that morning.

"Good morning," she said, signaling him with her eyes. "Are we going to have a good flight?"

He answered, "Everything looks clear and calm."

She ached to kiss him. He felt the electricity between them, and said, "Excuse me, I've got to get up on the flight deck," and left.

Vernon Justus, his bones aching from the cold, crawled out of the SuperCub's cockpit and scowled at the gray dawn. He felt the sting of moisture on his cheeks.

"No snow, damn it," he growled. "Clear up. We want a nice day for the President. Plenty of sun."

The wind mocked him with more sleet.

Justus went over to the P-38, stripped back part of the plastic tarp. Her metal skin was dripping wet and numbingly cold against his palm.

"You fire up good," he told the fighter. "No vapor

lock, no water in your carbs. You pay attention to me."

Distantly, he heard the thunder of a jet breaking the sound barrier.

23

With less than ten minutes until the President's arrival time, Air Force One's commander completed his final walk-around.

He had started on the flight deck and worked his way back, examining every foot of the plane's interior, nodding and speaking quietly to crew members and passengers.

Outwardly, the flight deck, which held seating for five crewmen and an extra observer's seat for the President, or other VIPs, was similar to that of any intercontinental 707. But a closer examination would have revealed the extra communications equipment, the code machines, and the slow-scan TV system. A pilot would have noticed extra instruments, additional controls—for the modified wing, the extra fuel tank switchover, and particularly the caged red switch labeled "capsule." It had been added only months before, after Anderson had Boeing install a new system which was, until now, a tightly held secret.

Colonel Thomas Anderson had always been disturbed it was taken as gospel that the President would be safer remaining aboard the plane in an emergency. True, it is almost impossible to bail out of a stricken jetliner. But, during any crash, there would usually be a period of time—a minute, perhaps only a few seconds—when the Aircraft Commander, realizing that there was no hope for the plane, might still have time to eject the one passenger whose survival was essential.

So Anderson rode roughshod over the "business as usual" detractors and scrounged the necessary funds for his personally designed survival system for the President. "Guys walk away from fighter crashes every day," he argued. "So can the President, if it ever comes to that."

He would inspect the capsule when he reached the President's compartment. Meanwhile, he left the flight deck and stood in the small compartment which opened, through the forward hatch, to the boarding ramp. The Presidential Seal had already been affixed to the door. He poked his head into the two airline-type toilets. They were sparkling clean, and stocked with towels, soap, and (he noted wryly) female necessities. Beyond the johns was the forward galley, which would serve the President and his guests.

"How's it going?" he asked TSgt. Ed Miller, the ranking Steward.

"Fine, sir," said Miller. He nodded toward the young woman who was helping him stack trays of pastries and coffee. "It's nice to have a woman around the house."

"Airman Nemath," said Anderson. "Your first flight, isn't it?" His eyes held no reminder of their meeting in the parking lot.

"Yes, sir," she said. "I've been looking forward to it." Until now, she had served only at on-ground luncheons for visiting dignitaries, congressional cocktail hours, and VIP meetings.

"Glad to have you aboard," he said.

To Angie, it sounded as if he meant it.

Anderson stepped into the next compartment, which held ten seats, now filled by the five Secret Service men, four Air Force security guards, and Lieutenant (jg) Olivia Matthews.

The walls were ivory, and a blue-green rug covered the floor. The dark blue seats were similar to those in first-class sections of any well-run commercial airline.

"Good morning," said Anderson. The Secret Service men nodded; the Air Force men chorused, "Good morning, Colonel."

Liv Matthews smiled. Anderson said, "Welcome aboard, Lieutenant Matthews. Glad you could make it."

One of the Secret Service men squirmed slightly. He knew how close his own presence had come to bumping the Navy nurse onto the advance plane.

She answered, "Thank you, Colonel." The words were spoken calmly, but it was as if they were a private confidence between them.

Anderson passed down the corridor between the port hull and the President's thirty-five-foot-long compartment.

He let himself into the office. Ten feet long, it held a blue sofa along the wall of the plane which faced the President's kidney-shaped desk. It was cleared, except for a white telephone contained in a special housing with nearly thirty buttons. By pressing the right one, the President would be in instant communication with any number, anywhere else in the world.

The pecan-paneled walls facing the main visitor's compartment could be raised at the touch of another button, opening the President's office to the larger area.

Passing the private bathroom, Anderson glanced in. Everything was in order—scrubbed, supplied, scented.

The forward part of the compartment held the President's bedroom, with two single beds, two easy chairs, a table, a lamp, and another telephone. The light gray rug contrasted with the deep blue blankets, each with its woven Presidential Seal.

Anderson opened what seemed to be a closet and stepped inside. A light had gone on automatically when he opened the door.

He sat in a small blue contour chair. His weight activated a switch, and shatterproof plastic panels sprang from the walls and floor, surrounding him. A red button blinked at him from one of the chair arms, which had curved around him automatically like the safety bars in a roller coaster.

He was in the secret "capsule," which had been added to Air Force One, following his own design and instructions.

The capsule was now armed and ready for ejection. Were he to press that red button, the capsule—and its occupant—would be fired upward for several hundred feet—high enough for its self-contained parachutes to open even if the ejection took place at ground level. It would be a rough ride, but a survivable one. Hundreds of fighter pilots owed their lives to similar ejection units. It was only necessary that Air Force One be in a non-inverted position for successful separation of the ejection pod.

The unit had never been tested, except electronically—which indicated that all components were functioning. Its ejection might very well break the back of the 153-foot-long jet. But since it was intended for use only *in extremis*, that was a secondary consideration.

"Flight deck," he said in a normal tone of voice.

The Pilot answered. "McGowan."

"Checking capsule."

McGowan said, "I read capsule armed and ready to eject."

"Roger. Exiting capsule."

He pressed a green button which, situated on the rear curve of one chair arm, could only be reached with difficulty. It would be impossible to press it accidentally.

The restraining arms swung back, the red button blinked off, and the plastic panels retreated into their slots.

Standing in the President's bedroom, Anderson thought dourly that, if the moment ever came, the

President might well refuse to leave the plane and abandon his crew and passengers. He knew that he himself would never bail out while others were still aboard. That was the reason for the second "Eject" button on the Aircraft Commander's instrument panel. If the President hesitated to eject, Anderson could do it for him.

He made his way back to the main cabin, which held thirty-two seats for White House staff and visitors. Two of the front seats faced electric typewriters, which were used by White House secretaries. A Xerox machine on the right side of the plane could be removed to make space for two more seats.

The seats here were larger and more complex than those up forward or back in the press compartment. Placed in pairs, one facing forward, one to the rear, separated by a table, the chairs moved on tracks. A knob on the right side marked "T" allowed them to be positioned at any desired distance from the table. Another knob, marked "R," let the chair be reclined.

The ashtrays, with their "Air Force One" logo and the Presidential Seal, each held a book of Air Force One matches—which would vanish, unlit, into the pockets of Senators or visiting heads of state.

The compartment was, as Anderson had fully expected, neat and ready for takeoff. Already fully boarded, its passengers were sipping orange juice or coffee and munching pastries.

He opened the door to the press compartment after knocking and hearing a shouted "Come in."

Located in the rear of the plane, where noise and turbulence were the worst, it was still a prized accommodation. Most reporters traveled ahead on the advance plane—for two reasons. First, there simply wasn't enough room aboard the President's aircraft. Second, they had to be on the ground waiting when Air Force One arrived, otherwise they would not be able to get photos or videotapes of the landing and debarkation of the Chief Executive.

The reporters aboard would be denied actual landing coverage, although they could scramble from the rear hatch and be on hand when the President made his own exit from the plane. But this was more than made up for by the fact that they had actually flown with him, and if they were lucky, might have even shared an in-flight drink or cup of coffee. Whether or not they were allowed to come forward was at the whim of the President. Some, like Johnson, enjoyed their presence and played genial host. Others, such as Nixon, insisted on privacy and rarely appeared within the reporters' field of view. President Foster split the extremes. When working, he remained out of sight. At other times, he was friendly and available.

Sue Earhart, pointing at her watch, said, "It's five of nine, Colonel. Is everything on schedule?"

"As far as I know, ma'am," he said. "We had a communication from the White House that the President was boarding Marine One. He should be here any minute."

Seymour Pike asked, "What time do we get into Helena?"

"Nine thirty-four their time," said Anderson.

The AP man, David Braun, grinned. "Plus or minus fifteen seconds?"

Anderson laughed. "Do you guys still play that game?"

"Sure," said Braun. "You invented it, remember?"

"Well, if you lose your shirt, don't blame me," said the Colonel. He nodded toward the other reporters and said, "Once we're airborne, any of you who want to come up to the flight deck, buzz me. We can give you the grand tour one at a time." He indicated the President's photographer. "Mr. Williams knows the ropes."

"I know one thing," said John Williams. "I'm not

sucker enough to put my money in any arrival pool, unless I'm inside that fifteen-second line."

"What are you people talking about?" asked Sue Earhart.

Braun and Williams turned to her with glee. As Anderson left, he heard the AP reporter suggesting that ". . . we just make a little bet on how close the Colonel can hit his estimated time of arrival . . ."

Anderson smiled. There's one born every minute.

He arrived on the flight deck just as the President's helicopter touched down two hundred feet away.

He slipped into his seat and nodded at McGowan. "Here he comes."

Engines Three and Four, on the starboard side of the plane, were already running, generating power and heated air conditioning.

Into a microphone which connected to an Air Force ground crewman beneath the plane, McGowan asked, "Clear to start One and Two?"

The ground man looked around. Nobody was within range of the hot exhaust from the rear of the turbojets, or close enough to be sucked into the whirling turbines from the front.

"Clear on One and Two," he said.

Major Paul McGowan leaned forward and, with a feeling that approached joy, made preparations to bring Air Force One to complete and vibrating life.

After making two telephone calls, one to the Great Falls police and another to the regional office of the Federal Bureau of Investigation, Joyce Cox knew that only a personal appearance by her would generate any action. Nobody was even slightly interested that Vernon Justus had vanished with two airplanes, one of which was an operational fighting machine. They listened politely, told her they were writing down the information, that they would "look into it." She knew what that meant.

If she had access to another plane, she would have flown down to the dirt strip herself. But the two small planes which were stored in the hangar belonged to out-of-town salesmen, and Vernon had locked their ignition keys in his desk.

She bundled up against the wind and began the drive into Great Falls.

Advance Man Warren Rogers grumbled at his coffee. The night had been too short and had passed too fast. His eyelids felt like sandpaper. His tongue was apparently coated with long, mud-soaked fur. His limbs ached. His voice was hoarse from too many cigarettes and phone conversations.

The hotel operator was taking forever to put through his calls. Sam Milnes had commandeered his private line, and was shifting his Secret Service men around like chessmen on a board.

His first call that morning had been from the Governor's office, berating him for this "surprise" visit by the President. If it had been the Governor himself on the phone, Rogers would have heated up the phone lines. But since it was only an aide passing the message that the Governor would be at the airport to greet the President, the Advance Man held his temper.

Secret Service agent Sam Milnes had set up a conference call with more than twenty agents scattered across most of the United States. A chain of checkpoints had been deployed along Air Force One's route. The agents, with souped-up cars at the ready, had their radio ears tuned to a special frequency on which the exact location of the plane was constantly given. If Air Force One failed to reach its next checkpoint, the Secret Service men, siren screaming and radiophone alerting all local rescue units, would speed off in search of the missing aircraft.

A special transponder mounted aboard the plane alerted FAA Ground Controllers when the jet was on

AIR FORCE ONE   283

their scopes. Its rate of blink and the special AF1 symbol differentiated it from other aerial traffic. If the symbol vanished from a radar screen without having been passed on to another control area, an immediate emergency would be called.

Early in presidential flight, escort fighters called "Quail" used to accompany the executive plane. But now, because of its speed and height, Air Force One was considered relatively immune to attack. Only a few special situations had called for the use of defensive planes.

One had been on a trip to Florida by President Johnson. It occurred on February 27, 1964. The President, booked for a routine Democratic fund-raising dinner, was advised that intelligence reports indicated there might be an attack by a Cuban pilot. Although high officials doubted that Fidel Castro would authorize such an attack, it was always possible that it might be tried by an unauthorized military group. Johnson flatly refused to cancel the dinner, so unusual precautions were taken—including grounding 26000. Instead, the President and his party were transported aboard another VC-137C, with no markings. Unannounced stops were made, including a visit to Joseph P. Kennedy in Palm Beach instead of the scheduled landing at Miami. The presidential plane then proceeded to Homestead Air Force Base, outside the Florida city, and Johnson's party were helicoptered to Miami Beach with Air Force fighters "Quail" overhead.

The temporary Air Force One remained at Homestead overnight, under heavy guard. President Johnson returned to her for a secret dawn takeoff back to Andrews.

For the duration of his trip, three other identical planes, with their numbers painted out, were in the air over southern Florida to confuse possible attackers.

No fighters or confusion techniques had been considered for this morning's flight to Helena, Montana.

There was no reason to suspect that the mission would be anything other than routine.

Joyce Cox had not created even a ripple in the horizon-to-horizon security screen when she reported her missing boy friend and his fighter plane.

Nor did anyone connect the disappearance of an antique P-38 with the abnormally low altitude Air Force One would be cruising at today. With the VC-137C at 28,000 feet, the Lightning would have the advantage of several thousand feet of altitude—a favorite tactic of her World War II pilots.

When Sam Milnes checked in with Chief of Staff Arthur Cummings, a few minutes before the President was due to leave the White House, he reported simply that everything was in order, that there had been no incidents or even the usual threatening phone calls. "Everything's cool," he said.

He needed a new thermometer.

Air Force One strained at her leash. She was ready. Her wing span, stretching 145 feet and 9 inches, quivered under the thrust of her four Pratt & Whitney turbojet engines. They could generate enough power, gulping down 1,600 pounds of jet fuel an hour, to lift a payload of almost 167 tons.

Andrews runways and approaches had been closed since 8:30 A.M., and would remain closed until fifteen minutes after she had lifted off.

She was already six minutes late. This did not disturb her Commander, who knew he could make it up easily en route.

The escort vehicles were ready. One would drive in front of the plane while it was taxiing. Two fire trucks and an ambulance would follow, actually chasing the jet down the runway during its takeoff. More than once, safety-glass windshields had been pitted by the flaming blast of the plane's four engines.

But now Marine One had arrived, and the White

House staff were debarking and boarding, as the crew prepared to start engines One and Two.

The only agent in the Great Falls office of the Federal Bureau of Investigation was young and friendly. He was also quite inexperienced. The other agents had all been siphoned away to cope with the President's arrival at Helena.

He had served Joyce Cox coffee, listened to her confused story, and now asked her to repeat parts of it.

"You say that someone called you and said that everything was going according to plan, but that nobody would be hurt, particularly the President?"

"Yes," said the young woman uneasily.

"The President of what?" asked the agent.

"I don't know. Maybe—"

He smiled. "Maybe the President of the United States?"

"Well, he's coming to Helena today and—"

"And naturally you want to protect him."

"Well, of course!"

"Against your friend, Mr. Justus?"

"If that's what he has in mind, yes."

"But didn't you just tell me that he was hiding out from bill collectors?"

"That's what he said. But that was before I got the call."

"Didn't he, at one time, make threats against the officers of his bank?"

"I told you he did."

"Well," said the young FBI man, "one of those officers is the bank president, isn't that right?"

She chewed her lip. "I guess so."

He spread his hands. "Believe me, Miss Cox, I appreciate your concern. Whenever the President appears anywhere, people see shadows behind every tree. It's only natural, and not to be ashamed of. We'd rather you come to us with something that isn't real than to conceal something that is, for fear of being embarrassed. You're to be commended for the trouble you've taken."

"I guess you're right," she said. "I listen to myself talking, and even to me it doesn't seem possible. I mean, Vernon's just somebody trying to make a living flying."

"I'm talking with our field supervisor in an hour or so," he assured her. "To ease your mind, I'll mention this to him." He glanced at his notes. "I have your phone number. If I need more information, I'll call."

"Thanks," she said. "I bet he's back there waiting for me now. He must have got caught in the dark, and put down in some farmer's field."

He followed her to the door. "Drive carefully, Miss Cox. It looks like snow out there."

"I will," she said. "Bye."

He waved, and went back to his desk. Yawning, he put his notes to one side and began going through the early mail.

It looked like it was going to be a long day.

The main hatch slammed shut.

"He's on board," said Anderson. At the same time, he and McGowan looked at the digital clock set between them, so it would not be confused with flight instruments.

It was nine-eleven, Eastern Daylight Saving Time.

"Start Two," he said.

"Starting Two," repeated McGowan.

The inboard engine rumbled and caught. The RPM needles wavered, steadied.

"Two is steady," said McGowan.

"Start One."

"Starting One."

McGowan repeated the ritual, saying the necessary words, although both pilots were now communicating with that sixth sense men on the flight deck acquire early in their flying careers.

An intercom bell sounded. Anderson pressed a button. "Yes?"

Angie Nemath's voice said, "Sir, the President is in his cabin and secure."

"Thank you," he replied. To McGowan: "Let's move it."

"Taxiing power," said the Pilot.

Air Force One shuddered under the increased energy, and then began to move slowly, at eight miles an hour, toward the runway.

Her commander said quietly, "Prepare for takeoff."

A I R   F O R C E   O N E
BOX 1776
ANDREWS AFB, WASHINGTON, D.C. 20331

TO: All Passengers

FROM: Aircraft Commander

Welcome aboard.

For those experiencing their first flight, traveling aboard the Presidential Aircraft is very similar to commercial flights. Food and beverages are available from the Flight Stewards, as are magazines and books.

Two portable typewriters are available for use by members of the Press. Simply request them from a Steward. Communications with ground telephone lines are also available on an availability basis. However, their use is conditional on land line charges being charged to your own or to your employer's number.

Smoking is permitted in all areas of the aircraft except when the No Smoking light is lit.

Please ask for anything you need, and enjoy your flight.

THOMAS ANDERSON, Colonel, USAF
Aircraft Commander

She was alive now. The juices pulsed through her—oil and jet fuel and hydraulic fluids. Her muscles gathered strength—four turbofans vibrated with enough power to move an ocean liner. Her eyes and ears were alert—their radar scanning the area, their radio capturing the racing electrons from the airwaves, their altimeters and barometric pressure gauges searching the sky and terrain.

In the rear compartment, where a martyred President's body had been flown from Love Field in Dallas to this very Air Force Base, four reporters and a photographer tightened their seat belts. They waited for takeoff where history had once bled, and were unawares.

The main compartment held its passengers in comfort, tinkling glasses of orange juice making an oriental musicale as obbligato to the whine of the engines. Every seat, every table, had its share of memories. Here, the first version of the SALT treaty had been discussed. Over here, while flying around the world, President Johnson had won $93.40 playing blackjack with Liz Carpenter. Back here, en route to China, President Nixon dictated confidential memos to be sent to John Mitchell. And here, Gerald Ford once spilled an entire glass of milk down the neck of Pierre Trudeau.

In the President's compartment, how many secrets had been whispered? How many hot-line telephone calls had gone out over the scrambled circuits, nudging the world closer to, or further away from, nuclear war? How many Presidents had, unseen, belted down a quick drink to calm trembling nerves, to soothe twitching stomachs? How many moments of quickly snatched passion had these two beds encompassed? How many hours of sweat-drenched, nightmarish sleep?

In the forward compartment, where the Secret Service, security men, and Nurse Lt. (jg) Olivia Matthews sat, secretaries had once worked. Fully grown men, returning from that fateful November day in Dallas, had wept.

And, on the flight deck, where Colonel Thomas Anderson's hand reached for the levers that would move this giant, complex creature of aluminum and steel and wires and transistors, fully a dozen of the world's best pilots had spent their working hours holding, with tender fingers, the leashes of a spirited, graceful thoroughbred.

Air Force One moved slowly toward the runway.

PART THREE

Flight Path

———————

24

"Let's go," said Anderson.

He advanced the throttle levers. Jet fuel raced through the lines and, in the combustion chambers, ignited. The howl of the turbojets deepened. Air Force One seemed to surround the noise, sucking it deep into her body for strength.

"Injection," said the Aircraft Commander.

"Water injection," repeated Paul McGowan. He threw the proper switches and distilled water flooded into the engines, where, mixed with compressed air, it expanded. The superheated steam whirled the turbojets' compressor blades faster. The sound was now the scream of some primal beast.

"Ten thousand RPM," reported the Pilot.

"Let's taxi," said Anderson.

"Roger."

McGowan pulled back on his control yoke. Anderson released his own and took charge of the control which would steer the jet's nose wheels. Until Air Force One had reached nearly a hundred knots, her control surfaces would not be effective. Anderson would aim her down the runway and steer her exactly as a driver does a car.

"Rolling nicely," he said.

The chase ambulance and the fire truck were dropping behind, he saw from the corner of one eye.

The voices of the men were lifted above the scream

of the jets. "I have one hundred knots," said Mc-
Gowan.

"Roger," said Anderson. He took the control yoke
in both hands. "I have control," he said.

"Thirty seconds," reported McGowan. "One-twenty
knots."

Air Force One had eaten up three quarters of a
mile of runway 19. She was watched by thousands of
eyes. When the President's jet took off, even jaded
professionals interrupted their work for a moment
to help wish her into the sky.

"V-One," said McGowan. This was the point at
which Anderson must decide to commit to take off,
or to kill power and start tapping on the brakes. From
now on, if he changed his mind, there would not be
enough runway to stop.

"V-One," repeated Anderson. This meant that he
planned to continue the takeoff run.

The plane seemed to lighten, to skate over the
harsh surface of the runway. She was eager to rejoin
her natural element.

"One-fifty," said McGowan.

She wanted to fly. But Anderson held her down.
Her escape from the surly bonds of earth would be
that much easier when he released her from his grip.

They had flying speed now, and then some. Mc-
Gowan said, "Rotate."

"Rotating," repeated Anderson. Slightly—almost
imperceptibly—he drew back on the control yoke.
Air Force One's nose rose gently, nibbling at the sky.

With this increased angle of attack, she found the
once-resisting air now shouldering under her wings
and lifting her with unmeasured power. She surged
forward, and her main wheels lifted off. The runway's friction gone, her speed increased, and the
ground fell away from her.

Non-pilots always hissed in their breath when, as
he climbed out only yards above the runway, a jet

pilot retracted his landing gear. They did not realize that the gear was useless in the event of a power loss, that the plane was better off with the extra lift which came as a gift because of reduced drag. The brutal truth was that without enough runway remaining to land on, wheels were more of a hazard than a help.

"Two hundred knots," said McGowan.

"Up flaps," said Anderson.

"Flaps up," repeated McGowan.

"Air Force One requesting 28,000 feet, proceeding to Mill Grove Intersection," said Anderson. "DV departing Andrews area."

"Roger, Air Force One," said the ATC Controller. "You are cleared to continue on your present heading and level off at 28,000 feet. I will hand you off to Cincinnati Control in eleven minutes."

"Thank you," said Anderson. "Air Force One out."

The Controller would have known merely from the designation of "Air Force One" that the President was aboard. But Anderson's reminder of a DV—Distinguished Visitor—insured prompt clearance and extra care in monitoring the flight.

"Climbing through six thousand," said McGowan. "Smoking light?"

"Kill it," said Anderson. He would leave the seat-belt warning on until they had passed through 15,000. Above that, turbulence should not be a problem. Meanwhile, the Stewards could start moving about.

A red light blinked on TSgt. Lester Dent's central communicator panel.

He tapped a button. Into his headset microphone, he said, "Yes, Mr. President?" Paused. "Right away, sir."

He punched up a code series, pressed a large square indicator that read: SCRAMBLE. Then he signaled the President with three beeps on the intercom buzzer, since he was now blocked out—as was everyone in the world except the one being called—by the President's scrambling device.

McGowan noticed from the corner of his eye, and smiled. "He's starting work early," he commented.

"Not as early as the place he's calling," said the Radio Operator. "It's around two A.M. there."

The Commanding Officer of the nuclear submarine *Urchin* held the Hushphone receiver close to his ear. It was plugged directly into the scrambler block of his private communications panel.

"Yes, Mr. President," he said. "I understand completely. I will activate in precisely one hundred and thirty-five minutes. I will then submerge and proceed with my scheduled mission."

He paused, listening.

"No, sir," he replied. "The missile carries no warhead. It will self-destruct well outside the final red line of intrusion. There are both timing and inertial guidance circuits to insure this. In the event both should fail, your defensive radar bursts will detune the homing devices, and the missile will impact into the sea before it can intrude into critical air space."

Another pause.

"No, Mr. President. In such cases we never advise NORAD or SAC in advance. The effectiveness of such action depends on surprise."

He waited.

"Thank you, Mr. President. *Urchin* out."

"Twenty-eight thousand right on the dime," said Paul McGowan. "Our airspeed's lousy down here, though. Only 480."

"We're fat," said Anderson. "We ought to have more than 31,000 pounds on final."

By this, he meant that they would have that much reserve fuel over Helena Municipal Airport. Enough to meander up and down the entire western third of the nation, if necessary.

Air Force One, at normal altitude, burned around 1,600 pounds of jet fuel an hour. With the increased drag, and lesser efficiency of the jet engines at this lower height, consumption was increased by almost 10 per cent.

Suddenly, and switching off his intercom mike so only Anderson could hear him, McGowan said, "I don't feel right about this flight."

Anderson switched off his own intercom. The other men on the flight deck noted the action, but accepted the desired privacy as the pilots' right.

"Say again," Anderson suggested.

"I can't put my finger on it. Here's you and me, going right to the line. I braced you about performance, and I won't be surprised if you lower the boom about Angie."

Anderson's lips went taut at the young woman's name. "You'd better believe it," he said. "We don't play that kind of game on board this plane. You've just bought that girl a transfer. And maybe one for yourself."

"Fine," said McGowan. "And while you're at it, how about one for you and that nurse of yours?"

"Keep your voice down," said Anderson. "As for Lieutenant Matthews, that situation's a bit different. I didn't arrange for her to be transferred to this mission. Nor is there anything going on between us." He hurried to add, "Not that I'm accusing you and Airman Nemath of anything either. I'm only concerned with the propriety of an officer of this command openly fraternizing with an airman—of the opposite sex—whom he personally had helped to be assigned."

McGowan did not answer. Yes, he remembered, it *had* been he who suggested that Anderson appoint a woman to the crew.

"All right," he said finally. "Let's table both of these issues. They're really personal. But what about this weird passenger list we've got? Four media people who out and out hate the President, yet he actually invited them aboard. Senator Philip Hopper, who's been trying to scuttle Air Force One ever since he got the presidential itch. We're heading into enemy territory, landing at the capital of a state whose Governor doesn't want us within a million miles. We're flying thousands of feet low because of an inverted ozone layer. Tom, there's just too damned many little things piling up. And you know what that can mean."

Anderson knew very well. It was axiomatic among fliers that small mistakes pyramided until they broke your wings and threw you down from the sky.

Cautiously, he said, "I think you're overreacting, Paul. But you're right—maybe we both made too much out of those personal matters. Let's just stay sharp and make the best of this flight. We'll sort the rest out later."

"Those are the operable words," agreed McGowan. "Staying sharp."

Anderson nodded, and both men switched on their command intercoms again.

In the Situation Room—the heart of the White House—an officer said, "The President's entering the Central Time Zone."

A sergeant nodded and adjusted the hands of a special clock, which showed the exact time wherever the President happened to be.

It was the linkage between this room and Air Force One which one presidential aide called "war risk insurance." Without a "Go" signal from the President, the nation was virtually defenseless. Only the Chief Executive has the authority to respond to a fast-moving threat. It is his finger which must punch up the orders—to launch a nuclear retaliation to sneak attack. The United States, already at a disadvantage because of an often-stated policy of never mounting a first strike, had only precious minutes to scramble the giant B-52 bombers, to launch the missiles from their silos and underwater nuclear submarines.

Three of the eight communications aboard Air Force One connected with the Situation Room.

Aboard the plane, Arthur Cummings had just demonstrated one of these direct links to Senator Philip Hopper, who merely shrugged. At his side, Sue Earhart, who had just spoken with a friend at Number 10 Downing Street in London by merely pressing a button, was more impressed. Communications were her business, and she recognized first-class equipment and service when she saw it.

Cummings indicated the phone she had just used and said, "Some of the boys still call this link the Mac-Jack Line."

"That's a strange name."

"It was first installed for Jack Kennedy, to talk with Prime Minister Macmillan. Some things hang on. Officially, it's the 10 Downing Street direct linkage."

She smiled. "Mac-Jack's more colorful."

He touched another button. "And speaking of colors, this automatically triggers the Hot Line between the President and Moscow."

"I thought that was only in doomsday movies," she said.

"Direct phone conversations may be," said Cummings. "In this case, whatever the President says is translated by an interpreter in the Situation Room, who puts it on a special teletype wire connecting with the Soviets. Not as fast as voice communication, but more reliable and less open to mutual error."

The Senator looked around the President's small

office. "I thought it would be bigger," he said. "Where *is* the President?"

Cummings nodded toward the bedroom. Its door was closed. "He's relaxing for an hour or so. He never got to bed last night. Perhaps we'll be able to join him later. He left a call for ten-thirty Washington time." He glanced at his watch. "That's forty-five minutes from now."

"Surely," said Hopper, "no one person, not even the President, needs *all* this redundancy in communications. What's wrong with one direct line to the White House?"

"And if that line failed, Senator?" asked the Chief of Staff.

"All right, two or three. All of which could easily be installed in a chartered aircraft."

Cummings sighed. "You obviously aren't aware of the complexity of keeping the President in touch with not only the White House but every military command around the world—not to mention direct lines to the heads of state of our Allies."

"And," put in Sue Earhart, "our enemies. Remember the Hot Line."

"Actually," Cummings went on, "on foreign trips, we often have a communications aircraft accompanying us, because even the gear aboard Air Force One isn't adequate."

"It cost a million dollars," snapped the Senator. "Why isn't it adequate?"

"The President isn't the only one using these communications links," said Cummings. "There's constant traffic in both directions from staff personnel." He indicated the larger compartment to their rear. "Right now, I'd say that most of our eight main circuits are in use."

"This other telephone plane," said Sue Earhart, her sixth sense for a story angle tickling her, "I guess it's got a nickname too?"

Cummings nodded. "We call her Talking Bird."

"Ah," said the reporter. "Named after one of the Johnsons, I presume."

In Montana, Joyce Cox had arrived back at the small airport, disturbed and dissatisfied by her conversation with the young FBI man in Great Falls.

She poured a cup of hot water over a spoon of instant coffee, stirred it, and sat down to think.

What was Vernon really up to? If he had merely hidden the P-38 out, why had he flown back—if he had—with the SuperCub?

To guard the World War I fighter?

She shook her head. That was senseless. How long could he camp on that dirt strip, in the cold?

Perhaps he'd gone somewhere else with the Super-Cub. To raise money, perhaps by selling the plane? But no, it was too heavily mortgaged for that. He *must* have returned to the dirt strip.

And if that was so, it was barely conceivable that he might be planning to leave the SuperCub there and take off with the Lightning to . . .

Grimly, she put down her coffee, found a hammer and screw driver, and began pounding away at the top drawer of the battered office desk.

"You take care of the forward compartment," TSgt. Ed Miller told A1C Angela Nemath. "Don't offer anyone drinks. They're not allowed to have them. You'll have it easy. Just lunch and beverages."

"Who said I wanted it easy?" she retorted. "Anyway. I'm supposed to stay close to the President."

"We're *both* supposed to stay close," he reminded. "I'll be in the center compartment. With you up here, we've got him surrounded."

"What about the flight deck?"

"Can you handle it?"

"Of course I can. It's just that—"

He grinned. "I *thought* you knew how to take care of aircrews."

She flushed. "What do—"

"Word gets around," he said. "Parking lots aren't the most private places in the world."

Before she could make a sharp reply, a signal bell rang, indicating that a Steward was wanted on the flight deck.

"You handle it," said Miller. He turned back to the trays of food he was preparing.

Trying to push down her anger, Angie hurried forward.

Each step she took over the, to her, stationary plush of Air Force One's blue carpet actually carried her a tenth of a mile closer to Helena, Montana.

The Deputy Administrator of the Federal Aviation Administration stared with disbelief at the order Clarence Willoughby had just handed him.

"You can't mean this, Mr. Administrator," he protested.

"Put it on the wire," said Willoughby. "No bells. It's a routine regulatory, in force until further notice."

The Deputy Administrator was unaware that Air Force One was, at that moment, en route to the municipal airport at Helena, Montana. If he had been, he might have taken stronger measures. As it was, disagreeing with the order, he saw no choice—after having protested it—than to do as the Administrator had instructed.

He went directly to the teletype room, where he told the operator to put the order out to all Air Traffic Control Centers and airport control towers.

The operator did as he was told, but he shook his head and muttered, "The shit's going to hit the fan over this."

*   *   *

Angie opened the door to the flight deck and went inside.

"Yes, sir?"

Anderson said, "Would you mind brewing up a fresh pot of coffee, Nemath?"

"I have some left, sir."

He smiled. "Give that to the Secret Service. They never know what they're drinking anyway."

"Yes, sir," she said. "I'll make some more. Ten minutes?"

"You've got it," said the Aircraft Commander.

Chief Warrant Officer Fred Stewart snapped awake from a half doze in the advance plane.

A crewman was shaking him by the shoulder.

"Hey, Chief. Get your tail forward. You've got a phone call."

"Me?" mumbled Stewart. "Who from?"

Awed, the crewman said, "The President. He wants to speak with you personally."

Stewart shrugged off his seat belt and hurried to the flight deck. Although he had been, for months, within a few yards of President Howard Foster, he had rarely spoken with him. The President would nod, and then it would be as if Stewart were part of the wallpaper.

He took the receiver and heard a series of snarling warbles and chirps. When he yanked it away from his ear, the radioman said, "It's scrambled, Chief. Press that red button."

Stewart did, and said, "Mr. President?"

He listened for a moment, nodding, and answered, "Yes, sir, I understand. I wondered why I got bumped up here, but now I get it. You can count on me, sir."

He waited another few seconds, said, "Good luck to you too, sir," and hung up.

The radioman asked, "What did the Man have to say?"

Stewart laughed. "He said to tell you deadbeats to

give me the number one meal on this flying junk-yard, and none of those messhall box lunches. Or else."

"Or else what?" glowered the crewman who had awakened him.

"Or else you'll all be shipped out to Iran," said the Bagman, smiling broadly.

The crewman, not sure if he were bluffing, joking, or telling the truth, opted for the safest course.

An hour later, Chief Warrant Officer Fred Stewart ate very well indeed.

Seymour Pike, Scott Meadows, and David Braun were now being given the super-communications dog-and-pony act too, while the Senator and Sue Earhart had been taken forward to the flight deck.

Their guide was the young press secretary, Morton Bailey. He fumbled with eagerness. Once, Pike got him off to the side and hissed, "Take it easy, chum. It's only the first quarter."

"I'm impressed," said Braun. "I've read about this gear, but it's another thing to see it in action." He had just reached the chief of the AP office in Hong Kong by simply dialing the number. "But, Mort, isn't this overkill? Surely he can get by with less."

"He tried, remember?" said Bailey. "It just didn't work out. We had a real snake pit, with communications men all over the place. No commercial plane can be lashed up to do the job right. You know the President. He kept his word. But he realized it was a mistake."

Scott Meadows indicated the large compartment, with its luxurious seats and paneled walls, "So is this. Maybe he needs efficient communications, but isn't this luxury a bit much? The country's heading for the poorhouse as fast as inflation can take us, and yet our leader enjoys this aerial yacht in a style that went out with the railroad robber barons and their private cars."

Unwillingly irritated, and surprised at it, Seymour Pike said, "What would you have him do, Scott? Get a steel cable and wingwalk all the way to Montana? Besides, we're enjoying these frills more than he is. I notice you're already on your second screwdriver."

The New York Times man nodded, frowning. "You got me there, Speedy. All right, Mort. Let's get on with the guided tour."

The press secretary, knowing that the flight deck was presently fully occupied, said, "Let's have some more juice and relax. Maybe it'll work on your consciences to see how hard the White House staff are working while you sit around drinking the President's booze."

In far-off Montana, Joyce Cox managed to pry open Vernon Justus' desk drawer. She fumbled through the tangle of keys there, found the one marked "Harper —Bonanza." That would be the red Beechcraft with the two radios. If only it were fueled.

The wind had freshened, and stung her face as she ran toward the hangar.

Air Force One passed over Dayton, Ohio.

25

In Helena, Montana, Advance Man Warren Rogers took a welcome break. He had just completed his walk-around of the Great Northern Hotel, and was as satisfied as he ever let himself become. He had inspected several of the rooms, chosen randomly, and was pleased to see that, while they were clean and neat, no ostentatious preparations, such as fruit baskets and Bourbon bottles, had been made. He gave the hotel manager a mimeographed memo to place in each room.

The wording was polite, but the message was absolutely clear: Do not order from room service unless you or your newspaper is prepared to pick up the tab. He'd gone on to note that a twenty-four hour snack and bar service had been set up in Room 308, which doubled as the Advance Man's office. He warned against giving laundry or dry cleaning to the hotel valet, since departure for Washington might be announced on an hour's notice. He urged that all portable typewriters, suitcases, and camera bags have their owner's name firmly attached. He welcomed the presidential party to Helena, on behalf of the White House staff and the good citizens of Montana.

Presumably the reporters would interpret that to include Governor Claude Hoskins, although he had yet to hear from the Governor's office. There had been no further word from Arthur Cummings, though, which probably meant that Hoskins was making good his promise to meet Air Force One at the airport.

Rogers checked his watch. By now, the President's plane should be crossing the Mississippi.

The Governor's hostility worried him—although he realized it was actually to combat this very hostility that the President was coming West. The mayoral race was only an excuse. Governor John Connally had been against John F. Kennedy's 1963 visit to Dallas—although his wrath was primarily directed toward Lyndon B. Johnson. Still, the tour had bought JFK his coffin.

And much the same had happened in Los Angeles in 1968. Mayor Sam Yorty had long held a grudge against the Kennedys—had, in fact, supported Nixon even though he, the Mayor, was a Democrat. When Robert Kennedy hit the primary trail, Yorty used every trick he knew to make Los Angeles an unpleasant stopping-off point for the candidate. Not only did Yorty refuse to give Kennedy's motorcade a police escort—a courtesy, and even necessary security measure, normally provided to presidential candidates—he actually had the L.A. police ticket every car in the motorcade.

Rogers, keeping in touch with his old friends, had shared a few drinks with Kennedy's staff.

Then came the confrontation in the Ambassador Hotel's kitchen between the young Senator and Sirhan Sirhan.

Bob Kennedy had no hope of living. By 3 A.M. Steve Smith, Pierre Salinger, and the rest of the Kennedy regulars had already started to make arrangements. Callous it might have seemed to others, but to professionals, who abhorred confusion and disorder—and Bob Kennedy was the most professional of all—it was an inevitable action.

Talking quietly with Jerry Bruno, one of the best

advance men in the business, Warren Rogers heard Bruno blaming himself.

Bobby had always liked to move through crowds. His staff and his security men disagreed, and tried to protect him. But, as Kennedy had said more than once, "If somebody wants to kill me, he's going to find a way to kill me. I won't live from day to day with a constant threat." He often accused his staff of finding mysterious ways of moving him from one room filled with thousands of people to another also filled with people, without his having seen any of them.

Ironically, Bruno pointed out, it was while ducking through a kitchen to avoid the Ambassador's crowd that Kennedy was shot.

And, like his brother, it happened in a city governed by a hostile politician.

So, on the morning of June 6, 1968, when the Senator's staff and privately paid security men brought Kennedy's casket down to the lobby of the Good Samaritan Hospital, they were surprised to find a group of Los Angeles policemen waiting.

Rogers, watching, saw one of Jerry Bruno's rare displays of anger.

A police lieutenant demanded to know what the Kennedy people were doing. Bruno said they were escorting the dead Senator, and the policeman said, "No, they're not. *We* are."

Bruno's temper blew the top off his thermometer. "Like hell!" he said. "You didn't escort him when he was alive. You won't now that he's dead."

My God, thought Rogers. It's like the scene in Parkland Hospital, with that two-bit official insisting that the President's body couldn't be removed to Washington, and with an actual armed confrontation looming between the President's men and local cops. It's happening all over again!

The argument continued, and when Bruno realized

that the only way to get rid of the Los Angeles police-men, swarming all over the lobby and parking lot, would be to shoot them down, he capitulated and allowed the charade of an escort to proceed.

Now Rogers himself faced a similar welcome for his President. The Governor had not authorized state police to escort Foster from the airport to the hotel.

Grimly, the Advance Man wondered what would happen if some nut with a high-powered rifle got lucky.

Probably, like Jerry Bruno, he would find himself fighting off unwanted state police body escorts.

Not, he thought fiercely, if *he* could help it. Governor or not, nothing was going to go wrong on this end.

The special intercom beeper which signaled a call from the President's compartment sounded, and Anderson replied.

"Yes, sir?"

He listened for a moment, replied, "Will do, Mr. President." He switched off the intercom and added, "Well, I'll be damned."

"What's up?" asked McGowan.

"The President's scrapping our cockpit procedure. Do you know what he wants us to do?"

"Start selling tickets?" McGowan's voice was anything but humorous. Senator Hopper and Sue Earhart had spent ten minutes on the flight deck, most of it with him fielding their questions while the Command Pilot pretended great preoccupation with flying the plane and examining the instruments.

"You're not so far wrong. Until we start our descent, or unless we hit weather, you and me will alternate cockpit time with strolling around back there playing genial, all-knowing Captains."

"Hell," said McGowan. "And I forgot my medals. 'On your left, folks, you can see Mount Trashmore, an artificial mountain constructed entirely of Schlitz beer cans.' " His voice changed. "Seriously, Tom, what's up?"

"I think," said Anderson, "that the method in our Leader's madness is beginning to emerge. That sly bastard is snowing those turkeys. He's putting on a show." He adopted the voice of a carnival barker. "See the Eight, count 'em, Eight, Marvelous Communications Systems! Count the hash marks on our skilled Pilot's arm." He called over his shoulder, "Sergeant Dent, has there been any heavy-up on outgoing traffic?"

"You bet, sir," said the Radio Operator. "Those tourists are burning up the circuits."

"I think you're right, Tom," said McGowan. "Well, at least that makes me feel a little better about the bad vibes I've had about this flight."

"What's our position, Carl?" Anderson asked the Navigator.

Glancing down at the map, which he had just updated, Birney said, "If you look down to the left, you'll see Hannibal, Missouri. Mark Twain country."

"How's our time?"

"We've made up those few minutes." Birney consulted his How-Gozit chart—which, as its name implied, provided a continuing overview of speed, position, fuel, and time. "Fuel burn's a little high, but nothing to worry about. We'll hit Helena maybe two thousand pounds light, if these head winds keep up."

"Good," said Anderson. "Paul, why don't you take the first shift? Go back and mingle for twenty minutes. Don't lie unless you have to."

"Yes, *mein Kapitän*," said the Pilot. He hesitated. "Listen, don't take this wrong."

"What's that?"

"You're all right?"

"Absolutely, Major."

"All right, I said not to take it wrong. It's just that I don't trust autopilots."

Anderson chuckled. "Neither do I, especially when I remember that every piece of equipment in here was designed, built, and installed as the result of contracts awarded to the lowest bidder."

At Helena Municipal Airport, the ATC tower chief stared, with open disbelief, at the regulatory communication which had been placed in his hands.

"Where the hell did this come from?" he demanded.

"Direct TWX from Washington," said his assistant.

"Verify it," said the tower chief. "Don't those idiots know we've got Air Force One scheduled in here this morning?"

"I guess not," said the assistant. "Shall we contact the President's plane directly?"

"And let them know how fouled up our operation is?" said the tower chief with biting sarcasm. "Just burn those knuckleheads' asses and get this thing straightened out. It obviously doesn't apply to Air Force One."

But, twenty minutes later, he was advised that it did.

One of the first things a flier learns is never to pass up a bathroom or a meal. The distance between each opportunity is sometimes numbered in thousands of miles.

So the first thing Major Paul McGowan attended to when he left the flight deck was a visit to the lavatory just outside. He finished, washed, adjusted his tie, and then—hearing the clink of cups—peered into the galley.

Angie was stacking empty juice glasses.

"I smell that fresh coffee," he said.

"Paul! Aren't you supposed to be up front?"

"The boss ordered us to mingle." He made sure

nobody could see them, patted her hip. "You look great in uniform."

"That's what all the boys say," she told him, trying not to meet his eyes, handing him coffee instead of pulling him to her as she wanted. Her voice lowered. "Is it all right leaving the Colonel up there alone?"

"Of course, Airman!" he said. The words echoed in his mind. Anderson had used them to him. Now he passed them down to Angie. "I'm sorry, that didn't come out like it was supposed to. He's fine, hon. So are we. That bit in the parking lot doesn't make any difference. Tom understands."

"I wish I did," she said.

"You will. The word is that we'll lay over tonight. I'll figure something out—"

She shook her head. "No, you won't. It's too dangerous. Every reporter in Montana will be there."

"I don't mean for bed," he said. "Just to talk." He brushed a kiss against her cheek. "Don't worry." He sipped his coffee. "I'd better get back there and play Airline Captain."

She squeezed his hand. "All right. Maybe tonight. Except, Paul . . . there's one thing."

"What?"

Trying to keep from laughing, she said, "We've absolutely got to stop meeting like this."

CMSgt. Juan Hernandez was worrying about money.

Over the weekend, his four-year-old Sportsvan had developed an alarming thump in the rear end. Suspecting shocks, Hernandez had put the van up on jacks and found nothing wrong with the suspension system.

Monday, his repairman down at the Texaco station gave him the bad news. Unless he put at least two hundred dollars into the transmission, his van would probably expire noisily one day soon instead of shifting into third as it had been instructed.

This was one more bill on top of all the others. And it had to be paid. The Hernandez family relied on the van. Helen had car pool two weeks a month and there were seven kids on her list. She couldn't drop out, because that would mean driving Nel and Frank twice a day on her own. And there was no way to stretch the Vega to a size capable of handling seven grade-school students. Hernandez authorized the repair; he had to.

With $737.40 a month base pay, augmented by allowances for quarters and subsistence, the Hernandez family had, like so many others in the lower middle class of income, gradually slipped into debt. In his case, the situation was worse than merely owing money that creditors were becoming increasingly aggressive in dunning him for; if word were circulated to his superiors about his obligations, it might well result in his being shipped out of the 89th.

The worst of all was the loan company he had, taking their word about complete secrecy, borrowed two thousand dollars from last fall. Although he had missed only two payments, which he had later made up, Hernandez had, just this morning, examined his latest statement and was angry to find that he still owed, according to the company's figures, more than he had originally borrowed. Tack-on charges for credit checking, insurance, advance interest, notary fees, and a crushing "discount" which had diminished the amount he'd actually received, had put him in worse shape than he had been when he took out the loan. The money was soon gone, but the obligation remained, and now the company, reminding him of his vulnerability as a member of the 89th Wing, was hinting of more drastic action than dunning letters and obnoxious telephone calls.

Hernandez thought he knew a way to get out from under. Everything would hinge on what happened today.

*　*　*

The Beechcraft's tank was half full—plenty for the flight Joyce Cox had in mind.

As she taxied out onto the blustery runway, her mind was jumbled. I'm stealing an airplane, she thought. I must be crazy.

She waggled all the control surfaces. Ailerons, rudder, horizontal stabilizer.

Well, she decided, *one* of us is crazy. Either me or Vernon.

The wind was across the runway, so she had to crab into it as she applied takeoff power.

The Beechcraft rose into the sky with the slow grace that only prop planes can achieve. Jets are speed racers, substituting speed for form. They do not fly, they are projectiles. Only light planes have that magical power of leaving the earth gently, with the sadness of a lover rising for a dawn departure.

At that moment, Air Force One passed over Des Moines, Iowa.

26

"We're at our assigned altitude now, Senator," said McGowan. "Twenty-eight thousand feet."

"Isn't that low?" asked Hopper. "I thought you normally fly above thirty thousand."

"Normally. But for the past few days the ozone layer has dipped lower than usual. It's not dangerous, but if we accidentally flew through it, you might have symptoms similar to hay fever."

Nearby, Sue Earhart said, "Those damned aerosol cans are what caused it."

"Possibly, ma'am," said the Pilot politely. "But at this time of year, the ozone usually comes down a bit."

Nervously, Hopper said, "Since we're flying lower than we should, doesn't that mean we might run into a plane coming the other way?"

"No, sir," said McGowan.

"How can you be sure?" asked Sue Earhart.

"Disregarding all the usual safeguards, such as looking out the windows, watching radar, listening to traffic communications, I can give you the answer in two words," said McGowan.

"What words?"

"Neodd and Sweven," he answered.

She repeated them, puzzled. "They sound Swedish."

"Mnemonics," he said. "Like Posh."

"Posh means fancy," she said.

"When the only way from London to India was on a boat through the Suez Canal, it meant Port Out—

Starboard Home. P.O.S.H. You see, ma'am, the north side of the boat was always the cooler one, without the sun beaming into the cabin. Those *were* the fancy cabins, I guess. The posh ones."

"Thank you, Major," she said archly. "My education has been furthered. Now what about those other two jawbreakers?"

"Simple," he said. "A thousand feet of separation is always maintained between opposing directions of traffic. Neodd and Sweven help us remember the right altitude for each direction. North and East—Odd. Neodd. South and West—Even. Sweven."

She lifted her screwdriver. "Brilliant," she said. "And on such children's pig Latin rides the monolith of our entire technological world." She sipped. "What happens if yon brave pilot forgets his mnemonics?"

"This plane carries three independent altitude reading systems. The usual barometric altimeter, which samples the air pressure and relates it to sea level. A second radio altimeter, which operates like sonar, bouncing a signal off the ground below. The third is angled forward, to warn us of any clouds filled with mountains. The radio altimeter is hooked up to a signal which goes off any time we drop more than fifty feet below a predetermined altitude. It's set at 28,000 now. If we go down to 27,949 feet, it starts yelling at us."

Suspiciously, the Senator asked, "Do regular airliners have these fancy devices too?"

"Most of them, Senator. Those that don't, should. I've never understood how any company can risk losing a nine-million-dollar plane, three hundred lives, and probably six hundred million dollars in lawsuits, just to avoid paying for a thirty-thousand-dollar automatic terrain detector."

Hopper, patiently, said, "There are finite limits to the weight an airplane can carry. There are similar limits to the amount of money which can be spent on any one flight. Accustomed to the usual 'no questions asked' spending procedures of the military, you may not comprehend the calculated risk, in the free enterprise system, a carrier must accept as an alternative to unreasonable costs."

Irked, McGowan said, "Maybe you're right, Senator. But I can sure as hell comprehend what a bloody pile three hundred body bags can make."

"Welcome up front, Mr. Pike," said Anderson. "Sit down over there."

"Over there" was the Pilot's right-hand seat. Seymour Pike slipped into it, awed by the control yoke which moved mysteriously at the command of the autopilot. He squinted out the tiny windows.

"I thought you'd be able to see more," he said.

"First time forward?"

Pike nodded. "I've flown light planes, gliders—sailplanes—stuff like that." He glanced around the crowded instrument panels, the control-packed pedestal between the two seats, the Flight Engineer's panel with its dozens of gauges and switches. "This is some difference."

"It's like anything else," said Anderson. "After a while, it becomes almost automatic. One flick of a needle over there in the corner hits my eye like a flashbulb." He indicated the yoke. "Want to fly her?"

"With the President on board?" Pike shuddered. "Not on your life."

Anderson lowered his voice. "You didn't really come up here to peer out our little windows."

"No. I may have overreacted the other day. Our friend the Senator has been mouthing off pretty good, but that's about all. He had a meeting with a bunch of TV and publishing biggies. One's on board today. Sue Earhart. I think you can take it for granted that he's going to see that anything which goes wrong on today's flight will get the widest coverage."

Anderson smiled. "But so would you, Mr. Pike."

Pike nodded. "If it were pertinent. If it were in some way a danger to the President or to the nation. But I wouldn't count the whiskey bottles in the locker, the way Hopper did half an hour ago. And I hope you can trust Major McGowan's lip, because Sue is sure as hell pouring on the charm and pumping him for everything he knows." He frowned. "I don't think it was smart of you to send him back there into that rat's nest. Up here, you guys are gods. We imagine you with unlit pipes clenched in your jaws, making life-and-death decisions in dead calm voices. The reality, with a slight case of five o'clock shadow, isn't the same."

"It wasn't me who sent him back," said Anderson. Wondering if he were wise, but deciding to trust this young reporter, he went on. "The President ordered us to mingle. He's got some reason for exposing the very nerve centers of this mission to that—as you put it so well—rat's nest. I hope he's right."

"So do I," said Pike. "Oh, I picked up on one other thing. Hopper's been as thick as honey with Clarence Willoughby."

"FAA Administrator?"

"One and the same. Is there any way the FAA could louse up your mission?"

Anderson considered the question. "I don't see how," he said finally. "We've always had a good working relationship with the FAA. They have no real control over our aircraft or our bases. Hopper may have been picking Willoughby's brain for something he could use himself, mudslinging."

"Well, I thought I'd mention it. I'd better go back. They'll think I'm joining the Air Force."

"We'd be glad to have you." Anderson grinned.

"Like hell. Listen, Colonel, by the time I left, even the Marines breathed a deep sigh of relief. Well, keep 'em flying." He slipped out of the Pilot's seat and left.

Birney said, "What the hell is going on today, Tom? This plane is turning into a guided tour at Disney World."

Before Anderson could answer, his intercom crackled. It was Paul McGowan.

"Tom? I'm coming forward. You'd better get ready to come back here. Senator Hopper wants to talk to you privately, and there's blood in his eyes."

"Push the steaks," TSgt. Ed Miller told his Stewards. "We've got enough for everybody. I'm only making four Veal Toscana, and one of those is on hold for the President. Or shove Poor Boy sandwiches and gumbo. Just watch that Creole mustard. It's hot."

"Jeez," mumbled one Steward. "Why can't we serve catered trays like the airlines?"

Miller ignored him. This particular complainer was on his short list for transfer out of the mission.

Assuming that there would be a mission from which to transfer.

The White House Situation Room's Duty Officer took the direct call from Omaha.

His opposite number said, "General, we have an ignition report from an area in the Barents Sea at your coordinates 971. It's raw data, just down from the Pole Star satellite. We have no report of any American nuke subs in that vicinity. I would suggest that you consider going to standby for Yellow Alert until we can verify further."

"Roger," said the Duty Officer. "Confirm standby for Yellow Alert. Out." He punched another button. "This is Situation. Give me the President."

Vernon Justus had no coffee to warm him in the cold Montana morning, but he had a pint of Old

Crow, which burned his throat and made him forget about the chillness of his toes.

He sat in the cockpit of the P-38 Lightning, listening to the radio. He was not enjoying rock music, or early news. Air traffic information crackled over the radio's speaker. Communications between Helena Municipal Airport and the planes arriving and departing. Reception was good at this time of the morning. Later, when the Heavyside Layer had constricted its radio-bouncing invisible wall around the earth's circumference, he would not be able to receive long-distance signals. But now, before the rising sun destroyed his range, he had actually intercepted a routine call from a Sioux Falls, South Dakota, controller to the Pilot of Air Force One, advising the Pilot that Sioux Falls had acquired ground control of the presidential flight.

And, because Air Force One was 25,000 feet higher than the ground station, he heard the Pilot's reply quite clearly.

"Roger, Sioux Falls Control. On course, airspeed 518. Altitude 28,000. Present ETA for Helena, nine thirty-four."

Justus snapped up from his half doze. 28,000! Air Force One was more than five thousand feet lower than he had planned.

He whipped out his charts and began calculating the approaches to Helena Municipal. With Air Force One entering the area at only 28,000, he might not have to delay his attack until she was already on her glide slope. He could top 28,000 easily. And that meant that he might be able to intercept his target well outside the normal radar scan of the civilian airport. He would show on ground control tracking scopes as unidentified traffic, but only for a few critical moments.

He smiled tightly. Yes, it would work. Because, unknown to him, an unusually low ozone layer had changed his life and that of every person aboard the President's airplane.

Advance Man Warren Rogers took the unexpected call still wet from the quick shower he had permitted himself.

"Rogers," he said.

"Sir," came a voice. "My name is Lipton. I work out at the airport, in Air Traffic Control."

"So?"

"Sir, you *are* President Foster's representative here in Helena, aren't you?"

Well, thought Rogers, I've been called worse. "You might say so," he admitted.

"I must talk with you."

"So talk."

"Not on the telephone, sir."

"Well, I'm in Room—"

"Sir, I'm on duty here at the airport. I can't leave. But you must speak with me. It involves the President and Air Force One."

"Mr. Lipton, since you know the President is due to arrive shortly, you must realize how busy I am."

"I know, sir. And I wouldn't bother you. Except, if you don't get out here right away, the President may not be arriving at all."

Rogers hesitated. His work was largely done. But to leave it by request of a mere telephone voice? Yet he could not ignore what had been said.

"Mr. Lipton," he said, "you hang up. I'll call you right back."

"Good. My number is—"

"I'll look it up," said Rogers, breaking the connection. It was the oldest trick in the world to call someone, giving a false identity, then offer "Call me back to check," giving the number of a phone booth somewhere.

He flashed the hotel operator. "Get Sam Milnes up here right away."

The operator, already thrilled by the thought of being on the presidential "staff," answered, "Right away, Mr. Rogers."

"And then I want the Air Traffic Control tower at the airport. A Mr. Lipton."

Waiting, he ran over his arrangements for the luncheon. It had been deliberately planned so that a goodly number of Helena citizens would be unhappy. The first rule of an Advance Man is that a stadium which holds sixty thousand people—say, the New Orleans Superdome—and which attracts more than thirty thousand people to see the President, is still (according to the press) only half full. On the other hand, when some 1,000 people attempt admittance to a room—such as the one here at the Great Northern—which can seat 850, that is an "overflow crowd." Numbers mean little; appearances are vital.

In his career, Rogers had used curtains to mask off thousands of seats so that an auditorium might appear jam-packed. He had closed off balconies, out of sight of TV cameras. He had learned never to put up police barricades in spots where they might not be mobbed. To the world, the visit of a President must seem a great event, with standing room only.

More than a thousand luncheon tickets had been distributed—"sold" would be more accurate—for today's luncheon. And the banquet room would not hold two thirds of them.

So they would be seated in the halls, and in cubicles. All would be accommodated—and all would be crowded, harassed . . . and absolutely thrilled that they were among the few who could be fitted in.

Nor would Rogers ever count on a local politician or even a friendly Senator to fill the hall. He trusted Bill Guthrie, but he had made sure—after he'd reviewed the list Guthrie gave him of invited guests—

that each ticket holder had been contacted and recon-firmed. The money raised at today's inexpensive $40-a-plate affair—adding up to some $5,280 for the Great Northern Hotel itself, based on $4.80 per serving, in-cluding one drink—would be delivered to the coffers of the Democratic National Committee. A portion would be returned to help finance William Guthrie's campaign for Mayor. The rest would be used for Committee expenses, including the approximately $11,000 it would reimburse the government for the use of Air Force One. Assuming a donation of $10,000 to Guthrie, the Committee would be more than $17,-000 ahead. Some of this would go to defray expenses still not paid off from the Elect Foster campaign last year.

His phone rang.

"Mr. Rogers?"

"Yes, Lipton?"

"Sir, I can't impress on you too strongly—"

"Hold it down," said the Advance Man. "I'm on my way."

The District Supervisor was not amused with the young FBI man's assessment of Joyce Cox's attempted report.

"Did you tape it?" he asked.

"No, sir," said the young man. "She didn't have any-thing real. We've seen a hundred just like her."

"You bet we have," said the Supervisor, "and one of them was Lee Harvey Oswald. Do you realize that if—and I know it's a long reach to that *if*—something happened, and we didn't have a record or a way to show that we'd tried to do something, our asses would all be in a sling?"

"I guess so," said the younger man.

"Can you reach her?"

"I have a number."

"Get on it."

"Sir . . . suppose I do contact her. What then?"

"Get it in writing, damn it. Haven't you learned anything? If it isn't on the record, it doesn't exist."

"You can count on me, sir."

The Supervisor said something rude.

Arthur Cummings noticed something from the corner of his eye. It was Morton Bailey, nodding toward him.

To Lieutenant Commander George Agee, and Sue Earhart, with whom he had been discussing the virtual flying sick bay Air Force One carried in three large emergency cases, Cummings said, "Excuse me for a moment? I'm being paged by our energetic press secretary."

Sue said, "Buzz off, but remember, I want to know what all this stuff costs."

He left her turning the same question toward the flustered Navy doctor.

"What's up?" he asked Bailey.

When Cummings pushed the proper button, the President was already on the line. The Chief of Staff listened without comment, then, at a question, said, "Yes, Mr. President. I'll handle all the details. I understand that we have your authorization to put the Defense Commanders on Yellow Alert."

The President hung up, and he was speaking directly with the Duty Officer in the special room at the White House.

"Repeat what you've heard, General."

"Omaha reports a positive missile launch from an underwater platform in the Barents Sea. It occurred at minus two minutes."

"Do they have a trajectory?"

"Negative. They're working on it."

"When do we get that data?"

"In another three minutes."

"All right. Place SAC and NORAD on Yellow Alert. You heard the President authorize this action?"

"I did, sir."

"Do we know if the missile is air-breathing or solid-fuel?"

"Negative."

"And so far there had been only one?"

"Yes, sir."

"Very well, General. Keep us posted. We are shifting this frequency to Emergency Override."

"So shifted," said the General.

"Air Force One out," said Arthur Cummings.

In the Barents Sea, far from land, the Captain of the *Urchin* turned to his Executive Officer and said, "Sam, have we just gone crazy?"

"Not by my book," said the other man. "We had our orders. We carried them out."

"Meanwhile," said the Captain, "the Soviet radar has our bird on their screens. Suddenly this isn't the healthiest piece of ocean in the world. What do you say we go down deep and slither out of here?"

"My sentiments exactly," said the Executive Officer.

Joyce Cox came over the mountain ridge and saw, far below her, the dirt strip. The ice and snow made it look like a half-healed scar drawn along the mountain's flank.

She banked the Bonanza and lost altitude. From this height, she could not be sure if the Lightning was still there. She saw the SuperCub, parked at one end of the runway. Its vertical stabilizer was full to the left, and the ailerons were reversed, to stabilize the plane against the wind. But it did not appear to be tied down. That wasn't like Vernon. One heavy gust, and the SuperCub could be overturned.

She swooped down over the dirt strip, her eyes fixed on its edges.

Yes, there it was. Vernon had peeled off the plastic tarp. The P-38 still crouched in its wide spot of the strip.

She buzzed the fighter at fifty feet. The cockpit canopy slid back, and as she swept past, she saw Vernon Justus staring up at her.

Joyce waved, but he did not wave back.

Air Force One passed high above Pierre, South Dakota.

———————————————

27

As Anderson entered the President's airborne office, the door to Foster's cabin opened and Liv Matthews slipped out.

"Making house calls, I see," said Anderson.

She smiled. Indicating her black bag, she said, "Blood-pressure time. We grab at him every chance we get."

"How's it holding up?"

"Normal, for a man his age and with his worries. How's yours doing?" She made a joking move toward him and he drew back.

"Later," he said. Then, winking: "After I've had some exercise."

"Promises, always promises."

"Is he in a good mood?" Anderson asked, nodding toward the President's bedroom.

"Butter wouldn't melt in his mouth. He's up to something. He took three phone calls while I was in there, and each one made him purr like a big old pussycat."

"Well, I hope I don't have to splash cold water over him."

"Why?"

He told her about the request from Senator Hopper. She frowned. "I know it's wrong," she said, "but I keep hoping that man will walk out on the in-flight movie. At 30,000 feet."

"I might help hold the door." He paused. "I had a pretty rough call from Marty."

"This morning?"

He nodded. "It was short and sweet. She wants a divorce."

"Oh, Tom, I'm sorry."

"Are you?"

She met his stare, then shook her head. "No. If you want the truth, I'm not at all sorry. And it's not just selfishness. Tom, you know I've never meddled. And I never tried to come between you. But anyone could see that she wasn't right for you. I'm not criticizing Marty—but the two of you made a mistake, and it's about time you both realized it. Now, maybe—"

He waited. "Maybe what?"

"Nothing," she said. "I'd better report to the Commander. He has to write everything down in the President's chart book."

Anderson would have asked her to stay, but at that moment Senator Philip Hopper came in.

Without greetings, Hopper said, "Am I interrupting the Colonel's physical?"

"No," said Anderson curtly. "I'll see you later, Lieutenant."

"Very well, sir," said Liv. She left.

Anderson always remained polite to guests aboard the plane, and he tried to be so now. "You asked to see me, Senator?"

"I certainly did. Colonel, what exactly is going on aboard this plane?"

"I'm afraid I don't understand."

"I'm equally afraid you do. I've been in the Congress for nearly thirty years. Do you seriously think I'm so stupid that I don't recognize a setup when I see it?"

Keeping his voice calm, Anderson said, "Senator, nothing has been 'set up' so far as I know. Except for a slightly lower altitude because of the ozone layer, everything aboard this aircraft is proceeding according to standard operating procedure."

"Oh? And is it standard operating procedure to have, not one, but two young women aboard? Is it standard operating procedure to give the press and visitors guided tours of the flight deck—and to encourage them to try out the communications equipment? Is it standard for your Air Force Master Chief back there to be whipping up Veal Toscana?"

Anderson managed a smile. He lost either way. If all this *were* standard, Hopper would cry "Waste!" If he said it wasn't, then the accusation would be "Fraud!"

"To be honest," he said, "I would assess it about half and half. If we had a Chief of State aboard, things might be even fancier. But if we were deadheading with nobody but crew and Air Force personnel, we'd all be eating box lunches."

"As well you should."

Anderson said, "I wouldn't push that too hard, sir. It's my understanding that one of the Veal Toscanas is especially for you."

It was the wrong response. Hopper was in no mood for joking. He bit out, "I find that offensive, and almost hinting of bribery, Colonel!"

"I'm sorry. It wasn't meant that way. Is there anything else, Senator?"

"Yes, there is." Hopper had slouched down in the chair behind the President's desk. He looked as if he were attempting to repossess it. He indicated the nearby sofa. "Sit down."

Anderson would have preferred to stand, but the tension was high enough without that implied discourtesy. He sat.

"All right, sir," he said, waiting.

Hopper toyed with one of the telephones. Trying to be casual, he said, "As I remember, you always have alternate landing fields."

"Naturally."

"Civilian or military?"

"Both, sir. If we have to divert from a destination which has already been secured by advance Secret Service parties, we prefer to land at a military installation."

"For reasons of security."

"That, sir. And for communications."

"Suppose—say, because of weather, or an accident on the ground—the Helena airport were shut down today. Where would you land?"

"Malstrom Air Force Base up at Great Falls. If we had enough advance warning, we could probably still get the President to Helena on schedule."

"How?"

"By chopper. Or if ceilings were too low for that, by motorcade."

"Would you recommend such an alternative?"

Anderson considered the question. What was Hopper getting at? Did the Senator know something that Anderson didn't?

"No, I wouldn't," he said. "I don't like changes in plans. My own recommendation would be to cancel the appearance and fly back to Andrews. But, you must know, I'm only in charge of the plane, not the President's activities. I can sugggest, but I have no control over ground procedures."

"Suppose you wanted to return to Andrews. Would you have enough fuel?"

"Normally, yes. But with today's low altitude . . . no, I wouldn't risk it. Remember, I have to consider the possibility of another diversion back there. No, I'd have to refuel. But that only takes a few minutes."

"Thank you, Colonel," said the Senator. "Please understand that, in my criticism of this plane, none of it is aimed at you personally. It's obvious that you're an outstanding officer."

"Thank you, Senator," said Anderson, rising. And

thinking: Like hell, my friend. When you bad-mouth my plane and my mission, you're bad-mouthing me and my crew. "Nice talking with you."

Seymour Pike, relaxing in the large center compartment, said to Sue Earhart, "How do you like the red-carpet treatment?"

"It's nice," she said. "Obvious, but nice. It didn't fool Hopper."

"And why do you think our friend the Senator has chosen this particular nettle? Foster has other weak flanks."

"But none that he made such an issue of in the campaign," she replied. "If Hopper can demonstrate that Foster was dishonest about this particular presidential perk, he can give the impression that's the normal way our new Prez does things."

"And naturally you're going to help him do it?"

"That was my intent. And you? *Inferno* isn't exactly pro-Administration."

"No, but we like to believe that we burn selectively. Sometimes, believe it or not, we even come out on the side of the pigs."

"I envy you members of the Young Journalism," she said.

"Why?"

"You can use words like that without flinching."

"You've used them yourself."

"Yes, with a deliberate intention to offend, and with a personal feeling of revulsion. But you grew up with such tags. They're part of your language."

"If you're trying to insult me, Miz Sue, ma'am, you're doing a good job. Believe it or not, I have my own personal copy of Roget's Thesaurus. When I use a particular word, I know its synonyms. Like yourself, I use street talk for effect."

"Do you plan to use any of it to describe this lovely little junket?"

"I'm not sure. I usually wait until all the cards are dealt before I call my hand."

"How Humphrey Bogartish of you."

He got up and, with a jaunty wave, answered, "How Bette Davisish of *you*."

CMSgt. Juan Hernandez leaned toward TSgt. Lester Dent and asked, "Les, can you patch a telephone call for me?"

Dent hesitated. "Hell, Juan," he said. "You know that's strictly against regs."

"It's important."

"You'll have to make it fast, before the CO gets back up here."

"I will."

"Okay, what the hell? I've been a private before. What's the number?"

Hernandez gave it to him.

Dent chuckled. "That'd cost you a bundle for long-distance, if we weren't patching through MARS." This was the acronym for Military Affiliate Radio System, which—operated by hams in the service in conjunction with civilian amateurs—made it possible for servicemen to place worldwide calls without the high costs of land-line telephones.

He switched to the ten-meter band and began calling, "CQ, CQ."

Lieutenant Colonel Carl Birney made his half-hourly position check and marked it on his charts and the How-Gozit. Air Force One was within half a minute of its scheduled flight path. They were picking up some head winds now, and he called McGowan on the intercom and alerted him to the fact.

"Thanks," said McGowan, adjusting a minor increase in thrust to maintain their airspeed.

"Sergeant Dent," said Birney, "let me have Report frequency."

"Roger," said Dent. "You're on."

Speaking quietly, the Navigator broadcasted the position and speed of Air Force One.

Five miles below, a team of Secret Service men relaxed. Their responsibility was over. Now the next team down the line could worry.

When the discreet light indicating that the President wanted service came on, TSgt. Ed Miller hurried into the President's compartment. Twenty seconds later, he hurried out, his face beet red. He found A1C Angela Nemath and, angrily, blurted, "He wants *you*. Get your tail in there, on the double!"

Surprised, she put aside her tray and hurried back to the presidential compartment amidships. Behind her, she thought she heard Miller whisper, "Bitch!"

He stepped into the forward galley, trembling. This was exactly what he had expected! He'd served two Presidents with skill and absolute loyalty. But the minute some split-tail came on board, all that went out the window. They couldn't keep their goddamned hands off her, filthy-minded old men!

Okay, he thought. The hell with them. He had been wavering all weekend, and even more so in the past two days. But now he knew that he had made the right decision, and was glad of it.

When Angie returned to the forward galley, she found Liv Matthews there, pouring herself some coffee.

"Oh-oh," said the nurse. "Caught in the act."

"That's okay," said the blond girl. "Can I get you anything else?"

"Yeah," said Liv. "A lead girdle. Ever notice how those Secret Service guys have eyeballs that go right through you, like X rays?"

"I know," said Angie. "I'm scared to make a sudden move when they're around. I swear to God, that one over there by the window is sleeping with his eyes open."

"I'm really not that familiar with them," said Liv. "This is my first flight."

"Mine too," Angie admitted. "You're the President's nurse, aren't you?"

"In a way. I work for his doctor. And you're the first female stew they've ever let on board this flying White House."

"Probably the last," said Angie. "When the President asked for me, I thought the Chief Steward was going to flush me down the garbage chute."

"Slight case of jealousy?"

"More than that," said Angie. She peered out of the galley to be sure nobody in her compartment needed service. "I guess he feels somehow threatened. As if I wanted his job."

Liv smiled. "Don't you?"

The younger woman flushed. "Okay, maybe I would. But only if I'd earned it. I know I'm junior face on the totem pole around here. All I want is a fair chance like everybody else gets."

"Is that what you told the President?"

Angie laughed. "I didn't tell him anything, except yes sir and no sir, and how much I liked working for him. He's really very nice. He only called me in to welcome me to Air Force One, and to ask me to tell Sergeant Miller that he wasn't feeling too hot and to please not to try to outdo the Diplomat for lunch. I don't look forward to telling Ed that. He's already steamed at me."

"You'll do fine," said the nurse.

"So will you," said Angie. Flustered, she went on, "I mean, we've all heard about you."

"I see."

"They tried to bump you off the flight, that's the story. I'm glad they didn't. Us girls have to stick together. There's only two of us."

"Don't you count Miss Earhart?"

"Her?" Angie's nose wrinkled. "She's a *reporter*."

"I've watched you often, Miss Earhart," said Anderson. "You're much more attractive in person."

"Is that supposed to be a compliment, Colonel?"

"What I mean is, you look terrific on TV, but no camera could do you justice."

She gave a groaning sigh. "I'm afraid you're just getting yourself in deeper and deeper, Colonel Anderson. I appreciate the compliment, I think. But would you go up to Walter Cronkite and tell him how handsome he is?"

"No, because it isn't true. He's dignified."

"Why must appearance make such a difference?"

He shrugged. "I don't know. If it really doesn't matter, why do you put on makeup and have your hair done?"

"Because dreary network policies, and narrow minds like your own, expect me to. I'd be just as happy in blue jeans and a plaid shirt."

"I doubt very much, Miss Earhart, if you've ever so much as worn a pair of jeans."

"That's Ms., if you don't mind."

"I do mind, but I'll call you anything you wish."

"How *macho* we've become."

"Look," he said, "maybe I'd better go back up front and do what I know best, fly this airplane. I'm certainly not making your day."

"On the contrary, you're cheering me up immensely. I thought all I'd see on this trip was bowing and scraping. It's nice, if a bit argument-making, to run into somebody with a mind of his own. Tell me, Colonel—"

"Since we're now on an argument basis, make that Tom."

"All right, Tom it is. And so is Sue. Are you for real? I mean, I know they call you the 'fifteen-second

Edwin Corley
336

man,' and all that jazz. But is the ramrod posture, and the knife-edged blue uniform, and the iron discipline —is that really you?"

"A part of me. Not all. It's the part I wear when I'm on the job."

"And now you'll tell me that what you do, this bit of piloting the President around, is important."

"Sue, it's probably the most important thing I could find to do with my life."

"Why? Foster's only another man. Why should he have all this at his fingertips when kids are starving in the ghettos and in West Virginia?"

"Because he's not Howard Foster, he's the *President*, and like him or not, he's what we've got, and if we don't back him to the hilt, things can only get worse, not better. Sue, I've flown three Presidents in my day —two full-time—and the one thought that keeps hitting me is not how much he's *got*, but how much more he *needs*. You probably see this plane as a big boondoggle, with free lunch and dancing girls for everybody. Well, it's not. It's a tool. If you don't like the man up there in that cabin, put your own in. But I'll bet that when you do, you'll want him to have every available possible instrument of communication and mobility. You can afford to be partisan. I can't. Whoever's up there, he's *my* President, and he gets one hundred per cent."

"Level with me, Old Fifteen-Second."

He laughed. "If I can."

"Is this trip really necessary?"

"I think so."

"And there's no more efficient way to handle it?"

"Sure there is. We try harder every time. But the answer isn't in chaining him to the White House the way the Senator wants to."

"You're very persuasive. Tell me, off the record, exactly what do you think of Senator Hopper?"

"*Off* the record? I've been burned before."

She crossed her heart. "On my honor as the best expense-account forger at UBC."

"I think Senator Hopper is a loudmouth who wants champagne service on a beer budget."

"Shall I tell him that?"

He looked down at her. "Will you?"

Her eyes softened. "Of course not. I said it was off the record."

"Thanks. Some advice. I think you've hooked up with the wrong team. Hopper doesn't have the stuff to ever make that big second effort. Foster will eat him alive."

He touched his flight cap and turned toward the flight deck.

"Colonel—Tom—" she called after him.

He turned. "Yes?"

"After this flight, some of us might go on waivers."

"That's fine," he said. "Me, I'm a free agent."

He left. Morton Bailey, who had just passed by, asked her, "What was all that about?"

She said, "Football talk, sonny."

Summoned to the President's office, Arthur Cummings lifted the phone which connected him via a scrambled circuit to the White House Situation Room. Foster was still secluded in his bedroom.

"Yes?" said Cummings.

"Sir," we've just received a trajectory plot from NORAD."

"Let's have it."

"It's a low, suborbital track, curving along the Soviet mainland, but well out of her air space, crossing the Arctic Ocean."

"Heading where?"

"If the present flat trajectory continues, the missile will enter our territory near Point Barrow, Alaska."

"Could it be aimed toward the oil fields?"

"Affirmative. We'll know more in a few minutes.

We have two spy satellites shooting infared pictures. They'll pinpoint the actual track more accurately than radar."

"Have defensive systems been notified?"

"Yes sir. We're on full Yellow, standby for Red Alert."

"Very well. Hold at standby. You will not, repeat, will not, go to Red Alert without confirmation from the President."

"Acknowledged," said the Duty Officer. "Situation Room out."

"Air Force One out."

Cummings put down the phone.

He sensed a presence. He looked up. Senator Philip Hopper stood there.

"*AR*thur," said the Senator. "What's all this about a Red Alert?"

A few miles north of Mount Rushmore National Monument, Air Force One left long white contrails in the subzero cold at 28,000 feet.

28

Although it was early—only eleven-fifteen, Washington time—TSgt. Ed Miller started his Stewards—and Stewardess—to serving lunch. He was coldly angry because of the message Angie had brought him from the President. Sarcastically, he had asked, "And what would you suggest that I serve him? Coddled eggs and a Bromo?"

She replied, "Chief, I'm only relaying what the Man said."

"The President! What the *President* said."

She had heard him call Foster the Man only yesterday. But she bit her lip and did not continue what might have turned into a nasty argument.

Actually, lunch was in order. Everyone aboard the plane had gotten up unusually early and, except for coffee and pastries, had eaten no breakfast—with the exception of Senator Philip Hopper, who invariably consumed a bowl of bran and milk immediately upon rising.

Miller decided to serve the veal to the President anyway. He softened its northern Italian flavor by adding a scoop of Minute Rice.

Since there was room, and at a nod from Mort Bailey, the reporters were invited to remain forward and enjoy their meal with the White House staff.

On the flight deck, Anderson said, "You go ahead, Paul. I'm not very hungry. I'll take the second sitting."

They both knew that by the time two hours had passed, Air Force One would be on the ground, and Anderson would be lucky to get a radar-oven cheeseburger. But the offer was also an order.

"What's my choice?" McGowan asked.

Angie said, "Ed's pushing Veal Toscana as the gourmet special. But if I were you I'd take the steak."

"Steak it is."

"Rare?"

Anderson almost looked around, controlled the impulse. It was obvious this young woman knew McGowan's tastes in food.

"Fine," said the Pilot.

Birney ordered steak too, and so did TSgt. Dent. Hernandez asked for the Poor Boy sandwich.

"Nemath," said Anderson, "suggest the veal to Lieutenant Matthews. I think she's the gourmet type."

"Yes, sir," said Angie. "Would you like some more coffee?"

"Tomato juice," said Anderson. "With a little hot stuff."

"One Virgin Mary," she replied.

As she left, a buzzer sounded from Anderson's control panel.

"Yes, Mr. President?" he answered.

He listened for a moment, then said, "Very well, sir. If that's the way you want to handle it."

When he clicked off the intercom, McGowan asked, "What's up?"

"Some kind of UFO alert. The sort of thing we'd keep quiet."

"But?"

"But he wants to go public. When things start happening, he wants the press and the passengers—which is to say, our friendly neighborhood Senator—in on the action."

McGowan sighed. "My mama told me there'd be

days like this. But she didn't say they'd come in bunches, like grapes."

"You may have to fly her for a while. He wants me back there when and if."

"No sweat."

Anderson turned to the Navigator. "Carl, from now on, update your position every ten minutes. Anything could happen. We might divert, we might even head back to Andrews."

"If that's what you plan," said Birney, "you'd better make your turn within the next six or seven minutes. That's our point of no return."

"What if we take a chance and go up to thirty-three?"

"Too late. The fuel burn during the climb would cancel out any savings once we got there."

"Okay. Just keep us on the map."

"It's done," said the Navigator.

Casually, Arthur Cummings asked, "What Red Alert is that, Senator?"

"The one you just referred to."

"On the telephone?" Twisting the knife, Cummings went on. "You must have overhead only part of my conversation. I was discussing contingency plans with the Situation Room. Whenever the President is away from the capital, the various Defense Commands often use that as a jumping-off point for tests of our response system."

"So that's what you were discussing? A test?"

Carefully, Cummings said, "I'm not at liberty to say, sir."

Suspiciously, Hopper asked, "Have you received a report—a message—from the FAA?"

"No, sir. Should I have?"

"Never mind, then. But I want to know more about this Red Alert. As a United States Senator, I have a right to know."

"Yes, sir, but I don't have the authority to tell you any more than I have."

"Then I want to speak with the President."

Cummings looked toward the closed doors. "He's not available now, Senator."

"Why not?"

"I really don't know. But he left orders not to be disturbed."

Hopper's voice rose. "All right, stonewall me. I've had it before. But this time, Cummings, you're fooling around with the wrong boy. I know all about this scheme—dazzle us with your nine-million-dollar toy and send us home with souvenirs, keep us happy and quiet. It isn't going to work. I promised my people that I was going to be on the last flight of Air Force One. And that promise holds."

Cummings merely stared at him. Hopper waited for an answer, and when he did not get one, drew himself up and said, "Count the minutes, Mr. Cummings."

Advance Man Warren Rogers stared at the regulatory communication which had been given to him by George Lipton.

"What kind of shit is this?" he asked. "They've got to be kidding."

Lipton said, "That's what I thought. But I ran it through Washington again, and it came back the same way. Effective immediately, only FAA-certified pilots are allowed to land at civilian airports which use Air Traffic Controllers."

His head whirling, Rogers said, "But military pilots are certified."

"No, sir. Some are, but most aren't."

"Maybe not some Air National Guard fighter jockey. But surely Colonel Anderson—"

"Is not FAA-certified. I had it checked, Mr. Rogers. That's when I decided to call you."

"Jesus Christ, he's been landing at civil airports all

over the world for ten years. Are you trying to tell me he's not *qualified?*"

"Of course not. He's merely not *certified.* There's always been an informal understanding between the civilian and military areas that military pilots were qualified at least to FAA minimums, and usually above. But there wasn't anything actually on paper in hard regulations. It was a status quo which nobody disturbed."

"Until today. Who rocked the boat?"

"The Administrator himself. Clarence Willoughby. And, you might as well know this, he'd have my job if he even guessed that I was talking to you."

"In other words, there's no way you can disregard this order."

"None whatsoever. Unless it's rescinded, I'm going to have to refuse landing permission for Air Force One."

"Suppose I get the President on the line. He can override this piece of crap."

"That was my first thought," said Lipton. "But he can't."

"He can fire that son of a bitch," said Rogers. "Then he can instruct the new Administrator to cancel the regulation."

"I suppose so. But that would take time. And Air Force One's ETA is in less than an hour."

"Can you get this Willoughby for me?"

"I'll try," said the tower chief.

But Clarence Willoughby was out of the office, and unreachable. And while the Deputy Administrator agreed with Mr. Rogers, and deplored the new regulation, he had no authority to alter or rescind it.

In the White House Situation Room, where the clock which kept pace with the President's own time had been pushed back another hour to Mountain

Daylight Saving Time, the Duty Officer took another report from Omaha.

The unidentified missile was still on a course which would take it near, or over, the oil-rich North Slope of Alaska.

The SAC B-52 bombers which, since the easing of the Cold War and the SALT treaties, had been standing down in greater numbers—only 10 per cent of the bombers were normally aloft at any given time—were being brought to full readiness. Missile silos were being buttoned up, linked to the outside world by underground cables which would carry the signals that spelled peace or destruction. The roving nuclear submarines had submerged, and were now in communication through the huge, miles-square low-frequency radio system which had been buried beneath the Minnesota forests.

Around the world, code books and sophisticated radio equipment were only a spoken order away from the furnace. The United States had not been on a full Yellow Alert since the Cuban Missile Crisis. The machinery creaked, but it still worked.

This had happened at the worst possible time, with the President aloft in Air Force One.

But the communications links between the Situation Room and the President's plane held.

Warren Rogers tried to call the Commanding Officer at Malstrom Air Force Base.

He could not get through. The base switchboard seemed to be shut down. He tried three times, without getting an answer.

When he dialed the White House direct, and asked to be patched through to Malstrom, he was politely but firmly refused.

"Patch me onto Air Force One," he said finally, angry that he had to take the final step remaining to him. When an Advance Man had to go running to his President for help, he wasn't a good Advance Man any more.

CMSgt. Juan Hernandez felt better after eating his sandwich. The phone call had helped to calm him too. Now the money worries were over.

It had been a hard choice. They'd been holding those nine acres near Fairbanks, Alaska, for more than five years, planning to put up a cabin and, one day, to retire there.

But today's problems were more real than tomorrow's dreams. In the phone patch arranged by Sergeant Dent, Hernandez had spoken with a grumpy, just-awakened real estate man who had been showing the property.

"If you'll take fourteen thousand for the package, you've got a buyer," said the broker.

"All cash," insisted Hernandez.

"That's what you said you wanted," said the real estate man. "If you'd take back some paper, I could get you eighteen, maybe twenty."

"No, no," Hernandez had said. "You know the story. I need the money now."

"Okay," said the broker. "I'll get a thousand binder today. As soon as you sign the papers, I'll collect the rest. You should have payment in full by the end of the month. Although, as I said, if you could hold on until June, I—"

"No, thank you," said Hernandez. "When you get the binder, could you wire it to my wife? Less your commission, of course."

The broker hesitated. But, after all, it had been he who sold the property to Hernandez originally.

"We don't usually do that," he said. "Oh, what the hell. You're a good risk. Otherwise, you wouldn't be flying on the President's plane. Okay. You ought to have the money tomorrow morning."

Hernandez thanked him and nodded to Dent, who signed off.

Now he finished his Poor Boy sandwich and watched the instruments which told him how his airplane was functioning.

The needles were in the green. Everything was fine.

Governor Claude Hoskins prepared to leave for the airport. At first, tired, he had considered canceling his appearance. After all, the President would not be arriving anyway.

But then it occurred to him that the effect of his being stood up by Foster, because Air Force One was not qualified to land at even this minor airport, might be more newsworthy than absence. He had made some notes for a brief address which he planned to deliver to the disappointed reporters.

He recognized the risk in defying a President of his own party. But it was a justifiable one. Future political trails were closed to him unless he broke out of the regional fences and became a national figure. This confrontation with Foster—spiced by the shadow of inefficiency and waste which was being cast by Senator Hopper—might break those fences for him.

Hoskins was not sure he could trust the ambitious Senator. But, then, he had no real choice in the matter. Without Hopper, he would not be preparing to make an address on national television.

The Governor of Montana yawned, and buzzed for his limousine.

Joyce Cox found the right frequency on the Bonanza's number one radio, and heard Vernon Justus yelling, ". . . Come on back, Bonanza. This is Bandit One."

That was his favorite handle. She responded, "This is Angels Two." A private joke, which he had once made about her cleavage. "We've been worried, Bandit One. What are you doing down there?"

Static hashed the reception, then she heard him say, ". . . keeping guard so nobody trashes the Lightning. What the hell are you doing flying Harry's Bonanza? Over."

"Had to find out what happened to you," she said.

"Well, come on down. We'll talk on the ground."

"Roger, Bandit One. What's the wind?"

"Calm. Make a straight-in approach."

"Okay. Angels Two out."

He did not respond.

Joyce made a circular pattern and approached the dirt strip about two hundred feet above the terrain.

Down near the middle of the runway, she saw Justus's voice crackled from the radio.
to be off, and there were two black stick-like objects jutting from the housing.

Instead of settling and flaring out, she kept her altitude. Closer, she saw—projecting from the center section of the Lightning—two ugly black machine-gun barrels glinting in the early-morning sun.

Justus's voice crackled from the radio.

"What the hell are you doing, baby? Get on down here."

Instead, she banked off to the right and, frightened, heard herself shouting over the emergency frequency, "Mayday. Mayday. This is an aerial emergency. Does anybody copy? Mayday!"

Racing the sun toward the Pacific, Air Force One passed over the South Dakota-Montana border.

29

When Warren Rogers was patched through to Air Force One, he was told that Arthur Cummings was busy on another call.

What the hell, thought the Advance Man. This is actually flying stuff anyway. He asked to speak with Colonel Thomas Anderson.

"Good morning," said the Aircraft Commander. "What's the good word in Helena?"

"I can't use it on the air," said Rogers. Quickly, without embellishment, he related what he had just been told by the tower chief. He finished with "I hate to get the White House involved. I thought maybe you could come up with an answer. They can't do this, can they?"

"It looks as if they have," Anderson said quietly. His mind raced back over the dozens of tests, examinations, check rides he had taken over the past months. "I'm afraid your tower chief is right. I've been qualified, but not certified. It's a technicality, that's all. But if there's a new FAA regulation forbidding uncertified pilots landing privileges, your Mr. Lipton has no choice. He has to go by the regs."

"Hell's bells, he can't keep the President circling around up there while we try and get the regulations changed."

"My guess is, we'll divert to Malstrom. Let's put that into effect as a probable backup. Get the chopper and your security people alerted."

"I can't. Malstrom's not answering the phone."

"Say again?"

Rogers explained his two attempts to reach the Strategic Air Command base—by direct phone and through the White House.

Anderson said, "Stay where you are, Mr. Rogers. I'll contact the base direct, and get back to you."

He nodded at Sergeant Dent, who had been monitoring the conversation. "Get me Malstrom Control."

"Yes, sir." The Radio Operator keyed his microphone and called, "Air Force One to Malstrom Control. Come in, please."

There was no answer. He tried again, with the same lack of response.

"Sorry, sir," he told Anderson. "They're not answering."

Dent raised the Helena tower again, and Anderson told Rogers, "You're right. Something's wrong out there."

"Maybe this'll help," said the Advance Man. "Lipton checked, and for the past twenty minutes or so, there hasn't been a peep out of Malstrom's tower—and there isn't any incoming or outgoing air traffic."

"I think I know what's up," said Anderson. "Hold down the fort, Rogers. I'm afraid the White House is going to *have* to get involved."

He clicked off his microphone and told Dent, "Get Mr. Cummings up here on the double."

Then, to McGowan, he said, "Big trouble."

"How's that?"

"Malstrom's buttoned up tight as a drum. I think they've gone to an alert."

"Mayday," called Joyce Cox. "Doesn't anybody copy?"

"Goddamn it, get the hell off the radio!" shouted Vernon. Her voice continued, almost overriding his own.

He turned up the RF gain on his own radio. The extra Radio Frequency power let him whistle into the microphone, overloading the frequency and blotting out her transmission. It would work for a few moments—the mountains were probably blocking her full signal anyway—but if she climbed higher, it was only a matter of time before her message was received and answered.

He primed the fuel pumps of the twin Allison engines and popped the starter selenoids.

The fighter's props whirled, the engines backfired, and caught.

Still whistling into the microphone, he taxied to the dirt strip's end, stood on one brake to bring her around, and began his takeoff run.

Concentrating on the transition from ground to air, he forgot to whistle for a moment, and heard her voice clearly:

"There is danger to Air Force One. They're going to shoot her down. Warn Air Force One . . ."

Savagely, he blasted a piercing whistle into the mike.

The FAA's Administrator was tracked down at the Le Consulat restaurant, in the Embassy Row Hotel. A strolling guitarist had just played the haunting theme from *Forbidden Games,* and was now embarking on a ballad by Jacques Brel.

Clarence Willoughby was not glad to hear the voice of the Deputy Administrator.

"I told you there'd be hell to pay," said the Deputy. "I just got a call from the President's Chief of Staff, aboard Air Force One. He demands that the landing regulation be canceled immediately."

"No," said Willoughby. Nervously, he remembered the promises Senator Hopper had made. Well, he had better come through with them, or Willoughby was a man without a job. "Mr. Cummings has no authority to make such demands."

"But he speaks for the President."

"In a matter like this, only the President can speak for the President. And even then, he can only request. He can't force us to rescind the regulation."

His Deputy's voice broke. "Mr. Administrator, I told you at the beginning that I disagreed with this matter. I still do. It's only fair to inform you—"

"Go ahead and write your memo," said Willoughby, wise to all the devices used for covering one's own tail. "Predate it, if you want to. Just remember one thing. If, in the long run, this regulation turns out to be desired and accepted, those who opposed it are going to look a bit silly, aren't they?"

Unhappily, the Deputy Administrator said, changing his destination in midstride, "What I meant, sir, was that Mr. Cummings warned me that if I didn't comply with his request—"

" 'Demand' is the word."

"Anyway, he threatened to have the President call direct."

"To order you to cancel the regulation?"

"Yes."

"You can't. You don't have the authority. And don't think you can switch him off to me. I'm leaving the moment I hang up. I'll give you some sound advice, if you'll take it."

"What?"

"Do what I did. Get your ass out of that office and lay low for the next three hours."

Willoughby hung up and, without waiting for a check, threw a twenty down on the table.

Just as he retrieved his coat from the check girl, he heard the phone at his table begin to ring again.

He hurried from the restaurant.

Arthur Cummings, sitting on the extra flip-down seat, said to Anderson, "You guessed right. Malstrom is on Yellow Alert, standing by for Red."

Anderson whistled. "What happened?"

"Unidentified missile headed right for Prudhoe Bay. Ever stop to think what an aerial nuclear blast would do to an oil field that size? It'd still be burning at the end of the century."

"But why just one?"

"One's enough. I agree with you, Colonel. It does seem like putting all their eggs in one basket. But maybe they thought they could sneak a single bird in under our radar, drop her right down one of our oil rigs—and take out a big chunk of the pipeline in the bargain."

"Why? Things are more settled now than they've been for years."

"Exactly. But remember, Colonel, we have no way of knowing *whose* bird we're tracking. The atomic club has grown. Let's say the Third World would like to see the major powers at each other's throats, then step in afterward and pick up whatever's left. It's possible."

"Excuse me, sir," said Sergeant Dent. "The restaurant manager says that Mr. Willoughby just left."

"I'm not surprised," said the Chief of Staff. "He was smart enough to know that his mealy-mouthed little Deputy had rolled over for me."

"I suppose the only thing we can do is tell the President," said Anderson. "He can break through Malstrom's radio silence by using the entry code."

"That code is changed every day," said Cummings.

"Doesn't the Bagman have it?"

"He does. But the Bagman is aboard our advance plane."

Now Anderson realized whose face it was he had been subconsciously missing all morning.

Warren Rogers was damned if he was going to sit around waiting for somebody else to pull the chestnuts out of the fire.

He had already called Sam Milnes and explained the situation. The Secret Service man was livid with fury.

"You sit right there, Warren," he yelled. "I'll be right out with a couple of men. When we get through with them, those controllers won't be in any mood to endanger the President."

"Calm down," said the Advance Man. "I'll take care of this end. What I want you to do is send a couple of your best men over to Malstrom. Even if the base is buttoned up, there has to be somebody in authority at the main gate. Let them know about Air Force One's diversion. If we can't call in, they must certainly be able to call out."

"We'll use the chopper," said Milnes.

"Not directly to the base," said Rogers. "Try the nearest town, get a car there. If you show up on their radar, those trigger-happy kids might just shoot you down."

"All right," said Milnes. "But before we leave, Warren, I might as well tell you, I'm going to put out a signal advising the President to turn around and go home."

"My sentiments exactly."

"I know you busted your ass getting ready here, but—"

"Listen, Sam, stop apologizing. Tell Cummings I concur with your recommendation. Just get moving."

"I'm on my way," said the Secret Service man.

Seymour Pike drew Sue Earhart aside and said quietly, "There's something very funny going on aboard this airborne luxury liner. I sense icebergs ahead."

"My antennas are already extended, good buddy. The traffic into the President's office, and up to the radio room, is almost as heavy as the Long Island Expressway at rush hour."

"Your friend the Senator was trying to camp in there, but I notice that they heaved him out. His face looks like a solar eclipse."

"I heard him tell one of the Stewards to remind Cummings that he still wants to speak with the President."

Pike shrugged. "I think I'm a good reporter, but I ask once to see the Man, and then I wait my turn. Apparently Senators don't have as much manners as us power-crazed media."

She laughed. "*I'm* media. You're only the press."

"Okay, Ms. McCluen, what do your rabbit ears pick up?"

"Nothing good. I think something big's going on."

"Hopper? He's the original big wind."

"Something *outside* this plane. And, with my luck, I'm trapped up here."

"You could be in worse places. If anything happens, you're right next to the Man with the big stick."

She made a wry face. "Do you think he'd let us in on it? If things hot up, it's back to the rear of the bus for us."

Seriously, he said, "From what you said before, I think you've laid down your ax for Hopper, and you're going to put on your straight-lady hat again."

"Maybe. I thought we were using each other, which is okay. But now I get the very distinct impression all the using was from him to me. I don't like that shit."

He smiled. "Also, maybe you weren't liking yourself too much either? Isn't it nicer to be on the side of the angels?"

"*Your* angels? Why, that rag of yours—"

He touched her lips. "My strength is as the strength of ten, because my heart is pure. Unfortunately, I can't say as much for most of *Inferno*'s staff."

"Let it drop. Speedy, do you really think Foster would let us in on the action if anything happens today?"

"My hunch is that he will. Somehow, I have the vagueish tickle in the back of my head that all this has been choreographed. And we're not merely spectators, we're part of the main action."

Before she could answer, a Steward came over to them and said quietly, "Excuse me. If you folks want another drink, you'd better order it now."

"Thanks, I'm fine," said Pike. "But why?"

Before answering, the Steward addressed Sue Earhart. "Miss Earhart?"

"Nothing."

To Pike, the Steward said, "Chief Miller informed me that the galleys are going to be closed down for a time."

"Any reason?"

"The President's orders," said the Steward. The gold-on-blue Presidential Seal on his blazer was just inches from Pike's eyes. The young reporter made a mental note that whenever an instruction was conveyed by anyone wearing that seal, the words seemed to take on an authority of their own.

"That's reason enough," he agreed.

Warren Rogers reached the Deputy Mayor of Helena.

"Mr. Judson? I've got a problem. It's serious."

"Go ahead," said Peter Judson, not one to waste time.

"I need the board of governors out here at the airport pronto."

"All of them?"

"It's urgent. I don't want to say too much on an open line, but I promise you, their time won't be wasted."

"I'll do my best," said the Deputy Mayor.

"We don't have much more than twenty minutes," said the Advance Man. "Half an hour at the outside."

"I'll get them there," promised Judson.

He hung up, called in his secretary and told her to get everybody in the office busy tracking down the five board members.

"I'm on my way to the airport," he said. "Have them meet me there in the VIP Lounge."

This was the private club maintained by the airport for the convenience of visiting celebrities, and in which most press conferences were held. Various consumer groups, whom Judson considered to be idiots, had been campaigning for years to outlaw the club on the grounds that if the ordinary tourist passenger couldn't use it, no one should be permitted to enjoy it. To Judson, that was on the order of a hitchhiker claiming that, since he could afford only hamburger, nobody else was to be allowed steak.

He tried to remember the lyric from Gilbert and Sullivan. How did it go? A song from *The Gondoliers:*

When everyone is somebodee, then no one's anybody.

The P-38 Lightning lifted off smoothly and began her climb-out.

Vernon Justus shouted into his microphone, "Joyce, get the hell off the horn. I mean it. Make a one-eighty and land. Now!"

When he released the mike button, he heard her, still calling, "Come in, anybody. Mayday!"

Goddamnit, why wouldn't she listen? He hadn't gone through all this, burned himself up making plans, sacrificed everything to keep this plane airworthy, just to have her scuttle it all at the last minute.

He keyed his mike, to block her transmission. He was now level with the Bonanza, which was half a mile ahead, flying due east.

"Joyce, I'm not kidding. Turn back and land right now. And get off that radio!"

Perhaps she was holding her key down continu-

ously, and was unable to hear him. She stayed on the
eastward course, and when he let up on his own button, he heard her repeating the Mayday call.

He poured on the coal, overshot her, and dipped
down in front. He waggled his wings. There was no
way she could miss that.

He radioed, "Turn that Bonanza around and land,
Joyce. I'm telling you, this is your last chance."

She banked to the left, and as he turned with her,
he thought: It's about time she got some sense. He
was glad that he did not have to hurt her.

"You don't seem too upset by all this, Mr. Cummings," said Anderson.

"Crisis is my daily diet," said the President's Chief
of Staff.

"Not Yellow Alert brand. That's just two steps away
from total war."

"Precisely. And only one man is authorized to take
those two steps."

"The President," said Anderson. "Well, if that missile's homing in on the North Slope, he'd better figure
out which way to walk pretty soon."

"He will," said Cummings. "I'm sorry we had to
include you in this deception, Colonel. The President
felt that the fewer who knew the truth, the better
chance of preserving secrecy. But the cat'll be out of
the bag any minute now. I hope that bastard Hopper
chokes on his veal, after all the trouble we've gone to
on account of him."

"I'm lost," said Anderson. "In more ways than one.
And I've got to make a decision on the destination of
this plane in a couple of minutes."

"Hold off on that," said Cummings. "I think it'll
all work itself out."

"In case you guys don't realize it," said Carl Birney's
laconic voice, "you're on Command channel. Every
one of us up here can hear you."

"That's all right," said Cummings. "Just keep what you hear to yourself."

"I take it," said Anderson, "you aren't in any big sweat about us setting down."

"No," said Cummings. "But I'm frosted by that toady Willoughby. I'd prefer for us to land at Helena. Still, Malstrom will be just as good."

"May I remind you, Malstrom is buttoned up."

"It won't be for long," said Arthur Cummings.

The Bagman was reading a John D. MacDonald paperback when the radio operator came back for him.

"You're one popular dude," said the radio operator. "Guess who wants to talk with you again."

"My pal, the President?"

"Right again. I don't know what it is you've got. It sure ain't beauty."

Stewart rattled the briefcase chained to his wrist.

"It's this, baby."

"What's in there, your lunch?"

"Almost right. Try spelling it l-a-u-n-c-h."

The radio operator took three beats to get it. Then he said, "Hey, friend, don't even joke about that!"

Arriving at Helena Municipal Airport, Governor Claude Hoskins was surprised to find the VIP Lounge occupied by Warren Rogers, and two busboys arranging chairs.

One of the Governor's aides advanced on the Advance Man, his face stern. "Who are you?" he demanded. "The Governor's going to use this room."

"Wrong, bub," said Rogers. "The President's going to use it. The Governor is welcome to hang around if he wants to." He flashed his White House credentials. The sight of the blue Presidential Seal was enough to turn the aide's backbone to water.

"Ah, you must be Mr. Rogers," said the Governor of Montana, thrusting out his hand. Rogers took it, and felt sweating coldness on Hoskins' skin. "I'm sorry if there's some misunderstanding. I assumed that, since the President isn't arriving after all, that the lounge would be free."

"Who said he's not arriving?"

"Why—it's my understanding that a new regulation applying to military aircraft—"

"I'd be mighty curious, Governor," said the Advance Man, "to learn how you know about that particular regulation, since it hasn't been made public either here or in Washington."

"My morning briefing—"

Disgusted at the man's lame lies, Rogers cut him off. "Well, forget your briefing, Mr. Governor. The President will arrive, on time, and I'm sure you're looking forward to a few moments alone with him." He turned to the busboys. "Son, put those last four back there, near the john. I don't think the Governor wants to be caught in the crowd."

"Well, I'm glad my information was wrong," said Hoskins. He retreated for a hurried conference with two of his assistants, one of whom cast a bleak stare at Rogers and hurried out of the VIP Lounge.

That bitch!

Vernon Justus had thought she was turning for a downwind landing on the dirt strip. Instead, she was spiraling for altitude, and her airspeed was so low that he could not turn with her without stalling out.

He made a straight run, picking up speed, and snapped the Lightning into a steep turn, gaining altitude as he did so.

Justus was too busy flying to whistle into his mike. He heard her still calling for help.

Then, chillingly, he heard a voice answer.

"Mayday caller, come in. This is Helena Tower. Come in, please."

"Thank God," came Joyce's voice. "Put this on tape. I'm at a little dirt strip near—"

Justus keyed his own mike, hoping he could override her.

"Break, break, break, break!" he yelled. Anything to blast into her signal, make it unintelligible.

He dove toward the Bonanza at nearly three hundred miles an hour. Deliberately, he swept over her with less than ten feet of clearance. He turned and saw her wings dipping violently as the slipstream bounced the Bonanza all over the sky. Now maybe she'd straighten up and listen to him.

But, as he made his turn, he heard her voice defying his threat. "Warn Air Force One. There's—"

"Break, break, break!" he shouted. He was high above her now, and the sun was behind him. The white wings of the Beechcraft were frail against the backbone of the mountain.

The Bonanza grew in size. He saw it through the ring and cross hairs of the aerial gunsight.

"Break, break, break . . ."

There was no other way. She was still clawing for altitude. Something had gone wrong in her head. He had to stop her, or she would ruin everything.

The Bonanza's wingspread filled the inner circle of the sight.

He uncaged the gun switch, and pressed the red button.

A stream of fifty-caliber bullets chewed their way across the wing and fuselage of the Beechcraft. It lurched, as a main strut gave way, and plunged, in a terminal spin, toward the snow-clad mountains.

In her panic, Joyce must have clutched at the microphone, and for a horrible moment he heard her voice screaming, "What's happened? Oh, my God, I'm falling! Help me! Jesus, someone help me!"

To blot her from his hearing, and his mind and memory, Vernon Justus shut off his radio.

Air Force One had just crossed the Little Big Horn River, and its Custer Battle National Monument.

30

Air Force One's center compartment was not crowded, but with the addition of the four reporters, the official photographer, Senator Hopper, and the Aircraft Commander, it was no longer the sprawling lounge it had been earlier in the flight.

Lieutenant Commander Agee and Liv Matthews sat at the rear. She had been in the forward compartment when Anderson came off the flight deck with Arthur Cummings.

"You go back," said Anderson. "I'll be there in a minute."

Cummings nodded and left. Anderson beckoned Liv over to the aisle between the President's compartment and the port side of the plane. Outside, the air rushing by at more than five hundred miles an hour made a harsh swishing noise.

"I think we're going to have quite a show back there in a couple of minutes. Join the fun."

She hesitated. "Are you sure that's wise?"

"Nobody'll even notice you. Except for me."

She smiled. "That's the best offer I've had all day. All right, Tom. You go first. I'll follow in a minute or so."

"Nope. We go in together. Come on, Navy."

"What happened to Flo?"

"She got bumped back at Andrews."

He led her down the long aisle and into the center compartment. He was right. Except for an occasional nod from a staffer, she was ignored. She found an empty seat near Agee and sank into it, while Anderson sat up front near the wall of the President's office.

Hopper cornered Art Cummings. "I thought I told you I wanted to see the President."

"You will," said the Chief of Staff archly. "Any minute now."

"Mr. Cummings," warned the Senator, "I've had all I want of tricks and games. My patience is exhausted."

Calmly, Cummings said, "Please simmer down, Senator. You know as well as I that I only carry out the President's orders. If it makes you feel better to growl at me, fine. But if you want to get anything done, why not save it for the boss?"

Hopper sat back, his lips tight. But he did not address Cummings again.

Seymour Pike, who sat next to Scott Meadows, whispered, "It's like opening night at Lincoln Center. Lights . . . Music . . . Curtain!"

"He puts on a good show," agreed the *Times* man. "But I think I'll wait until the reviews are in before I buy tickets."

"*Buy* tickets? Scott, you and me and the rest, *we're* the reviewers."

"I guess we are at that," said Meadows.

Sue Earhart sat near Morton Bailey. He sipped a cup of coffee nervously.

She touched his arm. "Down, White Fang," she said. "You look ready to jump out a window."

"Maybe I should." Touched by her warmth, he lost, for a moment, his professional distance. "I might have more future that way."

"Mort," she soothed, "you're doing a good job. Believe it or not, most of the press corps actually likes you."

"Sure. Because I'm easy to push around, and trap into conflicting statements. I know they're getting ready to ease me out. I just wish I had the guts to quit

first. Do you realize, I don't have the faintest goddamned idea what's going on here this morning? Nobody bothered to tell me. 'Just keep them happy,' they
said. I might as well be a social director in the Cats-
kills."

Sue, not wanting to lie to him or hold out unrealistic hopes, said, "Why *don't* you leave? If you
quit while you're ahead, you could just about name
your own terms on any paper or magazine in the
country."

"I don't quit because Foster asked me not to."

"Do you do everything Big Daddy asks?"

Slowly, he nodded. "Yes."

Then, realizing who he was, and where he was, he
stiffened. "I'd better circulate," he said. "They'll be
starting rumors about us."

Sue Earhart laughed. "Maybe your boss will lend
us his bedroom."

He patted her shoulder and went forward, toward
Seymour Pike and Scott Meadows.

Sue looked after him, thinking: Poor little bastard.
Then she stiffened too. Come on, baby. Don't start
feeling sorry for the natives.

John Williams, the President's personal photographer, was circulating too, snapping off candid photos
with his motorized Nikon. He also carried a Canon,
with its mirrorless reflex viewing, for use in intimate
situations when the mirror slap of the Nikon might
prove too loud. He called the Canon his "church
camera." He was shooting Color Negative #5247 today. It gave him an actual ASA rating of 125, which—
with the fast Nikon lens, f-1.2—let him get good color
negs in any situation where it was light enough to
read. His two-man lab in the White House basement
could then make color prints, slides, or black-and-
white glossies.

He caught a nice image of the Aircraft Commander
pointing out the window, with Senator Philip Hopper

nearby. It looked as if Anderson were telling the Senator to go take a flying leap.

While Williams' only job was photographing the President and everything that happened around him, he had a keen sense of news—coming as he had from a youthful career on *Life*, and then specializing in tough photo essays for such magazines as *People* and *Time*.

He saw the world through the lens of a camera. Whatever was out of the frame didn't exist.

And, just now, he realized that he had not seen one man he'd intended to focus on today.

Where the hell was Christopher Healy, the junior Senator from Montana?

Joyce Cox had no parachute. Even if she had, it would have been impossible for her to bail out of the wildly spinning wreckage of the Bonanza as it hurtled down toward the jagged face of the mountains below.

She had stopped screaming, and now fought the controls. They were lax and unresponsive. With one wing crumpled over the cockpit, she could not see most of the time.

Repeatedly, she slammed in opposite rudder, trying to correct the spin. The Bonanza did not respond.

I'm going to die, she thought.

It was a calm realization, all fear stripped away. She felt only sadness that the man who had trembled so often in her arms had now turned against her and killed her.

She wished now that she had not, reflexively, tried to help an unknown President, at the price of Vernon's love, and her own life.

Her mind seemed to pull away, and it was almost as if she could see the broken plane falling from the sky.

It was so like a crippled bird, struck down by a hunter's birdshot. She had seen them tumble often, in the annual quail and partridge hunts. And now she herself had become one of the wounded.

The Bonanza struck the side of the mountain.

It was a glancing blow, with much of the impact soaked up by the one still-whole wing. The airplane avalanched down the side of a steep cliff, which absorbed much of the impact's inertia. Like all mechanical accidents, the impression to its human passenger was a series of bone-jerking blows and hollow thumping noises.

Then silence swooped down over the mountain again, except for the annoying buzz-fly noise of a fighter plane high overhead.

TSgt. Ed Miller did not like this sudden congregation of passengers in the center compartment. Air Force One was only an hour or so out of Helena, and this rearrangement of seating interfered with his plans.

Dessert and coffee had not been served yet, and the requests for after-dinner drinks had not even begun to come in.

Time was his enemy, and it was running out on him.

He wished the President would start his show and get it over. There was work to be done.

He looked at his watch and, silently, urged: Hurry up!

Sam Milnes and another Secret Service agent clutched the sides of their seats as the Air Force helicopter seemed to stand on its side over the village of Ulm, Montana. It was just a few miles southwest of the Air Force base, which they had decided not to overfly or even pass, for fear of being picked up on radar and perhaps shot down. Nobody knew what might be going on in the minds of the Malstrom anti-aircraft gunners.

The Ulm Sheriff, after examining their credentials, closed up shop and sped them up Interstate 15 toward the base's main gate. "Thought something funny was going on," he said. "Most mornings, those jet bombers shake the eggs right off your plate. Been real quiet this morning."

He had the patrol car at an even seventy. Still, even with the heavily posted 55 MPH signs, he passed few cars.

"Folks figure it's their money, and their gas," he explained. "That Mr. Nixon, he railroaded the limit through, but to the normal guy, it looked like all that happened was that his oil company buddies got richer while the rest of us got poorer. So now, instead of thirty cents a gallon, we're paying sixty-five, seventy. More than double. People feel like, after they've spent all that extra money, it's their right to waste it, piss it down the mountain, whatever they want. They're the ones who paid for that gas, that's what they say."

Milnes, mildly irritated, said, "But you're a law officer. Don't you enforce the limit?"

"For safety, yes. But this highway was built for eighty-five, son. I'm doing seventy now, legally because we're on an official run. But your regular car would be crawling along here, doing only fifty-five. If a driver's weaving in and out, crossing the line—hell, I'll pull him in for doing thirty. But your good driver going sixty, sixty-five—he don't have to worry about me."

Dryly, Milnes said, "You're a credit to your profession, Sheriff. Isn't that the cutoff up there?"

He pointed to a sign that read: "This Exit for Malstrom AFB, HQ 24th Air Division."

"So it is. Got to talking and forgot where I was going."

The Sheriff of Ulm, Montana, screeched off the Interstate at a good 45 miles an hour on a ramp marked 25 MPH.

*   *   *

The reporters were beginning to congregate in the Helena Municipal Airport's VIP Lounge.

Governor Claude Hoskins bit his lip, but made no comment, when it became evident that the President's Advance Man was running this show. It was Rogers who guided the reporters and TV announcers and technicians to the bar, which had been hurriedly set up.

"Sandwiches are on the way," said Rogers. "Meanwhile, have a blast on the Democratic National Committee."

One reporter said, "I had the impression the Governor was going to make an address here today."

Roger winked. "Doesn't he always? As far as I know, he's only here to meet the President. But why don't you ask him yourself? The Governor may have other ideas."

Hoskins, who had been advised by one of his aides that a phone call to Washington and another to the Control Tower had indicated the new FAA regulation to be in effect, had decided to wait. He made himself cordially available to the press, and fielded their questions with generalities and evasions. No, he had nothing new to report on the rumor that he might be available soon for national office. Nor had he decided whether or not to run for a second term as Governor next year. No, there was no bad blood between him and President Howard Foster. Hadn't he come here at this early hour to welcome the President?

Rumors that the President might not land at all? Nonsense. But he would check into them immediately.

That was his escape hatch.

He made it clear to all that he was imbibing only plain coffee, and had just been served his second cup when a familiar face caught his eye.

He hurried over. "Martin, it's a pleasure. What are you doing out this early?"

Martin Lloyd, one of Helena's leading bankers, shrugged. "All I know," he said, "is that there's apparently an emergency meeting of the airport's board of governors."

"Today? Here?"

"They practically dragged me out of bed," said Lloyd.

"Why? What's the emergency?"

"I don't know," said the banker. "Do you have any idea?"

"Not a hint," said the Governor. "Excuse me." He hurried over to one of his aides, whispered instructions.

The aide left in a hurry.

The drone of the P-38 Lightning's engines was beginning to falter. Vernon Justus read an altitude of 32,400 feet. He could push higher, but only at a great increase in fuel consumption. The old rubber oxygen mask was bitter in his mouth, and the cockpit heater wasn't working properly.

The chart he had plotted indicated that he was due east of Helena, near White Sulphur Springs. According to his estimates, Air Force One should begin her letdown further eastward, near Harlowton. He intended to remain south of her track, so the sun would be behind him. He would have at least five thousand feet of altitude as an advantage.

He was sorry that he'd had to deceive his partner, who had kept insisting that nobody be hurt.

When Justus finished with Air Force One, he intended that everybody aboard her would be dead.

He had no illusions about the possibility of his own survival. Justus knew that within minutes F-104s from Malstrom would be swarming around him. Perhaps, if he cooperated, they might allow him to land and be captured for trial.

But he had no intention of cooperating.

So far as he knew, no P-38 had ever faced an F-104 in combat. It would be interesting to see how well they were matched.

It happened suddenly, without warning.

The walls surrounding President Foster's office suddenly slid up into the plane's ceiling, and almost as if by magic, he was revealed, sitting at his desk. Behind him, in one of the easy chairs, was a younger man with closely cropped hair.

Most of those in the central compartment had seen the President in person before. Still, especially after the buildup and the sudden discovery, almost like the rising of a theater curtain, his entrance was spectacular.

Foster was a tall man, perhaps ten pounds overweight for his rangy six-two frame. His face was angular and his eyes were set deep into his cheekbones. His hair was salt-and-pepper, and combed straight back. His clothing was conservative, but not dull. The jacket was singlebreasted, and the trousers had no cuffs.

He smiled. "Watch this," he said, and pressed a button.

The desk, and his chair, rose perhaps a foot straight up. Now he was higher than his audience, and his presence dominated them.

"Lyndon invented that little gag," he said, pressing another button to depress the desk again. "He wasn't above a little psyching out of his troops. Neither am I, but I don't need levitation."

He indicated the man behind him. "Most of you have met Senator Healy of Montana, I believe. I apologize for stealing him from you this morning, but we had some important matters to discuss."

Healy, without emotion, nodded toward the reporters. They nodded back. The message was clear: We'll get you on tape or paper before this bird lands.

"I apologize too," the President went on, "for being unavailable to you for most of this flight. Let me get right to the point, and if there's time later for questions, I'll take them."

He held up one finger. "At this moment, our country's defenses have gone to what we call a Yellow Alert."

There were murmurs from the audience, most of whom knew what a Yellow Alert was.

"We have done so," said Foster, "because our early-warning systems detected an unidentified missile, presently approaching us over the polar regions. It is aimed, approximately, at the oil fields of Alaska's North Slope. It is, I repeat, unidentified. It is apparently unmanned. We also know, approximately, where it originated—in the Barents Sea, north of the Soviet Union."

Sue Earhart asked, "Mr. President, does that mean it's Russian?"

"I'll answer questions later, Miss Earhart," he said. "But I was about to continue by saying that we're certain that it is *not* Russian. So far, there is only one missile, and not even the Soviets would be foolish enough to launch such a meager attack from a point close to their own borders."

Determined, Sue interrupted. "That's not enough reason to take a chance that it might be a Russian probe."

"You are certainly a persistent young woman," said the President. "Won't you humor one who is older, if not wiser, than yourself and let me present this in my own manner?"

Flushed, she sat down. Seymour Pike patted her knee, and she plucked his hand away and dropped it like an offending blossom which had been deposited on her leg.

"The reason I'm so sure that the missile isn't Russian," the President went on, "is because I know who it *does* belong to." He smiled at Sue. "That's your cue to ask, 'Whose is it?'"

She shook her head. "No, sir. Twice burned, forever shy."

"I'll bite," said the *Times*. "Although I've got a hunch."

"Which is?"

"It's ours?"

Foster nodded. "On the button."

"But why?" asked Scott Meadows.

"A not-so-routine test of our defense systems," said Foster. "We've done it before—with low-flying bombers, with what appeared to be blowups of our spy satellites. And with dummy missiles, programmed to probe our frontiers without actually intruding. Today's UFO was actually launched from the Barents Sea by the nuclear submarine *Urchin*. It's set to impact safely offshore. If, for some almost impossible reason, the guidance should malfunction, our own high-intensity radar signals will detonate it in the air some fifty miles away from the coast."

Seymour Pike said, "What if that should fail too, Mr. President?"

Foster shrugged. "The missile still couldn't do much damage. There's no warhead."

Pike said, "You know that, sir, and I know that. The question is, does the Strategic Air Command know that?"

I don't believe it, thought Joyce Cox. I'm alive!

She was as much a part of the twisted wreckage of the Beechcraft Bonanza as the broken metal itself. Her left arm flamed with agony, and she could see part of a broken bone protruding from her wrist. There was no feeling in her legs at all.

Joyce tried to move, but all she could manage was to lift her one good arm. With it, she tried to pull some of the wreckage aside, but she had no strength.

The stench of raw gasoline choked her. She coughed, and saw flecks of blood on the snow.

The mountainside was cold.

Calmly, she said, "I simply must get out of here."

She began to wriggle backward, attempting to pull herself out of the nest of tubular steel and aluminum. Within a very few seconds, she was forced to stop and gasp for breath. When she breathed too deeply, her chest hurt. Her breath rattled in her ears, as if she had a bad cold.

A distant voice said, "Mayday, do you copy?"

The radio was still working!

She fumbled for the microphone, choking on the fumes from the ruptured fuel tank. If she could put out a call, give her location, they would come and find her.

Joyce found what she was looking for. She breathed shallowly for a moment, cleared her throat, making sure she would have enough voice to broadcast for help.

Ready, she pressed the Push-to-talk button.

Somewhere, in the shattered case of the radio, a spark arced from a broken wire and with an almost physical *WHOOOMPH!* the gasoline vapors trapped in the fuselage ignited.

As the flames swept toward her, Joyce shut her eyes and her mind screamed, *It's not fair! Now now, not after all that happened!*

Then rationality left her and for a few seconds she was a babbling, pleading, animal creature that was soon blackened and consumed by the uncaring flames.

"What do you mean, you won't relay a message to the base CO?" demanded Sam Milnes.

The Officer of the Guard, who had been summoned to the main gate of Malstrom AFB by a sentry, returned the Secret Service man's credentials. "I'm sorry, sir," he said. "If you're actually who you say you are, you know why I can't."

"I represent the President," said Milnes. "Alert or not, he's still your Commander in Chief. I demand to speak with your Commanding Officer."

"Sir," said the Officer of the Guard calmly, "we are acting under orders from the Joint Chiefs, approved by the President. This base is under a defense alert. Our security posture does not permit visitors, messages, or any other form of communication. I'm not even supposed to be out here talking with you now."

"Well, you've already made that mistake," said Milnes. "So why don't you be a good fellow and take us to your CO?"

He made a move toward the young officer, who backed away.

"I wouldn't do that, sir," said the OG. "You're in the sights of half a dozen M-16s."

From the corner of his eye, Milnes sensed movement. He recognized professional military attention to orders.

"Look," he said. "Just tell your CO this. Radio Air Force One. That's all he has to do."

"Air Force One can radio us," said the officer. "I'm sorry, but you have to leave. Now."

One of Milnes companions started to make a protest, but the Secret Service man waved him back.

"Let's get to a phone," he said.

The President said, "SAC doesn't know just yet, but they will. You see, an attempted penetration of our defenses is only effective if it's kept utterly realistic until the very last minute."

He turned to Anderson. "Colonel, what's our arrival time at Helena?"

Anderson hesitated. "Forty minutes or so, Mr. President. But if I could see you for a moment—"

"Is there a problem?"

"Possibly. If—"

Foster spread his hands over the audience like a benediction. "Say it right out, Colonel. That's the purpose of this get-together. To show the press—and our distinguished colleagues—that this mission has nothing to hide."

"Nothing to hide?" sputtered Senator Hopper. "What have you been doing all day but hide from us the fact that you're pulling a snow job with all the fancy toys on board this flying town house?"

"Keep your blood pressure down, Phil," said the President. "You're turning red." He turned to Anderson. "Go ahead, Colonel."

"It seems, Mr. President, that the FAA has come out with a new regulation, effective this morning. No uncertified military pilots are allowed to use civilian fields."

"I see," said the President. "And I presume you aren't certified."

"No, sir," said Anderson. "Most of us are qualified to standards higher than those required by the FAA. We just don't have their paper work."

Foster looked to Arthur Cummings. "I presume you've already had a conversation with Mr. Willoughby?"

"No, sir. He's in hiding. And his Deputy doesn't have the authority to override the regulation."

"Do I?"

"Legally? No."

Foster pinned Hopper with his gaze. "Do you have any suggestions, Senator?"

Hopper said, "I understand there's a military base within easy range."

"Malstrom Air Force Base," said Anderson, to the President. "It's a SAC base, however, and because of this sneak attack you've set up, the base is under wraps."

"What does that mean?" asked Foster.

"They're not answering radio calls. Or telephone calls either. My information is that the only way you can get through is with the entry code carried by the Bagman. Excuse me, I meant your Codes Officer."

"That's no problem," said the President. "Chief Stewart is aboard the advance plane. I've already radioed to have him standing by. He'll relay the code to me, and I'll give it to you so we can contact Malstrom." He nodded toward the audience. "Actually, that's much the same demonstration I had in mind for our honored guests. You see, Senator, I know all about your low regard of this mission. It may have been a bit melodramatic, but that's exactly the reason I rescheduled the defense probe, to coincide with this flight. To make matters more difficult, Mr. Cummings and I decided to place the"—here he smiled—"Bagman on another plane, to demonstrate how essential the communications systems aboard this plane are to keep the government in touch."

He reached for the telephone. "You'll be allowed to listen in. That's a first, I presume."

But before he could punch up the correct button, McGowan's voice came over the ceiling loudspeaker.

"Colonel Anderson, report to the flight deck immediately."

Foster pressed a button. "This is the President. What's the problem?"

"Well, sir . . ."

"Out with it."

"Yes, sir. Radar shows that we have an unidentified fighter plane shadowing us."

Air Force One was then passing over the Musselshell River, near White Sulphur Springs, Montana.

31

"This kind of Sunshine Law I can do without," mumbled Seymour Pike. He was referring to a new law in some states which prohibits closed sessions of regulatory groups. This session aboard Air Force One certainly was not closed.

Anderson had just asked, over the open intercom system, "How do you know it's a fighter?"

"Radar shows that it's pretty fast, and damned high. And Carl made an eyeball check with his starscope. Colonel, you're not going to believe this, but it's a World War II P-38 Lightning."

"Is it closing?"

"Negative."

"Then we'll be outrunning it soon. Those fighters topped out around four-fifty, as I remember."

"Straight and level. In a dive, she could overtake us, and she's got five or six thousand feet to burn."

"Maintain course," said Anderson. He looked at Foster. "Mr. President, I'd suggest that we get that SAC entry code and contact Malstrom. I'd appreciate a covey of Quail as soon as they can get them here. That joker up there may just be a sightseer, or only some old-plane nut blown off course. But let's not take chances."

"You're right," said the President.

Senator Healy got up to make room for Anderson.

Air Force One's Chief Steward, TSgt. Ed Miller, was standing near the President's desk, holding a tray with a napkin over it. He stepped into what had, before the walls rose, been the presidential office and said, "Excuse me, Mr. President."

Foster, puzzled, but not alarmed, leaned back to give the Steward room.

The napkin fell from the tray, and revealed the .38 Police Special Miller held. He clicked the hammer back.

"Everybody return to their seats," he said. "Mr. President, move over to the sofa."

Anderson tensed.

"Don't try it," said Miller. "I've got hollow-points in here."

Senator Philip Hopper leaped up. "What the hell is this?" he demanded. "Another one of your 'demonstrations?' "

Sue Earhart hit him in the stomach with her elbow. He choked.

"Sit your ass down," she said. "This is serious."

With the President between him and the passengers in the center compartment, Miller backed toward the bedroom.

Calmly, Anderson asked, "What are you doing, Sergeant?"

"It's simple," said Miller. "You can land this plane on a five-thousand-foot strip, isn't that right, Colonel?"

"Perhaps," said Anderson.

"Don't fool around!" Miller almost shouted. "You've bragged about it often enough. Well, now you've got your chance to prove it."

Before Anderson could answer, the President said, "Don't fool around with this man, Colonel. Let's find out what he wants."

"Thank you, Mr. President," said Miller. "Believe me, I don't want anybody to get hurt. Especially you. Your Navigator was right, Colonel Anderson. That's a P-38 up there, fully armed and capable of blowing this plane right out of the sky. But that's not our idea."

"Suppose I sit down," said the President, lowering himself onto the sofa, "while you tell us what your idea is. Take all the time you need, son. Nobody's going to rush you." He looked at the Aircraft Commander, and the White House staff. "That's an order."

Their stunned faces stared back at him.

"Go ahead, Sergeant," said the President in an even voice. "We're listening."

"Due northwest, up near the Canadian border, there's the Blackfeet Indian Reservation and the International Peace Park. Colonel Anderson, have Colonel Birney get out the charts. And no radio calls. My friend up there in the P-38 can copy them, and if he hears anything at all, even a request for weather, he'll blast this plane apart. Do you understand?"

"Completely," said Anderson. "Keep it cool, Sergeant. We'll do what you say."

"Good. Tell him to plot a course for Cut Bank. There's a good strip there."

"That's a commercial airport," said Anderson. "The strip's longer than five thousand."

"I know," said Miller. "Give the Colonel your instructions, sir."

"The yellow button," said the President. He was too far from the desk to reach the intercom and telephone system himself.

Anderson relayed Miller's orders. When Birney began to question him, Anderson said, "No questions. And maintain radio silence. No exceptions."

After he had finished with Birney, Anderson turned to Miller and said, casually, "You realize that if your buddy blasts us, you go down too."

"Do I, Colonel?" asked the steward. "Not necessarily."

He jerked his head toward the President's bedroom.

The capsule, thought Anderson. And of course Miller
knows all about it—he was one of the two Stewards
designated to help Foster in case of an emergency.

Who was the other? He remembered: A1C Angela
Nemath.

"What do you want, young man?" asked the President.

"What does anyone want?"

"Money?"

"Yes. And immunity."

"I can't grant immunity," said Foster.

"The hell you can't. Your buddy Ford let Nixon
off the hook. Boy, that's what really frosted most of
us. We scrape along, nickel and diming it, and bang!
The crookedest no-good in the world gets caught,
appoints his buddy to the office, and gets off scot-free.
They even paid him a couple of million to go on TV
and brag about what he'd done."

"That was a long time ago," said Foster.

"Not for Vern, and not for me."

"Vern? Your friend up there in the fighter?"

"Sure. What does it matter?" Miller laughed.
"You've got to know his name to pardon him."

Carefully, Arthur Cummings said, "Mr. President,
the Sergeant has a point. Taking into account miti-
gating circumstances—such as the fact that no one has
been hurt, and if he gives up peacefully—you could
issue an executive order of immunity."

"Very well," said Foster. "What do you say, son?"

"What do I say? Shit, that's what I say. Vern warned
me against your tricks. Mr. President, I've been flying
you politicians around for nearly four years. I've seen
everything you can imagine. Hell, if I wanted to I
could put half your friends on Capitol Hill in the
slammer. So don't play nicey-nice with me, trying to
get me to put this pistol down."

"All right," said Anderson. "Assuming we proceed
to Cut Bank. Then what?"

Miller grinned. "Long before we get there, we're down on the deck under the radar. There's a short strip out on the reservation near the Indian Office. That's where you really set down. From there up to the Canadian border is only a jeep ride."

Probing, Anderson said, "You've obviously planned this for a long time."

"That's all you know. From the weekend till now. That's all the time we had. If the flight had been going somewhere else, we'd've planned for that."

So it's all improvised, thought Anderson. His eye caught Cummings'. The Chief of Staff gave a slight nod.

"About this matter of money," said Cummings.

"One million in cash," said Miller. "That's fair; considering you get back a nine-million-dollar airplane, not to mention"—here, he waved the muzzle of his pistol at the compartment—"all these important people."

"What about the President?"

"He won't be hurt. Not unless you make us, or unless you get all excited and do it yourselves."

The President said, "I believe we can work things out. But first, Sergeant, I have to cancel the SAC alert."

"No way. Sir. No radio in or out."

"If I don't cancel, and something goes wrong, the country might be thrown into war. You wouldn't want that."

"Why should I give a damn? What's this country done for me? Or Vern? He got his ass shot off for this country, and now he can't even afford fuel for his plane. Whose fault is that?"

Keep them talking, that was the cardinal rule in dealing with terrorists. Anderson asked, "How did you meet Vern? Is that his full name?"

"It's enough for now." Miller tapped the President on the shoulder with the pistol.

There was a surge of motion in the compartment. Words were one thing. But when he actually touched the President, even Senator Hopper found himself leaning forward, looking for a chance to jump the Steward.

"Stay easy," warned Miller. "Meet him? I went hunting. He flew us in. We got along real good. He opened my eyes to a few things. That was last year, with the last President. Too bad we couldn't get it together then. I didn't like that one at all. He was the original cheapskate."

"Sergeant," said the President, "it seems to me that this is all one great misunderstanding. Think about it, before you get in any deeper. You haven't yet gone past the point of no return. If you and your friend have just grievances, we can find some way to resolve them. I give you my word on that."

"Never mind your 'word,' sir. What I want to see is your signature on that paper of immunity."

So intent were everyone's eyes on Miller that only Liv Matthews, in the rear of the compartment, saw the bedroom door behind the steward begin to open slowly.

Anderson said, "We can't just proceed to Cut Bank without contacting Air Route Control Center. The minute we stray off course, they're going to start asking questions."

"Let them ask. And let them guess. That's part of the plan."

The President said, "Colonel, I want no one hurt as a result of this. You make sure your crew understands that. Mr. Cummings, you take care of the Secret Service. They aren't even to get out of their seats. Is that understood?"

"Yes, Mr. President," said Cummings. He had caught sight of the slowly opening door too. His muscles tensed, as he prepared to move.

The gap in the door was now wide enough to reveal

Angie Nemath, with a tray in her hand. She had been clearing the cabin after the conference between the President and Senator Healy.

Her face was white. Her lips trembled. She crept toward the sofa, the tray raised with its hard edge aimed, like an ax, at Miller's head. She lifted it.

Perhaps someone's eyes shifted, perhaps she made a slight noise, perhaps Miller felt a draft.

Whatever the reason, he whirled and, seeing the shape of somebody close behind him, panicked.

Whipping up the pistol, he shot her.

The tower chief drew Warren Rogers aside. "We just got some strange traffic," he said. "Somebody yelling 'Mayday.' A woman, we think. She said something about Air Force One."

"What?"

"I'm not sure. I played back the tapes. I think she was trying to give a warning. But she went off the air. We haven't been able to raise her since."

Rogers thought for a moment. He didn't have time to try and contact Sam Milnes.

"Radio the plane," he instructed. "Relay what you just told me. Tell Mr. Arthur Cummings, the Chief of Staff, that I recommend turning back or landing elsewhere."

"Malstrom's still off the air," said Lipton.

"I know. But he's got fuel for almost anywhere. I don't like the smell of this. Too many things are getting fouled up."

"I think I agree," said the tower chief.

"You won't get in the soup over this?"

Lipton shook his head. "They told me *not* to let her land. How can they get mad if I tell the pilot to go someplace else?"

"That bastard's getting closer," said Birney. "Why aren't we taking evasive action."

"Anderson said not to," said McGowan.

"We'd still better alert him that the fighter's closing," said the Navigator.

A radio voice said, "Air Force One, come in, please. This is Helena Control."

Dent said, "Sir?"

"Don't answer," said McGowan.

The voice called again. Then, realizing no answer was forthcoming, said, "I have a message for Mr. Arthur Cummings. Mr. Warren Rogers says to divert the flight. Repeat, divert to another field. We have received unconfirmed transmissions warning of danger. If you copy, please reply."

Dent said, "I can confirm reception by keying my mike, sir."

"Better not," said McGowan. "That character up there may be pretty sharp. Just keep a heavy ear working. I want to hear any messages aimed our way."

He keyed the intercom. "Colonel Anderson?"

To his surprise, he got no answer.

The shot had been deafening in the confines of the compartment. It came so suddenly, without warning, that most of the viewers were stunned.

Not so Anderson. He leaped at the Steward. Miller twisted and slammed the barrel of the pistol across the Aircraft Commander's forehead. Anderson reeled back, stunned. Blood trickled from his hairline.

Angie, who had been slammed back against the edge of the door by the bullet's impact, clutched at her left shoulder and fell, soundless, to the blue carpet.

The President half rose, and found himself looking down the barrel of the pistol.

"Don't move," warned Miller. "Nobody move."

Two ignored him. Lieutenant Commander Agee, his ever-present black bag clutched in one hand, started for the office area. Behind him, Liv Matthews hurried toward the crumpled figure of Anderson.

"Get back," warned Miller.

"I'm a doctor," said Agee. "That girl needs help."

"I'll blow your ass off," warned the Steward.

"No, you won't, son," said the President. "Let him help her."

Miller hesitated. Angie, shock wearing off, felt pain stab into her, and groaned.

"All right," said Miller. "But get her out of here. Back there in one of the chairs."

Agee pointed at the two nearest men—Senator Healy and Press Secretary Bailey. "You two, give me a hand," he commanded.

Miller pushed back against the plane's bulkhead, keeping the pistol pointed toward them as they lifted the young woman carefully. Blood from her wound splashed down and matted the carpet.

Sue Earhart stood up. "You lousy little son of a bitch," she said, starting forward.

"Stay back," Miller warned.

"Shoot me too," she said. "You get your kicks that way, little man? Shooting helpless women? Come on, blow my guts out. Maybe you'll get your rocks off. How long has it been, punk? Since your mama caught you beating your meat?"

She had sensed the truth about him, and come too close with her taunts.

"No-good bitch!" he shouted, raising the .38.

As he fired, Seymour Pike hit Sue with a blind-side clip, and she fell out of the bullet's path.

"That's enough!" boomed the President. "Everybody back in their seat. Except for you, Agee. Take care of that girl."

The Navy doctor had already torn Angie's shirt blouse and was applying compresses to the ugly blue-tipped wound through her shoulder just above the collarbone.

"As for you, young man," said Foster, turning to Miller, "bring yourself under control. You won't get what you want this way."

Anderson, whose head was being bathed by Liv Matthews, flickered his eyes open. The compartment was a blur. What the hell was going on?

He heard voices. One said, "I want this bird on course for Cut Bank."

Foster pressed a button. "Major McGowan," he said, "change course for Cut Bank, Montana."

"Yes, sir," said McGowan. Then: "What's going on back there? My instruments show that we're losing cabin pressure."

Anderson sat up and glared at Miller. "You stupid bastard, you've shot a hole in the skin. We're decompressing."

"Quiet!" said Miller. He listened. From the rear of the compartment, a hoarse whistling sound was heard.

"Plug it up with something," he ordered.

David Braun, the AP aeronautics writer, said, "It's right here. Give me a napkin."

Someone did, and he soaked it in a cup of coffee. He found the hole and, carefully, slipped the napkin up the pecan paneling. As it touched the hole, it was sucked in suddenly. He swooped his hand down and got an orange-juice glass, clapped it, open side forward, over the napkin, which was tearing into shreds. The whistling noise stopped.

"Miller," said Anderson, "you've flown long enough to know that we've got to take her down. That whole bulkhead could blow out any minute."

"Quiet, goddamn it," snapped the Steward. "Let me think."

"While you're thinking, let's get down to a safe altitude," said Anderson.

The President touched the intercom button, looked at Miller.

Miller hesitated. "All right," he said. "But not too low."

"Twelve thousand," said Anderson. "Descend at eight hundred feet a minute."

The President said, "Major McGowan, the Aircraft Commander instructs you to descend to twelve thousand feet at eight hundred feet a minute."

"Yes, sir," said McGowan's voice. "Commencing descent."

Agee, who had given Angie a pain-killing shot which put her to sleep, said to Miller, "You didn't hit any bones or major blood vessels. She ought to be all right."

"I didn't mean to hurt her," said Miller. "I didn't want to hurt anybody. You pushed me into it."

Anderson said, "It can't be helped, Miller. Because of what you're doing, you'll always be pushed. And every time you are, you'll fight back, until somebody's killed."

Miller hesitated. "I couldn't call it off now if I wanted to. Vern wouldn't let me."

"How could he stop you? You're his ace in the hole. Miller, I can outrun him in this plane. Without your gun down here, he hasn't got a chance. That's why he needed you."

"That Lightning's fast," said Miller.

"So are we. How about it, Miller? Forget what you had in mind. It's not in the cards, you know that. Let me go back to the flight deck and shake that P-38."

"If you do, what'll happen to me?"

"I don't know. But you'll still be alive."

The President said, "I'll do my best for you, young man. You have my promise, in front of these witnesses."

Senator Philip Hopper thundered, "You have *my* promise to see you on Death Row for skyjacking!"

"Phil," said the President, "sit down before I suggest that some of your fellow passengers *sit* you down."

"All right," said Miller. "I trust the Colonel. You go up front and see what you can do. But if you can't get rid of that fighter, I'm sticking with Vern."

"Just lower the hammer," said Anderson.

Miller looked at the cocked pistol, released the hammer, with his thumb holding it back from the striker. "I'll keep it ready," he promised.

Liv helped Anderson to his feet. The blood was still trickling down his forehead.

"Are you sure you're all right?" she asked.

He pressed her arm. "Right enough," he said.

"Be careful," she whispered.

Unsteadily, he began moving up the corridor beside the President's compartment, toward the flight deck of Air Force One.

To Vernon Justus, holding his altitude, it was as if Air Force One were slowly sinking away beneath him.

They're going down, he realized.

Unaware whether or not Ed Miller had undertaken the plan they had agreed on, and which actually did not concern him, he had been enjoying the slow stalk of the huge jet. Even from this distance, her size was immense.

Checking his compass, he saw that the President's plane was slowly changing course. Poor Ed Miller. He really intended to go through with the kidnap plan. Even working aboard the plane, viewing its security day after day, he apparently believed it was somehow possible to outrun the feds, with their computers and worldwide network of informants. To salve his conscience, Justus had originally planned to make the strike on a flight when, forewarned, Miller would be on sick call. But when the Steward insisted that he had a means of escaping from the plane "if something goes wrong," Miller's fate was lumped in with the others aboard.

Now, obviously, he had made his move—and apparently succeeded, for otherwise why would the plane be turning?

He lowered the nose of the P-38. He didn't want to let his target get too far ahead, or he might not be able to catch it.

On the flight deck, Carl Birney said, "Tom, we've passed one checkpoint without clearing it. All hell's probably breaking loose down there right now."

Anderson, strapping himself into the left seat, said, "I know. But that kid's gone crazy. He put a hole through the fuselage. And he shot that girl Steward." Then, numbly, he realized what he had said. "Paul, I—"

McGowan stiffened. "He *what*?"

"Take it easy, Paul. It's just a flesh wound."

McGowan was unbuckling. "That creep, I'll—"

"Harness up, Major!" said Anderson. "We've got a planeful of people to try and save. Read off that altitude."

Choked, McGowan said, "Passing through 27,000. What the hell's going on, Anderson?"

Concisely, Anderson explained what had happened. When he mentioned the P-38 fighter, Birney said, "And I don't think he likes our descent, Tom. He's closing faster."

"Let's take a chance," said Anderson. "Dent, give me a broad frequency. He's close enough that we ought to raise him, even on the wrong channel, with bleed-over."

"Roger," said the Radio Operator. "You've got it."

Into his mike, Anderson said, "Escort, this is Air Force One. We have received your instructions and are complying. Sergeant Miller is in command. Do you read?"

He waited, then repeated the message. There was no answer but the rush of static.

As Air Force One passed through 26,000 feet, Anderson gave up. "If he hears us, he's not interested," he said.

That was not so. Vernon Justus, at the controls of the P-38, was interested. It was just that he had other plans.

It had now been almost six minutes since he intercepted the President's plane. So far he had heard no radio communications which disturbed him.

But that couldn't last. Especially now that Air Force One had broken radio silence.

He felt the same chill in his stomach that had thrilled him so long ago, in those South Pacific skies. *This* was reality, not the daily scuffling and boredom. He had been bred and trained for this—and then, obsolete, had been tossed aside.

Well, not before he made one final triumphant kill.

He nosed the P-38 into a steep dive and watched the airspeed begin to increase.

So this was where she had come, through a series of events that, taken on the basis of chance, might have occurred only once in twenty million flights.

An ozone layer had moved down because of the winter's chill. A hostile Governor had raised the necessity of the flight. An angry man had joined his hatred with the fury of another. A President had, to influence those who doubted her need, manipulated circumstances intended to prove her worth, but these were now endangering her existence. A pilot flew, when he knew he should not.

Her side already wounded by a bullet hole, Air Force One tried to slip earthward, to safety.

*   *   *

The P-38 came out of the sun, with machine guns blazing.

Air Force One took the attack 24,700 feet over Fort Logan, Montana.

32

On Air Force One's flight deck, Anderson had found a way to put out a distress signal.

"Activate Seventy-seven," he told Dent.

Most large planes now carry a tiny transmitter called a transponder, which allows ground controllers to identify them on their radar screens. By switching to the SOS position, 77, a double image appeared on the controller's scope. It was a cry for help. And there was no way the P-38's pilot could pick up the 77 signal.

But for Anderson, and for Air Force One, it was already too late.

On his first pass, approaching from above and the rear, Justus stitched a row of fifty-caliber bullets down the left side of the plane. They smashed through the overhead, walking along the left row of seats, down the corridor between the President's compartment and the hull, and into the forward compartment. Justus, pulling out of his dive, missed the flight deck.

The fighter streaked past the jet, rolling over and doubling back for a second pass.

The first attack touched only one person in the center compartment. Seymour Pike, bending over to see if he could help Agee with the wounded girl, was struck just behind his right ear by a fragment of shattered bullet.

In less than a second of elapsed time, all the dreams

and the future were gone and the young reporter lay dead in the aisle. The wound was so small it hardly bled. But by the time Agee put a thumb against his carotid artery, Pike had no pulse.

In the forward compartment, one Secret Service man was wounded in the leg. His seat partner tore open the man's trousers and found a pressure point to stop the bleeding.

In the President's compartment, TSgt. Ed Miller felt the bullets slamming against the jet's hull and screamed, "What the hell's happening? What's he doing?"

President Howard Foster leaned forward and plucked the .38 revolver from Miller's numb hand.

With the tables reversed, he said, "I'm afraid your friend's trying to shoot us down, son."

Arthur Cummings and photographer John Williams leaped toward the Steward.

Unarmed, Miller made a mewing sound and, looking frantically for escape, lurched into the President's bedroom. The sound of the lock being clicked home was audible through the compartment.

"Kick it down," said Cummings.

"No," said the President. "He's safe in there. There's no place for him to go."

Anderson's voice came over the speakers. "Everybody strap in. We're getting out of here."

Air Force One, stung by the machine-gun barrage, was only slightly wounded. Vernon Justus had underestimated how sound her hull was. With all controls and electrical systems duplicated, and each section of fuselage structurally isolated from the next, it would take a massive blow in exactly the right place to destroy the airframe's integrity.

More dangerous were the leaks from the pressurized cabin into the thin air outside. Each bullet hole bleeding air through the plane's skin was a potential explosive decompression.

The President disregarded Anderson's order to strap on a seat belt. He stepped quickly to his desk and pressed a button on the red telephone. "Get me the advance plane," he told the Radio Operator.

"Yes, sir," said Dent.

In a moment, Foster was speaking with the Bagman.

"Your instructions, Chief," said the President, "are to open the Code Bag. I will require today's entry code for SAC."

"Yes, sir," said Chief Warrant Officer Fred Stewart. "May I have today's password?"

But before the President could say, "Vesper," the P-38 attacked again.

In the White House Situation Room, the Duty Officer was told that contact had been lost with Air Force One.

"Helena Control reports an emergency 77 on the transponder signal," he was told.

"Scramble fighters," said the Duty Officer.

"Sir, Malstrom's buttoned up. Only the President can get through. We don't have the entry code."

"Alert Looking Glass."

"Yes, sir," said the aide.

The aerial command center, fully manned with senior military officers, was equipped to take over if the government's chain of command broke down, or was destroyed. The Duty Officer knew that he did not have the authorization to hand over command of the country's defenses until it was confirmed that not only was the President unable to act, but neither were his successors—the Vice-President and the Speaker of the House. However, it was prudent to open the lines of communication and to alert the flying generals to the potential threat.

The aide returned. "I've scrambled an Air National Guard squadron down at Butte, sir. They had two fighters on ready, and they're already on the runway. Four more will take off within ten minutes."

"Very well," said the Duty Officer. "Keep trying to raise Air Force One."

On his second pass, Vernon Justus was beneath the big jet, and attacking from the front. In Air Force slang, he was at "twelve o'clock low."

Justus was surprised that the President's plane was still in the air. A burst such as he had given her on his first run would have blown the average World War II bomber into flaming shards.

His earphones were crackling with radio traffic now. He heard someone aboard the plane calling, "Mayday, Mayday. Air Force One is under attack by unidentified P-38. We have wounded aboard. Mayday."

But, as the machine-gun bullets stitched their way up the jet's underbelly, the voice stopped abruptly in mid-word. Either the radioman had been hit, or his equipment had been damaged.

Justus held down the firing button and, as he swept past the jet at a closing speed of nearly eight hundred miles an hour, he saw a piece of Air Force One's horizontal stabilizer break off, exposing bare struts and torn control cables.

He made his turn, an Immelmann which swooped him up and around in a one-eighty, and firewalled the throttles.

If he didn't blast Air Force One out of the sky this pass, his ammunition would be exhausted and he would have no choice but to ram her.

"He's coming at us again," McGowan had shouted. "Dent, alert Air Route Control. We're diving."

The Radio Operator, without reply, began calling, "This is Air Force One. We're diving. Clear all traffic. Mayday. Mayday. Air Force One is under attack . . ."

"Will she hold together?" asked McGowan "We're as full of holes as a Swiss cheese."

"She'll hold," said Anderson. His breath came hard, and he felt sweat on his forehead. His skin seemed hot.

"Dive brakes and gear?" asked McGowan. That combination would get them down fast.

"Negative," said Anderson. "We've got to outrun the bastard. If we trade airspeed for vertical drop, he'll be all over us."

The course he had chosen was far more dangerous, because at high speeds the airframe would be subjected to increased stress. But one more pass by the fighter might well be fatal.

The plane's airspeed increased to almost six hundred miles an hour.

"Here he comes," said McGowan calmly.

It was like a scene from a John Wayne movie. Except that they were playing the part of the enemy.

The Lightning bored toward them, and as if in that same movie, they saw the flash of its machine guns.

"Hard left," said Anderson. He stood on the rudder pedal, and McGowan helped. At the same time, Anderson banked the jet to coordinate the turn. Hopefully, nobody back there was bouncing off the overhead.

On the flight deck, the sound of the machine-gun bullets slamming into Air Force One's skin was like listening to a series of hammer blows against the aluminum.

"Level off," said Anderson, coughing.

"Shit!" said Dent.

"What's wrong?"

"He got the radios, sir."

Although the operating portions of the communications system—the tuners and microphones—were in the radio compartment, the actual transmitters and power supplies were in what would have been a normal jet's cargo hold.

And a stream of the P-38's bullets had torn through the jet's belly, pulverizing the delicate electronic gear.

"Can you lash anything up?" Anderson asked. He choked, wiped sweat from his face.

"I'll try," said Dent, pulling connectors from their sockets and attaching them to other units.

"Tom," said McGowan, quietly.

"Red-line her," said Anderson, shoving the throttles forward.

"Tom, look," said the Pilot.

He pointed.

The light which indicated someone was in the escape capsule had come on.

Anderson clicked his intercom switch. "Mr. President," he called, "are you in the capsule?"

The President answered, "I am not, Colonel. Sergeant Miller has locked himself in the compartment. It must be him."

Anderson activated the connection to the capsule. "Miller?" he said.

All he heard was a frightened sobbing.

Vernon Justus saw Air Force One diving, and lowered the Lightning's nose to pursue her.

But his gunsight told him that the angle of deflection was increasing. Air Force One was pulling away.

He put the P-38 into a steeper dive. As the jet passed through the center of his sights, he squeezed off the last few rounds left in his magazines.

He saw his airspeed climbing. With any luck, he could pull out of his dive directly beneath Air Force One and ram her from below.

TSgt. Ed Miller, so terrified that a streak of wetness glittered down his trousers leg, sat in the capsule and said, over and over, "I didn't mean to. I didn't want to hurt anybody."

No one answered. Once, a voice said, "Miller?" But he did not reply.

It was too late. Vern was going to kill them all.

Miller did not want to die. He wished that he could begin this day over again. He would have confessed everything, warned the Colonel, prevented this flight from ever starting.

Suddenly it was all clear before him. The whole thing had been a pipe dream. He wasn't important enough, or tough enough, or lucky enough, to carry off something like this insane kidnapping.

Vern had used him, for his own purposes. He had intended, all along, to shoot down Air Force One. And Miller along with her.

"Bastard," he whimpered.

His heart contracted when he heard the, by now, familiar sound of machine-gun slugs slamming into the plane.

She'll break up, he thought.

He's not going to get me!

He uncaged the EJECT button and, trembling, pressed it.

Air Force One was at 23,000 feet when the capsule hatch popped open and the capsule ejected.

It was as if the jet plane had slammed into a mountain.

The bullet holes had been minor pinpricks, draining away her life-giving air in little trickles.

This new breach in her skin was a severed artery. It was, in effect, an explosive decompression.

The door to the bedroom crushed inward, tearing off its hinges. Like the vortex of a tornado, everything not tied or fastened down was swept toward its gaping suction.

President Foster's chair was bolted to the floor. He

clutched it back, and felt the breath torn from his lungs.

Cups, glasses, plates, papers—all were drawn into the chaotic maw of what had been, seconds before, the President's bedroom. And, as the air swept out, the cold poured in. Even with the leaks from the bullet holes, the temperature inside the plane had been a nearly comfortable sixty-two degrees.

Now, in seconds, that temperature dropped to zero. Frost clouded the windows.

Oxygen masks dropped from their concealed niches in the overhead. Some had the presence of mind to grab them and, with a yank of the hose to start oxygen flowing, place them against their faces.

Others stared numbly, and began to drift into the twilight world of anoxia, oxygen starvation. It was like dreaming, with no fear and no concern with reality. Unconsciousness would come within seconds, death in minutes.

On the flight deck, Anderson knew instantly what had happened. The capsule light had blinked out at the very second the plane seemed to fly into a solid surface.

"He's ejected," he shouted. "Dive!"

There was no option. As his own mask fell, and he reached for it, he knew that only minutes separated life from death for his passengers unless Air Force One came closer to earth—and warmth and breathable air.

"President's compartment . . ." he gasped. "Drop the walls."

Juan Hernandez flipped off his belt. "I'll get it, sir," he said. He had to almost crawl up the steep incline of the plane's deck, so steep was the dive. The door clicked shut behind him.

"Six hundred knots," warned McGowan. "Dive brakes? We're building up terminal speed."

"Brakes . . ." said Anderson. As his hand reached

for the control, he coughed, and saw blood spatter on his wrist. "Paul," he whispered. "Take her."

His mind whirled, and he blacked out.

But his voice, and his body, continued to perform. As he babbled, "Put her nose down, let's give them a real roller coaster," his hands clutched at the control yoke.

McGowan fought for command. "Carl!" he yelled. "Help."

Birney leaped to the space between the pilots' seats and tried to pry Anderson away from the yoke. "He's out of his head," he said. "Sir! Come out of it!"

"Yank his mask," McGowan commanded.

Birney pulled it off. In seconds, Anderson slumped unconscious. "Shall I put it back on?" Birney gasped.

"Get him on the floor first," said McGowan. He had now dropped the landing gear and had the dive brakes fully extended. The airspeed of the plane slowed, but her rate of descent increased. The altimeter was whirling through 18,000, and although the air was freezing cold and very thin, it would at least support life.

Hernandez had dragged himself down the corridor and into the President's compartment. He had to pry Foster's hands away from the seat back. Unceremoniously, Hernandez rolled the President out into the aisle. He found the switch which activated the walls, pressed it, and they came down, enclosing the compartment again. He crawled through the door, slammed it, and the shriek of the blown hatch abated somewhat. The main cabin was now semi-isolated from the near-vacuum of the bedroom.

It had been less than two minutes since Miller blew the capsule through Air Force One's roof. The passengers were still in a state of near-shock. Each had reacted differently.

Sue Earhart had thrown herself over Seymour Pike's body, as if to protect him. She felt trays and cups hitting her as the suction drew them toward the gaping hole.

David Braun, knowing instantly what had happened, got his oxygen mask on the moment it dropped, and then began helping others.

John Williams and Senator Christopher Healy tried to reach the President, but they were hurled to the floor by the force of Air Force One's dive. Both blacked out for a few seconds, until those close to them pressed oxygen masks over their faces.

Lieutenant Commander George Agee clamped a mask over Angie's face, then grabbed one for himself.

Arthur Cummings, thrown against Liv Matthews, bowed almost politely, and collapsed. She couldn't find another mask, so she shared her own with him in an aerial version of buddy-breathing.

Morton Bailey grabbed Senator Philip Hopper, who was trying to climb over the back of the seat in front of him. "Buckle up!" yelled the young press secretary.

When the Senator screamed something incoherent, Bailey said with delight, "You're hysterical," and slugged him. Then he buckled the stunned Senator into his seat belt.

Some of the White House staff remained calm. Others panicked.

But all were alive when Air Force One leveled out at 11,000 feet. Even in this emergency, McGowan had remembered "Neodd."

The plane was heading north, but now he began to correct his course. To Birney, he called, "Where's that bandit?"

"We left him way the hell up there," said the Navigator. "And it looks as if he's got company."

Air Force One's sudden acceleration surprised Justus, and when he began his pullout, he realized that he was going to miss her on the upward roll. He tried to correct, to turn his fighter back into a speed-gaining dive, but his response was too late, and he saw his target pulling away.

A movement caught the corner of his eye. When he twisted around, he saw an F-104 with Air National Guard markings flying off his port wing.

His radio crackled. "Throttle back, buddy, or you're dead."

Hesitating, Justus heard another voice. The message was anything but official radio traffic. "Bring her on down, turkey, or I'll blow you away. You're right in my sights."

Justus checked his mirror and saw another jet directly behind him.

Hell, he thought, his mind reverting back to 1944 and those cloud-filled skies over the Pacific.

"Fuck you," he yelled, "no Meatball made can catch a P-38!"

He slipped off on one wing, out of the jet's field of fire, and rammed the throttles to the wall.

"Take him, Walt," a calm voice said.

A heat-seeking missile left the weapons pod of the lead fighter. Trailing white smoke from its rocket engine, it homed in on the exhaust vent of the P-38's starboard engine and, in an explosion that tore the old plane into tiny fragments, impacted.

After a moment, the calm voice said, "No parachutes."

"Let's catch up with Air Force One," said the other pilot. He switched frequencies and began calling the President's plane, but there was no response.

The first voice said, "He must have got their radio. Pull up alongside and we'll shepherd them with hand signals."

The two jet fighters winged over and began the dive down to 11,000 feet.

It took more than three minutes for the fragments of the P-38 to tumble down to the Montana hills.

One, blackened by flame and soot, left a red smear across a cliff face.

Perhaps a Meatball—a Japanese Zero, so named because of the red circle of the rising sun—could not overtake a P-38. But the years, and technology, had.

33

"Air National Guard, do you copy?" asked TSgt. Lester Dent.

He received no response.

Carl Birney, who had taken over the left seat of Air Force One, flying copilot for Paul McGowan, shouted, "Dent! They're signaling back."

The two F-104s were waggling their wings.

"They copy you," said Birney.

"That means we're transmitting again," said Dent, who had been joining wires in a search to activate one of the radios. "We're just not receiving." He keyed his microphone. "Air National Guard, this is Air Force One. If you are receiving dip your wings."

"He did it," said Birney.

McGowan tried the radio, "Air National Guard, do you see signs of structural damage? Dip once for yes, twice for no."

Glumly, Birney said, "He dipped once, Paul."

Calmly, McGowan radioed again: "Once for serious, twice for moderate, three times for slight."

Birney reported, "Twice. Moderate."

McGowan said, "That's better than I thought." Into the microphone, he said, "Helena Control, this is Air Force One. Request clearance for straight-in landing. National Guard, relay message. Once for affirmative, twice for negative."

He peered past the Navigator, out the left window.

He could see one of the F-104s just ahead of his port wing.

In a moment, slowly, the fighter dipped its wings two times.

McGowan slammed the pedestal with his free hand. "Goddamned bastards!" he said.

The airman's motto that if something can go wrong, it will, was holding today.

Northwest of Alaska's North Slope, the incoming missile passed the coordinates where it should have self-destructed. A forty-three-cent switch, slightly corroded, did not make contact when ordered to by the onboard computer.

The dummy missile bored through the substratosphere toward Prudhoe Bay.

And the pyramiding of tiny errors continued. The missile's backup destruct system was tuned to a particular radar frequency which had been, until this month, in common use around the Distant Early Warning System's bases.

That frequency had been changed, however. And because *Urchin* was at sea, somehow the frequency modification had not caught up with the nuclear sub.

So, while the new frequency pinpointed the missile's location and course, to the missile, there was no radar at all.

Relentlessly, it closed in on its programmed target.

In the White House Room, the Duty Officer was told, "Air Force One's transmitting again. They were damaged by a fighter attack, but they're now in view of two Air National Guard planes, showing moderate damage. However, they can't receive."

The Duty Officer had just received the latest report on the approaching missile. The vast resources of the United States defense forces were only minutes away from Red Alert. He knew all too well that once a Red was called, the chances of devastating error would magnify.

He had already put in a call to Vice-President Arthur Rand, who was somewhere in Maine, fishing for salmon. Guides had been dispatched to hurry him to the nearest telephone.

Jake Dobbs, the venerable Speaker of the House, had been sent for and was on his way by squad car from the Capitol.

If contact could not be made with the President within the next few minutes, there was no alternative but to assume he was powerless. Direction of the government and the country's nuclear strike force would be taken from him and turned over to the next in the chain of command.

Anderson had recovered consciousness and was sitting up in the cramped open spot between seats and equipment. "How do you feel, sir?" asked Hernandez.

"Groggy," said Anderson. "Paul? What's happening?"

"We're on our way to Helena," said the Pilot. "Pretty well shot up, but still flying. Are you okay?"

"More or less," said Anderson. "Did we get clearance to land at Helena?"

"Negative," said McGowan. "But we have no choice. We're transmitting, but we can't receive. Dent's tried Malstrom, but according to the National Guard boys out there, there's been no response."

Anderson, groaning, pulled himself up. "Take it easy, sir," said Hernandez.

Birney started to slip out of the left seat.

"No," said Anderson. "You stay there. Keep helping Paul. He's in command."

McGowan started to protest, but Anderson stopped him. "I'm not fit to fly. You're doing fine. I'll go back to see how things are. Dent, keep an ear open. I may be on the horn."

Hernandez said, "The President's compartment is sealed off, sir."

Anderson said, "Then I'll use one of the secretary's phones in the main compartment."

"I'll be listening, sir," said Dent.

"Meanwhile," said Anderson, "keep trying to find some way for us to receive."

"I'm trying," promised the Radio Operator.

In the forward compartment, Anderson asked, "Anybody hurt?"

One of the Secret Service men said, "Johnson took a slug in the leg. He's okay. We're freezing our butts off, but that's all."

"Hang in there," said Anderson. To the Security and Maintenance men from the 89th, he said, "Get rags, wood, plastic—whatever you can find—and start plugging up holes. If you spot anything serious, like broken control cables, let me know."

He went back through the corridor to the main compartment.

The President, pinching his nose to stop a trickle of blood, nodded and said, "That was some descent, Colonel. Congratulations."

"They're owed to Major McGowan, sir. Anyone hurt back here?"

His face darkened when he was told about Pike.

"It was just bad luck, Colonel," said Agee. "The boy didn't feel a thing." He examined Anderson carefully. "Are you all right yourself?"

"No," said the Aircraft Commander. "I've known for some time that I suffer from porphyria. The oxygen starvation got me just now. I need something to keep me going for another hour."

Agee, obviously shocked, didn't speak. He reached for his bag, found an ampule, and broke it, revealing a throwaway hypodermic needle.

"I don't recommend this," said the doctor, "but once won't matter that much."

He waited until Anderson had rolled up his sleeve, and injected the drug.

Almost before the needle was out, Anderson had turned to the President. "Sir," he said, "we're transmitting now, but we still can't receive. I assume that the SAC alert is still holding. Do you want to try to reach Malstrom again?"

"It isn't just Malstrom," said the President. "It's every SAC base around the world. If everything has gone as it should, the missile has self-destructed by now. But if it hasn't—"

"You're a lunatic," shouted Senator Philip Hopper. "Is this the way you plan to run your Administration? By tricks and deceit? You've made one fine beginning!"

"For once I agree with you, Phil," said Foster. "I seem to have outsmarted myself. Well, unless we find someplace to put this plane down, Arthur Rand may have to pick up the pieces."

"Divert to another field," Hopper told Anderson.

"Malstrom's out," said Anderson. "Thanks to that FAA ruling, Helena's closed to military traffic. And I doubt if we can make it any further, shot up as we are."

Hopper lurched out of his chair. "I've got to make a call," he croaked. "I've got to call Washington."

"Who do you want?" Anderson said, picking up the telephone. "Dent? Hold on for an important call."

"Willoughby. FAA."

Anderson glanced at the President, who nodded. He handed the phone to the Senator.

Dent told Hopper, "I'll try, sir, but we can't receive. We'll just have to shove it out there and hope for the best. National Guard, if we get a response, give me two dips."

"Office of the FAA Administrator," Hopper said rapidly. "Mr. Willoughby. Hello? Hello?"

Dent said, "National Guard indicates that someone has answered."

Hopper almost babbled. "This is Senator Philip Hopper. Tell Willoughby to cancel that regulation about military planes landing at civilian airports. You hear me, cancel it! If he doesn't, I'll ruin him! I'll have all your hides! Tell him to forget everything I said. Malstrom wasn't supposed to be closed! If that ruling isn't canceled immediately, he's out on his ass!"

Foster took the telephone from his hand and, quietly, said, "This is the President. If you receive me, please contact Helena Municipal. We're landing with or without clearance. Thank you."

He put down the phone and smiled at the trembling Senator.

"Phil," he said, "if we ever get back home, you and me and Mr. Willoughby are going to have quite a little talk."

Had Air Force One only known it, the landing clearance at Helena had already been arranged by Advance Man Warren Rogers.

His statement to the five-man board of governors had lasted only two minutes.

"The President is up there in a plane that, from our current information, is damaged and carrying wounded. Some idiot in Washington, aided and abetted by this moron"—and he indicated the Governor of Montana—"has put our President in danger for political advantage. Malstrom Air Force Base is shut down because of a defense alert, and Air Force One has only one other place to land. Right here. The FAA says she can't. What do you say?"

The vote was unanimous, the tower chief, grinning, had run back to his office, and Hoskins' protests were almost unheard as he insisted that the board of governors had no right to overrule an FAA directive.

"Lloyd," he said to one of them, "you're letting me down. I thought you backed me."

"I did, Claude," said the banker. "But I must have been crazy. Oh, it isn't what you've tried to do that disgusts me the most. It's how stupidly you handled it. We must have been blind to support you. I think, when I see the boys downtown, we're going to have to reconsider everything we promised."

"I've got an idea," Dent told Anderson over the phone. "Our Quail tell us we're getting through to the advance plane, but the entry code is too complicated for them to get it over to us with wing dips. My slow-scan TV is working. I can contact some nearby radio ham who's into slow-scan too, the advance plane can give him the code, and he'll put it on his tube and beam it up to us."

When Anderson asked the President if that would breach security, Foster nodded. "Of course it will, but what choice do we have? The code's only effective today anyway. So let's go to it."

"Vesper," he said into the microphone, hoping it would be received by the Bagman. "Chief Stewart, this is the President. Listen closely . . ."

Meanwhile, Dent had gone to another frequency and was calling, "CQ, CQ, looking for Slow-Scanners. This is Air Force One, broadcasting in the blind. We have an emergency and cannot receive." He gave the frequency of his slow-scan receiver, and said, "Please, fellers, don't everybody jump on me. Let the first guy handle the traffic. This is an emergency."

Anderson and the President had gone forward. As Anderson opened the door to the flight deck, he heard Dent shout, "Yahoo!"

The Radio Operator pointed at the small TV monitor. Words were forming on it, like a teletype.

"He's got his camera aimed at a Selectric typewriter," said Dent.

They read, "KWC-8905 receiving Air Force One. What is your problem?"

Into his microphone, Dent said, "We need a message relayed from our advance plane. It will be in code, so copy carefully." He gave the meeting frequency, and said, "Air Force One standing by."

They waited for what seemed hours but by the aircraft digital clock was only slightly more than three minutes.

A new picture began to form on the TV screen.

"KWC-8905 to Air Force One. Code name, Vesper. Message follows."

Dent waited, notebook in hand.

The Selectric somewhere down there in Montana typed: "Hotdog and Catsup. 99-482-111-0. Ballgame." Then: "Message ends."

"Many thanks," Dent yelled into his microphone. "Air Force One out."

As the Radio Operator switched frequencies, the President said, "Find out who that ham operator is. He's earned gold-plated call letters for the rest of his life."

"Air Force One calling Malstrom Control," Dent radioed. "Hotdog and Catsup. 99-482-111-0. Ballgame."

The Air National Guard jet jinked up and down to attract attention, then dipped its wings once.

"They heard us," yelled Dent excitedly. Into his mike he said, "Just a minute, hold for the President."

It had taken TSgt. Ed Miller nearly eight minutes to reach the barren ground of central Montana. The capsule dropped, in free fall, for nearly 20,000 feet until the altitude-activated mechanism automatically deployed three bright orange parachutes.

Although there had been an oxygen bottle near his left thigh, Miller was too frozen by panic to use it. By the time the chutes popped, he was almost blue from cold and lack of oxygen. He was semiconscious when the capsule slammed into a snow-covered ridge.

The protective plastic sides sprang open, and he tumbled out into the snow. A bitter wind howled out of the north.

All survival instructions were stern about staying near the bright markers of the parachutes. Miller had forgotten them. Instead, he began breaking his way through the crusted drifts in a direction that he hoped was downhill.

For perhaps half a mile, it was. Then he realized that he had trapped himself in a box canyon, and that no matter which way he turned, he would have to climb.

Senator Hopper had buttonholed Sue Earhart and Scott Meadows.

"Deception," said the Senator. "He's put the country at the very brink of war, just to impress us with this plane."

"Wrong," said Meadows. "Events put us there. Sure, he was stacking the cards. So were you. The difference is, Senator, that President Foster pulled us out of the hole *you* helped dig."

Hopper, to Sue, went on. "I don't have to point out what a story this is. Attacking his own defenses by missile . . . putting SAC on alert . . . harboring a hijacker aboard his own plane—"

"Whoa," said Sue "All I know, Senator, is that we had the gun to our heads three times over, and the President and this crew and, yes, this plane, got us out of it. I agree with Scott. If this had been a chartered plane, we would all be dead right now." Her voice dropped. "Instead of just poor Speedy."

"But—you promised."

Sweetly, she said, "Darling, I was wrong."

* * *

The unarmed missile impacted two miles east of the Alaskan pipeline, fifty miles inland from Prudhoe Bay. If the President had not called off the alert, by now SAC bombers would have been orbiting their Fail-Safe positions. And, without word from the President, it was quite likely that the Speaker of the House —since Arthur Rand was still unlocated in the wilds of Maine—might have ordered what he supposed was a second strike against what was presumably the origination point of the missile, Soviet Russia.

Perhaps it even fell without sound in the forest, for, after all, there was no one there to hear it.

The nearest F-104 waggled its wings violently.

"Go, National Guard," said McGowan. "Do we have radio traffic?"

One dip. Yes.

"From Malstrom?"

Two dips. No.

"Helena?"

One dip.

"Are we cleared for landing?"

One dip.

"Many thanks," said the Pilot. He turned to Anderson. "Do you want to take her in, Tom?"

"No," said Anderson. "But I'll fly right seat for you."

Birney steadied the controls while McGowan released the yoke. After Anderson had taken over at the copilot's position, McGowan assumed the Command position of the left seat.

Helena Municipal was less than fifteen minutes due west. Air Force One had drifted down to ten thousand feet. "Sweven."

"Holding at ten thousand," said Anderson. "Begin descent in thirty seconds."

"Roger," said McGowan. He ran through his prelanding checklist. They were flying slower than normal because of the extended gear, which he dared not retract, for fear undiagnosed hydraulic problems might cause a jam.

Anderson consulted the instruments, which were the quiet guardians of Air Force One's safety from now until touchdown.

"Commence descent," he said.

It was odd, riding in the right seat after so many years. McGowan had his own way of flying. There were moves he made which Anderson would not have. But he could not fault the other pilot. McGowan was right on course, flying a badly damaged airplane without radio ears.

The National Guard planes kept pace with them.

McGowan said, "Quail, relay the tower's instructions. Helena Tower, this is Air Force One. Are we on your screens?"

One wing dip. Yes.

"I have us eleven miles from the outer marker." He had consulted a plaque which listed a series of airspeeds versus weight and drag. "I estimate Boundary Speed at one-thirty knots. Helena, give me wind speed. Quail, one dip for each five miles."

The nearest F-104 dipped its wings four times.

"That's a copy at twenty miles head wind."

A single dip of the jet fighter's wing confirmed his statement.

"Eight thousand," said Anderson. "A little high."

McGowan throttled back slightly. The whine of the jet engines lowered.

The President, sitting quietly on the extra jump seat, watched with fascination.

All this has been going on without my knowing it, he thought. I've argued, pro and con, for this mission, and I never even knew what it really consisted of. It isn't nine-million-dollar planes, or fancy communications gear, or even the pomp and circumstance of the great blue-and-white plane arriving at some foreign airfield.

It's men—dedicated, tireless, loyal, professional *men*. And, he added, remembering the wounded cabin attendant, *women*. Without them, none of this stuff is worth the paint to keep it from rusting.

Maybe Hopper and those media people learned a lesson today. But I learned a bigger one. I've been looking in the wrong direction. It's not as simple as cutting total costs. What I've got to do is utilize the tremendous commitment these people have. They're my secret weapon.

He heard Colonel Anderson say quietly, "Six thousand feet. You're thirty knots hot. Reduce airspeed."

Grateful, with the vibration that had racked her bowels now quieting down, Air Force One sank toward the distant patch of asphalt and concrete that was known as Helena Municipal Airport.

Far behind, Ed Miller found a cave. His lungs hurt from the thin, cold air. His pants were torn from the falls he had taken on the icy cliffs. He had tried to return to the capsule, but lost his tracks on bare rock slopes. Now he wandered in widening circles.

The cave was out of the wind. And it seemed warmer. It was a good place to rest for a while.

He crawled inside and huddled in one corner. There seemed to be a buzz in his ears. He shivered, until sleep covered him with a warm blanket.

He would be found the following spring, by a hunter attracted by a swarm of buzzards, orbiting the tattered flesh and gleaming bones dragged from the cave by wolves.

"Gear down," said Anderson. He knew it was already down, but the rule was to observe every item on the checklist.

"Gear is down and locked," said McGowan.

"ILS right on the money," said Anderson.

An Instrument Landing System approach was not necessary today, with the clear visibility, but Mc-Gowan had asked for it and, as Aircraft Commander, his request was an order. Meanwhile, Anderson monitored the landing visually. It was a method of landing which, when handled properly, was doubly safe.

"I have the runway in sight," said Anderson.

"Helena Tower, we have runway contact," said Mc-Gowan. "Are we cleared to land?"

The nearby fighter's wing dipped once.

"Cleared to land," said Anderson.

The plane buffeted slightly. Thermal activity was occurring, where great bubbles of warmer air broke from the ground and rose rapidly, to become cumulus clouds when they reached a height cold enough to condense their moisture.

"Twelve hundred feet," said Anderson. "Crossing outer marker."

"Fifty degrees flap," said McGowan.

Anderson activated the flap lever. The tail seemed heavy. He trimmed it up.

Another gust hit the plane, and it yawed suddenly. The F-104 began waggling its wings frantically.

Although he could not see it, Anderson knew what had happened. He said, "Reduce port thrust. We've just lost our left horizontal stabilizer."

Air Force One was close enough to the tower so that Rogers, watching through ten-power binoculars, saw the chunk of metal rip away from the plane's tail section. He was not the only one who saw it. The tower chief pressed an alarm button and shouted into a microphone, "Emergency landing! Fire gear, ambulances, get out there."

One fire truck and an ambulance had already been waiting on the service roads. Lipton's command sent half a dozen others roaring out of their garages.

The voice of an Air National Guard pilot crackled from the loudspeaker. "Air Force One has just lost a chunk of her left horizontal stabilizer. She's yawing badly. Gear is down. They're going to try and make it."

"Good luck, you poor bastards," whispered the Advance Man.

She tried to roll to the left, but both McGowan and Anderson fought her. Wounded, she trembled in pain, and they soothed her with gentle movements of the controls and with delicate blasts of her jet engines.

"Bug speed, one-ten!" called Anderson. They were dangerously slow as they passed the airport boundary.

McGowan advanced the port thrust a hair. He did not dare add more.

"Flaring out," he said.

She leveled off, thirty feet above the runway's hardtop approach. Some supply buildings, a fence—once these were cleared, they had nearly two miles of delicious airstrip in front of them. If only the gear had not been damaged, and held.

The gear touched, screeched, caught hold.

"Reverse thrust!" shouted McGowan. "Hit those brakes."

Anderson repeated, "Brakes."

McGowan had thrown the thrust levers forward, and now he pulled on the wing's spoilers, killing any lift the plane might still have left in its forward motion.

Tires squealed and burned with white smoke. One of the tandem wheels blew and left a strip of burning, tumbling rubber for half a mile down the runway.

By the time they had reached the primary turnoff for the terminal building, Air Force One was moving slowly enough for McGowan to turn her nose wheel and aim her toward the group of running ground

crew and Secret Service who had poured out of the
building.

Anderson began laughing.

McGowan, worried, turned to him. "What the hell?"
he asked.

Anderson pointed at his watch.

"Nine thirty-four, exactly," he said.

34

The President, flanked by Secret Service men and television cameras, left the plane as if the flight had been perfectly normal. He waved to the crowd, and had to be warned that time was short, to keep him from working the fence with a round of handshakes.

Before he left the flight deck, he told the crew, "You're all in for commendations. Maybe more."

The moment he was gone, McGowan began to unbuckle. "Handle the shutdown?" he asked Anderson. "I've got to see about Angie."

"Right," said Anderson. "Only, wait a minute." He tapped the woven wings on the left breast of McGowan's tunic. "I've always thought those sewed-on things were tacky." He unfastened his own silver wings and dropped them into McGowan's hand. "Try these."

"Tom," said McGowan, surprised, "what the hell do you think you're doing?"

"What I should have done a year ago," said Anderson.

"Shit," said McGowan. "We can't run this outfit without you."

"I'll keep running the outfit. If they let me. But it's up to you to fly the plane."

"Do you think there'll still *be* one after this?"

"Still?" asked Anderson. "Hell, there isn't any choice. As long as there's a President, there'll be an Air Force One."

* * *

Angie, barely awake, looked up at Paul McGowan.

"Hi," she said. "One of your nice Stewards shot me."

"Probably jealous," he said. "How do you feel."

"Crummy." Agee and the others had moved back to give them privacy. Through the rear hatch, four men were carefully removing Seymour Pike's body. Senator Philip Hopper sat in a rear seat, shaking his head and making notes on a sheet of Air Force One stationery.

McGowan said, "We're a little beat up, but we got here. Mostly due to Anderson and the crew."

"I heard you flew her over most of the high jumps."

"We all flew her," he said. "Listen, you're going to get well, you hear me? I can't do without you. That's all I could think of, up there on the flight deck, fighting myself to keep from dropping everything to come back here to you."

"Of course I'm going to get well, you nerd. What do you think this is, the last reel of *Love Story*? I've only got a little hole in my shoulder. Set the bone myself." In her joke, she had moved her arm, and she winced and tears came into her eyes. "Ouch."

He hugged her gently, careful not to touch her wound. "Baby, I love you. I'm staying with you until you're better, and—"

She shook her head. "No, Paul. You're flying the President home, because that's what you've got to do."

He could not disagree with her.

"All right," he said. "But you can't get rid of me. I need you. It's about time I admitted it. You can believe me, hon."

"I believe you," she lied. It was a form of hope, what she said. Maybe it would come true.

Liv and Anderson walked around the tattered plane. The fifty-caliber bullets had torn great holes in her body. Jagged chunks of aluminum hung like icicles from a Christmas tree. The sinews of her control cables were clearly visible through the gaping holes. Where the stabilizer had broken off, the stumps of ribs and main beams were twisted into doughy knobs.

"I don't know how she stayed in the air," said Anderson.

Liv held his arm. "There were too many great people rooting for her," she said.

He turned and took her away from there, to the main terminal.

"Why are you in such a hurry?" Liv asked.

"Because I'm not going to get caught in the same trap again," he said harshly. "That thing out there is aluminum and steel and plastic. It's only a machine, constructed by men to serve men. I'm goddamned if I'll get sentimental over it."

Her hand found his. "How about getting sentimental over me?"

"That's different," he said. "Liv—I've turned in my wings. Not officially, but that's only paper work. I'm grounded, baby."

"Good," she said. "Now I can stop worrying about you."

"I've got what might be a nasty divorce ahead of me," he said. "I don't make much money, and I never will."

"That doesn't matter," she said. "I'm independently wealthy."

He stared at her, and she kissed him.

"You're kidding," he said.

"No, I'm not," she said, with another kiss. "I've got a heart of gold."

A voice from the terminal's loudspeaker called, "Will the Aircraft Commander of Air Force One please report to the tower?"

"Whoops," said Anderson. "Hon, I've got to—"

She did not release his hand. "You've got to what?"

Slowly, he looked at her and smiled.

"Why, nothing," he said. "They're calling some other guy."

They towed her into an unused hangar, and photographers and reporters gathered and gasped over her wounds. They recorded her for the evening news, and then they left, and the doors were closed, leaving her to gloom and hours of quiet.

One afternoon, a tall man in Air Force uniform came and waved the sentries aside. He stood near her for a long while, looking. He did not touch her, although he could have gone up the ramp to do so. When he had looked long enough, he went away.

The winter passed, and when the birds and butterflies began making their nests in her shattered sides, more men came and, after photographing her from every direction, began, carefully, to dismantle her cabins for the Smithsonian Museum.

She never flew again.

AFTERWORD

Air Force One is fiction, but it did not start out that way. On the morning of February 19, 1970, my wife, Betty, and I went to the East Gate of the White House and were ushered inside. There we met Brigadier General Kenneth Hughes, military attaché to President Richard M. Nixon. I had been in correspondence with General Hughes regarding a book I had in mind about the President's airplane. His response had been moderately negative, but finally it was agreed that we should meet and discuss the matter further.

I had assumed we'd be doing so in his office. I was wrong. We went down to the West Basement, where Herb Klein, the President's chief of communications, joined us, and then a staff car whisked us to the Pentagon, where an Air Force helicopter was waiting. General Hughes, pointing out modestly that he had only gotten his chopper license the week before, took the controls and turned my hair white by taking us directly over National Airport at a meager 1,000 feet, with commercial aircraft flying below and *above* us.

At Andrews AFB, in nearby Maryland, Colonel Ralph Albertazzi, Aircraft Commander of the presidential plane, was waiting. He took us aboard the jet most popularly known as Air Force One—a modified Boeing 707 with the tail number 26000.

It was an odd luncheon we shared. Hughes and Albertazzi were polite, direct, but apparently opposed to my doing the book. Big "ifs" kept interfering. *If* I were permitted to research the book, I was to make no investigation into any other aspect of the 89th Wing's activities. (I had produced a stony silence by asking about "Night Watch" and "Looking Glass," two semi-secret operations conducted out of Andrews.) *If* I were allowed to continue, I must promise not to inconvenience or annoy President Nixon. And so on. But, as I met each of these possible objections, I sensed that I wasn't really getting to the center of their problem. I had already pointed out that I could do the book anyway, working from public and Freedom of Information sources.

Betty caught on before I did. Seated next to me by the port window overlooking the swept-back wing, she made a little doodle on her note pad and flashed it to me.

She had drawn: $$$$.

Someone was afraid I would zero in on the heretofore unrevealed amount of money the presidential air missions cost.

At that time, such an exposé was the last thing in my mind. To be honest, I was fascinated with the plane. It appealed to my love of gadgets, electronics, and flight. I believed then, as I still do, that it is absolutely necessary our President—*any* President—has the finest equipment money can provide. When I stood up and went into what I call, from some years spent presenting TV storyboards to bored advertising clients, my Eric Hoffer speech—in which every word is shouted or otherwise made to appear gigantically important—the effect was sudden. Actually, all I said was that I didn't give a damn how much the plane cost, it was well worth it. Instant relief, smiles, and fresh coffee for all. A few cleanup details, handshakes, and I was told that I would get the go-ahead.

When I asked for some form of identification to allow me onto the Air Force bases I intended to be visiting, I received only a knowing smile and the promise, "Don't worry. You won't have any trouble. They'll know who you are."

And they did. For months I strolled into tightly guarded areas with no more authority than an advance call giving my name and the purpose of my visit.

I had a ball for a while. Other writers viewed me with green-eyed envy. The book was announced and, from its simple inclusion in the publisher's catalogue, was instantly pegged for the number two spot by a large service which rents best sellers to libraries.

So why didn't I go ahead and publish my non-fiction biography of the world's most important airplane?

Two unexpected facts interfered.

A letter from the White House, signed by General Hughes, arrived bearing the unexpected instruction that my copy had to be cleared by the Administration. The reader must remember that this was before Watergate, in a time when a White House request was not easily ignored.

And I got to know the real people behind Air Force One perhaps a bit too well. At Andrews, and in Fort Worth, where I attended training sessions (and piloted the simulator in a landing only slightly better than the one described in the opening chapter of this novel), they were friendly, candid, and often indiscreet. I realized that if I printed everything I'd heard, some tails might be caught in the prop wash of official disapproval.

The combination was too much for me. I canceled the project and returned my publisher's advance, which left me in a deep hole since I had already spent thousands of dollars on research. I dug myself out by writing and publishing more novels—but Air Force One was never far from my thoughts or my heart.

I continued my research, but limited myself to that material which was available to any other reporter willing to dig. I wanted no special favors from the White House, because in the event I ever *did* write my book, I had no intention of submitting it for approval—or censorship.

But the problem seemed unsolvable. I mumbled about it over beers in nine countries. Then, one night at a party celebrating her latest smash, *Once Is Not Enough*, Jacqueline Susann said, "Stop fighting it, stupid. What you've got here is a novel."

Bless dear Jackie, who—unknown to most—was always outrageously generous and helpful to other writers. A novel fixed all my hangups. I wouldn't hurt anybody's career, because I'd be using fictional names. Besides, the Old Guard was all gone by now. And, except for actual personal security details about the President, I wouldn't feel under any obligation to submit my book for White House scrutiny.

So, after seven years of research and writing, *Air Force One* has finally landed. And its flight was assisted by many, in the air and on the ground. To name just a few:

Colonel Ralph Albertazzi, Aircraft Commander when I began my research, was always friendly and helpful.

Herb Klein, whose positive reaction toward the idea of such a book helped overcome adverse positions held by others less inclined to allow free access to the semi-secret activities out at Andrews.

Brigadier General Kenneth Hughes, who made the project live. I suspect he was acting under higher orders when he requested that the book be submitted for clearance.

And the other Pilots, Navigators, Flight Engineers, Radio Operators, and Flight Traffic Specialists of the presidential aircrew, who shared their opinions, professional knowledge, gripes, and an occasional cold brew with me.

The present Administration has been cordial, and I offered to let the aircrew and security personnel examine my specific sketches and details involving the presidential cabin. They declined, which surprised me. However, the reader may be assured that while the configuration of the fictional Air Force One is completely accurate in most respects, I have altered certain details to avoid pinpointing the President's location during flights.

For my medical expertise, particularly the dread disease which forced our fictional Aircraft Commander into his decision to step down from that precious left seat, I'd like to thank:

My nephew, Raymond Zekauskas, M.D., who—when still interning—came up with porphyria as a lovely way to put a pilot out of action in a high-altitude stress situation.

Dr. Arthur Ulene, consulting medic of the "Today" program, who confirmed the diagnosis and the subsequent effects on our hero. Porphyria is extremely rare, yet Dr. Ulene, as a resident, encountered two cases of the disease, and passed on his observations to me.

Dr. C. D. Taylor, our genial GP down here in Pass Christian, who added some common sense to all the needles and pills.

And all the others—Fletcher Knebel, who shared impressions of his own flights aboard Air Force One . . . novelist Roderick Thorp, who presented me with a stack of research material more than two feet high which he had gathered for another project . . . Robin Moore, who revealed backstairs hotel secrets about political lunches . . . the friendly staff of the American Airlines Simulator operation and the Stewardess School in Fort Worth . . . pilots of nearly every airline in the country, who shared their experiences with me in a hundred airport coffee shops . . . my stalwart assistant, Gail Scarboro, who nearly wore out one IBM Selectric on the many drafts of the book with never a complaint, only pleas for fresh ribbons . . . and, finally, my wife, Betty, who tried vainly to swipe a monogrammed martini glass from the plane, but had to settle for a book of matches.

Pass Christian, Mississippi.

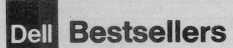
Dell Bestsellers

- [ ] **WHISTLE** by James Jones $2.75 (19262-5)
- [ ] **GREEN ICE** by Gerald A. Browne $2.50 (13224-X)
- [ ] **A STRANGER IS WATCHING**
  by Mary Higgins Clark $2.50 (18125-9)
- [ ] **AFTER THE WIND** by Eileen Lottman $2.50 (18138-0)
- [ ] **THE ROUNDTREE WOMEN: BOOK 1**
  by Margaret Lewerth $2.50 (17594-1)
- [ ] **THE MEMORY OF EVA RYKER**
  by Donald A. Stanwood $2.50 (15550-9)
- [ ] **BLIZZARD** by George Stone $2.25 (11080-7)
- [ ] **THE BLACK MARBLE**
  by Joseph Wambaugh $2.50 (10647-8)
- [ ] **MY MOTHER/MY SELF** by Nancy Friday .$2.50 (15663-7)
- [ ] **SEASON OF PASSION** by Danielle Steel ..$2.25 (17703-0)
- [ ] **THE DARK HORSEMAN**
  by Marianne Harvey $2.50 (11758-5)
- [ ] **BONFIRE** by Charles Dennis $2.25 (10659-1)
- [ ] **THE IMMIGRANTS** by Howard Fast $2.75 (14175-3)
- [ ] **THE ENDS OF POWER**
  by H.R. Haldeman with Joseph DiMona $2.75 (12239-2)
- [ ] **GOING AFTER CACCIATO** by Tim O'Brien $2.25 (12966-4)
- [ ] **SLAPSTICK** by Kurt Vonnegut $2.25 (18009-0)
- [ ] **THE FAR SIDE OF DESTINY**
  by Dore Mullen $2.25 (12645-2)
- [ ] **LOOK AWAY, BEULAH LAND**
  by Lonnie Coleman $2.50 (14642-9)
- [ ] **STRANGERS** by Michael de Guzman $2.25 (17952-1)
- [ ] **EARTH HAS BEEN FOUND** by D.F Jones .$2.25 (12217-1)

At your local bookstore or use this handy coupon for ordering: